Gradually the image took shape.

· ·

Finally the body was complete. Then, taking the special bone in both hands, he laid it in the center of the forehead, in the position of the third eye.

For a while he continued rocking back and forth, muttering a low incantation, then finally he rose and went to the window. Slipping to his knees, he pressed his face against the pane and stared out. Eagerly he scanned the heavens for the sign. Finally, his hopes exhausted, he sank sadly back onto his heels. The sky was empty. He glanced over his shoulder to the image laid out in ritual array, and a grim chatter broke through his clenched teeth.

Soon, very soon, the moon would be full. Then his duty could be fulfilled.

· ·

MICHAEL STEWART

BIRTHRIGHT

HarperPaperbacks
A Division of HarperCollinsPublishers

HarperPaperbacks   *A Division of* HarperCollins*Publishers*
10 East 53rd Street, New York, N.Y. 10022

A hardcover edition of this book was published in Great Britain by William Collins Sons & Co. Ltd.

Cover illustration by Steve Gardner
Step-back illustration by Jeffrey Terreson

First HarperPaperbacks printing: December, 1990

Printed in the United States of America

HarperPaperbacks and colophon are trademarks of HarperCollins*Publishers*

10   9   8   7   6   5   4   3   2   1

*This is for my wife, Martine,
and for our daughter, Amelia*

Acknowledgments

Especial thanks are due to the following, whose personal help I gratefully acknowledge:

In the USA: Dr. Stephen Jay Gould, Professor of Geology, Museum of Comparative Zoology, Harvard University; Dr. Alexander Marshack; Dr. David Nathan, Director, Boston Hospital for Children, Boston, Mass.; Professor David Pilbeam, Professor of Anthropology and Earth Sciences, Harvard University; and Dr. Oliver Sacks.

In the UK: Professor Colin Blakemore, Wayneflete Professor of Physiology, University of Oxford; Dr. Peter Collett, Department of Experimental Psychology, University of Oxford; Dr. David Geaney, Warneford Hospital, Oxford; Dr. Joe Gipps, Curator of Mammals, London Zoo; Charlotte Harrison, National Autistic Society, London; Dr. Michael Heaney, Curator of Western Manuscripts, Bodleian Library, Oxford; Dr. Georgina Mace, London Zoological Society; Dr. Myra Shackley, to whose work on *almas* and "wildmen" I am particularly indebted; and Dr. Chris Stringer, Department of Palaeontology, Natural History Museum, London.

I should also like to acknowledge my sincere thanks to my editors, Ed Breslin and Andy McKillop, and above all to my inspired publisher, Eddie Bell.

"Are human beings innately aggressive . . . ? The answer is yes."

—EDMOND O. WILSON, *On Nature*

• • •

"If Neanderthal man could be reincarnated and placed in a New York subway—provided he were bathed, shaved and dressed in modern clothing—it is doubtful if he would attract any more attention than some of its other denizens."

—WILLIAM STRAUSS and A. J. E. CAVE

BIRTHRIGHT

ONE

WINTER

1

THE BOY WATCHED THE FLAMES CURL TIGHTER
around the rigid body of his dead father. Beneath the
great bearskin mantle the blackened flesh had begun to
peel away from the upper bones. Fat dripping from the
point of an elbow sizzled into the embers. The face,
scorched of hair, slowly stretched into a living grin, and
for a brief moment the eyelids parted, revealing the whites
like two wolf-tooth beads. Fighting back his tears, the boy
squatted lower onto his haunches against the bare rock
and stared deeper into the blaze. He was determined to
catch the spirit taking wing. He stared so hard his eyes
burned, but he didn't blink. Slowly everything began to
recede into the background. Soon he hardly seemed to
hear the moaning of the wind around the crags or the
wails of the women huddled around the fire, or yet the
baneful wolf-howls of the menfolk as they stood with arms
upraised to the full moon. He barely even felt the hand
of his small sister reaching for his own.

"Atta," he implored.

As he watched, the flame suddenly burned through

the leather neck-thong and his father's precious flintstone, so sharp that it could skin a hare quicker than thunder followed lightning, dropped into the embers. Before it could splinter in the heat, the boy snatched up a stick and raked the stone aside. He would return it later, when the rites were done and nothing was left but bones and ash.

Gradually he raised his eyes to the sky and followed the gush of sparks into the clear night. He felt a stab of panic: had he missed the moment? He scanned the arch of the heavens for the new star. The Wolf, the Bear, the Great Crow... where was it? And then he saw it, just briefly. It moved across the sky, a fiercely blazing speck dragging a long trail of sparks. But then, instead of rising to its place, the shooting star began to fall back to earth, falling like a fiery spear, far away across the distant rocky peaks towards the land where the sun rose. And then, quite suddenly, it vanished.

The boy's heart leapt. His prayer had been heard. His father had not gone to join his ancestors. He was coming back.

•

Slowly Sam lowered the binoculars. Cold sweat prickled his skin and his pulse drummed in his temples.

A fire at *that* altitude?

He muttered aloud in disbelief, his breath freezing on the moonlit air. He stamped his feet and clapped his mittened hands to restore the circulation, but he quickly grew dizzy and nauseous and had to stop. At three thousand meters, the nights in the Transcaucasus were bitterly cold and the air was so thin that the least exertion robbed the lungs of breath and made the head swim sickeningly.

He wiped the frozen condensation off the eyepieces and focused the binoculars once again on the flickering pinprick of light just visible in the clear, bright night, high up on a distant, inaccessible crag.

It *was* a fire! Jesus Christ.

Slowly he swung the glasses around the horizon to scan the jagged mountain crests that stretched in ridge after ridge of inhospitable wilderness, a cold, empty landscape cast into surreal relief by the luminous pallor of a full moon. He was standing at the very top of the world, where the mountain-tops grazed the stars and the earth's atmosphere bled over into space.

He panned back again to the small flicker of light. A freak electrical phenomenon—some kind of St. Elmo's fire? Or a pile of dead wood, ignited by a bolt of lightning? But the peak was way above the tree line, and there was no sign of any storm. He stared so hard that the image grew indistinct. Just as he was about to lower the binoculars again, he froze. A shadow! He could have sworn he'd seen a shadow pass fleetingly across the light. Yes, there it was again! A figure of some kind. A living creature. He gave a sick jolt. Wild animals shunned fire. The only living creature to make use of fire was man. Could such a high, inaccessible and barren wasteland ever support human life?

He fumbled for his compass and took a bearing, then spread out his map on the frost-crusted rock and traced a line. The line ran just to the west of the bleak Gara Azhdaak, the highest peak in the whole vast and barren Gegamskiy mountains, one of the remotest regions on earth. Just beyond the peak, it passed directly through a tiny pencilled circle marked with a set of reference co-ordinates: 40° 19′ 35″ N; 44° 53′ 25″ E. A grim shiver chilled his spine. He'd made that reference mark himself. Back home in Boston.

With a shaking hand he folded the map back into his anorak pouch and scanned the black void that lay between himself and the tiny, elusive flicker high up in the far distance. Could he make such an ascent without proper climbing gear? He'd left camp with nothing in the jeep but some medicines and knick-knacks with which to trade favors with the nomads. How would he have explained to his Soviet colleague taking a load of ropes and crampons anyway? He'd left the other anthropologists behind writing up field notes while he'd taken himself off ostensibly to spend a few days studying a small tribe of nomads. Even if, in the full spirit of the new co-operation between East and West, he'd admitted to his real purpose, what would he have actually *said*? That he was off in search of *almas*? The man would have laughed. No one in the scientific community seriously believed these "wild-men" of the mountains actually existed, let alone that they were what he believed them to be. No: for the rest of the world these were just figures of folklore, figments of camp-fire tales. This was Soviet Armenia, after all, and the twenty-first century was just a blink away; barely fifty kilometers away there was a modern hydro-electric plant under construction, and the border with Turkey lay little more than a hundred. Be *real*.

Sam's jaw tightened. But then, they hadn't seen what he had. That satellite picture had been no flight of fancy. Besides, had anyone in military intelligence come up with a better explanation for the curious ring formation that had shown up so clearly on the computer enhancements? He gazed at the distant peak and his pulse quickened. A fire, made by man where no man could live.

Abruptly he slipped his binoculars away and, swinging his backpack onto his shoulders, with the light of the moon to guide his steps, struck out across the rocky shale.

❋

By the following nightfall, traveling laboriously across rough terrain in a zig-zag, up dry riverbeds treacherous with loose scree and down precipitous ravines bristling with spiky thorns and jagged rocks, Sam finally reached a smooth ledge that lay, by his reckoning, about a thousand feet directly below his target. There, in the lee of a great boulder, he decided to bivouac for the night. He built a small fire from the scanty scrubwood around and heated up a tin of baked beans. Then he curled into his sleeping-bag and, setting his back against the knifing wind, struggled between exhaustion and excitement to get some sleep.

In the small hours he awoke to find his whole body completely numb. He stumbled to his feet and rubbed his frozen limbs vigorously; he had to get moving, or he'd die of hypothermia. He ate half a bar of chocolate and drank a little of the precious water from his flask, which his own body heat had kept from freezing, then he packed up and, checking his bearings, began to search for a way up.

The moon had veered round to illuminate directly the rough grey mass that rose sheer and forbidding above him. As he scanned the rockface, despair surged through him. It was impossible. He might have been a fair climber in his younger days, but this wasn't the Adirondacks. The risk was insane. Slip and break a leg here, and he could kiss sweet life goodbye. But then he thought of the reward. If it was true, up there lay simply the most valuable scientific property that the world had ever seen. Get your ass up there, he muttered roughly. And so, gritting his teeth, he began the impossible climb.

•

Dawn had long broken, and under a pale sun the frost had already vanished from the outward-facing rocks to reveal crusted orange lichens and tiny violet-spangled flowers struggling forth from every crevice. Above, the sky was sharp with the cries of the scavenging birds he'd driven off the charred remains. Around him, the wind moaned eerily through the splintered crags. He stared about, giddy from the climb and dazed from the shock of the discovery.

He was standing on a broad, smooth rocky shelf that ran around a massive outcrop of rock, breaking the steady sweep of the mountain towards its peak. Though it curved out of sight from where he stood, he knew from the satellite enlargements that the shelf stretched in a large horseshoe. Around the edge ran a high, jagged parapet which effectively concealed it from any angle except overhead. Not far from the small pile of ashes and bones at his feet, however, the rockface had fractured, leaving a narrow gap like a missing tooth that lay along a direct line of sight to the point on the plateau far below where he'd first seen the flicker of fire. Had he been standing even a few hundred yards to either side, he might not have spotted it at all.

He shivered. Apart from clumps of wiry grass raked flat by the wind, no living thing stirred. Cautiously, filled with a mixture of dread and awe, he stepped forward towards the pile of charred bones.

The body lay on its side in a fetal curl, hands to

ankles and knees to chin. The skull was twisted so as to face upwards, the eye-sockets empty and the teeth bared. Tufts of scorched, mud-matted hair still stuck to the cranium. The fire had evidently died down before consuming the bones, and the birds had not yet quite picked the carcass clean. The gums were almost intact, and fleshy matter still lurked in cavities under the jaw and between the spinal vertebrae. On the ground around the skull, embedded in the ashes, lay a ring of small stones, arranged in a half-circle. His throat went dry. He'd seen just such a stone halo once before. At a burial site in Italy, not far from Rome. A Neanderthal burial site.

Then he frowned. Early man buried, not cremated, his dead. But then, in thirty-five thousand years, undoubtedly with some contact with moderns, wasn't some degree of cultural evolution to be expected? He turned back to the skeletons. The proof, as always, would lie in the bones.

Before disturbing anything, he took out his camera and shot off a reel of film. Then, very gingerly, he knelt down and reached out to examine a bone. It was a femur, clearly belonging to a heavy, robust adult male. But as he picked it up, it fell apart, split open down its full length. From the lack of charring on the inside this had evidently been done after the burning. There could be only one purpose for this chilling ritual: to suck out the marrow. He threw a nervous glance around him. This, too, he'd seen before, just once, at a similar site in Yugoslavia. It was generally taken as evidence of cannibalism.

Finally, he reached for the skull. Even as he picked it up he knew he had his answer.

It was a largish head, with thick brow ridges that arched over the eye-sockets. The nose had evidently been strong and prominent. The jaw was powerful, the cheek-bones heavy. The front teeth were relatively large and the molars small. From the side, the skull looked elongated, almost streamlined. At the back, a pit ran across the center of the occipital bone, with a well-defined ridge at the base. With a trembling hand, he felt the back of his own head. It was quite smooth. Like any modern skull.

The cry of triumph that broke from his lips was instantly snatched by the wind and flung away across the cavernous mountainside. He stood back, his mind reeling. He'd been right! Here, in stones and bones, was absolute, incontrovertible proof. Forced to retreat into ever more remote regions of the world, lost from sight for tens of millennia and reduced now to probably no more than a few pockets of surviving relicts, *Neanderthal man still lived!*

He spent the next hours meticulously photographing and recording every detail of the body, its orientation and the position of its bones. Finally, with the sun already declining, he decided he'd better make a move. With great care he began lifting the bones one by one into his backpack. As he dismantled the neck and shoulder blades, he noticed a small oval-shaped stone lying half buried in the ashes. It was made of flint, chipped to a razor-sharp edge, with a thong of hide threaded through a hole at the broader end. The leather was fresh and the stone itself bore no signs of fire. He shivered involuntarily. Someone had been back afterwards. He slipped the stone quickly into his pocket but, afraid it might get damaged, looped it over his neck instead. Finally, he strapped up the backpack and eased it gently onto his shoulders, then with a last glance about him, headed for the gap in the parapet and began the descent.

Going down was tougher than going up. Most of the time he climbed in shadow, where the rock was beginning to glaze with frost and shapes and distances played tricks with his vision. Soon his feet were so numb that he could only guess the toeholds. He glanced down. Beneath him, the mountain fell away in a long sweep of loose shale, ending in a sheer drop. Below that, grey mist swirled around the ledge where he'd bivouacked the previous night and blotted out the plateau stretching far below where, concealed in a rocky gorge, stood the jeep that would take him home with his world-shaking discovery.

With the light falling and the cold intensifying fast, desperately weary in every limb and fighting for breath after every exertion, he began to make mistakes. First, he put his weight on a loose boulder and lost his footing; as he writhed and twisted, the backpack swung against the rockface with a sickening crunch. He let out a howl of despair. Slipping it off his shoulders, he looped the straps around his wrist and, more carefully still, carried on downwards. Foot, toe, foot, toe he went, not releasing one until the next was quite secure. He'd made it down the first sheer path and reached most of the way across the broad sweep of scree when quite suddenly the ground slid from under his foot and he fell sharply backwards. Thrusting the backpack clear, he fought frantically to regain his footing, but the surface was a mass of loose pebbles. The more he struggled, the more he slipped. Slowly the whole mountainside began to slide downwards like a sheet, gathering speed as it went and carrying him helplessly along in a torrent of stones. He struck a boulder and flew head over heels into the air. The backpack was torn violently from his wrist. He wrestled and clawed in an effort to buck the landslip, but it was no use: he was

part of it, one rolling boulder among the rest, flung headlong in the same downrush. The roaring grew louder in
his ears. Stones spun wildly past his head. Violent shafts
of pain stabbed him in every quarter. The sky tumbled
crazily about his eyes. Covering his head with his arms
and curling into a ball, he gave himself up to the stone-
storm and waited for the one final jolt, greater than the
rest, that would bring the blackness and the silence.

•

The boy crept slowly forward. The man lay motionless on his back. Cautiously the boy inched closer, half
afraid he might suddenly leap up at him. He scented the
air, puzzled. An odd, sweetish smell. He lobbed a small
pebble; it glanced off the man's cheek, but he didn't stir.
Was he dead? Gingerly, the boy came up close. In the
low twilight, he peered at the strange figure. The hair on
the man's head and cheeks was a pale gold, the color of
bison grass in winter. And his skin, where it wasn't cut or
bruised, was white and faintly like the egg of a snow hawk.

Very cautiously, the boy reached out to touch his
face. The skin still warm. And then he gave a sudden
start. Something had glinted in the moonlight.

Around his neck, half lost in the clothing, the man
wore a flintstone. The boy reached forward, and let out
a gasp. It was the very same stone, with the very cord
he'd cut himself. Earlier, he'd gone back to the rock-ledge
to find the bones spirited away and the stone gone. Now
he understood. It was all so clear. His father *had* come
back!

"Atta," he whispered, overjoyed. "Atta!"

2

○

IN THE SMALL HOURS OF THE NIGHT, SAM CAME
around to find himself lying staring up at the stars. He
felt nothing except a weightless, floating sensation and
the strange, resigned detachment of a dying man. He
thought of the two women he'd left behind. Julia would
be shattered. She'd uprooted from England with her
daughter and come to settle over in the States with him.
She'd done everything she could to make him the wife
she believed he wanted. He'd put his heart into it, too,
but gradually, over the past year, they'd grown apart. For
her, the fault was that they'd never had a child of their
own: they never could have, either, since his illness that
summer. Well, now she could forget the adoption agencies. It wouldn't have been the answer, anyway. Because
there was someone else in his life: Max. How would Max
take it? She was a tough girl, but she'd miss him. She'd
miss the afternoons at her apartment, too, the clandestine
meetings at conferences across the country, the little
trips—like Venice. What a way to go! So much unresolved, so much left unsaid.

He stirred, and a blaze of agony shot through every fiber of his body. He forced himself to lie still while he took an inventory of the damage. His first thought was his stomach: had the cancer been jolted out of hiding? But his stomach didn't hurt; there wasn't even the ominous throbbing warmth that had first alerted him to trouble. He ran his mind over the rest. Right arm probably fractured; no sensation in the left leg; ribs stabbing like knives at every breath. He coughed, and a black clot spattered the ground beside him. As he eased himself carefully up on an elbow, he noticed that he was lying under a light covering of leaves and brushwood. He looked about, struck by the oddity. The moon had swung around, casting the mountainside in shadow, but even so he could see that the ground about was quite bare.

Then in a flash he remembered the backpack. He struggled painfully to his knees. The landslide had carried him close to the edge of the drop, where a boulder had broken his fall. He crawled forward and peered into the void below. He let out a howl: somewhere down there, far beyond reach, lay his prize, pulverized beneath the cascade of rubble. What about the film? He felt in his pocket: thank God, at least the canisters were still there. In the top pouch of his anorak he found his compass, the glass broken but the needle still true. And his pocket flashlight, dented but still working.

He struggled to his feet, shivering and nauseous and barely able to hold the compass steady. How the hell was he going to make it out? Suddenly he froze. What was that sound behind him? *A footfall?* He swung the flashlight around. For a brief instant a pair of eyes glowed back at him in the beam, then vanished, and he caught the fleeting outline of a stocky but distinctly human figure—perhaps a boy?—disappearing behind the rocks into the darkness.

Breathing heavily, he'd begun to move forward again when a sudden realization hit him with a sickening jolt. Those eyes had reflected back green, like a cat's. The human retina reflected red.

Shaking now in every nerve, he gritted his teeth and set out, inch by inch, upon the downward stretch. His head swam, and time and again his legs buckled under him and he blacked out with pain. Howling aloud at every jarring step and stumbling in a permanent semi-conscious daze, barely aware of where he was or what he was doing but determined to get out alive at any cost, he made his painful, laborious way down onto the flatter terrain. At one point, beyond the limit of endurance, he sank to his knees and was about to give up the struggle when he had the impression of an arm under his own, helping him up. Was he dreaming, or was someone really there? That half-human, boy-like figure he'd seen? Off and on during the nightmare hours that followed he had the sense that this strange, silent creature was walking with him, supporting and steadying him, but his mind was too foggy to register with any precision. When finally, with the first tinges of dawn lightening the sky, he found himself within sight of the jeep and, in a sudden moment of lucidity, cast around him properly, he could see no sign of a living soul and concluded that his helpmate of the night had just been a figment born of his pain-crazed mind.

In the First Aid box he found a bottle of painkillers and some rolls of bandage, and from the provisions chest he procured a bottle of bourbon. Soon he'd strapped himself up as best as he could and, with the pain dulled, began to think more clearly. First thing was to get medical help. For all the jogging and weightlifting he'd done to build up fitness, he felt just as weak as he'd been under radiotherapy. Did he have the strength to make it back to camp? His Russian colleague would get him to the hospital. Then came the next thing: should he tell him? No reason to. They were collaborating on research into nomadic tribal structures; their agreement said nothing about *this*. He'd get back home to the States as soon as he was fit to move; he'd publish a complete report of his discovery, supported by the photos, and on the back of the international storm of excitement that was bound to follow, he'd put together a team from his department and mount a full-scale expedition back here. In the world of science, the prize went to the man first into print. And it was *his* prize. He wasn't going to share it with anyone, least of all with the other side just because he'd happened to find it on their soil.

He clambered painfully into the driver's seat and hauled the door shut. As he spread the map out on the passenger seat, a tidal wave of fatigue crashed over him and the whole world began to swim out of focus. Leaning forward over the wheel, he sank his head in his hands and gave in to the relentless pull of sleep.

•

He felt himself being tugged from the depths of slumber by an insistent scratching sound. For a while his body fought back, refusing to come around, but the noise grew more and more persistent. Finally, he raised his head and forced himself to open his leaden eyelids. With a violent start he jerked awake.

A face, pressed against the window! Large, dark eyes staring in at him! A hand clawing at the windshield!

He shrank back, choking with horror. He'd never seen such a face before. Desperately he tried to read the intent in those strange, heavy-browed eyes. His mind flashed to the jack-knife under the dashboard. Slowly he reached out. The eyes sharpened at once. He froze in mid-motion. Then, quite suddenly, the face vanished. But as it did so, Sam caught a glimpse of the profile. The head was longish, almost streamlined, and though it was clearly a young, immature face, the brow was curiously prominent and the cheekbones noticeably heavy. His first, fleeting thought was that perhaps he had not, after all, imagined his elusive helpmate of the night who'd guided his stumbling steps. Then he trembled to the very core. This was no nomad boy, roaming the wilds. No: he recognized the unmistakable shape of the head and those distinctive facial features. And he, of all people, knew what they meant.

One of *them?* Down *here?*

Rooted to the spot, he honed his ears for any sound to tell where the boy had gone. All was silent but for the low whistling of the wind in the eucalyptus trees. Then, without warning, the face appeared at the other side of the jeep, where the window was half lowered. It stared in at him, holding his gaze steadily.

Sam now studied him more carefully. Most striking of all were his eyes, which glistened like two coals so black as to appear almost violet. The pupils seemed to fill the whole iris, like those of a cat in the dark, making his stare eerily penetrating. From his head a matted thicket of wiry reddish-black hair straggled out in all directions. His forehead sloped steeply down to pronounced eyebrow ridges and continued in an unbroken line, almost in Roman fashion, to a strong, straight nose. His nostrils were slightly flared and the cleft above his upper lip appeared relatively deep, and this, together with the fullness and prominence of his lips, gave his face a Levantine, almost sensual look. His skin was weathered to a fresh tan and his cheeks were quite smooth but for a dusting of the lightest down. At a guess, he couldn't be much over twelve. His general build was extraordinarily robust for such an age, though: beneath the rough fur tunic he wore, his shoulders were broad and sturdy, and his arms, which hung bare, were visibly muscular and ended in square, powerful hands.

Jesus Christ Almighty.

Terrified of making a wrong move that would scare the boy off, Sam slowly eased his face into a gentle smile. Desperately he mustered the smattering of American dialect he knew.

"Hi," he croaked. "What's your name?"

The boy's brow furled into a frown. He made no response.

Remaining quite still, Sam repeated his greeting in Russian, then in Turkish, but he met with a blank expression. As he spoke, the boy peered in more closely. Curiosity seemed to be battling with caution. He took a half-step forward. Finally, he uttered his first sound. A strange low, soft grunt. It carried the inflection of a tentative question.

"Atta?"

Same felt his flesh prickle. Get some kind of communication going! What should he reply?

Mimicking the boy's tone and intonation as closely as possible, he repeated the sound.

"Atta," he replied.

Instantly, the boy's eyes sharpened with suspicion

and flicked uncertainly over his face and clothes, then slowly his frown relaxed and a cautious smile lit the corners of his mouth. Quite suddenly he stepped forward and reached a hand in through the open window. Instinctively Sam backed away, until he realized the boy was pointing to the flintstone around his neck. Gradually a realization began to crystallize. Nodding slowly, he took the flintstone in his hand and repeated the strange word over and over in a clear statement of affirmation.

•

On a groundsheet beside the jeep he laid out some rough bread, crackers, a couple of Hershey bars and several cans of beer. To these he added a collection of the trinkets he'd taken along as offerings of friendship to the nomads—a hunting-knife, some cooking pots, small bags of boiled candies for the kids and a rag-bag of jeans and tee-shirts in various sizes. Beside him on the ground he set the small dictaphone he used for recording interviews and notes; the camera, to his intense frustration, had been lost with the backpack. Swilling a handful of painkillers down with more bourbon, he squatted on his ankles in nomad fashion and settled down to wait for the strange kid to come forward.

At first the boy hung back shyly in the shade of a tall eucalyptus, his gaze watchful and fearful. Feigning to ignore him, Sam switched on the tape machine and, observing him out of the corner of his eye, began to record his impressions.

"I have here a male youth," he began softly. "Height about five foot, weight around one hundred and ten, age roughly comparable to a twelve-year-old. Overall build rugged, stocky, the mountain-type. Legs-to-torso ratio appears low, hand-to-forearm high. Clearly a cold-adapted physique. Cranium fairly long and low-set, with a relatively small development of the mastoid process and a large bistephanic supra-orbital projection . . ."

Gradually, the boy inched forward. He stopped at the edge of the groundsheet, where he stood for a long moment, his large dark eyes flicking over the assortment of objects. Moving smoothly and carefully, Sam opened a beer and drank a little himself, then held it out. Cautiously, the boy reached forward and took the can. For a while he examined it with a look of intense fascination. Sunlight glinting off the bright aluminum evidently caught his eye, for he began to play with the effect, turning the can this way and that while the fizzy amber liquid spilled out onto the ground. A smile of delight slowly spread over his face. Then, quite suddenly, he put the hole to his lips in exact imitation of Sam's action and took a mouthful. He choked violently and spat it out at once, clutching the can tightly as he doubled up. The can crumpled in his grip as if made of tissue-paper. Recovering after a moment, he examined it with renewed curiosity and, dropping onto one knee, ran a forefinger through the small puddle of beer caught in a hollow in the rocky ground. He licked the finger thoughtfully. The taste seemed interesting. He repeated the action. Slowly the smile returned and broadened into a grin. The grin broke into a chuckle, the chuckle into a full-bellied laugh. Despite himself, Sam began to laugh, too, quite captivated by the simplicity of the boy's wonder and delight.

He opened another can and held it out. This time the boy stepped onto the groundsheet and squatted down beside him. But Sam's smile had begun to harden. This changed everything.

This was his prize.

•

He spent the next hours in a surreal daze, lurching between elation and exhaustion, while he worked on reinforcing the boy's trust. The flintstone worked like a magic charm; he only had to display it when he sensed he was pressing him too far or too fast and at once the unquestioning trust would return and the fearfulness give way to a simple desire for fun. The boy was fascinated by novelty and could make anything an object for his play. He was easily excitable, too, and Sam performed all the tricks he could think of to keep his interest alive.

All the time, though, he was wrestling with the problem of how the hell to get him out. Could he get him drunk? Not easily. Could he drug him? He had enough Luminal in the medicine box to knock out an army, but how, realistically, could he get him to take it? Then there was the problem of crossing the border. How would he get him across without papers? Even if he managed to find an uncharted route over the mountains, what if they were stopped? Or broke down? Or simply he himself couldn't make it? How would he explain this weird, wild creature dressed in crazy fur-skins and gabbling incoherent gobbledegook? In despair, he was reconciling himself to returning empty-handed or, worse, surrendering him to the Soviet scientific establishment, when he noticed the boy had pulled out a maroon tee-shirt with *Harvard University* emblazoned on it and was holding it up against his chest, as though measuring it for size. At once he saw his chance. Could he get the boy actually to *put it on?* And if the tee-shirt, why not the jeans, too?

Taking off his anorak and sweatshirt, he began a laborious copy-cat ritual of dressing and undressing. Puzzled at first, the boy gradually responded to the game. Coaxing and teasing him by stages, Sam finally succeeded in getting him to put on the unfamiliar new clothes. When the dress was complete, he could hardly suppress a wry smile: certainly, the kid looked a bit wild and strange and distinctly muscular for his age, but, cleaned up a bit, he'd hardly turn any heads on the streets back home in Cambridge.

The pain was beginning to return in waves, and he knew his time was running out. Acting as normally as he could, he began packing everything up into the jeep. The boy joined in as part of a new game. Finally, Sam climbed into the back and beckoned him aboard. But here the boy hesitated. Sam tried everything he could think of. He pulled comic faces, tapped tunes on the bases of the pans and finally held out a bar of chocolate. This enticed the boy forward and, with a playful grin, he swung himself in. Carefully, Sam changed places so that the boy was now on the inside, against the grille separating the back from the driver's cab, then he quickly slid out onto the ground and slammed the door shut. He'd got him! There was a puzzled cry and a certain amount of shuffling about, but he hurried round to the front and hauled himself into the driver's seat. Swallowing the last of the painkillers, he gunned the engine into life and, with just one good hand and one good foot to drive by, steeled himself for the final supreme effort. He glanced up in the rear-view mirror. The boy's eyes returned his look steadily—puzzled at the unfamiliar new game and yet still implicitly trusting. Sam gritted his teeth. Sorry, kid, he muttered. Got to do it. You're my ticket to Stockholm.

The journey was a nightmare through hell. The horizon swam in and out of focus before his eyes. One

moment the track ahead lurched up to meet him and the
next it fell away into an abyss, and each jolt sent a blaze
of pain shooting through the very roots of his body. He
navigated more by guesswork than the map. Across the
river Razdan to Elar. From Arzni to Agara. To Mastara
and Nov-Artik. It seemed interminable. From time to time,
he looked up to find the boy staring at him, the bewilderment now turned to fear, or he'd glimpse the short,
powerful fingers, whitening around the grille, and he'd
turn back and address himself more determinedly to the
road ahead. Finally, at some unmarked point south of
Anipemz, after an agonizing ride down a long, winding
dirt track, he realized he must have crossed the border,
for when he came to a road he found the signposts had
changed to Turkish. He let out a peal of elation. He'd
made it!

It was barely five miles into the safety of the West,
however, that he hit the fateful bend. The track plunged
steeply down a hill, veering left at the bottom. He missed
a gear and, with his single hand, he simply hadn't the
strength to hold the steering-wheel through the tightening
bend. The rear wheels suddenly broke away and the jeep
skidded on the soft, sandy track. It lurched briefly back
on course again, then slewed around broadsides across
the track, where for a second it seemed to stop, poised
in mid-career. From behind, a howl pierced the air and,
glancing up in the mirror, he saw the flash of eyes wild
with raw terror. Suddenly, as if caught up by its own
momentum, the jeep came alive again and flipped over
onto its side. It skated gracefully a full hundred yards
further on until, with slow and terrible irrevocability, it
shunted head-on into the side of a large outcrop of rock,
hurling him forward into the windshield and the blackness
beyond.

As the dark engulfed him, his final desperate thought was: Cray! *Tell Cray!*

•

Max cast a final glance around the small compound in which the gazelles were corralled, awaiting release. They moved about in their newly formed groups, scenting the air nervously. Though kept in the reserve for ten days now, the animals had been bred in captivity and the sounds and smells of the rocky foothills of the Himalaya were still a strange novelty. The males prowled around, butting the palings with their long, slender horns, shadowed closely by the more timid females in small, graceful shoals. One large male from the Minnesota Zoo stock was trying to dislodge his radio collar, and she made a brief note on her clipboard; he'd soon forget about it, though, once out in the wild.

She ran through her check-list one last time. Everything seemed in order. The animals were fit and ready for their new life. It was anyone's guess, though, if the extra string of chamois genes they'd been given would be expressed properly; modifying an animal's genes *in vivo* was really more of an art than a science. Still, if only one of the groups adapted to the harsh new environment and survived to breed in its own turn, the project would have been a success.

She called across to her research assistant.

"Okay, Steve, let them out."

The young man opened the gate at the side of the pen. For a moment, the gazelles hesitated. Then the large male stepped outside, tailed by his small coterie of females, and a moment later all forty of the sleek, dun-colored creatures were in the open. Again they appeared to hesitate, as if torn between the security of captivity and the instinctual call of freedom. Then, quite abruptly, the herd broke into a run and headed for the hills. Some distance away, the lead group stopped and turned, and the large male raised his antlers briefly in salute, then in unison they wheeled round and ran off at a gallop until the whole herd had disappeared from view, merging into the dusty slopes that stretched away towards the mountain ranges and the far hazy distance.

For a while Max scanned the horizon through her binoculars until she could see no more sign of movement. Beside her, the assistant stood tuning in the radio receiver to the faint clatter of electronic signals. Finally she lowered her glasses and breathed a deep sigh of satisfaction. She'd done her part; it was now for the zoologists and local trackers to take over. But as she looked around the empty compound and the deserted, rolling landscape all about her, she was struck by a profound sense of loneliness. Instinctively, she fingered the antique gold bracelet Sam had bought her in Venice—when was it?—no more than ten days ago. Where would he be right now, she wondered, and what might he be doing? She raised her gaze to the sun, now reaching its zenith, and before she could check herself for such an adolescent thought, she felt a moment's comfort to imagine that somewhere under the same sun he, too, might be wondering just the same.

3

―――――――――――○―――――――――――

"NOW FOR THE WEATHER IN THE BOSTON AREA THIS Monday morning. You've heard it before, folks: more precipitation on the way..."

Julia snapped off the radio and glanced out of the car window at the sky glowering yellow and leaden over the roofs of the shopping mall. Always the weather, every ten minutes. Wind-chill factors and winter storm watches. As if she didn't have enough of it at home, with Sam and his thermometers and barometers inside and out, not to mention that box for measuring rainfall in the middle of the garden and that ridiculous anemometer thing perched on top of the flagpole. Perhaps here, in the States, this land of extremes, the weather really did spell life or death, whereas back home it didn't. (Why did she still call England "home"?) It was early February, and the winter had broken all records for severity. Everyone had become obsessed with the statistics, and whole conversations were conducted in inches of precipitation and degrees below.

She felt like this every time Sam went away and left her with her thoughts. Relax, she told herself: everything's fine. Sandy's grades might be disappointing, but she'd always been a sporty rather than a bookish girl, and, anyway, she loved her new school and was making plenty of friends. Sam would be back in a fortnight, full of traveler's tales; he'd sweep them up in his enthusiasms and they'd feel once again part of the ebb and flow of life. Why then, Julia asked herself, did she feel so uncomfortable?

She only had to look out of the window at the large white clapboard houses set back from the road, presenting one façade after another of columned porticos and elegant windows immaculately preserved since colonial days, to know the reason. She didn't *belong*. It felt so different here from the relaxed, cosmopolitan neighborhood into which she'd arrived with Sandy four years before. At that time Sam had been living in a large, shabby old house in the heart of Cambridge, barely a couple of minutes' drive from the Yard, with a Professor of Divinity on one side and a marine biologist on the other—between the devil and the deep blue sea, he'd chuckle.

Then, about two years ago, things started changing. He became involved in some big, secretive project. For a while he shuttled constantly back and forth to Washington, and well-dressed men in black limousines would arrive at the house and disappear into his study for lengthy meetings behind closed doors. As Professor of Anthropology at Harvard University, his salary was generous but not enormous, yet quite suddenly they seemed to have a great deal more money. New cars appeared in the garage, Mayan artifacts replaced the wart-hog tusks and nomadic rugs decorating the living room and even a special safe had to be installed for the necklace he gave her that Christmas. A new house became the inevitable next step. And so, last spring, before his sudden illness, they moved out of the Boston city area to the small, well-heeled town of Lexington. For Sam it represented the proud heart of American tradition and values. Her daughter Sandy, for her part, found it snobbish and exclusive, and at first that had caused her problems integrating, but at least it was America and that was all that finally mattered. But for Julia, one step deeper into New England had been one step further away from the old one, and now, with Sam absent, she felt a stranger in her own neighborhood.

With a sigh, she swung the estate wagon down the track. She had no right to complain. There were plenty of people far worse off, people who didn't have a thousandth of what they did. She thought of the disturbed and maladjusted children she dealt with every day at the Unit. All the upset she and Sandy had suffered over the divorce and the problems in settling into a new life over here were insignificant in comparison.

The house came into view. Like its neighbors, it dated back two centuries, but twenty years previously it had been repositioned further up the slope from the river and at the same time completely rebuilt, so that now it squatted lower and more comfortably into the contour of the land, offering two floors at the front and three at the back. Yet for all that she did, laying out an English rose garden, entertaining twice a week, keeping the place filled with flowers and fun, she sometimes felt it was more like a smart country club than a *home*. A home needed children. Sandy was a wonderful girl and a joy to have around, but she wasn't *theirs*—Sam's and hers. Now, of course, it was too late . . . Abruptly, she stemmed that line of thought. She was taking practical steps to remedy the situation, and it was best left like that.

She pulled up outside the house and, grabbing an armful of shopping, hurried up the front steps. From the outside she could hear the phone ringing, but by the time she'd punched in the right number on the alarm panel— Sam was forever changing the code—it had stopped. She began unpacking in the kitchen. A note Sandy had stuck to the fridge door made her smile: "This refrigerator contains the four main food groups. Fast. Junk. Frozen and Spoiled." No problems in absorbing the culture there. She glanced at the clock: she'd better hurry or she'd be late for her afternoon at the Unit.

The phone rang again. This time she caught it.

"Mrs. Wendell?" A man's voice, strangely aspirated, wheezing.

"Speaking," she replied.

The voice at the other end tautened.

"William Cray here. I don't know if you remember me."

"Of course I do."

She pictured him clearly: a smallish, precise man with silver-gray hair and extraordinarily laser-blue eyes. Exuded, almost literally, a smell of power. Spoke in a hoarse semi-whisper, the result of a war-wound—she'd noticed a scar on his throat, above his neck-tie. One of Sam's well-dressed visitors. An old college friend, apparently. He'd asked once if she was a royalist; she'd been so taken aback she'd just laughed.

"I thought I should come myself," the man went on, then broke off. The edge in his voice made her pulse quicken.

"Something's wrong," she guessed in alarm.

"I'm calling from the car..."

"Is it Sam?" she blurted out.

"Stay right there, Julia. I'll be with you in ten minutes."

•

Sam opened his eyes a fraction. A naked lightbulb overhead seared the roots of his eyeballs. In the background, voices jabbered in an unfamiliar tongue. The powerful smell of hospital disinfectant made him feel nauseous. He struggled to raise his head. The face of a dark-skinned girl fringed by a small white cap veered in and out of focus. What was happening? *Had they got through?*

"You lie still now, Mr. Wendell," said the nurse in broken English.

He clutched her by the wrist, but she gently unclamped his grip. A moment later, he felt the sharp sting of a needle in his arm and gradually the face and the lightbulb and the jabber of voices receded into a single dull, distant blur.

•

The boy crouched beneath the window, as still as stone. The dog stood off, scenting him suspiciously. From its belly came a low growl. Its ears were flattened, the hair on its spine bristled and its lip was curled back to reveal vicious fangs. It began to bark and paw the earth. Still he didn't move a muscle. The dog grew angrier. From the darkness a voice shouted. Then the boy let out a long, slow call, half whistle and half hum, like the moan of wind across the mouth of a cave. Within a moment, the dog's barking hushed to a soft growl. Then, cocking its head from side to side, it came forward and nuzzled his face affectionately.

He listened acutely to the noises floating in on the cold night breeze. Eyes keened, he scanned the darkness; though the moon was obscured by a frosty haze, not the tiniest movements in the furthest shadows escaped him. Finally, he rose slowly to his feet and looked in through the window.

On a bed, lit by a low bluish light, lay the man.

The boy reached forward, but his hand met an invisible barrier, like a screen of ice. It rang hollow to the tap. The figure within didn't stir. Working his fingers into a chink at the bottom, the boy gradually raised the frame. Stealthily he slid his body through the gap and dropped noiselessly onto the floor inside.

The man lay unstirring, his face grey as ash. Thin red and white threads fed into his nostrils and his arms. The boy reached forward and laid a hand on his forehead, over his closed eyes and down his fair-stubbled cheeks, lingering a moment at his lips, then down his chin to the flintstone around his neck. Then, pressing his hand in his own, he knelt down and shut his eyes tight against the tears.

•

Julia watched from the porch as the black limousine disappeared down the drive and became quickly absorbed into the curtain of falling snow. She gripped the door-post, unable to move, scarcely even aware of the bitter cold or the strange muffled silence that had descended with the snow. Sam had been involved in an accident. He was lying critical in some village hospital half across the world. "We're taking care of everything," William Cray had told her. "You stay right here. We'll have him back in no time."

Abruptly, she turned indoors and strode to the study. Even as she entered the maroon-painted room with its studded leather chairs, book-lined shelves and the large partner's desk with the gold-framed photos of their honeymoon in Venice, she was stabbed by a terrible foreboding that he would never walk into this room again. Suddenly it seemed empty, disembowelled. She found herself wondering how she would cope if the worst happened—how Sandy would cope, too. She'd rebuilt their life once; she couldn't do it a second time. She should never have let him go off on that crazy adventure, at least not until he was quite sure he'd got over his illness completely. She'd spoiled their last evening by raising the issue again, and it had provoked an upsetting quarrel. Were those parting words to become his final memory?

Snap out of it, she told herself severely. Sam was basically tough and resilient; sheer bloodymindedness would pull him through. Besides, William Cray had got a contact-man out there fixing things on the spot. He had done his best to reassure her; goodness knew what strings the Foundation—or whatever he called his outfit—were able to pull. But this was to avoid facing up to the gravity of the situation. Under pressure, William had admitted that Sam was "very critically ill." How could she possibly stand by at home, idly waiting and praying? Sam needed her. Where in heaven's name was Kars?

Quickly she scanned the shelves for an atlas, then reached for the phone. Within fifteen minutes she had fixed her itinerary. The five-thirty shuttle to New York would connect with an overnight flight from Kennedy due to land in Ankara, Turkey, at six the following morning. Catching an internal flight at eight and hiring a car at the other end, she could possibly reach the hospital soon after midday, local time.

By four she had called Sandy at school, explained what had happened and arranged for her to stay with the Blanes next door while she was away, and within half an hour she was on the turnpike, heading for Boston. By ten past five she'd reached Logan airport, parked the estate wagon and was heading briskly for the shuttle.

•

The nurse had just come on duty. Though it was only five in the morning and still dark outside, the hospital was beginning to stir. She adjusted her cap in the cracked mirror and smoothed the creases of her uniform. The American was some kind of VIP.

She tapped on the door out of courtesy and let herself in. She'd barely taken a step inside when she let out a sharp exclamation. Beside the bed, caught by surprise, crouched the figure of a boy. His tee-shirt was torn and bloodstained and an ugly wound oozed through his thick-matted hair, but it was the cast of his face that shook her most: he looked more animal than human.

She rushed over to the bed. The patient lay stiff and still and his flesh bore a greyish, translucent pallor. Instinctively she reached to feel his neck artery, but she already knew the answer. She glanced at the drips—nothing appeared dislodged—then at the boy. What in heaven's name was he doing there? And then she noticed the small oval stone hanging around his neck. She recognized it at once: the man had been wearing it when he'd been brought in. She understood. The boy was a thief. A wretched gypsy kid who'd stolen in from the fields to pilfer from the sick and the dying.

She pressed the alarm knob, and within moments two orderlies came running in, followed by a senior nurse and the doctor. Having quickly checked the patient over, the doctor turned to interrogate the boy. He uttered nothing but strange, incomprehensible grunts; he seemed bewildered and confused by the commotion, and his large, dark eyes were moist and filled with anguish.

"Take him to the Director's office," snapped the doctor. "And clean him up."

When the orderlies laid hands on him, he made no attempt to escape. But when they tried to march him out of the room, he began to struggle violently, crying out vociferously in a strange dialect she'd never heard before. The closer they dragged him to the door, the more he fought and screamed, as if nothing would tear him away from the man he'd robbed. His strength was phenomenal. He threw off the two fully grown men with ease, but again, instead of making his escape, he scrambled back to the bed and clung defiantly to the dead man's arm, jabbering away all the time in the same old gibberish. The doctor finally called for a straitjacket, and eventually they dragged him, kicking and howling, out of the room.

Then the doctor beckoned to the nurse and, with the screams dying away down the corridor, they turned their attention to the corpse on their hands.

o

Julia was met at Ankara by a young man from the US Embassy in a Brooks Brothers suit and wingtips, who smoothly steered her through passport and customs control and onto her internal THY flight. At her final destination, she was once again surprised to be met, this time by a rangy, ageing lumberjack with yellowed eyes and the abused complexion of a man who had lived life hard. William Cray's man. He introduced himself as Carson.

Carson took her bags to a beaten-up old sedan badly parked outside the entrance and helped her in. Unhurriedly, he steered the whale of a car through the reckless swarms of motorbikes and *dolmus* taxis, and even when they reached the open road, with Kars signposted eighty kilometers away, he scarcely increased speed. He chatted in a leisurely way about himself, his young Turkish wife and the living he made dabbling in kelims and meerschaum pipes, and it was only when finally she frowned pointedly at her watch that he seemed to appreciate her urgency.

He looked across at her and shook his head.

"I guess they didn't tell you in Ankara," he said in a slow, regretful voice.

At once she understood. The world spun sickeningly about her. Her own voice sounded very small and far off.

"When . . . when did he . . . ?"

"Early this morning. In his sleep. Peacefully."

It isn't true! she howled inwardly. It wasn't possible. This was all unreal, a dream. She wasn't really here at all. It was just some appalling illusion, a cruel trick of her senses, a projection of her foreboding. Then she caught the look on his face and turned abruptly away. She felt sick, suffocating. She'd known this all along; some terrible whisper in her ear had told her. She had willed him so hard to hang on, to wait just until she'd got there, telling him that every minute was bringing her closer. But he hadn't managed to. And now it was too late. Too late even for one single word.

They continued slowly to the hospital, in silence. There was no hurry for anything. Life had ground to a halt.

•

The Director, a short, swarthy man in a starched white coat sat nervously stroking his moustache as he offered his condolences. He spoke of the will of God, as if to stress it wasn't the hospital's negligence. Carson leant against the window, translating.

But Julia was hardly listening. She veered numbly between belief and disbelief, between wanting to know the particulars and wanting not to know, between the torment and confusion of her own thoughts and the clinical rectitude of the white-coated figure sitting opposite. She found her stare locked onto the small box containing Sam's personal effects lying on the desk between them. She felt repelled yet mesmerized, as though these remnants were somehow actual bits of the man she'd loved. There was his Rolex, his pipe, the fountain pen she'd given him on their first anniversary; there were the anti-this and anti-that pills he took whenever he went into the field; his map, folded and crumpled; his wallet, too, battered and blood-smeared, with the money carefully separated and listed—crisp dollars, grubby Turkish bills and some Italian lire notes (Italian money? she wondered fleetingly). There was his small pocket electronic notebook, too, evidently dented in the accident, and a miscellany of other bits and pieces: airline ticket, passport, driver's license, dictaphone tapes, traveler's checks and a few canisters of film. What remained of his clothes, she gathered, had been placed in a chest in the mortuary, along with the equipment salvaged from the wrecked jeep.

The Director moved the box closer, indicating it was hers to claim, but she couldn't bring herself to touch it. With an understanding nod, Carson reached forward and took it. Then the Director opened his desk drawer.

"And then there is this." He held out a curious small object.

She took it. It was a sharp, oval-shaped stone strung on a leather lace. She turned it over in her palm. Its rim had obviously been chipped to form a cutting edge. Was it some kind of primitive blade? It could have come right out of the specimen drawers at the Peabody Museum, one of those endless shards of broken flint which, under the spell of Sam's imagination, became scrapers and burins and other wonders of Stone Age craftsmanship.

"Your husband came in wearing this thing around his neck," Carson translated. "They tried getting it off him, but he wouldn't have it." He paused while the Director said something, his face wreathed in regret. "Seems there was an unfortunate incident in the night," he went on. "Someone got into Sam's room. A thief. Tried to make off with this medallion thing. They're holding him here, in case you want to press charges. Mrs. Wendell?"

She rubbed her eyes. What did any of this matter?

"If nothing was stolen, I'd let the man go," she said.

"The boy," corrected Carson. "Some gypsy kid." He exchanged a few words with the Director, who was tapping his temple with a slantwise grin, and added, "Seems the boy's nuts. Out of his mind. Cuckoo."

"Then the poor lad needs help, not punishment," she responded sharply.

"We're talking about looting a corpse here," he reminded her.

"I'm sure the corpse doesn't give a damn."

At this, the Director gave a puzzled shrug and, rising to his feet, asked if she would like to see her husband now.

He led the way out into the corridor to a separate complex of prefabricated buildings. Here there was none of the hubbub of patients' families milling around the wards; instead, two orderlies in white fatigues posted at the main door screened all who entered, while others within chaperoned sombre, shuffling patients around like prison wardens. Halfway down the corridor, the Director stopped outside a door. It was locked and bolted. He opened a narrow sliding panel and glanced inside, then beckoned her forward with a brief remark. Carson translated.

"That's your 'poor lad'," he said.

She peered in through the slit. The room was small and bare, lit only by a naked lightbulb and a narrow, barred window set high in the wall. Although there was a mattress and a bench, the boy squatted on his ankles on the floor, his back to the door. His matted reddish-black hair had been shaven in a broad swathe, revealing an ugly deep gash running across his scalp, stained orange with iodine, while on the floor in the corner lay a blood-stained bandage he'd evidently ripped off. All the time she'd been observing him, he hadn't moved a muscle.

She turned anxiously to Carson.

"Something's wrong with that boy."

"They had to tranquilize him," he replied.

"How did he get that terrible cut?"

Carson shrugged. "They can't make head or tail of the kid," he said.

"Have his parents been told?"

"They can't trace any parents."

"And they're going to turn him out, just like that?" She was aghast.

The Director looked surprised when Carson translated.

"But you wanted him released," he responded.

"Not if he's got nowhere to go and no one to look after him."

"Mrs. Wendell, this isn't the United States. Thousands of children in this country don't have homes. They survive."

"Surely there's something we can do?" She addressed this appeal to Carson. "We can't just turn our backs on him."

"Live out here, ma'am," replied the old roughneck, "and you'd soon drop those soft romantic notions." He took her elbow. "Come on. They have their ways, we have ours."

She bit her lip. Perhaps, she shouldn't interfere in other people's lives. She had her own to straighten out, and right now that was lying dead in the mortuary. That was where she had to start to piece it together again.

•

The afternoon had passed in an empty, timeless continuum. There were endless official papers to sign, and always Carson was on hand, easing through the red tape with a nod and a wink here and few dollar bills there. He went off for an hour or two, but when he returned he appeared uncharacteristically agitated and caused a great stir about the place. She retreated to the ante-room to the morgue. He found her there and told her that a vehicle was arriving in the early hours of the morning to take her and the casket to a nearby Turkish military airbase, where a USAF transport plane, diverted on a flight homeward bound for the United States, would pick them up at 0500 hours.

It was now late evening. As she sat quietly in the

ante-room, composing herself for her final farewell, she thought of Sam and the deep pride he felt in being born an American. Now, for the first time, she felt she properly appreciated what it meant. She felt filled with gratitude for all the help Carson and Cray and, by extension, their nation had spontaneously offered. Would her own country have done the same had Sam been British and Professor of Anthropology at Oxford? She thought back to all the times she'd mocked him for taking his patriotism so seriously—all that raising and furling of the flag and the hand on the heart pledging loyalty to his country, right or wrong—and she felt that, when stripped of the jingoism, there really was something admirable, even enviable, in the spirit of nationhood, the sense of belonging to one gigantic, polymorphous family which, at times like this, served and protected its own. It was a side of him she'd never properly appreciated, and now, at the end, it was what served him best.

Slowly she rose to her feet. As she opened the door, a heavy smell of formaldehyde hit her. The morgue was in darkness but for a low red safety light and the last of the dusk filtering in through a small, half-open window. For a moment she stood on the threshold, letting her eyes grow accustomed to the dim light. In the center stood a large marble slab on which lay the rough wooden coffin, open, its lid propped up against the wall...

Suddenly she froze.

A movement, right there, in the shadows beneath the slab!

She choked back a cry. Was she imagining it, or could she see eyes burning at her out of the dark? Slowly, to her horror, the shadow came alive. A hand detached itself, then an arm, rising above the form of the slab and coffin, the silhouette of a head with a mop of wild, tangled hair. As the head turned, she caught a glimpse of the profile, and instantly she recognized the boy she'd seen through the door panel, the boy caught thieving. Surely they'd let him go, hadn't they? Had he come back?

A wave of pity flooded through her. The poor boy obviously had nowhere to go. What could she do? Give him money? She'd left her purse in the Director's office. As she fumbled through the pocket of her jacket for anything to give, her fingers touched the curious stone he'd sought to steal.

"Here," she said, stepping forward. "Take it."

The boy made no move at first. By now she could see better and began to make out more about him. He wore a tee-shirt inscribed *Harvard University*, of all things. Had he plundered it from the scene of the crash and somehow hitched a ride on the truck which had taken Sam to the hospital? Then she saw the blood-stain on the shirt. Oh God: had Sam run him over? But he must have been wearing it *before* the accident. Had he then been in the jeep with Sam at the time?

Her whirl of thoughts came to an abrupt halt. The boy had risen to his feet. Slowly, with cat-like movement, he reached out a hand. For a moment they stood with their hands only inches apart, and the thought flashed across her mind that he was going to snatch the sharp stone and attack her with it, but as she looked into his large, deep eyes and scanned his strange, unfamiliar features, she realized that he was the one who was afraid.

"Take it," she repeated in a whisper.

With a soft grunt he took the stone and gazed at it for a long moment with a look of respectful awe. Turning, he carefully laid the stone inside the coffin. Then, with a long, choking sob of grief, he sank back into the shadows whence he had come.

When she'd finally winched up the courage, she stepped forward and peered in the coffin at the loosely swathed body. The flintstone lay neatly arranged on his chest. His face appeared calm and composed, but the harder she stared, determined to fix the image on her mind for ever, the more an uneasy feeling grew that the calmness was merely the superficial stillness of a corpse and that behind the frozen, waxy mask lay something quite else, some half-formed cry, gagged in midutterance. Desperately she struggled to read that last message. To whom, about what? A cry of pain? A cry of final terror in face of the great unknown? Or some howl of frustration at something unresolved, unachieved? It was the look of a drowning man in an empty ocean as the lifebelt slips ineluctably from his grasp.

She looked away. She was projecting. Seeing faces in the fire. Then, trying to ignore the thought of the other presence in the room, she drew up a chair and settled down to keep vigil. She had just closed her eyes and was saying a prayer when she felt a hand reach for hers. The skin was rough, yet the touch was strangely pliant. Squeezing her eyes shut against the tears, she clasped the hand tightly, grateful for the silent comfort.

●

Hugging the outside wall tightly, Carson peered in through the small low window. In the dim light he could just make out the shape of the woman slumped in a chair, her eyes closed. Then he caught sight of the other form huddled at her feet and drew back sharply. So, his hunch had been right. He'd searched the hospital high and low; if the boy was anywhere, it had to be here. With Sam Wendell.

He flexed his grip. Any minute now the men would reach the morgue. With any luck they'd flush the kid out right into his arms. He sank back into the shadows and waited.

While packing up Sam's personal effects for the flight, driven by simple curiosity, he'd played the dictaphone tapes. The anatomical stuff had gone over his head, but one thing was clear as daylight: the boy Sam Wendell had described there was one and the same as the boy who'd sneaked into the hospital here. He'd thought fast. What the heck had the professor been up to, smuggling a boy across from the other side? The kid might just be a gypsy from the wilds, but technically he was a Soviet citizen. This was one hell of a sensitive border. Sooner or later someone over there would report him missing, or someone this side would recognize his gobbledegook, and the next thing there'd be a nasty little international incident. He'd driven home and got on the scrambler to Langley right away. While waiting for instructions, he'd developed the film. He'd put through another call. This time to William Cray. And then the shit really hit the fan.

A sharp rap from inside the morgue broke his train of thought. The men were coming for the casket. Julia rose and opened the door. Then it happened, almost too fast. Suddenly the window flew open. In a single, agile movement, a small, stocky figure slithered out and dropped to the ground. Even before Carson moved, the boy had seen him. With a howl of terror, the boy scrambled to his feet. But he'd taken no more than two, perhaps three, steps when Carson was upon him and grabbing him by the shoulder, brought the side of his hand down in a short, hard jab to the base of the skull.

4

O

THE FLIGHT SEEMED INTERMINABLE, BUT IN A WORLD robbed of dimensions time had little meaning for Julia. She could sit there in that droning metal tube for eternity, for all anything mattered. Sam was dead: how could the impossible be true? All those things she'd meant to say and do were now to remain forever unsaid and undone. All marriages went through periods of storm and calm, and for the past year they'd had their share of rough weather. But she'd been determined not to let her second one drift onto the rocks in the way of the first. She'd recognized the pressures of Sam's work, with its late hours and frequent travel, and she'd done everything to ease the burden and keep the family home fires burning for him. Just after the move to Lexington his illness was diagnosed, and during the short, intensive treatment, they'd grown close again. But this brush with his own mortality had left him with a feverish desperation to live every moment to the full. He'd thrown himself into his life and work like a drowning man, and the chasm between them had gradually widened again. She'd understood and bided her time. But now, suddenly, time had run out. The clock had stopped, with the pendulum stuck in mid-cycle. She could never have forseen the cruelty of fate to reprieve a man one moment, only to strike him down the next. A man still in his late forties, too, with his best work yet to come. Life, as he'd remarked the day he got his discharge, was actual, not actuarial.

The illness had left him with another legacy, too. He had always wanted a child together, the love-child of an older man whose first family had long grown up and left home. But she'd always said, *Wait*: wait until Sandy was getting along better, wait until she herself had become established at the Unit, wait until the new house was properly fixed up. Each small postponement had seemed perfectly reasonable on its own until suddenly events overtook their plans. She'd never forget that first day the trouble was diagnosed: late into the night, they talked through their lives and made plans for the future, and she pledged to give him a child. But she was cheated even of that promise. True, they caught the cancer early and the cure was total, but the radiotherapy left him unable to father a child. Having pledged to give him a child, she took recourse in adoption. So, she had them placed on the books of several agencies in New York and the Coast—not in Boston, though, as he'd stipulated. That was four months ago. Nothing suitable came up, and they began talking of looking to other sources, perhaps Mexico, or Brazil. Now, of course, all that was perfectly academic. It would be just her and Sandy from now on.

She stared out of the airplane window. Sandy would be desperately upset by Sam's death. She'd taken to him from the outset. He personified the America she yearned to adopt, and he provided the practical entrée into it. He spent time with her, sharing his passions and interests with her, sometimes he'd take her to the Department with him, too, and she'd sit in on his lectures or rummage through the endless trays of fossils and prehistoric bones in the collection. Before school on the very morning the fateful call came through, for instance, she'd made a round of the anenometers and barometers in the garden, despite the bitter cold, carefully noting the readings in his special book for his return. With her craze for Jell-o and Froghurt, her pride in her school and its sports teams, her love of bleached denims and floppy sweatshirts and, of course, her ubiquitous Walkman, she was virtually indistinguishable from any other American tenth-grader. That was largely Sam's influence. How would she react now that he was gone? Might she be persuaded to consider returning to the home country? They could sell up and go back at a moment's notice. There was always an American school in London, if re-entry into the English educational system was a problem. She'd put it to her. Yet she could foresee her answer. For Julia herself, the reason for staying might have gone with Sam, but for Sandy America was now the home country.

The plane had begun its descent, and the buzz of excitement from the other passengers, mostly servicemen returning from duty abroad, rose in pitch. She glanced around the eager faces. They all had loved-ones to meet them, family and friends to welcome them home, a whole rich life awaiting them. She sat up. This wouldn't do. She took out her compact and lightly made up her face. She looked tired, and a thread of silver caught her eye among the waves of fair hair, but she wasn't badly preserved for a woman of thirty-eight, and single. She tightened her eyes shut against the sudden tears and allowed her body to sink with the plane until, with an abrupt jolt, they hit the runway.

•

As they drew to a halt and Air Force ground transportation vehicles converged on the plane, she noticed a black limousine with dark-tinted windows and a small flag on its hood emerge from the side of the terminal building and roll slowly across the tarmac. It pulled up a short distance away and waited, its exhaust billowing in clouds on the cold, clear morning air. She gathered up her belongings, collected her small overnight case from the steward's closet, and headed for the door.

A blistering cold wind whipped her face, bringing tears to her eyes, and she had to grope her way down the steps. By the time she'd reached the bottom, a figure had detached itself from the car and was advancing towards her. It was William Cray, deep in a black alpaca coat. Peeling off a glove, he took her hand with a courteous smile. The touch sent a curious shiver through her. He scrutinized her quickly, intensely. She felt a momentary confusion of feelings.

"Hello, Julia," he said with warmth.

"This is so kind of you," she murmured. His gaze flicked over her shoulder to the aircraft behind. She understood. "I'm sorry," she said. "You're meeting someone else."

"Of course not!" He beamed his penetrating blue eyes back upon her. "I've come to see you through the formalities. You must be beat. You won't want to wait in line with a bunch of rednecks."

"I'm really so grateful. For everything."

"Sam was a very valued friend, Julia," he replied with quiet emphasis. "And a great loss to all of us who shared his convictions." Beckoning to the driver to take her suitcase, he steered her towards the car. "Hurry in out of the cold."

As she turned, she followed his glance back towards the plane. The tail section had been swung aside to open up the loading bay, and fork-lift trucks were maneuvering into position beside a ground ramp. Should she wait for the coffin? He must have read her mind.

"I'll see that they have the casket sent ahead," he said, reaching for the car door. "To your home?"

She swallowed. "I rather think not."

"Of course. Just give them the address when everything's settled."

"I will. Thank you."

She was bending to get into the car when a sudden brief shout from the plane behind arrested her. She turned. A scuffle appeared to be going on inside the cargo bay.

"Hurry on in." Cray was pressing her forwards.

But the shouting grew louder and, a moment later, two burly servicemen in military police uniform came down the ramp half dragging and half carrying between them a small, stocky, writhing, kicking figure. Cray moved to help her into the car, blocking her line of sight. But she had recognized the wild, matted hair and beneath an Air Force denim jacket, the torn maroon tee-shirt.

She started forward.

"My God," she cried. "It's that boy!"

Even as she spoke, a medical orderly hurried forward and pressed something into the boy's arm. Almost at once he fell quiet and, with buckling legs, allowed himself to be marched off to a waiting military ambulance.

Her mind was reeling. How had he got there? What was going on? She grasped Cray's sleeve.

"That's the boy from the hospital in Turkey! What's he doing here? What are they doing to the poor wretch?"

Cray hesitated a split second before replying.

"Looks like they got a stowaway," he said with a mild shrug.

He must have climbed aboard on purpose, she thought. He didn't want to be parted from Sam. She forced Cray to meet her eye.

"Hey, they can't just haul him off like that."

"Julia, please. It's none of our concern." He steered her finally into the seat and hurried around to the other side. Across the tarmac, the ambulance sped away. "They'll probably just put him on a plane back home," he added with finality.

"But he hasn't *got* a home! Your man Carson said so. This is perfectly dreadful."

"Don't *worry*, Julia." He addressed the driver. "Drop me off at the commandant's office. Wait while I get Mrs. Wendell cleared. Then take her on to Lexington and come back for me."

Suddenly she became aware of her ill manners.

"I really can't accept," she protested. "I'm depriving you of your car."

"Don't give it a thought. I've got things to take care of here." He read her anxiety. "Listen to me, Julia. Whoever that kid is, he'll be looked after okay. Put it out of your mind. You've got enough to think about as it is. Now go home and get some rest."

●

*"Praise the Lord I'm a believer hallelujah folks verily
I say unto you it's a blessing to share the Word of God
in the Boston area..."*

Julia stared with venom at the neck in front of her.
An ugly, parboiled neck, square from skull to collar. She
really must stop being so wretchedly English. She could
easily tap him on the shoulder and ask him to turn the
radio off, but she knew she wouldn't, for fear of hurting
his feelings. But he wouldn't feel hurt: he was getting paid
to drive her, and that gave her the right to travel however
she liked. A perfectly simple commercial transaction, just
like a billion daily interactions that took place in this country. William Cray's help, for instance, was merely part of
some *quid pro quo* for what Sam had been or done. But
what about those who had nothing to hide? The boy, for
example?

She turned to look out of the window. The recent
snowfall had frozen, adding another layer to the drifts
piled on either side of the highway. To her right lay acre
upon acre of swampland, bristling with the tips of bul-
rushes and bracken and glazed with a pearly sheen of ice
which, here and there, caught the bright morning sun in
a dazzling flash. To her left lay woodlands of oak and
spruce, maple and willow, snow-locked and stretching
into the mauve-blue distance. As ever, she was struck by
the sheer beauty of the country.

As she stretched her gaze across the whitened landscape, images of the incident at the airbase kept flashing
across her mind. She simply couldn't put the boy out of
her mind; she felt somehow responsible for him. She
thought back to her conversation with William Cray as
she was leaving. He'd returned to the car and handed
her her passport, duly stamped, and she'd tackled him

again. She couldn't leave things there.

"What'll happen?"

"Charles here will drive you home and then . . ."

"I mean, to that boy?"

"They'll repatriate him, I guess," he'd responded in a terse, almost offhand manner.

"But he's got nowhere to go and no one to go to," she'd protested.

He'd made a display of concealing his exasperation.

"Julia, we're talking about an illegal immigrant. Besides, they think he's Armenian. That makes him a Soviet citizen."

"What about *glasnost*?"

"Exactly. The Soviets will expect us to send him right back."

"Maybe he's seeking asylum."

"Come on, does he look like a political refugee?"

"So they're going to ship him back to Armenia?"

"Or wherever they found him."

Thinking back to the *Harvard* tee-shirt, she'd begun to see it all very clearly.

"I think Sam found him," she'd said quietly. "He deliberately brought him out. I don't know why, but that's my belief."

"That's all somewhat academic," Cray had responded crisply, then mollified his tone. "Julia, there's nowhere he could stay here. If he's got no folks out there, he's not likely to have any over here either."

"There are charities, William. Agencies?"

"For a savage from the boondocks? Be real."

"Someone would adopt him. A family would take him in."

"Tell me," he'd asked softly, fixing her with his penetrating stare, "why are you so concerned about this boy?"

"Sam meant to help him. And I think he was very attached to Sam, too. I feel in a way responsible."

He'd allowed a brief silence to fall, then reached for the door-handle.

"Get home and get some rest, Julia. I know how you feel. You have a kind heart and you mean well. But don't get hung up on this kid. There's nothing you can do. It's out of your hands."

Now, as she gazed out of the car window across the frozen wastes, she heard her own voice saying, *I think Sam . . . deliberately brought him out. I don't know why, but that's my belief.* Gradually, she began to wonder if, after all, she had a hunch why he'd done this. Could it be possible that he'd meant not just to bring him out, but to bring him *home*?

Who *was* this boy, and why him? She thought back with emotion to the vigil they'd kept together over Sam's body. He'd been a stranger but he'd brought her the comfort of a son. What had he meant to Sam, and Sam to him? Perhaps Sam had taken pity on him, befriended him, possibly even saved his life. Certainly, there'd been a powerful bond, otherwise why would the boy have kept coming back? What would drive a poor, ignorant boy to fight to stay beside the dead body of a man he could hardly have known? And then to follow him aboard an airplane, surely the most terrifying ordeal for a gypsy kid from the wilds of nowhere. What could the poor child have been suffering, too, enclosed in a vast metal bird soaring high above the clouds? Only the power of love could inspire that devotion. The boy must have loved Sam. And Sam, in turn, must have loved the boy. Without any doubt, Sam had had a plan for him.

As she stretched her gaze to the snow-capped hills in the pallid, mauve distance, she heard herself repeating. *A family would take him in.*

Of course!

The clarity of the idea dazzled her. It was so obvious, so *right*. Wasn't it the very thing Sam had wanted?

Why not *their* family?

Instantly, she wished she'd never had the thought. Fine, with Sam around to be a father to the boy. Fine, too, if they *had* a proper family. But they didn't any more. She was a single parent with an only child. What kind of a family was that to bring a young boy into? And what about Sandy, who might accept the idea in principle but would respond differently when presented with the actual choice. Besides—and this thought came as some relief—it wasn't a real possibility anyway. At that very moment the boy was probably being put aboard a plane back out east, and the whole thing, in William's phrase, was academic.

In her mind's eye she saw again the look on Sam's face in death, that desperate, tormented frustration, the face of a man who'd died bursting with a message he could never tell. And once again the nagging question returned: why would Sam have taken such pains—even risked his life, and, as it turned out, lost it—to rescue this gypsy boy and smuggle him out? Why else except to make him the son they couldn't have and hadn't been able to adopt?

•

Julia lay in bed, as she had done for the past three nights, staring at the same sentence on the same page of her book, unable to see beyond the marks to the meaning. On the bedside table, the alarm clock showed it was gone two o'clock. Beside it, a bottle of Sam's Luminal insidiously offered the promise of sleep. She knew she wouldn't take any; she didn't believe in pills. Behind stood the photograph of Sam she liked most, the one taken in his study in their Cambridge house showing him enthusing over some primordial skull. She closed her eyes to see him better. That was the Sam she'd fallen in love with: animated, electric, full of pride and energy. The flush of a toilet dragged her back to the present and its sorrowful reality, and she turned back to her book.

She'd begun the sentence again when she heard the creak of a floorboard in the corridor outside. Sandy put her head round the door. Her long, expressive face was full of concern.

"I saw your light," said the girl. "Are you okay?"

Julia returned a wan smile. "Can't you sleep either, darling?"

Sandy shook her head with a swirl of her long fair hair. She came over and sat on the side of the bed. She wore a knee-length tee-shirt imprinted with the icon of a rock star, and on her fingernails she had painted small dabs of pink lacquer in the mode of the current school craze. Her blue-grey eyes were drawn. She'd taken the news quietly, almost in a matter-of-fact way, but the wound had clearly cut deep. The same afternoon she'd taken herself off on a five-hour walk, and when she'd finally returned she was calm and strong. Over the following days, Julia found her reinforcing her own calmness and strength.

Strength in her resolve about the boy, too. She'd checked with Cray: he was still in the country, at some holding center while the repatriation paperwork was being processed. She'd discussed it carefully and at length with Sandy, and Sandy had agreed—if not with wild enthusiasm, at least without reluctance. She wondered if it was fair to ask the girl to make a decision of this importance anyway, with the shock of Sam's death so fresh, but they had to decide or they'd lose the chance. Even so, when she called William Cray to say they'd made up their minds to try and adopt the boy and to beg him to do all in his power to make it possible, he'd held out no great hope it could be done and told them to expect a negative.

She took the girl's hand. She had to be quite sure.

"Sandy," she began, "you would say, wouldn't you? We won't do anything without your absolute agreement."

"Not that again, Mom. I said okay. If it's what you want."

"But is it what you want?"

"I thought we'd agreed. You always go over and over things. It's simple: we've decided, so let's do it."

Things are never simple, my sweet child, Julia thought to herself, however they might appear from the perspective of a fifteen-year-old.

"It's a big step," she warned.

"Do give me some credit," she said with an impatient sigh. "I know it won't be easy. He can't speak a word of English and he sounds pretty bizarre, to say the least. But it'll be something worthwhile to work for. Just what you need right now."

"Sam wanted it. I'm quite sure."

"That's really not the point, Mom. The real question is, do you? It's okay to think about adopting when we were all a family, but you've got to decide if you want to burden yourself. It's okay for me: I've only got a couple of years and then I'll be in college. But you've got your own life. You're young, Mom, and you can start again . . ." She checked herself. "Sorry."

"No, no, you're right. I've thought about all that."

"Then it's settled, and no more worrying. Come on, pack it in for the night." She closed her book for her and laid it aside. "Try and sleep."

"You too, angel. God bless."

"Night. Mom."

The girl switched off her bedside light and, with a light kiss on her forehead, tiptoed out of the room. For a while, Julia stared up at the shaft of moonlight thrown across the ceiling. If it really came to the point, she thought, it might just work out.

°

A tumbler of bourbon in his hand, William Cray stared out at the traffic twenty stories below, gliding in a noiseless stream down Pennsylvania Avenue and converging on the Capitol in the distance. Even at two in the morning the nation's capital was throbbing. The sight of ribbons of white headlights and red tail-lights forging into the indigo backdrop of the starry sky beyond always stirred him. It was the American flag, writ large.

He turned back to his desk and drew the lamp closer. He reached again for the magnifying glass. *Extraordinary.* No doubt about it. The curious oval stone in the photograph, lying in the chest cavity of the half-burnt cadaver, was the very same stone as now lay on the blotter beside his tumbler.

He leafed slowly through the rest of the sheaf of blow-ups. A wild, empty, craggy mountainscape. A pile of charred human bones, taken from every angle, first as a group, then each individually. Then, oddly out of sequence, the shot of a woman. Long dark hair. Early twenties. Intelligent face. Hazel eyes smiling over the brim of a wine-glass. Sitting at a table, outlined against a window arch. Behind the sun setting over a lagoon. Venice? He moved on to the next photograph: a man's private life should remain private in his death.

He reached for the paleontologist's report. For the fifth time he read it, trying to read between the *caveats* ("the limited evidence available appears to suggest..." and "without actual specimens in hand for positive radiocarbon dating...") for any interpretation he might have missed, any conceivable explanation other than this utterly incredible, shattering bombshell.

He turned to the small tape recorder. His old friend's voice was hardly recognizable; in parts, it rambled incoherently as though he was drugged, and in others it trailed off as if he'd wandered away from the recorder. But all along he could hear the urgency crackling through the tiny speaker. Sam had known what he was on to all along. He'd even hinted as much at their lunch at the F Street Club the day before he'd left on the trip. He'd been studying satellite photos of the area he was visiting and something had been preoccupying him deeply. He wouldn't divulge what. "But just wait, William," he'd said with deadly cool. "I'll bring you back something you won't believe. The biggest thing since Genesis. The ultimate test case."

Turning off the tape, he reached for the report on the boy. Carefully, point by point, he compared it with the transcript of the tape—the shape and cast of the boy's head and features, his physique and general build, his bizarre manners and behavior, the puzzle of his unidentifiable language...

He rolled the bourbon thoughtfully around his glass and stared out at the night sky. All was silent but for a gentle, persistent bubbling coming from the large tropical aquarium set into the panelling behind the desk. His thoughts turned to Julia. Damn the woman: a typical sentimental Englishwoman, looking for a crusade. Why couldn't she stick to doing her good works at that kids' mental home? She'd been on the phone, pestering him, twice a day. He'd told her the boy was being held in a halfway house, pending inquiries—and that was the truth. Well, partly the truth: the inquiries were of a biological, not a diplomatic nature, and the house was, in fact, a laboratory whose research lay in that twilight region halfway between commerce and government. Then, late that afternoon, he'd returned to his office at the Foundation headquarters to find her on the phone, holding.

"Sandy and I have discussed it fully," she'd told him simply. "We're absolutely determined to adopt that boy if we possibly can. We want to bring him up in our house, as one of the family. Yes we, ourselves. We need your help, William."

He'd fudged as best he could, saying it was really out of the question.

But *was* it out of the question?

Eliot Lovejoy was the main obstacle. He was thirsting to get his hands on the specimen. But biological and physiological data were only part of the extraordinary story this boy could tell. The bigger questions were ethical and behavioral, to do with how a genuine primitive would react to the aggressive and competitive impulses of a modern social environment and what that, in turn, would teach us about our own essential nature and the structures best suited to control it. And how better could *that* be studied than by placing the boy out there in society—indeed, in an actual real-life family? He was far too unsocialized to enter a proper household yet, but given a few weeks, or as long as it could be spun out, he could be tidied up, trained, conditioned...

He glanced at the desk-clock, recording the different time zones around the world, and reached for the phone. He'd speak to a couple of the other directors.

5

"MOM? THE CAR'S HERE." SANDY WAS CALLING FROM the living room. "Are you coming?"

Julia was in the study, unpacking the box of Sam's personal effects that had arrived earlier that morning. She winced. As bad as being called Mom was being yelled at from two rooms away. But then, she was living with an American teenager; wasn't that what she'd been wanting?

She stared at the insignificant relics of Sam's life lying on the leather-topped desk. His Rolex, his pipe, his pocket map . . . Distantly she wondered if there hadn't been more—a pocket dictaphone and some rolls of film? Maybe they were in the crate with the stuff from the jeep. What should she do with it all? Everywhere she turned were stacks of his stuff to be sorted through. A huge pile of mail forwarded from the Department filled a corner of the desk; even working through that would take ages. It wasn't going to be easy, tying up the loose ends of a life brought down in mid-flight.

A postcard projecting from the pile caught her eye. The picture showed a surly camel against an arid desert landscape. It was addressed to Prof. Sam Wendell, Peabody Museum, Divinity Ave., Cambridge, Mass. and bore a Pakistani stamp.

> Hi! Finally made it! Mules lame, guides corrupt. All I can do to keep them from butchering the gazelles for meat. I share a sleeping-bag with half the creepy-crawlers in creation. Steve's great. Foraged for wood for 4 hours so I could shower. Not quite the Danieli, but could it ever be? See you before you get this.
>
> M.

She turned it over. Who was "M"? One of his students, perhaps. Looked like a woman's writing, but you couldn't tell: all Americans seemed to write in an identical copperplate. The Danieli—the hotel in Venice? Sam had taken her to Venice for their honeymoon. Quickly she slipped the card back into the pile. The memory was too sweet and too painful.

The door burst open and Sandy came in. She had tied her long fair hair back with a black ribbon, and beneath the designer coat she'd borrowed from Kirsty next door she wore a white shirt with a black bootlace tie.

"The car's here," she repeated impatiently, then checked herself. "You okay?"

"Fine."

The girl glanced at the box of Sam's stuff and fixed her severely with her grey-blue eyes.

"Let's get the funeral over with and then we'll clear everything out. Being maudlin won't bring him back."

"I'm not being." She was toying with his old-fashioned spirit cigarette lighter. Suddenly she smashed it down on the desktop. Objects in the box jumped, and on the edge of the desk a silver photo-frame toppled face down. She clenched her jaw. "I'm not maudlin. I'm angry."

"Angry?"

"At him. Why did he have to go on that trip? He knew the risks. I told him, it takes a year to get over a serious illness, but he didn't listen. Field trips are for younger men, I said. You can imagine how he took that! So off he gallivanted. It was so *thoughtless*. In a family, you have to think of the others, the ones you leave behind."

She looked up, expecting to see shock on her daughter's face. Instead, a frown of sympathy puckered the young girl's forehead.

"You're bound to feel angry when you put so much into one person and then they die," she replied quietly. "I feel let down in a way, too. But it proves how much we loved him. That's the way I think of it."

Julia reached out and squeezed the girl's hand. She felt stirred to cement this moment of fellow-feeling by proposing an adventure. But even as she spoke she knew she'd picked the wrong tack.

"What you say we go back home for a decent holiday when it's all over?" she suggested. "We'll stay at Claridge's and do it properly. Get a taste of the old place."

"We can't afford it, Mom."

"Hang the money!" She gestured around the room. "Look at this great big house and all this stuff. We don't need anything so grand, not just for us. We don't even *need* to be here."

"England's boring."

"It's civilized, at least. Here, if you don't have money
and influential friends, you're nobody. I've seen that in
the last few days. Over there, it's different. People judge
each other by what they are, not by what they've got."

"You're being sentimental. It's all changed over
there." She took her arm and pulled her away from the
desk. "Come on, for heaven's sake! You'll have to pay
the grave-diggers overtime."

"Alexandra!" she cried, shocked. But she was smiling, too, as she followed her daughter out of the room
and down the corridor, past the dining room where the
caterers were laying out the buffet lunch, pausing in the
hallway for her coat and gloves, then out into the crisp,
still morning air and to the black limousine waiting to take
them to the chapel.

°

Sam had been popular and well connected, she
knew, but she was astonished by the number that had
made the journey to the spacious, colonial-style chapel.
Half Cambridge seemed to be there: colleagues and pupils from the Department, his assistant Bernard, students
from other faculties, friends, and former neighbors, even
the coach of the football team he'd avidly supported and
the manager of the deli in Harvard Square where he
stopped every morning for bagels and coffee. There was
one young woman, too, who cast her a long, intense
glance as she walked down the central aisle, a tall dark-
haired girl with an alert face and a creamy complexion
accentuated by brightly reddened lips. At the end of the
service, Julia turned to Sam's old friend the Professor of
Linguistics, Walter Schreiber, sitting in the row behind,
and asked if he knew who she was. Walter flushed and

fumbled for a reply; he believed her name was Maxine Fitzgerald, he said, and she was a geneticist at the Massachusetts Institute of Technology. Julia cast the young woman a friendly smile; it was pleasing to think how widely Sam had been known and admired.

Others had come from further afield. Sam's brother and his wife had come from Virginia, though their plane was delayed and they arrived as the mourners were filing out of the chapel to the graveside. And William Cray had flown in from Washington, bringing with him a man he introduced as Dr. Eliot Lovejoy, a lean, avuncular figure with a slight stoop and the face of a bloodhound. She felt touched that he had made the journey and sorry at the circumstances that had brought them together. Maybe, when all this was over, she might get to know him better and to discover the side of Sam he'd known. When offering their condolences, people spoke of Sam with such special warmth that she felt a pang of something close to jealousy to think of how much of him she had not known. It was as if she'd had her Sam and they'd had theirs, and both were gone, lowered into the earth inside that ornately carved coffin. No one would ever know the complete Sam.

In contrast to the funeral service in the overheated, airless chapel, the interment itself was brief, for an Arctic wind scoured the graveyard, whiplashing the huddled figures with frozen particles of snow and rime. Julia felt detached, as though she were viewing the scene from afar. Numbly, she gazed over the cemetery, a gently undulating landscape laid out more like a golf course than a graveyard, and, to one side, cordoned off by a line of cypresses, the cloistered Garden of Remembrance, and she found herself thinking once again that this was just the set of a film she'd stumbled in upon, with Sandy and the other actors playing their parts in the fiction, and that any moment the director would cry *Cut!* and real life would resume. It was not the real *her* who, standing bareheaded in the teeth of the cold, stepped forward as the final words were uttered commending the departed's soul to the life everlasting and cast a single white rose into the pit. Nor were they the real selves of those people standing back at a respectful distance from the open chasm, their faces set hard in expressions of grief and sympathy. And yet there was one sound that carried about it the terrible ring of reality—the rhythmic, hollow thud of earth falling upon the coffin lid.

As the gathering broke up, William Cray stepped forward and taking her arm, accompanied her down the path toward the line of limousines. Sandy took her other arm. As they neared the end, he stopped, allowing the main press of people to pass and pay their condolences, and then drew her to the side. Triumph gleamed in his startling pale blue eyes. She felt gripped by a hypnotic fascination.

"Good news, Julia," he said. "I believe we can work it out."

"Work it out?"

"The adoption."

"Ah." She tore her gaze away and flashed a glance at Sandy.

"I wanted you to know right away," he went on eagerly. "I know how much this means to you. And would have meant to Sam, God rest his soul." He paused, his eyes hardening. "You're the only hope that poor kid has, Julia. Now is not the time, I know," he said, leaning closer, "but a lot of people pulled a lot of strings for you on this.

That's how much they thought of Sam."

"I'm very touched," she mumbled. "We both are, aren't we, darling?"

Sandy nodded, but said nothing.

"There is one thing, though," he went on, raising a cautionary finger. "Don't expect to have him quite yet. We can't bypass all the channels. He'll be staying in for a while longer. Like quarantine. But the agency will handle all that." He opened the car door and held out his hand with a bright smile. "I must ask you to excuse me, Julia. I won't be able to join you. I have to get back to D.C. by this afternoon."

"Of course." She took his hand. "Thank you, William. I do appreciate all you've done."

He turned to Sandy. "Goodbye, young woman. You've made a brave and generous choice."

Sandy shook his hand in silence, and with a courteous bow he left. After they'd settled into the car, she muttered, "Brave and generous, *hah!* You'd think he wanted us burdened with that kid."

"We don't *have* to be," responded Julia automatically.

"Oh, for goodness' sake, mother, stop it! It's what you've been angling for all along. Just stop trying to lay it all on me. I said I'll go along with whatever you want, okay?"

She turned away and stared out of the window. Julia looked out through her own side, wondering how she had got into this vicious trap. Was it because Sandy spoke her mind in the way any American child was brought up to do, whereas she herself never expected people to say what they meant? She'd read layers of subtext into Sandy's words that probably just weren't there, so that even now, with the deed all but sealed, she didn't really know whether the girl was really saying Yes or No. Everything was topsy-turvy. She wasn't hearing her daughter any more.

The car slowly pulled away. Lost in her troubled thoughts, she suddenly found herself looking into the gaze of the tall, dark-haired young woman, standing a short distance away and fixing her with that same intense stare as in the chapel. Gradually as she held her eye, her stare softened into a careful, almost complicit smile.

•

Max turned right off Massachusetts Avenue and nosed her red Rabbit down Brookline toward the Charles River. To her right, in a narrow no-through street off Putnam Avenue, stood the condominium in which she lived. A couple of blocks to her left lay the main complex of the Massachusetts Institute of Technology and, directly overlooking the river, stood the drab, rain-streaked Sixties lab block which housed the Department of Biogenetics where she worked.

She'd flown in from Pakistan the previous afternoon and still felt mildly disoriented, and yet she already had the feeling she'd never been away. The weather had grown colder in her absence and the buildings one degree grimier where the clapboard had trapped the snow, but nothing else had outwardly changed. The same steady coil of steam still rose from the manhole cover outside her house as though a dragon breathed beneath the street, the car in the parking bay alongside hers still bore its tattered bumper sticker ("Guns don't cause crime any more than flies cause manure") and electric Yuletide candles still burned in the window of the first-floor apartment below her own.

And yet things had changed for her, inwardly. As soon as she'd arrived, she'd called Sam on his direct line at the Peabody Museum. His assistant Bernard had answered. At first she hadn't believed the terrible news. She'd called back and spoken to his secretary for confirmation. She'd even obeyed an invincible urge to call his home in Lexington, giving a fictitious name. Julia had answered; she'd been very precise and restrained and relayed the simple facts. It *was* true. And now, to banish any doubt, she'd just witnessed his casket being lowered into the ground.

She slammed the car door hard in anger and pain. Huddling into her overcoat, she headed for the steps that led up the side to her front door. She'd better start getting used to life without Sam.

Inside her apartment, she kicked off her shoes and fixed herself a herbal tea in the kitchen while she listened to the messages on her answering machine. The first was from Gerald, her head of department. He spoke close into the receiver in a tone full of intimate innuendo.

"So, the dove has returned?" The reference was to Project Noah, the endangered species project, but the double meaning didn't escape her. "I need you to bring me up to date. How about a working supper? Call me. Ciao."

For God's sake, she muttered to herself. She would see him in the labs in the morning, in professional hours. She reached for the pile of unopened mail. Letter, bills, circulars—nothing interesting except a card from Murray, the researcher with whom she shared her lab. He was in Cleveland, Ohio, giving a paper to a conference on a breakthrough technique he'd developed in his part of the vast national project for mapping the entire human genome. The card was an old black and white photo of Crick and Watson in Stockholm receiving their Nobel prizes, only he'd overlaid Watson's head with his own. Murray stooped, wore boffin glasses and had a complexion cratered like the moon. But he was brilliant at his work and had a good heart, too.

She tossed the envelopes aside and went to the living room. She needed a decent drink. She poured a large, neat Stolichnaya and, putting on a record of Strauss's "Four Last Songs," sank into the sofa and waited for the vodka to take effect. Right. She'd clear out all evidence of Sam, the photos, the mementos of sneaked weekends at imaginary conferences, the bathrobe and toothbrush he kept there, even the small stock of his favorite malt she'd laid in. She'd develop a new set of friends. She'd change her hairstyle, redecorate the apartment, throw a party and make a wall-hanging out of the Afghan silk drape Sam had brought her back on an earlier trip, which now lay as a covering on the bed. She'd parcel up the books he'd lent her and send them to his home with a note of condolence. And she wouldn't listen to any more of this high-romantic German stuff. Abruptly she rose and turned off the music. Her new life started here.

6

A SLOW, STEADY DRIPPING SOUND WOKE JULIA. HER immediate thought was that a pipe in the loft had frozen and burst, but as she lay trying to pinpoint the source she realized it came from outside: water was dripping off the eaves onto the window-sill. With a surge of delight, she leapt up and threw open the curtains.

The thaw had begun. Beneath a dazzling mid-March morning sun, she saw that the frozen carpet of snow lying across the sloping garden had shrunken, revealing large patches of tousled green. Small rivulets veined the crust in a delicate latticework. A thick clump of snow slid from the bough of a nearby fir tree and fell wetly into the soft mush below. She opened the window and inhaled the fierce, crisp air. A line of footprints scuffed a sloppy trail through the slush down to the river, returning in a different direction through the woods: Sandy had been for her run. The air stung her cheeks, the light seared her eyes. Stretching her gaze to the line of trees beyond in the piercing crystal air, she felt she could see the very finest twig on the furthest branches. The clarity of the light here still startled her, in contrast to the murky mistiness of England; it aroused in her an irrepressible sense of excitement, too, as though in a land where you could see forever, anything was possible.

She dressed quickly, impatiently, for today she had a lot to do. Today the boy was arriving.

As she was coming downstairs, she heard the phone ring, but Sandy had hung up by the time she reached the kitchen: it was a wrong number. The girl handed her a glass of orange juice.

"You look as if you need this," she said.

Julia switched on the coffee machine she'd prepared the night before.

"You know," she smiled, "one day I really will come jogging with you."

"Running," corrected the girl. "I wouldn't. It'd finish you off."

"What's happened to Scott these days?"

"He trains down the track."

"Don't worry, you'll soon have a running mate. He's quite a tough little chap."

"He *looks* like one, you mean." Sandy took the English muffins out of the toaster and turned with a swirl of her blonde ponytail. "Don't you think they should have let us meet him properly? A couple of visits in—what?— six weeks isn't my idea of getting to know my future brother. Admit it, Mom, we don't know the first thing about him. Talk about a blind date!"

"He's been in quarantine, you know that."

Sandy gave a derisory snort.

"They're worried he's got rabies, or what?"

"That's the regulations. These things take time."

Adoption agencies were snowed under with work,

as she knew from experience, and processing an application could take ages. Anyway, William had called and very sweetly and patiently explained the reasons for the delay. First, the boy was an alien, without papers, or any known parents or relatives, and that was causing headaches for immigration. Then the Health Department had insisted on a quarantine period and on running its own medical checks. The usual choke-up of red tape.

"Tell me," she began more brightly, "what do you think of 'Adam'?"

"Adam who?"

"As a name. We can't go on call him 'this boy'."

Sandy sighed impatiently. "Why don't you just call him Sam and be done with it?"

"That'll be his middle name," replied Julia, refusing to rise to the taunt. "Adam Samuel Wendell. It's got a certain ring, don't you think?"

She blew her fringe out of her eyes.

"Very classy, Mom."

A brief silence fell, filled by the sputtering of the percolator. Adam: that was the name she'd been going to give Sandy if she'd been a boy. A good, firm, *basic* name. She glanced at the girl, then looked away. Once again she asked herself if this thing was going to work. She'd been increasingly worried about what she'd let them in for. Hints from the adoption agency, not to mention her own trained observations during the visits, warned her that the boy could be quite a problem. She'd suspected from the first that he might be a little backward, that his strange grunts might conceal some language handicap, but precisely how far this was an abnormality she couldn't yet tell. The boy—Adam—was not your average European or American twelve-year-old. He would undoubtedly have special needs to be catered for; Sandy had her own needs, too, and these were bound to come into conflict. This was going to require some delicate balancing. She'd lain awake these past nights as the day drew inexorably closer, worrying it over and over until she was exhausted and the problem itself grew worn so smooth that it seemed to slip from her mind's grasp. Today, some time in the afternoon, the front door would open and she'd come face to face with her new charge. Until then, she simply didn't know what to expect. She had tried insisting on seeing more of the boy, only to meet with a polite but immovable brick wall. She hadn't pressed it too far; in a way, she didn't want to know too much too soon. She'd made up her mind, and however odd or disturbed the boy turned out to be, it would make no difference to her. In fact, as Sandy observed, she hadn't made up her mind so much as made up her *heart*: the poor lad looked so lost, so lonely, so desolate. Sandy said it was like going to a stray dogs' home. Still, underneath the worldly wisdom of adolescence, maybe she felt touched with pity, too.

Julia poured a large black coffee. Sandy saw, and frowned.

"You go on about drugs, Mom," she said, "but what's caffeine? Plus you don't eat. Here," she handed her a buttered muffin and intoned, "take, eat . . ."

"Don't be profane," reproved Julia.

"Well, it is sort of the Last Breakfast."

She searched the girl's serious eyes.

"Sandy, listen. We're only taking him on for a trial period, remember. If it doesn't work out in a month or so . . ." She trailed off.

"Yes? What then?"

"Well, we'll have to find him an alternative home."

"You said we'd just send him back. See—now we're taking responsibility for him. We'll never get rid of that."

"Not at all. It's explicitly agreed."

"Be realistic, Mom." She shrugged. "Well, whatever happens, we'll cope. We always do."

"Right," agreed Julia, her heart sinking.

•

Julia fussed around the large, airy living room plumping up cushions and straightening the books and magazines on the coffee-table. For a while she busied herself re-arranging the flowers but, suddenly dissatisfied, took them all out and exchanged them for vases from the hall and study. She went around the room dusting and polishing, taking special care over the fine old ebonized drinks cabinet, the antique hickory escritoire and the mantlepiece with its precious Chinese porcelain vases. In the kitchen she cleared the work surface, stacked the plates and cutlery in their cupboards and drawers and tidied away the olive oil and blueberry vinegar and other condiments, although she knew she'd be needing them later. Then, feeling it looked too bare, she took out plates and cutlery again and laid the table. For tea, or supper? Would they have put him on a regime like at the Unit—spaghetti rings, hamburger, french fries, milk shakes, eaten at five-thirty? Well, here he would eat as Sandy and herself did, proper food at a European hour; he'd eat with them, as one of them. As she put out the paper napkins and stood back, she felt a brief stab of pain, remembering the last time she'd laid that table for three.

She returned to the kitchen to call the Unit—she was taking this as her fortnight's vacation and she was worried about one of her cases, a ten-year-old autistic boy who'd had a bad seizure the previous afternoon—but something was wrong and she couldn't get a line. She went to Sam's study next door to try the phone there. On the threshold she hesitated, shocked by the ravages she herself had wrought. Previously an oasis of calm and order, a temple to reason and knowledge, lined from floor to ceiling with books and decorated and carpeted entirely in a uniform *eau de nil*, the room now lay bare and stripped, the shelves empty and the books crammed into packing cartons or stacked in haphazard piles on the floor. She was intending to donate them to the Peabody, but she had to sort and list them first. She bit her lip; she should have done it all in one fell swoop, and before now, too. And yet, part of her wanted them to stay there, sharing their proper place with the rest of the apparatus of his profession—his specimen cabinet, his computer terminal and all the mass of papers and lectures and articles that represented the sum of the man's achievement. They *were* him: how could she throw them out?

She glanced directly through the window. On the lawn beyond the gravel drive, in a direct line of sight, stood the flagpole. Since the tragedy the floodlights had remained off at night, with the flag at half-mast. Abruptly she crossed to the desk. She'd go out later that very morning and raise the flag. And she'd get down to sorting out the books once for all. Today the mourning was over.

She lifted the receiver, but still could get no line. She tried calling the operator, but the line itself was dead. Or was it? In the background she could hear a faint but distinct sound like air bubbling through water. Puzzled, she replaced the receiver. She'd give Adam's new bedroom a final check and then, if it still wasn't working, go to the Blanes' next door and report the fault.

The spare room was separated from Sandy's bedroom by a bathroom of its own and commanded a fine view over the lawns sloping down to the river and the woodland beyond. She'd had it redecorated and fitted out with shelves, a desk and a large toy chest. In the cupboard lay an assortment of loose-fitting clothes she'd bought, guessing the size—jeans, tee-shirts, sweatshirts, a tracksuit, even a pair of sneakers the woman in the shop had said would fit a well-built twelve-year-old. In the toy chest, being uncertain of his stage of development, she had set him up with the common essentials—crayons and a drawing-book, Lego bricks and Disney character toys. As she unwrapped a poster a colleague from the Unit had well-meaningly given him, showing space ships zapping one another in a galactic war game, she frowned: somehow she didn't think a backward gypsy boy from the remote wilds of the Caucasus would relate to that. Not yet, at least. She was furling it up again when the phone rang. She hurried down the corridor to her own bedroom to take it, filled with sudden anxiety that it might be the agency saying the whole thing was off.

It was William Cray. He'd been trying her all morning, he said, but her line had been down. There was something he wanted to discuss with her before the boy arrived. A lot of people at the Foundation had been very fond of Sam, he told her, and they'd decided to set up a small trust in his memory. They'd wondered whether to endow a Fellowship after him, or possibly offer travel grants for anthropological studies, but when they'd heard about the boy and the special interest Sam had taken in him, and now that he was being adopted into the family, they felt here was the ideal opportunity for their support.

"You'll have additional expenses, Julia," he insisted. "Money for the boy's special needs. For his education. For medical treatment. In fact, as far as that's concerned," he hurried in, "I've already spoken to Ralph Singer. He's agreed to take him on. He's the best. But you already know that."

She frowned. Sam had thought the world of Dr. Singer and gave him the prime credit for his recovery, but she'd never liked the man. He had dead eyes.

"You won't pay a dime, Julia," Cray was saying. "We'll cover his fees."

"I really can't allow you to do this," she protested.

"Don't deny Sam's friends the means of showing their appreciation."

"But I don't need financial help," she responded, conscious of sounding ungrateful.

"Don't stand on your pride, Julia. Any help is more than willingly given. Sam meant a great deal to a lot of people."

"Well, that's very kind of you all, then."

He heaved a satisfied sigh.

"Good. So, everything's set. Let me just wish you the best of luck."

"Thank you, William. I suspect we'll need it."

"Oh, by the way, I called about your phone line. They're sending along repairmen to fix it. Well, goodbye, Julia."

As she replaced the receiver, she stared at the Star Wars poster in her hand. What *was* a child from the wilds of nowhere going to make of this culture?

•

"Martha Walker. Hello again, Mrs. Wendell." The smartly dressed young woman on the doorstep smiled, showing perfect teeth, and held out her hand. Julia remembered her from her visits to the agency, where she fielded her questions with the practiced skill of a politician. She gestured to an impassive mouse-haired woman of middle years, standing on the step below her, dressed in a white hospital coat and carrying a medicine bag. "And this is Nurse Reed."

Julia looked around in perplexity.

"Didn't you bring him?"

With the briefest inclination of her head, Martha Walker indicated a white sanatorium van parked in the driveway. Sunlight glinted off the gold laminate on the windows.

"Let's go through the formalities first," she advised.

"Of course. Do come in."

Julia showed them into the living room. They refused refreshment. She signed, unread, the papers put in front of her. Martha Walker conducted the business in a cool, professional manner. She referred to the boy as the "adoptee child," the "case in question" and even "client 1577/B," until finally she seemed to run out of appellations.

"We don't have a name yet?" she asked, skimming through her papers.

"Adam," replied Julia firmly. "Adam Samuel."

"Adam suits him perfectly," murmured the woman drily, noting down the name. "Now, Nurse Reed will take you through the medication packet."

The nurse opened the medicine chest and took out a bottle of pink tablets.

"For his anxiety attacks, use the Valium here," she began in a flat voice. "If you find it peps him up instead, and it might, go for one of the alternatives—Librium or

Tranxene. In an emergency, you've got your Largactil right here." She pointed to a hypodermic syringe and a small batch of sealed vials. "One shot will usually zap him out."

Julia's mouth had gone dry. At the Unit they used drugs occasionally to control the extremes of behavior among the more manic and hyperactive children, though she'd always claimed that meant they'd failed. The nurse finished her catalogue and Martha Walker resumed her briefing.

"Okay, now for some behavioral abnormalities you may find distressing," she began in a clinical tone. "Whatever you make him wear, he'll want to tear it off. He hasn't quite reached puberty yet, but he can still cause embarrassment."

"I think I can cope," said Julia stiffly.

"I was thinking more of your daughter," replied the woman, unruffled. "Then there's the business of his domestic habits. He's had some of the rougher edges knocked off him, but I'm afraid he's far from being fully socialized. You'll learn for yourself about his eating and sleeping manners, but I should mention house-training." She held Julia's eye for a deliberate pause, then shifted her gaze out through the window. "Luckily you have plenty of open space here. You'll find it distasteful from time to time, but at least, by and large, he is discreet about where he chooses to mess."

"I see."

She swallowed. My God, she thought, what are we taking on? All right at a place like the Unit, specially set up to cope with cases like this. But at *home*? Martha Walker must have read her thoughts, for as she closed her file with a snap of finality she cast her a faint smile, half sympathetic, half pitying.

"I've been in the adoption business ten years, Mrs. Wendell," she said, "and I've never had a case like this. In my view, the boy should be institutionalized. He may be no more than twelve—or so our doctor estimates, based on his teeth—but he's got the physical strength of a college jock. At the same time, in terms of his ability to manage himself, he has the developmental level of a two-year-old. And as for speech, well, that's just plain gobbledegook. You certainly couldn't call it *language*." She looked casually around the room. "Pity about the porcelain. That'll have to go, of course. Nice rug. You spent what for it? Ten thousand dollars? Buy yourself a ten-dollar plastic groundsheet, Mrs. Wendell. And I'd advise plastic slip-covers for your chairs if you value your chintz."

"I do have some experience of problem children," said Julia tightly.

"Then I'm sure you'll do fine," replied the other woman without conviction, closing her briefcase. "Just think of him as an undomesticated animal with the strength of an ox and the manners of an ape and you'll make out nicely."

"I don't think that's a very proper attitude to take."

"Wait till you clear up the shit, dear," replied Martha Walker sweetly, rising to her feet.

Too taken aback to respond, Julia followed the young woman out through the front door into the crisp afternoon. The nurse went ahead and opened the back of the van. She lowered some steps and went inside. There was a long pause and a sound like the dragging of a heavy sack. Julia hurried forward just as the boy emerged into the daylight. She stifled a gasp.

He looked terrible. His face was bleached the color

of ash, and beneath his prominent brow ridges his eyes rolled around, listless and unfocused. His body tone was so slack that the nurse had to support him down the steps. His hair had been cropped even more closely than before, and the weal from his head wound, though healed, stood out, purple and angry. He was dressed in an orange sweatshirt, jeans and trainers, but he wore them oddly askew, as though he'd been browbeaten into wearing them. But it was his expression that most shocked her. Gone was the quick, wild brightness in his eyes and the alertness of his manner that had struck her so forcefully at first sight. When finally he saw her and half-registered who she was, he merely let out a pained whimper and made no attempt to come forward.

Martha Walker cleared her throat.

"Meet your new son, Mrs. Wendell. Not the prettiest sight, I know. You've got a few hours until the sedation wears off; then the fun and games will start. Nurse, settle him down inside, will you?"

Julia reached out to take the limp body in her arms.

"No, leave him to me."

As she took his hand, she noticed the skin on his wrist bore abrasion marks, as though chafed by a rope or metal clasp. She looked up sharply.

"He had to be restrained at times," explained Martha Walker in a matter-of-fact tone. "You should also keep a watch on doors and windows. Especially at night. He seems to sort of come to life after dark." She hesitated briefly, as if uncertain whether she could abandon her brief quite so abruptly, then took a step towards the van. "There we are, then, Mrs. Wendell. He's all yours. You know where to reach us if he becomes completely un- manageable. Well, good luck."

With the boy clutched tightly to her, Julia stood in the middle of the drive, seething with outrage, as she watched the two women climb into the van and slam the doors. Gouging out a tight U-turn in the gravel, they headed away down the drive and were soon lost from sight. Hoisting the boy's arm over her shoulder like a soldier carrying a wounded comrade, she helped him unsteadily indoors and into the living room, where she eased him gently into a chair. She knelt down and scanned his face anxiously. His eyelids were sluggish and his head lolled heavily. What had they done to the poor creature?

"Adam," she whispered. "Adam?"

His lips moved, but at first no sound came out. Finally, with a great effort, he managed to squeeze a strange, guttural croak from the back of the throat, before his head sank onto his chest.

"Atta?"

She felt a spurt of encouragement. He'd tried to copy! Copying sounds was the way every language was learned, from the very first word an infant uttered. The stupidity and arrogance of that woman from the agency! You could work miracles with disturbed children provided you gave them your love. *She* plainly had no love for anyone but herself; she resorted to drugs, in place of care and understanding.

She stayed beside him for some moments until she saw he had fallen fast asleep, then she went to fetch a blanket, for the poor boy was as cold as stone. On the way, she picked up the medicine pack, meaning to throw it in the garbage. Then she thought again: they might come and check up. She'd stow it away in the cabinet in her bathroom, in case. She glanced at her watch. If she hurried she could get the supper made before he woke up. And before Sandy came home and saw her new adopted brother.

•

At first it seemed the hounds of hell couldn't have awoken the boy. First, two telephone repairmen arrived and spent an hour crawling all over the house, hammering and shouting to each other from one room to another. Then one of them accidentally set off the burglar alarm, though she couldn't imagine what on earth they were doing fiddling with that. But Adam slept through it all. Until close on five, when the light began to fade and the first hint of twilight crept out from the woodland.

She was in the kitchen preparing Cajun chicken for supper when she heard a crash. Without stopping to take off her white apron, she dashed into the livingroom. In the doorway, she froze. Adam stood by the fireplace, his back to her. In his hand he held one of the precious porcelain vases; a coffee-table lay upended at his feet. He raised the vase. She stood rooted to the spot, mesmerized by the look on his face as he put the vase close to his ear and tapped it sharply with his knuckle. A note of perfect purity rang out. He tapped it again, harder. In the mirror she could see a smile slowly spread across his strong, prominent features, a smile of such simple wonder and delight that she found herself quite captivated and momentarily forgot her anger. Maybe music was one way through to him: Sam had quite a record collection of tribal stuff, Andean nose-flutes and Himalayan cymbals...

He caught sight of her in the mirror, and started violently. With an eerie chattering sound, he backed away. Then he turned and saw her in the doorway. His eyes widened in shock, disbelief, and something close to fear. Suddenly he let go of the vase. It fell into the hearth with a terrible crash.

"No!" she cried, springing forward.

He backed into a table, sending a lamp crashing to the floor and scattering small ornaments everywhere. This seemed to startle him further. He cast about him frantically, to find himself trapped. As abruptly as at the flip of a light-switch, his mood changed and he stood his ground and began pumping his arms up and down in a warlike fashion, while from deep in his chest came a low, threatening growl.

"Stop this at once!" she yelled, quaking with rage.

She took a pace forward. Suddenly, as though she'd overstepped some threshold, he went berserk, lashing out with his fists and feet in all directions. Books, magazines, photos, ashtrays, *objets d'art*—anything movable or fragile joined the maelstrom. Her own fury welled up uncontrollably. She'd strike him, she'd beat him, she'd teach the little brute a lesson. But from her experience she knew that the moment you met force with force you had failed. Struggling to control herself, she stood still and softly called his name. He stopped and stared fixedly at her, though refusing to meet her eye. Suddenly it dawned on her that his terror-filled gaze was locked onto her white apron. Quickly she untied it and threw it onto the floor. For the first time, he raised his eyes to hers.

As rapidly as it had flared up, his tantrum abated. When she now stepped forward, he made no protest but let her take him in her arms. Together they sank onto the sofa, where he curled up, shivering and whimpering, with his head buried in her lap. My poor, poor boy, she thought. What have they done to you at that place?

Some time later, dimly through the tumult in her mind she heard footsteps in the drive hurrying up to the house. A key in the lock, a flurry of coats and bags, then a familiar call.

"Mom? Yoo-hoo. Where are you?"

Sandy.

She couldn't respond, she couldn't even move, only wait for the inevitable. The girl's steps clattered across the hall tiles towards the living room. There was a gasp. She stood in the doorway, taking in the scene, her face wide with horror. Her hand flew to her mouth.

"Oh my *God!*"

Julia looked up with all the composure she could muster.

"Sandy," she said, "this is Adam."

"Christ, Mom! You can't be serious!"

"Adam, this is Sandy."

The boy looked up. His large, dark eyes scanned the girl before him. His nostrils widened, as if to scent the air. Sandy stepped tentatively forward, seemingly unable to tear her gaze away from him. As though drawn by some invisible force, she reached out her hand.

"Hi, Adam," she said in a brittle rasp. "Welcome to bedlam."

Slowly, cautiously, Adam extended his own hand. His expressive face was filled with yearning and mistrust, curiosity and fear, but above all profound bewilderment. For a moment their hands hovered an inch or two apart, but as they finally touched Sandy flinched and withdrew quickly with a small cry, almost as if she'd touched an electric fence. She stepped back and, never taking her eyes off him for long, surveyed the devastation with disbelief.

"Things make take a little time," said Julia.

Without a reply, Sandy set about tidying up. In a tight silence, she restored the fallen ornaments and righted the tables and lamps, then knelt down and began picking up the pieces of the shattered vases. She moved about the room with her back to them, but Julia could see her face was white and her eyes were wide with shock. Distraught to the point of numbness, Julia clutched Adam tighter and gently rocked him back and forth. There was nothing whatever she could do or say.

•

The boy crouched beneath the window, staring up at the dark night sky. Behind him, the bed lay untouched; beside, his night clothes lay in a pile, unworn. The light of a full moon on the wane flooded the room. Suddenly a radiator gurgled noisily. He leapt back, startled. After a moment, he crept gingerly forward and prodded the metal plate with a finger. He tapped, and it returned a muffled ring. He shook it, but it remained fixed. Somewhere deep in the bowels of the house something throbbed and shuddered, drawing his attention away. Outside, a bird gave a long, plaintive hoot. A puzzled frown puckered his heavy brow.

He crept soundlessly back to the window and looked up at the sky with silent yearning. He craned his neck to see more. Sinking to his knees, he pressed his face against the cold pane. He scanned the stars back and forth, he scoured every inch of the heavens in vain as his frown gradually deepened with sorrow and despair.

TWO

SPRING

7

○

JULIA WENT TO TAP ON THE DOOR BUT, REALIZING THE absurdity of it, let herself straight in. Adam lay curled up on the floor beneath the window, his knees tucked under his chin and his knuckles pressed into his eyes. He was naked but for the short pants she'd put on him beneath his pajamas; the pajamas themselves lay torn and buttonless on the unused bed. She stepped quietly across the carpet and stood over him for a moment, reluctant to wake him and start the day's struggle. She thought back to the tantrum of the previous afternoon and the scene, too, at bath-time. Martha Walker hadn't said anything about a phobia for water. He'd fought and screamed when she'd tried to wash him, and even a wet washcloth had made him howl. She thought, too, of the bruises on his back and legs and the angry purple and yellow needle-marks all over his buttocks and inner arms. She should have absolutely insisted on having him sooner, or at least on overseeing his care. He was her adopted *son*, not some quarantined animal she'd been waiting to have delivered. She recalled the woman's words, *just think of* *him as an undomesticated animal*, and she clenched her teeth in fury. Unforgivable!

Suddenly, she became aware he was staring at her behind his knuckles. She started: how could he be awake and keep so rock still? She assumed a pleasant smile.

"Morning, Adam. How are you today? Aren't you cold?" She laid her hand on his shoulder; oddly, his body was quite warm. He flinched at the touch. "Easy, now. There's a terrible draught coming from that window."

She drew the curtains fully, letting in a bright swathe of sunlight, and went to the cupboard; the clothes he'd arrived in were ripped and caked with the previous night's attempted supper. As she passed, she swept up the pajamas. God knew what he'd been used to wearing, but until he got accustomed to normal clothes she'd do better to give him tough, loose-fitting things without buttons or buckles. She chose a large gray floppy sweatshirt that Sandy had worn in ninth grade and, opening it for his head, advanced towards him. He wriggled away.

"Come on, Adam, you've got to get dressed. You can't go around like that. Now, over your head..."

He refused, and the more she pressed him the closer his temper grew to breaking-point. Make a game of it, she thought. She sat down on the floor in front of him and made pretence of putting it on herself, then invited him to copy. Back and forward went the sweatshirt between them as his delight grew, until finally she managed to get it on him. She thought back to his reaction to the mirror the previous day. He'd better start getting used to everyday things right away.

"Here, take a look at yourself."

She swung open the wardrobe door. On the inside was fixed a full-length mirror. At first he frowned and cocked his head on one side in puzzlement, then gradually as some kind of recognition grew he began to grin. The reflection grinned back. Suddenly, with an excited chatter, he reached out toward it. As his hand met the cold glass, he gave a small surprised grunt, but as he withdrew his hand and the image followed suit, he let out a peal of laughter. Within a moment this, too, had become a game. He swayed back and forward, pressing his face against the surface and gibbering incomprehensibly. Then an idea seemed to occur to him. Gripping the door, he peered round the back. No one was there. He uttered a high-pitched cry and repeated the trick, over and over again, and his laughter, a trilling, tinkling cascade of sound, rose to fill the house. Infected by his simple delight, Julia found herself unable to stop laughing, too, until tears of mirth filled her eyes. She heard a step behind her, and as the mirror swung back, she caught a glimpse of Sandy in the doorway. She turned. The girl had been watching, a tight half-smile frozen on her face.

•

Adam seemed to take note of his surroundings for the first time. He allowed Julia to lead him by the hand across the landing and down the stairs that led directly into the large open-plan living room. He had no evident recollection of the room from the previous day. He hung back at the foot of the stairs, his large dark eyes flicking this way and that. Odd, small features seemed to attract his attention—the intricate pattern of the Persian rug, the tassel of a lampshade, a rainbow of light sprayed up the wall from a cut-glass vase. He appeared to take in the nearest objects first, and it was a moment before his gaze reached across the room to the full-length windows that gave onto the broad, balustraded deck and, beyond, the expanse of open ground leading to the dense belt of woodland that separated their property from the Blanes'. At the sight of the outdoors, he started forward, but she grasped his hand tightly and steered him out across the hall and toward the kitchen.

"Breakfast first," she said firmly. "What would you like? Juice? There's orange and grapefruit. And cereal? Corn flakes, puffed wheat, Rice Krispies, porridge, oats…"

Sandy was by now in the kitchen, sitting on a bar-stool over a bowl of cereal and a sports magazine. Opposite her, she'd laid out a single place-setting; since Sam died, they'd formed the habit of taking breakfast at the bar counter rather than at the round table. Separately, on the table, lay a plastic bowl, spoons and polystyrene cup.

She looked up from her magazine as they entered, and sighed.

"Mom, do you really think he understands? You're wasting your breath."

"Treat him as though he understands, and he'll get there a good deal quicker." She moved her own plate and cup down onto the table beside his. "Now, Adam, what's it to be? Corn flakes?"

She had gone to the cupboard and was reaching in among the shelves when she heard a sharp exclamation, followed by a howl of frustration. The boy was wrestling with Sandy for her bowl. As he wrenched it out of her hands, milk and cereal shot across the floor.

"Brute!" she cried. "Look at him, Mom! Here, you pig: give it back!"

"Gently, darling. Don't shout at him. He doesn't understand."

"I thought we're supposed to treat him as if he did."
She sprang forward and snatched the bowl back. By then
he'd discarded it anyway and was crawling on all fours
after the food on the floor, picking up the flakes and
smelling each one carefully before putting it in his mouth.
She pulled a face at him. "Adam? Here, boy! *Woof,
woof.*"

"Sandy!"

"Well, look at him. God, I don't know."

She reached for a floor-cloth and bent to wipe up
the mess. But he pushed her away, jealously guarding
his store. With a snort of disgust, she threw the cloth
down and went back to her magazine.

"Come on, Adam," Julia intervened. "Sit up here
like a good lad. Look, here's your own corn flakes." She
rattled the packet as she poured a helping into the plastic
bowl. "You have yours. Let Sandy have hers. Darling,
pass your bowl over."

"I'm not hungry," replied the girl dully, without looking up.

"Have an egg, then. Or toast. You need a proper
start."

"No thanks."

Julia turned to the boy, unable to avoid venting some
of her annoyance on him.

"Come along now," she began briskly, "sit up. *Sit.*
In the chair. Like that. Watch: look at me. I'm sitting in
the chair. Right, *you* sit in the chair. No, wait, I haven't
put milk on it yet. Milk. Don't you want milk? Of course
you want milk. Don't grab. Here's a spoon. *Spoon.* No,
you use it like this. Here, I'll show you. It's okay, I'm not
going to steal it. Look, watch how I do mine. No, *not*
with your fingers. It's going all down your front. Sandy,

pass me a dishcloth please. Quickly."

The girl lobbed a cloth over. "I'd get him a bib," she muttered.

"No, Adam, you don't need the whole packet. You've got enough there. Keep in your chair. Sit down, or you'll spill it everywhere! Oh, *blast* you."

Adam took the cereal packet and the bowl over to the corner and squatted on his heels, stuffing his mouth full with his hands. She drew a deep breath. Suddenly she felt a desperate need for coffee. As she reached for the percolator switch, she caught Sandy's despairing grimace.

"Talk about Planet of the Apes," mumbled the girl and reached for her school bag. "Let me get out of this madhouse."

"Give it time. We can't expect results overnight."

"So we live in a zoo till then?" She checked herself. "I'm sorry," she went on more quietly. "It's just not quite what I expected. A younger brother, you said. You had no idea either, admit it. We were stupid, going into this thing blind."

Julia reached for her hand and gave it a reassuring squeeze. The touch was only feebly returned.

"It'll work out, I promise. Come on, or you'll miss your bus. Got everything?"

"Yup." With a final glance at Adam, Sandy headed through the door. In the hallway she turned to her mother and whispered, "Don't you think he looks a little... *funny*? There's something *about* him. Something in his face. Spooky." She shivered. "Sure you'll be okay alone?"

"Of course! We get far worse at the Unit."

She lingered. "You know, Mom, he's not going to fit in with us, I can see it. The Unit's where he really belongs. It's set up for people like him."

"Sandy, he's only been here a few hours. Give it a chance. Don't rush to conclusions." She opened the door and gave her a kiss. "Now hurry away or you'll be late. Have a happy day. Love you."

"Love you, too, Mom."

She stood on the doorstep watching the long-legged young girl running down the driveway, her heels kicking up the slush and her ponytail flying in the crisp morning air, until she'd disappeared out of sight. Then she turned slowly back indoors. She'd better take stock. So far, they were only heading for trouble. But what could she do? To give Adam up would be to fail him, and herself. To keep him could be to fail Sandy.

•

Food, it quickly occurred to her, formed such an imperative in Adam's life as to provide the perfect tool for conditioning. First, she had to find out which he most liked. Over the next few days she tested his preferences. She compared honey and chocolate against lemons and bitter fruit, and quickly she found he had a powerfully sweet tooth. Next, she tried salty cooked meat, anchovy paste, olives in vinegar, and discovered he had a deep aversion to savouries. She ransacked the fridge for small samples of meat, chicken and fish, for vegetables, raw and cooked, for fruit and yogurt and cheese. She tried him on bread and muffins, and on pastries and cakes. By the end she had concluded he was broadly like any twelve-year-old boy and liked best the food that was worst for him: candies, cream buns, fatty hamburgers and french fries and, to drink, Seven-Up. He made her smile with his bizarre combinations—tomato ketchup on a doughnut, for instance, and maple syrup on baked potato.

He ate greedily, well beyond the point of satiety, as if driven by a deep anxiety. When her back was turned he hoarded scraps in his pockets and squirrelled away crusts in small hiding-places. Had the idiots at the halfway house used hunger to underpin his 'socialization'? But he was partly driven by curiosity, too, a patent eagerness to try out new things for their own sake. This she found one of his most appealing characteristics, given her experience of many of the children in the Unit with their apathetic spirits and lethargic appetites. There again she caught herself making these comparisons. Where had the assumption that the lad was subnormal come from in the first place? True, five minutes of his rude and crude manners was enough to convince anyone he was socially maladjusted—but was he psychologically, too? In what way *was* he backward? The agency had offered no proper analysis. He was bright and quick and, for as long as she could spin out a game, attentive, too. And yet he seemed to inhabit his own private mental universe in which the world was ordered by quite different principles. Out of the small clues she picked up along the way she began to build a picture of a stranger from another race or age, one whose world was founded on concepts and premises quite alien to our own. A creature—and here she stifled a shiver—who was among us but who was somehow not *of* us.

And then he'd tease her by playing back at her a game of her own devising, and he'd beam his radiant smile and laugh his silvery waterfall of laughter, and she'd find herself once again intrigued and captivated and she'd berate herself for clouding psychological fact with metaphysical fancy. He *was* one of us, a boy basically like any other, with the same drives and motives and the same sense of fun and play, only a boy who had been dragged out of his own familiar surroundings and thrust into a world where, bereft of the means with which to communicate, he was all too readily taken for stupid and backward.

He was neither of these, and it didn't take her long to establish that to her own satisfaction. At one point, for instance, she'd taken him to the bathroom to try the rudiments of training when he spotted the mirror on the wall. Evidently recalling the earlier game, he began dancing up and down in front of it, chattering to the reflection. Then he tried prying it off to look behind, but it was screwed to the wall and this made him pause to reflect. He peered more intently. He shut his eyes; then opened them again; the image was still there. He bared his teeth, and the face bared its own back. Then he reached out, but instead of touching the glass he began slowly stroking his own head, feeling the bristly stubble where he'd been shorn. He must have touched his scar, for he winced. He did it again, though, as if to make sure, and then he turned away from the mirror and felt around his head like a man feeling for his hat. Clearly, he'd seen from the reflection that he looked different from how he imagined himself. Didn't this show quite convincingly that he had actually *recognized* himself? That was not such a dumb trick at all. Many backward children—indeed, among the animal kingdom, all but the higher primates—were unable to achieve this. But unquestionably Adam could.

And yet he remained remote, lost in the impenetrable fortress of his own mind. How could she get through? Language had to be the key. She began considering taking lessons in sign language—they regularly used it at the Unit—though however complex and rich a language like Ameslan was, it would only ever connect him with a pitifully small number of people. But as she listened more carefully to the noises he made, she gradually began to see patterns. Were the sounds actual words? Did his "plain gobbledegook" have a structure and carry meaning? Had Martha Walker been wrong to say derisively, "You certainly couldn't call it *language*"? If it was a known language, there was no one better able than Sam's old friend, the Professor of Linguistics, to tell her that. If not, it still could be something he'd made up for himself, as children did who were removed at an early age from the society of others. Either way, somebody could surely decode it. The key must be to get him to link his own sounds for objects with the corresponding English words. Such became her plan. But almost at once it broke down: he seemed to make different sounds to denote the same things and, more confusingly still, the same sounds to denote different things. In the end she gave up; after all, you didn't need to learn Chinese to teach a Chinaman English. Whatever got him talking quickest was best. Once he could talk, the avenues into his mind and soul would lie open. It was only a matter of time. Time and patience. And, above all, love.

•

"Sorry? I didn't quite catch your name." Julia held the receiver closer and jammed a finger in her other ear. Adam was bashing a cooking pot against the side of the stove. "Maxine Fitzgerald?" The name rang a bell. "Excuse me a moment." She put her hand over the receiver and yelled, "Stop that bloody noise!" The boy cowered back, as though expecting a blow. "I'm sorry," she continued into the phone. "Yes, of course. Fine. I'll be in."

As she replaced the phone, she recalled the striking young woman at the funeral standing cool and watchful and slightly apart from the other mourners. Distantly she remembered wondering at the time if this attractive lady was the mystery sender of some postcard she'd turned up among Sam's mail, but now she realized she'd been far off the mark. This woman had been a colleague: they'd evidently been working on some project together. He'd lent her some books, she'd said on the phone, and she felt really bad at not having returned them. She was going to a dinner party in Concord that evening and could she drop them off on the way? Julia sighed with annoyance. She should have told her to send them direct to the Peabody; she had enough unsorted here already. She turned back to Adam. He was waiting uncertainly for her next response.

"I couldn't hear on the phone with that filthy row," she explained gently. She gestured to the telephone. "Phone. Telephone. Can you say that? Don't worry, we'll get there. Now, where shall we start?"

Objects. Nouns. Names of things. She picked up the pan and said the word. She put it back on the "shelf." She introduced him to the "stove" and showed him it was "hot." She led him to the sink and demonstrated the "tap," correcting herself to "faucet," and how it gave "water," though at the sight of water he recoiled in fear. Next, she took him to the "sideboard" and opened first one "drawer," and then another. Drawers intrigued him, and soon he was having fun pulling everything out onto the floor. This she indulged until he moved onto the knife drawer, where she had to intervene. A squabble developed. He snatched a small filleting knife. A dangerous note had entered his laugh.

"Adam, no!" she commanded. "Give it to me! Knives are sharp. Dangerous. Stop this."

As she tried to wrest the knife from him, it sliced deep into her finger. Blood sprang from the wound. Instantly his mood changed. His eyes widening with distress, he dropped the knife and, with a curious cooing sound, took her hand and pressed it tight. Within a moment the finger had stopped throbbing and the pain vanished. Finally he released her hand and gave her a strangely wise, knowing smile.

"Doesn't hurt a bit," she said in amazement. "Come along, let's tidy up."

Wrapping a piece of kitchen towel round the finger, she began putting the pots and pans back in the cupboard. She'd better tie up the knife drawer and do something about the breakables in the larder, too. God, she thought with a moment's irritation, it's like having a two-year-old again—child locks and kiddy catches. She'd better call the Director at the Unit, too, and ask to take more time off; she'd badly underestimated how long Adam would need to settle in. The Director had agreed to find him a place, but there was no way Adam was ready for that yet.

She glanced across at him; he was playing at putting things away, quite happy now. Once again, she was struck by how quickly his moods changed. He seemed to perceive and feel things absolutely directly. For him, things were exactly as they seemed, apprised at face value, without any mediation of thought or analysis, so that his mood switched as rapidly as the world he perceived changed about him. One moment he would be bursting with irrepressible excitement, the next trembling in abject fear, the next again riveted by some intriguing puzzle. His large, expressive face registered each passing emotion immediately and openly, as though he possessed no notion of concealment. At the Unit, she'd seen children as emotionally labile and children as expressively unmediated, but never both in the same child. This boy was special.

The afternoon grew dark early and a fine misty rain began to fall. She was in the study making some phone calls when a violent thud directly overhead sent her hurrying upstairs. She found Adam in Sandy's room, beaming with glee, with the drawers from her dressing-table upended and jeans and panties, tee-shirts and shoes scattered on the floor.

"For heaven's sake!" she cried in exasperation and brusquely shooed him out of the room, slamming the door after him.

From the corridor she could hear his bewildered whimpering. As she was putting the clothes back, a small wad of letters fell out from the folds of a nightdress. Letters in Sandy's writing. Love letters, apparently unsent, addressed to Scott Blane, the boy next door. Did Sandy have a crush on *Scott*? She'd never given the slightest hint of that. Julia sighed. They didn't seem to be able to *talk* as they used to. Over the divorce, they'd been like sisters together; now they were back to behaving as mother and daughter, polite but estranged. Was that just a stage in the growing-up process, or was Adam's arrival to blame?

Julia bundled the letters quickly back into the drawer,

then closed the door and returned downstairs. She found Adam squatting on the living room floor, happily tearing up magazines, all memory of the incident upstairs clearly forgotten. She paused for a moment in thought. Was this why Sandy had been so cool and distant with the boy ever since he'd arrived? Was she staying late at school again today deliberately to avoid him? She hadn't even invited Kirsty over once in the past days. Was she embarrassed by Adam and ashamed of the impression it would give Scott?

For a while she busied herself in the kitchen, making a cottage pie for the children's supper and quieting her anxieties in the comforting activity of preparing nourishment for her family. It would all work out in the end; she was only making things worse by imagining the worst before it happened.

From the living room came the sound of the television switching from station to station. She smiled to herself: Adam was fiddling with the knobs. Then suddenly her smile froze. Above the tinny babel of voices, she heard another short, choking cry. She was halfway to the door when a terrible scream pierced the air. The living room was in darkness but for the glow of the television screen. As she rushed in, she saw the boy stagger back and throw his hands up to shield his face. He turned and shot a desperate glance behind him. The curtains were open, and through the large glass sliding doors she could just make out the white balustrade of the deck and, far beyond in the darkness, the outline of the trees standing out against a stormy sky. With a stricken howl, he spun around and, before she could even utter a cry, he made a wild dash for freedom. He crossed the room in a flash and lunged bodily into the invisible door. There was a gigantic *crack* as he flew through the plate glass, followed instantly by a shattering *crash*, then a long drawn-out scream receding into the distance, and finally silence.

She leapt forward, but within two steps she fell over an overturned chair. As she was scrambling to her feet, she caught a glimpse of the television screen. A medical serial . . . figures looming menacingly in the frame, a doctor in a white coat. Without pausing, she rushed to the shattered window. A large, jagged hole had been ripped through the glass, and shards and splinters lay scattered over the deck beyond. Slashing her sleeve on the razor-sharp points, she clambered out onto the deck and stared out, aghast, into the blustery twilight. The boy was nowhere to be seen. She yelled his name, but the wind flung the cry back at her. She rushed to the edge of the wooden balustrade. Below, she could just make out a scuffed patch where he'd landed and, far away across the lawn toward the drive, his fleeting figure disappearing into the woodland. With a despairing cry, she threw herself over the balustrade and, twisting her ankle as she dropped to the ground below, hobbled up the slope after the fleeing form. She was just cresting the rise when a pair of headlights swung through the trees. Briefly catching the boy's outline in their beam as they turned, they headed slowly and steadily down the drive toward the house.

•

Max had made the drive to Lexington slowly, wondering at every exit on the highway whether she shouldn't turn back. She knew what she wanted to prove, but was this the way? For all her resolve to start a new life, for all the new dates and changes in her lifestyle she'd made, she hadn't been able to shake off Sam's grip. She heard his laugh, she saw his smile, she felt his presence everywhere. This was crazy. She'd always been in control of her feelings, and she wasn't going to let them get the upper hand now. Nearly two months had passed, and it was time to lay the ghost.

Betrayed already by the thumping of her heart, she drove at a crawl down White River Drive with its proud colonial mansions, searching through the rain-bleared windshield for the number. At the mailbox marked "Wendell" she gritted her teeth and swung down the drive. On the seat beside her lay a pile of books. She had her story ready. And yet, even as she heard the tires crunch on the gravel, committing her to the act, she knew she was deceiving herself. She was making this pilgrimage to add to Sam's life, not to close it down.

Suddenly, fleetingly, two small bright green spots glowed out of the darkness at her. Eyes caught in her headlights. A cat? A fox? Then she caught the flash of an arm. A snooper! She accelerated on to the house, a low building less pretentious than its neighbors, and hurried through the thickening drizzle to the front door. She rang the bell. No one answered. She hammered on the door. No one came. Then she caught sight of the figure of a woman in a pale dress over by the far trees, all but blotted out by the steadily falling rain, ploughing at a stumbling run through the grass. A long drawn-out call floated across from the woods.

"Adam? A-dam?"

The distress in the voice sent a chill shiver through her. Instinctively, she turned up the collar of her jacket and set off through the rain in the direction of the cry.

•

Julia called his name again more softly. Barely ten yards separated them. She took a step forward, but he shrank further back into the trees. The rain was falling heavily, sheeting through the naked branches and spattering the ground below to a mulch. In the low twilight she scanned him for injury. Blood streamed from his nose and a small gash across his forehead, but otherwise, superficially, he seemed miraculously unharmed. Perhaps the sheer momentum had carried him through before the glass could fall and lacerate him.

"Adam?" she called in a whisper, reaching out a hand.

But something behind her seemed to catch his eye, and he tensed, poised for flight. She turned to see a figure running across the open ground toward them. Maxine Fitzgerald! The woman came to a halt a short distance away. Her long dark hair was bedraggled, her jacket drenched and her shoes covered in mud.

"Keep back, please!" hissed Julia. "It's all right, Adam. Come here, love. Come on."

The other woman seemed to size up the situation quickly. She slipped unseen round the back of the boy, positioning herself between two trees so as to block off his escape. As Julia came forward and he turned to flee, he fell straight into her arms. Julia watched in astonishment as the woman pincered him expertly by the wrist with one hand and, drawing him close, pressed the flat of the other against the side of his neck. Almost at once he stopped struggling and a curious calm took possession of him, and he allowed himself to be taken without protest into Julia's arms. He was trembling uncontrollably.

"It's all right now," she comforted. "Come on, let's get you back home."

As she helped him back toward the house, she glanced at the other woman with grudging admiration.

"Where did you learn that trick, Miss Fitzgerald?"

"It's Max," she corrected. "I work with animals. They generally have a spot somewhere. With horses it's on the flank. I don't mean to say..." She broke off. "What happened?"

"He had an accident." They had reached the gravel drive. Ahead, lights burned from the kitchen and study windows. The bluish flicker of the television illuminated the living room. Her mind flashed back to the picture she'd seen on the screen. White coats. Like her own apron. "God only knows what they did to him," she muttered to herself.

"They?" queried Max.

"Oh, nothing."

Together they helped him indoors and into the kitchen. Julia laid him on the floor, with his head back to staunch the nose-bleed, and checked him over for fractures, then she called Ralph Singer. The doctor wasn't there, so she left a message with his service. She hurried upstairs for bandages and antiseptic, and when she returned the boy was sitting up with Max kneeling beside him, chatting to him as she gently wiped the blood off his face. Her tone was kidding and cajoling, but her eyes seemed to scrutinize him with a hardening interest. He replied only in soft, pained grunts.

"He won't understand you," said Julia shortly. "He doesn't speak English."

"Oh? Where's he from?"

"Turkey. Or thereabouts."

"*Nasil siniz*," said Max. Adam made no response. She glanced at Julia. "That's 'How are you?' in Turkish.

I heard you work with disturbed children, Mrs. Wendell. So, you get them from abroad, too?"

She felt obliged to correct the misunderstanding.

"Actually, Sam found him out there on his last trip. In the Caucasus. Or, I rather think he found Sam." She put down the bowl of water and held out her hand. "Do call me Julia. I'm being terribly inhospitable. Can I offer you a drink?"

"Don't let me trouble you."

"It's no trouble."

"Look, you've got your hands full. Why don't I just leave the books? Will you be all right?"

"Fine. Sandy will be home any minute anyway."

"That's your daughter." It was a statement, not a question. Max evidently knew already.

She nodded. "Well, just put the books in Sam's study. It's the first door on the right."

While Julia began cleaning and dressing Adam's cuts, Max fetched the books from her car. When she returned to the kitchen, she cast her a sympathetic glance.

"Looks like I'm adding to your workload," she said.

Julia sighed. "And then I've got all his stones and bones to sort through. Goodness knows how we'll manage that." She straightened. "Look, you can't go to dinner like that. You're soaked through. Let me lend you something."

Max smiled, a warm, friendly, trust-inspiring smile.

"Don't bother, I'm only seeing an old friend." She went to the door. "'Bye now, Adam. *Allah ismarladik.*" The boy blinked uncomprehendingly. "Well, good-bye Julia. Sure there's nothing I can do?"

"Sure, thanks."

The door closed and footsteps hurried across the

gravel. A moment later, the car started up and, with a brief sweep of headlights across the window, quickly disappeared from earshot. Julia thought back to the young woman's visit with fleeting puzzlement: odd that Sam should be collaborating with a geneticist who worked with animals. She sighed; she'd never understood the ramifications of anthropology, and it really only showed how she'd lost touch with him towards the end. She turned back to Adam; she didn't want to pursue that line of thought any further. All she knew was that this woman Max had been very warm and pleasant. She'd caught them in the middle of a crisis and, far from reacting with shock or suspicion, she'd taken the boy as he was and shown a kindly and friendly interest in him.

The ring of the phone cut across her thoughts. It was Ralph Singer, calling from his car. He was already on his way.

•

By breaking up cardboard packing cartons from Sam's study, Julia managed to block up most of the window before she ran out of tape. The glazers couldn't come until first thing in the morning, so they'd have to do with a gaping hole for the night. She'd cleared up the broken glass as best she could; the deck was still full of splinters, but she'd have to leave that for the daylight.

Adam was upstairs in his room. Dr. Singer had been and checked him over thoroughly. He'd said he'd had a lucky escape and looked okay, but he'd insisted she bring him in to the clinic the next day. She knew doctors rarely made house calls—and, when they did, it was a costly business. She felt unsure about calling on the generosity of the trust. An appointment at the clinic could only add to the bill. If it was necessary, she should cover it herself. But how was it necessary if the boy was okay? She had an inbuilt mistrust of all medical practitioners: the less they had to rely on them, the better.

She'd tackled the doctor on the need to take the lad in.

"Better safe than sorry," he'd responded.

"You mean, you're worried he's *not* all right, then?" she'd persisted.

"Mrs. Wendell, I pay a hundred thousand a year in insurance," he'd replied, "and I'm not looking for a negligence suit."

"Ah, I see: *you* want to be safer than sorry."

She'd tried to forget her instinctive dislike of the man, to ignore his false charm and empty eyes, but she couldn't. She'd begun to learn to read Adam's expression, too, and she could see he was strangely disturbed. At one point, he'd suddenly pointed at the doctor and let out a short, harsh peal of laughter, and she'd had the odd feeling that he had in some way *seen through* the man's façade. Still, she would take him in to the clinic in the morning. *She* wanted to be safe, not sorry.

She closed the curtains against the howling draught and turned up the heating, then went round systematically child-proofing the room. One by one she removed all the ornaments and breakables and put them on the upper shelves in Sam's study to be packed away later. She turned the Persian rug upside down and spread dust-sheets over the furniture. In the morning she'd buy more tape—fluorescent orange tape—and run it at eye-level along the other full-length windows. If this was not to be a no-go area, if they were to live like a family at all, then this had to be done. Until Adam had adapted to them, they'd have to adapt to him.

A sharp hammering from upstairs brought the reality home to her. She bit her lip. Sandy was fixing a lock on her bedroom door. The girl had come back late from her basketball team practice to find the place in shambles and she'd stalked upstairs to her room. A moment later there'd been a cry of rage, and she'd come running down in tears. Adam had been at her private letters! How dared he! How she *hated* the boy.

"This isn't a home, it's a hotel," she'd declared finally. "If we have to have a stranger here, then I'm locking my door. Don't expect me to be nice to him, Mom. He's a vile little monster, and I won't have anything to do with him. Ever."

Julia poured herself a small brandy and swallowed it like medicine. The dream was turning into a nightmare. With a final glance round the bleak and barren room, she turned off the lights and headed up to bed. As she passed Sandy's room, she saw her bicycle padlock hanging from a latch nailed into the frame. The light was on under the door. She tapped, but there was no answer. She called goodnight, without receiving a response; she could tell the girl wasn't asleep, for she could hear pages of a magazine being turned.

She carried on to Adam's room and put her head round the door. The boy was squatting on the floor beneath the window, muttering to himself in a low voice and staring intently at something in his hand. It was the photo of Sam she kept by her bed. Flushed with annoyance, she was about to step in and demand it back when she checked herself. His muttering had now risen to a rapid chatter. As she watched, he reached out a finger and very slowly, almost tenderly, he began stroking the picture. Only then did she realize with a jolt he was talking to *it*. Talking to Sam.

Very gently she closed the door and, overwhelmed by a confusion of feelings, tiptoed softly down the corridor to her own room.

•

Max sat nursing a Miller Lite, watching baseball on the television with the sound turned down. Beside her, the answerphone light flashed, indicating she had messages, but she wasn't interested in picking them up right now. At supper at her girlfriend's, she'd felt too distracted to concentrate on their conversation, and she'd made an excuse to leave early. She had to be alone to think. As she stared at the condensation misting the surface of the beer can, a convulsive shiver ran through her. She knew it wasn't the shock of meeting Julia and penetrating Sam's home life. It was that boy.

Her thoughts turned back to the last night she and Sam had spent together in Venice, and gradually a notion took shape in her mind, a notion so fantastic, so utterly crazy, that she broke out in a peal of derisive laughter. But her laugh quickly died, for she could find no obvious reason to refute it.

Sam had chosen a restaurant he knew, a heavily furnished, ducal establishment in a converted palazzo overlooking the lagoon. Toward the end of the meal, over a second bottle of *Venegazzu*, he'd begun talking of the field trip on which he was embarking the following day, a trip among the nomadic peoples of the remote Caucasus. He was perhaps the western world's expert on the region. During days spent trekking across the harsh terrain and nights huddled round the campfire, he'd collected innumerable folk tales. Now, in this improbably plush Venetian setting, he'd begun to recount to her the one story that had always intrigued him above all others.

He'd told her of the *almas*.

Far away in the remotest crags and wastes, beyond the furthest reach of modern man, there lived small, scattered pockets of wildmen of the mountains, known to the nomads as *almas*. These weird, shy creatures had been sighted fleetingly from time to time, yet no single specimen had ever been captured alive or dead. According to eyewitness accounts, they looked human—slightly hairy, stockily built, heavy-featured, but otherwise entirely human—but they lived in caves like animals. Where they came from was unknown; their origins lay lost in the mists of myth and legend. The nomads themselves took them for granted as an uncommon but perfectly natural part of the local fauna. Their accounts, however, were so interwoven with folklore that fact was inextricable from fantasy, and it was quite possible that these human-like beings were simply figments of folklore, mythical creatures sprung from the nomadic imagination. Except for one thing: the descriptions were extraordinarily consistent and were to be found among tribes across a wide band of the remotest regions of the world, stretching from the Caucasus in the west to Mongolia in the east—among tribes, that is, who could have had no possible intercourse with one another.

She'd listened, spellbound. She'd sensed in his speech the smoldering of a life-long ambition, a personal quest which he'd pursued quietly and obsessively, well away from the public gaze. And yet she'd had the feeling that he was holding something back. When finally he'd come to the end and the candles were sputtering, she'd leaned forward and whispered the questions she'd been dying to ask yet hardly dared for fear of the answer: *is it true?, are they real?* He'd stared into his glass for a long while before finally meeting her eye and, in a razor-edged whisper, replied, *Yes, Max, I sincerely believe they are. Absolutely real.*

And now, as the cold beer numbed her hands and the flickering screen held her gaze in a mesmeric grip, her thoughts turned to Adam. She thought of his strange physiognomy, his wild look and uncouth manner, his curious language . . . and she knew with absolute certainty that she had somehow to find a way to get a closer look at him. And then suddenly, abruptly, she laughed aloud again. She couldn't be serious! This was crazy! Absurd. Irrational. Sam had been telling *fairy-tales.* This was almost the twenty-first century, for God's sake! There just were no weird and wonderful creatures out there still waiting to be discovered. She'd better come down to earth. Taking a deep swig from the can, she reached forward and turned up the television.

8

SPRING THAT YEAR AS SANDY PUT IT, SPRANG. NO
sooner had the last lingering rim of hardened snow along
the driveway finally shrunk back into the grimy leaf-mold
than the first green shoots burst through the bedraggled
earth and the trees in the woodland around began to
swell with bud. And with it all the moment of decision
pressed relentlessly closer.

Julia witnessed the daily change with a shiver of
excitement mingled with unease. The heady smell of fresh
sap carried on the softer air filled her with such a sense
of hope that she would forget for a moment the trials of
the past three weeks since Adam had joined their household and she'd renew her faith that, with proper love and
understanding, everything would work out in the end.
And yet, as she looked out at the maples and birch trees
bristling into bud, and at the burgeoning ranks of poplars
in the plantation across the river, she was struck by an
unnerving feeling they were all closing in on her and,
unseen during the night, as if playing some sinister game
of grandmother's footsteps, they had advanced another

step toward the house. Then she'd focus her thoughts on the open ground between, on the pool, still covered over from winter, and on the rose beds lying beneath their protective straw, on the weird structure of logs and stones, too, that Adam had built at the edge of the trees, half hut and half cave, and she would bring all the force of her mind to bear on filling this buffer zone with space and life, as though by the sheer power of her will she could fight back the encroachment and restore her peace of mind.

Everywhere she turned she found cause for worry. First, there was Sandy. Sandy had taken to the new set-up very badly. Since the incident over the letters, she'd barely addressed a word to Adam. She acted as though he didn't exist. Perhaps to compensate, Julia found herself keeping up an endless one-sided patter to the boy, talking about this and that and often nothing in particular, just as one talked to an infant or a foreigner in the hope that they would pick up the inflection if not the actual meaning. For Adam was, in effect, both of these: an infant and a foreigner.

She worried about him, too. Sometimes she'd catch him looking so sad and lost and wistful. He did his best with a good will most of the time, and he brought his own curiosity and sense of play to his side of the bargain, but there was really so very much for him to learn and everything was so terribly alien. Would he have been happier if she had never interfered at all and let him be sent back to the life he'd come from? She just didn't know. She'd never before felt so paralyzed with doubt and confusion. There was no one to help, either. The Unit's developmental psychotherapist had come by several times—he'd paid another visit yesterday—but each time he left with a different diagnosis. If no one knew what was wrong, how could anyone know what was *right*? If the experts didn't know, how could she?

But when she felt despair overwhelming her, she'd pull herself together and remember that nothing was absolutely final. Her first loyalty was to her first child, and this venture had to be right for Sandy above all. Yet she badly wanted it to work for Adam's sake and, in a way, for Sam's, too—and then again, for her own sake as well, for she had vested so much of herself in its success. And so she threw herself with renewed energy into making it all work. There would be moments of real reward—Adam would achieve some small breakthrough, or she and Sandy would have one of their good old talks, or Max would come by and, with that special knack of hers, ease the family tensions—and for a short while, until it all fell apart again, she'd allow herself to think that maybe, after all, it did stand a chance.

As March turned into April, the trial period she'd promised Sandy came to an end and the day of decision dawned.

•

Morning sunlight poured in through the kitchen window. Sandy was packing up her school bag ready to go. Julia glanced at her watch: they'd be early for the bus, and that would give them a moment to talk off the premises. Adam was still upstairs; she'd taken to getting him up after Sandy had left.

"I'll walk you down," she offered. "Got everything?"

"Guess so." Sandy snapped the bag shut. "You haven't forgotten today, have you?"

"Forgotten?"

"The sports presentations, Mom."

"Ah, yes. That's today. So it is."

Julia frowned. How could she go to the school and leave Adam behind alone? Equally, how could she take him along too? Another small test of divided loyalties. She drew her breath to speak, but Sandy cut in quicker.

"It's all right, Mom. It doesn't matter."

"I thought it was mainly twelfth-graders, anyway."

"Other people's parents come along, too." She tossed her ponytail briskly. "Anyway, anything so long as you don't bring the Martian."

"Do stop calling him that. It's insulting."

"Insulting to Martians."

"He's coming along well," protested Julia. Say anything, she thought; just keep talking. "He already knows more than twenty words. I counted."

Sandy gave a fond smile.

"You're a real air-head sometimes, mother," she said. "Repeating things like a parrot isn't the same as knowing them."

"Well, it's a start."

They left the house in silence and walked down the drive one pace apart. In the woodland, blackbirds squabbled noisily and squirrels foraged energetically among the mulch of last year's fallen leaves. They reached the end without a further word and stood for a while at the roadside bus stop, watching the stream of large sedans roll slowly past. Sandy whistled softly, quite at ease, but Julia felt increasingly tense. How could she get through? There was always Max, a safe topic of agreement. Max was coming by at the end of the day. She had become quite a regular visitor. At first she'd come over to help sort out Sam's books and specimens, and this had developed into something of a friendship. Julia had warmed to the younger woman from the start, though she had to admit she couldn't quite see what was in it for Max. For themselves, though, Max brought a welcome breath of fresh air into the increasingly fraught atmosphere at home. Max showed a genuinely fond interest in Adam, too, in heartwarming contrast to the reactions from the neighbors, which ranged from quaint curiosity to unfeigned distaste. Sandy had grown to like her; she found her lively, interesting and good fun. In some ways she looked up to her as an elder sister and perhaps, too, derived from her a contact with an adult American way of life that she'd lost with Sam's death.

But even this failed to spark off more than a brief conversation, and soon they fell silent again. A short while later, Kirsty came hurrying out from their drive and joined them. A dark-haired girl of the same age as Sandy but in every way more precocious, she greeted Julia with an easy first-name familiarity that, rooted in English manners, Julia still found faintly uncomfortable. Immediately Sandy perked up and began chatting merrily. Wishing them both a good day, Julia turned to leave. On the way down the drive, she heard the note of a heavy diesel engine and she paused while the orange school bus made a brief stop. As it finally lumbered out of view, carrying the two girls in animated conversation with their friends, she headed briskly towards the house and her other child.

•

Once indoors, she hurried up the narrow stairs that led to the two small attic rooms under the eaves. Soon after his arrival, Adam had eschewed the spare bedroom with its centrally heated comfort, its large, soft bed and its en-suite bathroom, and he now slept instead in the cold, bare east-facing attic, among old rolls of wallpaper, offcuts of carpet, suitcases and empty packing-cases. This he'd chosen for his room—his lair, as Sandy called it. As she went up the stairs, Julia called out his name. Ever since the morning she'd woken him with a gentle shake and he'd reacted as though she'd come to attack him, she'd made it a rule to warn him well in advance she was coming.

"A-dam, A-dam," she called. "Morning, love. Rise and shine."

She always opened the door of his attic cautiously, too, never quite sure what she might find inside. One day she'd discovered him amid a pile of feathers, squatting over the headless corpse of a pigeon, his hands red with blood. Assuming he'd been devouring the bird, she'd snatched it up in disgust and tossed it out of the window. A wrong move. She was used to handling children's tantrums, but the suddenness and ferocity of his reaction had taken her by surprise. It had taught her how perilous it could be to cross him. He possessed his own very clearcut sense of right and wrong, and she had to learn to respect this, alien though it often seemed to her way of thinking. Later, clearing up the mess, she'd noticed streaks of blood on the floorboards forming a strange but very definite pattern: it was a rough circle with a triangle drawn inside, and it reminded her oddly of some marks she'd recently found etched on one of the bones when going through Sam's collection.

Twice she'd found him not there at all. The first time, he'd slipped out through the window and taken refuge in his garden hutch where he'd made himself a rudimentary bed of twigs and leaves. The second time had been far worse: he'd gone missing for two full days. Fearing what they might do to him, she'd held back from calling the police. It had come as quite a surprise when, early the next morning, a patrol car had turned up at the house out of the blue. At the time she assumed that one of the neighbors had spotted Adam and called the police, but no one ever mentioned seeing or reporting him. When he finally came back, of his own accord, in the middle of the following night, she could tell he'd been living rough in the woods and didn't look as if he'd been anywhere near habitation at all. How had the police known? The puzzle still lingered unsolved in the back of her mind.

Today, however, he was there. The room was freezing cold. He was sitting directly beneath the window, with his chin on his knees, as though he'd fallen asleep staring out at the sky. His bed, a simple mattress, lay untouched in the corner. To give him more space, she'd shifted all Sam's old stuff into the other attic—his tennis racquets and climbing gear and the boxes she'd filled with his old clothes and photographs and papers during the grand clear-out, including the carton that contained his watch, pipe and map and other personal effects from the accident. Bit by bit, however, it all seemed to be gathering back in Adam's room. What conceivable interest the boy might have in any of it was quite beyond her. Why, in particular, did he insist on keeping her small bedside photo? She'd retrieved it once, but within two days it was back up here again. She'd let the matter pass without making an issue; in a way, it was rather touching.

She could divine no principle behind his hoarding, either. It seemed altogether random and indiscriminate. Scattered around the small room was a whole magpie's collection of bright, shiny objects—spoons, coins, empty cans, an old bunch of keys, a piece of broken mirror, a car hub-cap and various baubles and bits of tinsel plundered from the Christmas decorations box. By contrast, in the far corner lay a heap of dead leaves and logs from the lumber stack behind the garage, while in the center was a small pile of rocks and stones which he seemed in the process of chipping into flakes.

She hesitated in the doorway for a moment, trying to place the strange, faint odor that permeated this room. It made her think of wet acorns in an old leather pouch. Sandy said the place stank like a kennel. She herself didn't find it distasteful, though, so much as puzzlingly reminiscent of something in the far reaches of her memory. Once she'd found some moldering pieces of fried chicken behind the mattress, but even when she'd cleared those out the smell still remained.

Finally she stepped inside.

"Adam? Are you awake?"

He opened one eye, birdlike.

"Right." She went to close the window. "We'll get you washed and dressed and then we'll have some breakfast. Corn flakes? Milk? Juice? Toast or muffins?"

She recited the usual litany. She knew he'd only eat cold porridge drowned in maple syrup, but she had to keep the one-way dialogue going. He responded merely in grunts. She had to assume these were intelligible: the moment she entertained the opposite assumption she knew she'd given up hope.

She reached for his hand and helped him to his feet.

"Come on then, my boy," she said.

•

The breakfast cycle took a good hour. Adam sat cross-legged on the floor in the corner of the kitchen. He hated chairs, and she wasn't going to risk a tantrum this morning. She managed to get him into an open-neck check shirt and jeans and odd-footed sneakers, and round his neck she'd tied an apron to catch the worst of the spills. His thumb was short and his fingers inflexible, so that he found it hard to grip objects in the normal way. He sat holding the spoon tightly in his left fist—he was clearly left-handed—but like young children he had difficulty in moving his wrist independently of his arm, so that most of the porridge ended up on the floor. That didn't worry him—he'd scoop it up with his fingers, which he found more convenient anyway—but it wasn't very hygienic and, besides, it revolted people, particularly Sandy. To show he'd finished, he upended the bowl onto the floor and, evidently curious to explore the effect, began smearing the porridge round with his fingers. Instead of reprimanding him, however, she took a cloth and showed him how to make a game of wiping it up, then rewarded him with a sweet biscuit.

It was slow, painstaking work. Full-time work, too, and that was another worry. She'd already used up her annual holiday entitlement and was on unpaid leave, but the Unit was already short-staffed and she'd promised the Director that she'd go back to her regular afternoons in a week's time. She was still planning to take Adam along with her, but she increasingly foresaw trouble. At the Unit he'd be under their authority, not hers, and she could see their methods wouldn't suit him. He was so very different from the other cases.

Moreover, if she had to drive him there and back each day—if he was to make any life in this country at all—he'd have to get accustomed to the car. The only time she'd driven him out before was to take him to Ralph Singer's clinic in Boston, and he'd been terrified; he'd struggled so frantically to get out that she'd almost crashed the car. If he really had been in the jeep with Sam at the time of the accident, could that be the root of his phobia? She sighed. Always questions, questions.

She shut him up in Sam's old study, now converted into a playroom, while she tidied up and made her phone calls. By the middle of the morning she'd finished, and she decided to start car-training again. He was fascinated by keys, and by jiggling her key-ring just out of reach, she managed to lead him in a dance out of the house and across to the car. There he hung back fearfully. She began fiddling ostentatiously with the ignition and before long, unable to overcome his curiosity, he sidled in alongside her and snatched the keys: he always had to copy everything himself. His grip wasn't precise enough, however, and he quickly grew frustrated at not being able to get the key into the lock. He began angrily jabbing and stabbing it all around. She took a deep breath and repeated the familiar routine to herself: *don't get angry, he's only frustrated because his ambitions are greater than his abilities.* And in despair, as the final card, *change the game.* She sat back and closed her eyes tight. The trick worked. Within a moment the din had ceased and she felt a tug on her sleeve. Suddenly she opened her eyes wide.

"Boo!" she said brightly.

He let out a silvery peal of laughter and tugged at her to repeat the trick. On went the game until ultimately she was able to reclaim the keys and start up the car. She allowed it to roll slowly forward in a wide-sweeping arc.

At first his deep-set, dark eyes widened in fear, but gradually he relaxed and soon he began to laugh. Round and round they circled, churning up the gravel on a tight lock, while his excited jabber rose to fill the bright morning air. Finally she eased the car down the drive, diverting his attention with the electric windows, until by the time she'd reached the road he seemed quite to have forgotten his panic in the delight of playing with the new toy.

She drove at a crawl down the broad tree-lined avenue, not wanting to risk a tantrum trying to get him into a seat belt. People on the sidewalk cast him strange stares. She glanced across at him, remembering how she had reacted herself on first sight. Though his hair had grown back and he was dressed like a typical kid of his age, nevertheless there was always something . . . odd, yet familiar, about his look, like an echo from a deep-buried memory or a long-forgotten dream. She turned her attention back to the road, feeling disturbed and uneasy.

As they reached the Grand Union parking lot, a cream Cadillac drew up alongside. Her heart sank. Out stepped Loretta, Scott and Kirsty's mother, a tall, angular woman wearing a pair of mirrored sunglasses the size of clay pigeons. She advanced, hands outstretched. Though she addressed her, Julia sensed she was studying Adam from behind her glasses. She began asking after her with exaggerated concern.

"No point in shutting yourself in like a nun, my dear," she was saying. "Sam wouldn't want that. Sandy's old enough to look after herself. And babysit the boy." Adam was staring at the woman, a grin inexplicably spreading over his face. "But then you're used to problem kids, dear," she continued with a sour frown. "Any time you want him out of the way, just call. We'll find him

something to do—polish the car or clean up the yard."
She touched her arm and leaned closer. "If there's anything we can do," she insisted.

Adam was actually laughing now and pointing. Julia
shook his arm.

"Adam!" she hissed.

Loretta began backing away.

"Well, I guess I'll see you later," she said tightly.
"Now excuse me."

With a hard glare at Adam, she left. He was still
grinning and gabbling some incomprehensible nonsense.
Julia felt on the point of slapping him.

"Behave yourself!" she snapped. She wrenched his
hand down to his side. "That's extremely rude. You'll
have to learn some manners if you're going to fit in at
all."

Angrily she marched him into the supermarket. He
followed meekly, looking puzzled and wounded. She was
pushing the trolley past the shelves when a thought
dawned on her. She cast the boy a slow, careful look.
Could he actually be *aphasic*? She'd read of cases of
aphasiacs who, when confronted with a politician speaking on television, for instance, would go off into apparently inexplicable hoots of laughter although they were
quite unable to understand the words as such. What happened was, they latched onto a mismatch between the
speaker's facial grimaces and the tone of his voice, between the mask and the modulation, and they knew intuitively that the words rang false. Now, Adam himself
wore his feelings on his face. It was one of his most
endearing qualities; it might be embarrassing, but at least
it was honest. Could it be that, though incapable himself
of any devious thought, he was highly attuned to sensing

falsehood in others and had thus detected the hypocrisy in Loretta?

Putting an arm round the boy's shoulder, she drew him toward her.

"Oh Adam," she sighed tenderly and sadly. "What are we going to do with you? You really don't belong in this world."

But then a more chilling thought followed swiftly. You could not lie to an aphasiac. They might not grasp your words and so couldn't be deceived by words, but they did grasp the expression behind them, and *that* could never be simulated or faked. If this was true of Adam, it meant that you couldn't lie to him and expect to deceive him: he'd see through you right away. And, given his rigid, fundamentalist ideas of right and wrong, what might happen if he didn't always respond with the same innocent derision?

•

Max accelerated into the dwindling sun as the Boston suburbs receded behind her. Beyond a narrow ribbon of houses and hoardings, of gas stations and fast-food joints, layer upon layer of virgin wooded slopes now stretched on either side of the highway as far as the eye could see. She felt irritable. The first results from the field had come through; she'd spent the day running an assay to refine the small fragment of the gene sequence and she'd had to break off in the middle to come out here. She'd cancelled an evening date, too, with a producer from NBC television she'd met recently researching a "New Genetics" program. Why *was* she taking such pains to cultivate the Wendell family?

To her own surprise, she found she was growing

genuinely fond of Julia. She hadn't meant to: she wasn't even sure she wanted to. It raised all kinds of issues of conscience that she could really do without. She kept telling herself that was all in the past, a closed chapter—the man they'd both loved was dead and buried—and yet whenever his name came up, as it constantly did in conversation, she couldn't help feeling a twinge of shame, even perhaps envy. Time and again she wondered whether to tell Julia the truth and clear the air once and for all. But always she decided against it. The truth would only cause her unnecessary pain. Julia had enough to cope with right now. For all her secure suburban setting, the poor woman seemed so at sea, so isolated. At that moment, Max put her foot down harder. *Bullshit*, she muttered aloud. You're not sorry for Julia. You're not keeping secrets so as to spare her feelings, either. You're not making friends with her family out of some respect, or regret, for Sam. The truth is, you're courting them because of Adam. That boy is what you're really interested in. And telling Julia about Sam would wreck your chances of getting closer to him.

Yet the closer she got, the greater the puzzle became. What *had* Sam meant to do with the boy? Bring him back to the States and adopt him, as Julia unquestioningly believed? Or, as she herself suspected, bring him back to *study* him? Had he been planning to wheel him round the Peabody from one department to another, examining his bone structure, his musculature, his metabolism, his behavior and, above all, his language, to find out where he fitted into the known taxonomy of Caucasian tribes, to find out *who he was*? She gave an involuntary shiver. Sam was dead, and maybe that was Adam's good fortune. But a question did not die with the man who'd asked it. Who precisely *was* this boy? In all honesty, given the right circumstances, wouldn't she leap at the chance of studying him herself? She glanced at the seat beside her on which lay a bag from a toyshop in Boston. There lay her answer. She was making the circumstances.

Finally she reached the long, clapboard house and rang the doorbell. Loud music drowned the ring, and no one came. She let herself in. The din came from Adam's playroom. She looked round the door. The boy was squatting on the floor, his face just inches from the television on which an episode of *Dallas* was showing. From time to time he traced a finger across the screen. Beside him lay Sandy's tape player, from which the *Walküre* were riding forth at full blast. She couldn't help smiling: everything about this kid was incongruous.

Julia's voice from behind startled her.

"Hello, Max. Sorry, I didn't hear the bell. I was upstairs with Sandy." She sounded weary and fraught and she stood erect, tensed. She advanced into the room. "Adam, would you please turn that down? *Adam!*" She muted the television and grimaced. "He's suddenly caught the music bug."

"Opera, too," remarked Max. "Soaps *and* classical."

"It's all the same to him," responded Julia with a faint smile. She reached to take the tape player from his grasp but he wrenched it back and a brief tussle ensued. "Stop it, Adam. That's enough now! You can have it on, but not so loud."

Max stepped forward and held out the toyshop bag.

"Here, Adam, I brought you something," she said. "No, don't tear the bag. *Open* it. Like this." She helped him take out the present. "It's an abacus. For counting. I'll show you." She sat down beside him and moved the wooden beads across the rods. "One. Say 'one.'"

"Un," grunted Adam.

"Two..."

"Doo."

"Three..."

Here he fell silent. Julia knelt on his other side and coaxed him gently.

"Zhee," he wheezed finally, then clapped his hands. Julia and Max followed suit, and Adam smiled with glee. They played this game until he grew bored and wanted to explore how far the rods would bend before breaking.

Julia met Max's eye, then glanced away. She seemed to wear an almost permanent look of anxiety.

"What did the shrink say?" asked Max, to break the silence.

"Infantile schizophrenia this time. Last time Adam was a maladjusted retardate. It's all words. To cover up the fact no one knows."

"Maybe they'll wise up when he goes to the Unit."

"If."

"If?"

Julia straightened. "If he stays, that is. It's touch and go."

"Sandy?"

Julia shrugged with weary resignation.

"It's her decision. This is first and foremost her home. If she wants to drop him like an unwanted toy..."

She broke off. This was not a conversation to be held in front of Adam, perhaps not even one she wanted to share with Max. Max felt her pulse quicken. She had no idea things had gone that far.

"I'm sure she'll come around eventually," said Max.

"I wish I shared your optimism, Max." She went to

the door. "Can I offer you a drink?"

"Thanks. Do you have any wine open?"

Julia led the way into the kitchen and uncorked a bottle. In silence she poured two glasses, handed Max one and raised her own in an ironic toast.

"Look," said Max, "why don't I have a word with her? It can't do any harm."

"As you please. I've done all I can. I'm at my wits' end."

"Don't count on miracles."

"I've long since given up counting on anything."

•

Max found Sandy sitting cross-legged on the bed, copying out a diagram of a neuron system from a biology textbook. Sandy pulled off her stereo headphones and shook her fair hair free.

"Hi, come in," she cried, thrusting the book aside. "All this stuff about axons and ions. What's the point if you want to be a zoologist? Did you have to do it?"

Max smiled. "You need to know how things work to really understand them."

"I've no idea how the phone works, but that doesn't keep me from making calls." Sandy cast her a sideways glance. "But that's not why you're here. Mom sent you."

"Wrong. I came to see how you are."

"Well, I'm fed up." She toyed with the ends of her hair. Max glanced around the room: a new basketball poster, some dying meadow flowers in a mug, the usual clothes and magazines strewn over the chairs and floor. "Maxie," resumed the girl in a more tentative voice, "do you think I'm being unreasonable?"

"I think it's very tough for you, Sandy."

Sandy gazed distantly out of the window.

"I sometimes wish I was one of your gazelles," she murmured. "Taken far into the wilds and set free. Sometimes when I'm out running I pretend I am. Leaping and bounding, all light and springy." She met her eye. "It must be wonderful to see them go."

Max nodded. "Sure. Running free for the first time in their lives. Breaking out and discovering a whole new world. It's kind of wonderful and scary at the same time."

"Zoos stink," said Sandy with sudden vehemence. "It's wicked to keep wild animals in captivity. I'd send them all back where they came from. Where they belong."

Max heard the underlying *cri* but chose not to take it up. Instead she began explaining why zoos were necessary and how, these days, they had become far less museums for amusing the curious public than breeding centers for keeping endangered species alive.

"Many species only exist in zoos today," she heard herself saying. "They can't be released because their habitats have vanished. In four or five hundred years, it's estimated that the world's wastelands will begin to expand again and the zoos can release the animals back then. But the genetic stock may be too weak through inbreeding. That's the hot question."

Sandy was sitting forward now.

"Well?"

"Who knows?" she replied, watching the girl carefully. "The point of our gazelle project is not to take the chance. See, the world's changing too fast—the wilderness is shrinking, habitats are dying, the globe's warming up, all that. A lot of species just can't adapt by natural selection quick enough. So we adapt them artificially.

Give them a hand up the evolutionary ladder. It's that, or extinction."

Sandy let out an angry sigh.

"I *hate* man," she said between clenched teeth. "We interfere with nature and make a mess, then we interfere again to straighten it out. It's a vicious circle. Why can't we just leave things alone in the first place?"

"You know why?"

"Because we're stupid, greedy and selfish. Even when we think we're being all good and moral, we're just kidding ourselves."

She'd been scratching her pen on the exercise-book, making savage, angular marks. Max could feel the ferment rising to a head.

"I don't know so much," she demurred.

"Look at Mom, for instance," retorted the girl. "She pretends to herself she's doing everything for *him*—and, of course, for dear Sam—but really it's all for herself. For her own satisfaction, her own image as this saint of charity. Adam doesn't need us. He'd be much happier back where he came from. Only she can't let him go. She talks about his needs when really it's *hers* she's interested in."

"That's too cynical, Sandy. Anyone can twist someone's motives to look selfish."

"But it's true! If only she were more honest! Those kids at the Unit: if she really cared about them she'd give *them* her precious charity. There's dozens of them and only one of him. All she cares about is feeling good inside. She had a real-estate man appraise the house the other day," she went on, growing flushed. "It wasn't because she has the faintest intention of moving to a smaller place—i.e. and giving up Adam—but just so it would look to me like she's keeping an open mind. She keeps saying we aren't committed to keeping him, but she knows that's not true. We committed ourselves the moment she signed the papers. When I tell her that, she acts all sanctimonious. 'Someone's got to look after the poor lad.' Sure, someone has to. Why not an agency, or the Unit, or someone whose job it is? Why does it always have to be us?" She checked herself. Her lip was trembling. "I'm sorry," she mumbled. "I don't mean to lay a number on you."

Max put her arm round the girl's shoulders. She could feel her body locked rigid with tension.

"I understand, Sandy. Like I said, it's tough."

"Thanks, Maxie."

"C'mon now," she said, giving her a gentle shake, "I have an idea. You know that old hunting shack out in Worcester County I told you about? It's in a helluva state, like no one's been there since Davy Crockett. I was planning on going out there Saturday and doing some spring-cleaning. Would you like to come along?"

"Just you and me?"

"I wasn't planning a party."

The shoulders gradually relaxed.

"Sure, I'd like that."

Max patted her comfortingly and rose to her feet. At the door she turned with a smile.

"I never understood about ions either. Someone somewhere does: that's all you need to know. Right?"

•

On the landing outside, Max hesitated. To her left lay the narrow stars that led up to the attic. She'd never actually been inside Adam's room. She listened for a moment to confirm he was still downstairs, then tiptoed hurriedly up the wooden steps. The first attic was a large, half-empty boxroom that smelled faintly of dust and boiler fumes. The other was clearly Adam's. There the smell was quite different—a sweetish, musky odor reminiscent of her gazelles.

From the threshold she glanced around quickly, furtively. Branches, logs, leaves, stones, odd glittery objects. As she took a step inside, she tripped over a track shoe. Bending to pick it up, she noticed fleetingly that the sole was heavily worn on the ball of the foot but hardly at all on the heel. Downstairs, she heard a door shut; Julia would be wondering if something was wrong. She put the shoe down and, with a final glance around, sneaked back out down the stairs. Sandy was right, she thought as she passed the girl's door: no one's motives were entirely pure. Altruism was really selfishness in disguise. Everyone had their own needs. Science was curiosity, and curiosity, by its nature, was self-serving; satisfying that was *her* need. Yet it was this that turned the world, that created civilization and culture, that had produced penicillin and pesticides and advanced man's span of life. The mess was a by-product of progress, but the balance-sheet still showed a vast net gain. Science could provide the means to utopia. And that, Sandy, was cause for hope, not cynicism.

She was coming down the main stairs when her mind flashed back to the track shoe in Adam's room. She'd often noticed the boy walked with a peculiar forward-tilting gait, and now she understood. Normally in walking a person put the heel down first and then the toes. Adam didn't: he walked *toe-first*. But her next thought stopped her in her tracks. Wasn't that how certain primitive tribes of African bushmen walked? And weren't those savannahs of Africa they inhabited the very cradle from which the earliest species of man had emerged? She thought back to the fairy tales Sam had woven over dinner that night in Venice, and she gave an uncontrollable shiver.

•

William Cray angled the small reading-light closer and settled back into the soft upholstery of the limousine to read the file. Out of the corner of his eye he saw Eliot Lovejoy's satisfied, confident smile. So, here was the final and full proof of the boy's origins from the samples taken at the "halfway house." Proof of the unbelievable so absolute as to make the most extreme skeptic believe. He appeared to study it carefully, wondering what approach to take. Eliot would demand the boy go back to the Center; he himself was determined he'd stay with the family. Everything was going so sweetly. Julia Wendell had not for one second suspected the fault on her telephone line was other than normal, nor that the telephone engineers who'd come to fix it were from anywhere but the utility company. And it was already paying dividends. The listening devices the men had planted were working well, as the first transcripts demonstrated. Barely a word could be spoken within that house that was not overheard.

Finally he closed the file and handed it back.

"I'm sorry, Eliot," he said quietly. "This doesn't change a thing."

He waited for the inevitable outburst. In the headlights of a passing car he could see the scientist's long bloodhound face contort with sudden fury.

"What the hell d'you mean?" he stormed. "It's the goddamn proof!"

"Eliot—"

The howling of a police siren forced a brief second's truce, then Lovejoy burst in again.

"I want that boy back in my lab, William."

"We're going to play it as we agreed. The boy's staying right where he is. That house *is* your lab, Eliot."

"Not for much longer. You read the transcripts."

"That's being taken care of."

William Cray paused. It wasn't being taken care of. He hadn't bargained for internal dissent between mother and daughter. The trial period was up, and if the girl cast her veto then Adam would be sent back to the agency. Eliot would get his specimen, sure, but that would put paid to the really interesting experiment. The social implications of this unique phenomenon were far more profound than the purely scientific ones. Besides, they had to take precedence in time order, since every day that passed the boy adapted further to his new environment and lost more of his essential natural responses. How could they learn all that he could teach them about innate human values and social instincts except by observing him interacting with society itself? Certainly not by incarcerating him in Eliot's labs. That must wait. He himself had originated the project: he had first right over handling it.

The tense, acrimonious silence lengthened. An ambulance passed with its beacon flashing, illuminating the other man's hard-set features. Cray frowned in thought. He had to find a way. Perhaps the agency could invoke some small print and refuse to accept the boy back. Or was there a subtler way? What about this Maxine Fitzgerald? He recalled the cool, watchful young woman at the funeral whom he'd recognized from the Venice photograph. How come she'd gotten so friendly with her paramour's bereaved wife? What was her angle? And there was always Julia herself. Maybe it was time to pay her a visit. He'd call her up and suggest dinner.

He turned to the scientist. It was critical to keep him on his side. After all, they both belonged to the Foundation and shared the same fundamental interest.

"Relax, Eliot," he said in a more conciliatory tone. "Just hold on. You'll get your material to play with. I guarantee."

9

MAX TOOK OFF HER READING GLASSES AND RUBBED her eyes. Morning sunlight streamed in through the lab window and reflected off the desktop screen, making it a strain to work on the text. She glanced at the clock on the lab wall; she'd better get moving if she was going to have any time at the shack. She felt weary and frustrated. She'd been hard at work composing the experiment approval application since before six. Paperwork was not *real* work. A cartoon pinned above her desk depicted Crick and Watson's famous double helix unraveling into a ribbon of red tape. That was genetics today.

Beside her lay a Federal Express document pouch filled with papers from the Bronx Zoo, the center coordinating the gazelle breeding program. Box files titled *Project Noah* lined the shelves above, crammed with applications, submissions, reports, memos and the endless registration forms and notifications that had to be sent to all and sundry—to the National Institutes of Health, the Recombinant DNA Advisory Committee, the Institutional Bio-safety Committee and every other watchdog of the environment, both official and self-appointed. The project was run under the auspices of the World Wide Fund for Nature and coordinated by the New York Zoological Society; ten major zoos around the world were participating, and the main scientific research was being funded by the National Institutes of Health. But that made no difference. The fact was, their work involved inserting genes of one species into living creatures of another, and that was enough to get every Tom, Dick and Harry clamoring to play judge and jury. They were introducing genes from a subspecies of the chamois, *rupicapra rupicapra caucasica*, into the dorcas gazelle, *gazella dorcas dorcas*, but from the reams of paperwork required to get permission to test just a single modification to the experiment already authorized, one would have thought the project was about recreating Frankenstein's monster. It wasn't even about creating transgenic animals. It conformed to the general moratorium on germ-line testing. None of the gazelles would be able to transmit the foreign genes to their offspring; the characteristics grafted onto them *in vivo* would die with them. Where was the danger in that? What kind of people did the public think scientists really were? The evil freaks of tinseltown movies, breeding horrific life-forms in labs, which then escaped to replicate uncontrollably? Scientists were decent, well-intentioned citizens like any others, men and women with families and loved-ones, people of conviction and conscience who wanted to see a better life on a better planet. Why didn't people ever quite *trust* them?

The distant slam of a door broke her train of thought. She looked up, puzzled; the labs were usually empty on a Saturday. A moment later, her lab-mate Murray burst in. His expression was thunderous, and beneath his wire-framed glasses his eyes were heavily pouched. He went to the coffee-machine; the flask was empty, and he swore. She handed him a Tab from her bag.

"How did it go yesterday?" she asked. "No, don't tell me."

For reply Murray dumped a thick wad of computer print-out onto the lab bench and sank into his chair.

"The creep's been hacking into my files," he growled.

"He wouldn't know how. Gerald's too dumb. He's a moron."

"He's an effing mother."

"Change your ID. Or lay a trap. Write a virus."

He wiped his glasses on his shirtfront and assumed an air of nonchalance.

"Too much dopamine, that's the problem with our pal Gerald," he said. "I think we could fix that, don't you, Maxie? Like vector his coffee?"

She laughed. "He really gets to you, doesn't he?"

"Screw him. C'mon, what's the good news?" He swung his feet onto the desk, spilling the dregs from a plastic cup. "You heard from the outback?"

"One male has knocked out a couple of rivals and grabbed their females. So at least it looks like they've begun breeding."

"That's what I envy about your stuff, Maxie. It's sexy."

"Ah, but you get the money."

He managed a chuckle. It was true: the big money in genetic research at the moment was on a gigantic project to crack the human genome. Codenamed HUGO, it aimed at mapping the entire blueprint for a complete human being. This was an international race with billion-dollar stakes. The Europeans and Japanese were already runners; funded by the Defense Department, the United States was still leading by a nose. By contrast, the field of endangered wildlife was all talk and no money. With a sigh she switched off her desktop computer and rose to her feet. As she passed his desk, she glanced at the stack of print-out with its familiar close-printed computer type cramming the page: CCAATGGATTCCATG . . . and so on—just four bases repeated endlessly in different combinations in an unbroken sequence. Here was just one fragment of the code to build one human protein but, taken collectively over three thousand million base pairs, it made up the formula for a complete human being. Gradually, systematically, the code was being cracked. And Murray was right in the forefront of it all.

"Where did I go wrong?" she sighed.

"Stick with it, Maxie," he replied. "Trouble with my shit is, it attracts the flies. Like Gerald. He's not always after your ass."

"You don't think?" She cast him a complicit smile from the doorway. "Do me a favor. While you're spiking our department head's coffee, fix his testosterone level, too, will you?"

With a laugh, he reached for the print-out.

"See you, kid."

"See you, Murray."

•

Max arrived to find Sandy had gone off to play basketball in her usual Saturday morning school "friendly." Adam was kicking listlessly around the garden, clearly bored. Julia was busy on the phone to the mother of one of the kids at the Unit, listening to some problem about day release. She came off the phone briefly to tell Max the latest news. The decision had been made for them. She'd called the agency earlier to discuss the options for Adam's future, only to be told that the probation period had expired by two days and the adoption had been formally registered. There was no going back now. Like it or not, Adam was Adam Samuel Wendell of White River Drive, Lexington, Mass. Julia's adopted son, Sandy's adopted brother. She hadn't had the chance to tell Sandy yet. She was going to have to pick her moment carefully.

Then the phone rang again, and she excused herself and hurried back to the study. Max couldn't help overhearing. This time it was evidently the kid's father; the child had been sent home for the weekend as part of a rehabilitation program, and already they couldn't cope with the terrible tantrums. They were in despair: what should they do? The firm, professional way Julia handled it impressed Max. Pity one could never solve one's own domestic problems, she reflected, in the way one could other people's. Through the window she saw Adam strolling desultorily up and down the drive, hands in his pockets, scuffing up the gravel. The perfect idea suddenly occurred to her. It would provide a perfect chance to spend some time alone with the boy and observe him in a new and unfamiliar environment. And Julia would reckon it a favor.

Hearing a lull in the phone calls, she put her head round the door.

"I can see you're buried up to your neck," she said sweetly. "Why don't I take Adam off your hands for a while? Go out somewhere."

"Would you? Get him to show you the dam he built in the river."

"I thought we'd take in the basketball. At school."

"Max, I'm not really sure . . ."

"Come on, Sandy's got to face facts sooner or later."

"Well, if you really feel you could manage." The gratitude in Julia's voice was unconcealed. "The moment he gives trouble, whisk him back home, won't you?" The phone rang, and with an apologetic smile, she reached for the receiver. "Take the estate," she said.

•

The sports center was enclosed by a vast glass canopy supported by a lattice of brightly colored tubular struts. Beneath lay an entire complex that included tennis, basketball and squash courts, a gymnasium and workout area and two pools, most with their own seating galleries, as well as a large, busy social concourse equipped with a snack bar and a small amusement arcade. The din of excited young voices echoed round the high canopy, broken now and then by a thrilled scream from the pool or a referee's shrill whistle from the courts. Adam was in wonderland.

She found the basketball court and sat him close beside her in the upper tier of seats, as far out of sight as possible. She could tell the game was in its closing moments. The teams were mixed and the play was ragged but enthusiastic. She recognized the coach as Scott, the older kid from next door. As she watched, Sandy gained possession of the ball. Instantly she was guarded. She bounced the ball on the spot for a second, then stuttered her feet, freezing the defender. The stutter became an explosive dribble as she suddenly burst past the other player into the open court. Still some yards from the basket, she grasped the ball in one hand and, in a single flowing movement, leapt into the air and lobbed it in a short, spiralling arc towards the target, where it glanced off the backboard, skimmed the rim of the net and fell vainly to the ground. A cry of surprise broke out across the court; evidently she didn't usually miss an easy jump shot. She flashed a laughing glance at Scott and beat her head with her fists in mock penitence. At that moment, Scott blew his whistle and the game came to an end. The players relaxed and gathered into small knots, joking and kidding among themselves.

Adam couldn't contain himself any longer. Before Max could stop him, he'd slipped from her grasp and was clambering down the steep tier of seats towards the front. She hurried helplessly after him. Sandy spotted him as he vaulted onto the court. The other players began to stop and take note.

The ball lay just beyond the baseline. In a flash he picked it up and began bouncing it up and down, but he couldn't catch properly and kept missing it on the rebound. Finally he gathered it in both hands and stepped out into the open court. Sandy pushed forward as he took a sighting on the far end.

"Give it here, Adam," she hissed.

But Adam ignored her. He had his eye sighted on the far end. Taking the orange ball in his left hand, he drew back his arm and, with a muffled grunt, punched it like a shot-put high into the air. Heads turned to follow its trajectory. The ball soared in a graceful sweep, almost grazing the floodlights, before descending in a perfect arc towards the basket. A gasp rose from the onlookers as it struck the rim, richocheted uncertainly in the mouth of the net, then with a shudder it slipped down the funnel and fell through to the ground below. There was absolute silence on the court as it bounced slowly away into the corner.

Scott was the first to speak.

"Jesus," he breathed. "Some shot, kid!"

Sandy cast Max a look of dumbfounded surprise. Max shook her head in genuine amazement. Gradually the kids recovered from their astonishment. They pressed forward.

"Whassyuhname?"

"Hey, Sandy, this your new kid brother?"

"I heard he's some kinda gypsy."

"Weird, man."

"Say, kid, where did'ya learn to play ball?"

Sandy pushed herself between them. She looked embarrassed, but more for Adam's sake.

"He doesn't understand too well," she said, steering him away.

"Let's see that shot again."

"C'mon, he fluked it!"

"Hey, Scottie, give him a play-off."

All the while, Scott had kept his eye fixed on Adam.

"You could be big," he said quietly. "Shoot like that you'll be another Magic Johnson." He turned to Sandy. "You never said anything."

"I didn't know. Anyway, maybe it *was* a fluke."

"Only one way to know." Scott gave Adam the ball he was carrying and pointed to the other end. "Okay, champ. Shoot."

Once again, Adam took a sighting and, with a short, sharp grunt of exertion, propelled the ball in a perfect twisting spiral towards the far basket. It slipped unfalteringly through the net and bounced away along the floor.

Scott cheered, the others laughed. Adam laughed,

too, in his uncomprehending way, full of the simple desire to please. Scott clapped him on the shoulder.

"Come down here next Saturday, and I'll show you some of the basics. What do you say, huh?" He paused, realizing he wasn't being understood. "Well, you can be deaf and dumb and still make it." He turned to the other kids. "What does it take to get to the top, you guys?"

"Practice!" they yelled.

"Make sure he practices, Sandy." He glanced over towards the basket. "Left-hander, too," he mused. Then he clapped his hands briskly. "Okay, team, let's wrap it up. Same time next week."

He headed away to the changing-rooms, and the rest of the group swiftly broke up. Sandy hung back. Her gaze was fixed on Adam with a new, keen curiosity.

"Son of a gun," she muttered. Then her tone grew more abrupt. "If Scott's going to start coaching you, Adam, you'll have to get into shape. You can come running with me in the mornings. And get some decent playing clothes: you can't wear that junk on court."

With a half-smile of puzzled disbelief, she turned and disappeared off into the changing-rooms, leaving Max alone with the boy in the center of an empty court.

•

The shack was reached up a steep, pebble-strewn track that had in earlier times formed the course of a river. It stood on a small, level clearing amid dense woodland. To the last, her father had kept nature at bay, but just in the few years since his death the clearing had begun to close over, so that now the rear of the building was enveloped in black spruce and balsam fir and the rough grass in front overrun with saplings. The shack itself was bare and spartan. The nearest phone was four miles away, at a small store that sold hunting equipment and which only opened seasonally. The electricity only functioned periodically, too, so that kerosene lamps were the standard form of lighting, ice in a drink was an unexpected luxury and as often as not supper had to be cooked over an open fire. For Max, it held memories of the happiest days of her childhood. It was here that she'd first fallen under the spell of her father's passion for wildlife. Since his death, finding it too painful to visit, she'd left the place virtually untouched. Her mother, who had retired to Florida shortly afterwards to live with her sister, herself since widowed, had never shown any liking for it—she'd found it too hot in summer and too cold in winter and altogether too dull for a city-dweller—and so, from as far back as Max could remember, it had always been *their* place, a retreat for just the two of them, father and daughter.

She threw the windows open to let in the warm spring air and went round checking for damage. Robustly built of thick-hewn lumber, the structure had withstood the seasons well. Apart from a broken window in the kitchen and a dead crow in the grate, a thin film of dust everywhere and an all-pervasive stuffy, unlived-in smell, the shack was just as it had been when she'd turned the key in the lock the final time. Leaving Sandy sweeping the main living area, she took a pile of rugs onto the porch to be shaken out. There she paused for a moment, gazing out over the tree-tops. Yes, it had been wrong to keep this place a mausoleum; a new broom, a new purpose, was needed. She'd never quite cut free from the influence of her father; even Sam, she recognized, had always been something of a surrogate. Now both men were gone and she was alone. Alone to find herself and her own, independent life.

A movement in the bushes caught her eye. It was Adam, bent forward in a semi-crouch, creeping silently up the track. Every now and then he'd stop and pick up a small, smooth pebble, examine it carefully and toss it back, then glide stealthily on a few steps. A natural hunter, she thought; a natural *stalker*. An amazing eye, too. Her mind went back to the basketball game that morning, and she marvelled at the turnabout in Sandy's attitude. Maybe it wasn't that straightforward, though. Sure, with Scott accepting him so readily and so publicly, Sandy could hardly maintain an overt hostility. Was she playing along until the boy condemned himself by some terrible or uncouth act, leaving it to time to prove her right? Yet it had been her own suggestion to bring him along on this trip; her mother had actually advised against it, arguing that it was far too long a journey. But in the event, Adam had sat in the back of the car without a murmur, playing contentedly with her Walkman as if for all the world he'd been on long car-rides all his life. Max cast a glance behind her, half-hoping to find a clue to her questions in the industrious figure within. When she turned back, the boy had vanished. He'd simply melted into the landscape.

A short while later, after they'd broken the back of the cleaning, she spread the blanket on the grass out at the front and laid out some drinks and cookies she'd brought along. She called Adam, but there was no reply.

"What if he's lost?" queried Sandy.

Max shook her head. "I don't think so. He's in his natural element here."

"Yes, more than at home. That's not his environment."

"Well, I guess he doesn't have much choice."

"*We* do. Anyway, I don't think it's fair to him, being

forced to fit into our way of life."

"Surely he's better off here than in whatever primitive backwater he's come from. It must be an improvement."

"Must be?"

Max let the question hang unanswered. She reached for a can of Seven-Up and, stretching out on the blanket, stared up at the infinite blue sky. The air was heady with the scents of spring and raucous with the chittering of birds. She hadn't felt such a sense of physical ease for so long. Gradually she became aware of a small, rhythmic chipping sound coming from the other side of the shack. Puzzled, she rose and went to investigate. Sandy followed.

She found Adam crouching over a small pile of dry twigs set in a hollow of earth against a fallen tree-trunk. He had a stone in each hand and was striking one against the other. To his side, the grass was flattened and stained reddish-black, and a short distance away lay the bloodied pelt of a rabbit, turned inside out like a glove. A strip of material torn from his sleeve lay on the ground beside him, furled and knotted to form a makeshift stone-sling, while next to it were three large, perfectly round pebbles. He turned at their approach and grinned. As he moved, she saw, behind him, a skinned rabbit, skewered along its length on a stick.

"Revolting!" breathed Sandy, backing away.

Adam turned back to the tinder and, bending forward, struck one stone sharply against the other and puffed hard. A thin spiral of smoke rose into the still air. He quickly piled on the wood, and soon he had a blaze going. Then he deftly fixed four crossed sticks in the ground to form a rack and laid the skewered rabbit on the spit.

Max knelt down beside him to observe him more carefully. She took note of the way he grasped the stones in his powerful grip and how he always struck the left one against the right. She noticed for the first time, too, a curious feature about his ankles—slight ledge-formations, knowns as "squatting facets," commonly found among aborigines and indeed among many other tribal peoples who squatted rather than sat. And strongly reminiscent of those, too, that Sam had once pointed out to her in the collection of prehistoric human bones in the Peabody...

Slowly she rose to her feet and retraced her steps, deep in thought. Sandy looked up as she approached.

"Don't you sometimes wonder?" she frowned.

"Wonder what, Sandy?"

"Who he *really* is. I don't see him as this simpleton gypsy. I don't even think he's quite... somehow... one of us."

"Sandy!" she scoffed gently. "You just find it hard to accept the fact that you've suddenly got a brother. Remember, I was an only child too. I know how you feel."

"Do you?"

A sudden guttural whoop prevented her reply. Adam came running round the side of the shack, carrying a large platter made from the bark of a fir tree. He came up to Sandy and laid the offering before her. The bark, furled into a semi-cylindrical shape, held small pieces of rabbit, lightly charred and neatly jointed. He picked among them carefully, then handed her the choice morsels.

"No thanks," she said, turning aside.

"Take it, Sandy," Max warned her quietly.

"I'm not hungry, thanks."

"Take it."

Reluctantly, the girl took the piece of char-grilled meat and, screwing up her face, took a small bite. Adam watched eagerly, his large dark eyes wide and expectant.

"Delicious," she said without conviction, then gradually her expression changed. "It really is, actually. You try some, Maxie. Hey, Adam, you really aren't bad at some things."

Adam was beaming. He moved from one to the other, piling their hands full, then, squatting back on his ankles, he devoured the carcass himself. Max glanced across to find Sandy looking at the boy now with a grudging smile that seemed, despite herself, genuinely fond.

°

Max returned the two home in the early evening and, refusing the offer of supper, made for the door to leave. In the hallway, Julia laid a hand on her arm.

"Listen!" she whispered.

Upstairs Sandy was bossily ordering Adam to be on parade in the morning at six-thirty prompt, dressed properly for a run, and that didn't mean barefoot and just in the boxer shorts he slept in. Adam's grunted responses suggested this was a one-way communication only; Max doubted how much he possessed a concept of the future anyway. But Julia was smiling. Those past few hours seemed to have smoothed away weeks of worry.

"They're *talking*, Max," she beamed. "I don't know how to thank you enough."

"Come on, I didn't do anything."

"Yes, you did. If you hadn't taken him with you this morning . . ."

"Don't jump the gun, Julia. Give it time."

"You're right. We must give it time."

The desperation in her eyes took Max aback. She hadn't realized how much of herself Julia had staked on making this enterprise work. She still found it hard to imagine why Julia should, finally, *care* so much. Why did she risk alienating, perhaps even traumatizing, her daughter just for the sake of giving a home to a strange kid out of some kind of obscure pledge to the memory of a dead husband? It didn't stack up. But then, without children of her own, she really wasn't one to judge. Parenthood, she'd often felt, was a door: the world divided between those on this side and those on that. Everything looked different once you'd stepped through. Try as she might to understand Julia, she never really would. And yet, even from the sidelines, she could see enough to tell her that the odds were laid heavily against. Wasn't this eagerness of Julia's to make a family based on a dangerous blindness? Couldn't she see that, however determined she might be to create a normal, harmonious home for Adam, there was something about the boy that was profoundly and fundamentally *ab*normal, that somehow he was not entirely—how had Sandy put it?—*one of us*? No one could remain so blithely unaware unless they'd chosen deliberately to shut their eyes to the evidence all around them.

As Max drove away from the house that night, she weighed up the evidence objectively, as a trained scientist might, and she found the pieces fitting into an inescapably clear pattern. And it was a pattern of which Julia, in her blind innocence, had not the slightest inkling.

•

Crouching in the half-light, Adam delved into the large cardboard box. Beside him, two packing-cases lay empty on their sides. An academic gown and mortarboard, several dress shirts in tissue-paper, a silk evening scarf, a khaki safari suit, a pair of ski pants and various other articles of clothing lay scattered on the attic floor. Rummaging deeper through the box, he pulled out a curious oval, ivory-colored object. His brow furrowed. He took it into the wedge of moonlight that spliced in through the small window. It was a flat slab of old, yellowed bone. The under-surface was perished into a hard, sponge-like lattice, but the top was smooth, and deep in the plaque was scratched a definite pattern—a triangle enclosed within a circle. He studied it carefully, tilting it this way and that. Then he let out a low, excited grunt and, with his breath coming in shorter bursts, began rocking back and forth on his heels, cradling the bone to his breast.

After a while, still clutching the bone, he pulled out a battered canvas holdall from beneath the bed and began taking out the contents one by one, arranging them carefully on the floor to make the shape of a human figure. The photo in the silver frame served for the head. Two small square passport photos for the eyes. A large, full-length shot taken in the regalia of Professor of Anthropology made up the torso. He lingered for a moment over a newspaper cutting, and after some deliberation placed it in the groin area. Gradually the image took shape. Photos from the obituary made up the arms and others torn from the back flap of book jackets the legs, while still others taken on expeditions into the wilds, driving a jeep or posing beside groups of nomads, filled in the rest. Finally the body was complete. Then, taking the special bone in both hands, he laid it in the center of the forehead, in the position of the third eye.

For a while he continued rocking back and forth, muttering a low incantation, then finally he rose and went to the window. Night had fallen, and stars shone like pinpricks in a shroud of darkness. Slipping to his knees, he pressed his face against the pane and stared out. Eagerly he scanned the heavens for the sign. From time to time the moving light of an airplane would briefly excite his attention, only to have its false promise betrayed a moment later. Finally, his hopes exhausted, he sank sadly back onto his heels. The sky was empty. The moon returned a blank stare, a bright, thickening crescent, waxing fast. He glanced over his shoulder to the image laid out in ritual array, and a grim chatter broke through his clenched teeth.

Soon, very soon, the moon would be full. Then his duty could be fulfilled.

10

○
───────────

THE UNIT LAY IN THE FURTHEST REACHES OF CAM-
bridge, up by the Charles River dam, but finding herself
with time to spare, Julia took a detour through the heart
of the city. She headed for the Common and, skirting the
university campus, cut back down a sideroad off Harvard
Street in which stood the broad clapboard house that had
been their first home. As she drove slowly past, she
pointed it out to Adam beside her. Converted into con-
dominiums after they'd left, the house had grown shabby
and dilapidated; litter lay caught in the overgrown yard
and loose telephone wires swung against the peeling
paintwork. Sam would have been appalled. In a downstairs window a sticker read, *Reborn in Christ*. She smiled
wryly: she could hear Sam's brusque Yankee voice saying, "If you're born in Boston, you've got no need to be
born again." Their neighbors had all moved, and older,
rustier cars now stood parked in the street outside. She
drove on, her thoughts fixed on Sam. What would he
have made of Adam? Would he have shown him a father's love, helped him to integrate better, championed

him in the neighborhood? Would he have approved of him going to the Unit, where she was now taking him? Probably not that. *Damn* him for dying on them! she thought with sudden asperity. She needed him. Adam needed him. After all, the boy had been his idea, his mission.

By the time the complex of low, modular buildings came into sight, however, she was feeling stronger and more composed. The idea might have been Sam's but the decision had been hers, and now it fell to her to see it through. She drew up in the parking area at the side and sat for a moment, controlling a nagging sense of unease. Ahead lay the playground, surrounded on all sides by a tall, climb-proof fence. A group of eight-year-olds was playing in the sandpit and on the climbing-frame. She knew each one intimately: they'd been there for most of their lives—and they'd probably remain there for most of the rest. Through the wire-glass windows, she could see a "class" at work—art, perhaps, or music? Art meant messing around with gummed colored paper and blunt scissors; music was hammering spoons upon upended metal pots and singing nursery rhymes. Through another window she could glimpse the small staff room, already fogged blue with cigarette smoke—these were exceptionally difficult children drawn from all over the state, and the job was notoriously stressful. The buildings themselves were faced in panels painted bright primary colors, the grounds were meticulously tidy and every effort had been made to present a clean, cheerful face. It struck a strangely false note.

Abruptly she reached forward and released Adam's seat belt.

"Come on, my boy," she sighed. "Let's give it a go."

•

The Director was a fitness fanatic with prematurely silver hair and a smooth, tanned complexion. He sat in a tracksuit and trainers, clenching a grip-strengthener, as he flipped through Adam's file. Comparing the conflicting diagnoses from the psychotherapists who'd visited the boy, he permitted himself the lightest frown.

Finally he came round the front of his desk and perched on the edge, and with an easy, frank smile gave Adam his welcome-to-the-Unit speech. They were there to help him, he stressed; he was to think of the staff as his friends. Adam smiled back, and the Director said how glad he was they were breaking the ice so quickly, when his smile gradually developed into a laugh. Julia recognized the laugh with alarm; she tugged at his sleeve and cautioned him to behave. But the Director betrayed no discomfiture; experienced at removing himself from the equation, he merely continued to chat smoothly and easily. All the while Julia could see he was watching the boy closely, and she could hear his mind thinking, as clearly as if he'd been speaking aloud, *Inappropriate responses . . . schizophrenia . . . so what's new?* When, a moment later, Adam grabbed the grip-exerciser, the Director played along, even admiring the power of his grip, while Julia knew he was really thinking, *Not paranoid, not manic either. What shall we go for? Settle for non-specific.* Finally he ushered them to the door, telling Adam that it was open to him at any time and adding that he could keep the grip-exerciser if he liked. She bit her cheek hard. Did it matter what labels you used, so long as you *cared*?

She took Adam from room to room, introducing him to the other children according to the ritual for newcomers. She could see he was growing increasingly ill at ease. His eyes darted about nervously and his hand was clammy and trembling. He refused to go inside one playroom where a mentally retarded ten-year-old was sitting body-rocking amid a pile of broken toys, and he shied violently away at the sight of another boy in the corridor, afflicted with total insensitivity to pain and heavily bandaged as a result of a recent scalding. Was there something innately unnatural about these children that he shunned? Or was it the atmosphere, what Sandy would call the *vibes* of the place? Already she was beginning to see this wasn't going to be so straightforward.

Yet when face to face with an autistic black girl of nine called Coral, his manner completely changed. Julia had managed to build up a mild attachment from this girl, though she recognized this was due more to habit and familiarity than with any perception of herself as an individual. Coral was now sitting in a corner of the recreation area with a box full of odd buttons, taking some out and arranging them on the floor, obsessively making patterns.

Adam seemed drawn to this small girl. Crouching down beside her, he watched her playing. She was oblivious of his presence, locked in a world of her own. Suddenly he reached out and picked up one of the buttons, breaking the pattern. Julia steeled herself for the inevitable tantrum. But instead, the girl looked up and, just briefly, met his eye. Autists were usually careful to avoid eye contact. Julia intervened.

"Adam, give her that button back," she said gently.

"Your button," said Coral in a flat, echolalic tone.

"She means *her* button," said Julia.

"Her button," echoed Coral, holding out her hand.

Obediently, Adam handed her back the button. She took it without any noticeable response and went on with her obsessive little game.

Julia left him there under a brawny young male charge nurse called Dan and, collecting a stack of case files from the records office, went off to the staff room to update herself on what had been happening. There she drew up a molded plastic chair and sat staring out of the window, unable to concentrate. Why had Adam reacted so differently to that small girl? Could he be marginally autistic, too? Yet he seemed perfectly able to form relationships: he was warm and loving and capable of showing his feelings, and he certainly engaged the world about him, rather than standing aloof from it. His world was far from the "empty fortress" of the autist's. Still, there was something she still couldn't put her finger on. Disturbed, she turned to the files and began reading.

She'd covered five or six cases when the bell rang for snack-time. A moment later she heard a violent commotion. Shouts, then footsteps hurrying past down the corridor. Filled with foreboding, she rushed from the room and raced down the corridor. As she burst into the playroom, she stopped dead.

The charge nurse had got Adam pinned to the floor in a arm lock, with his knee jammed against the boy's neck. Adam's nose was bleeding and his face was contorted in pain and rage. The other children clung to the walls, squealing and jabbering. Coral herself remained in her corner, numb and untouched, staring at the box of buttons lying scattered at her feet. Julia rushed forward and, with a furious glare, wrenched the boy free, then drew him away to the far side of the room where, amid the hubbub, she struggled to calm and comfort him.

○

The Director dismissed the charge nurse and turned to Julia.

"I'll have the pharmacist get him something," he said, reaching for the phone. "Make sure he takes it *before* he arrives each day."

"Wait a minute," she responded hotly. "You heard what happened. Dan took the box from Coral because it was snack-time. Adam simply misunderstood and went to help her."

"Aggression is a behavioral disorder, Julia. You know how we deal with that here. First containment, then conditioning."

Suddenly she snapped.

"Drugs aren't the answer," she retorted. "I don't want Adam to be one of your placid zombies, doped into submission. We should be able to get through by *understanding*."

The Director maintained his flawless smile, but his fingers whitened round his pen.

"Let's not get into that debate right now, shall we?" he said in a sweetly warning tone.

"It's high time these issues were faced."

"Adam is the issue." He tapped the file on his desk. "And whether we're right for him here. I wonder if he might not be happier somewhere else."

"He's a special child, and he needs special help."

"I have sixty-five other kids to think of, and each one of them is special. When we start making exceptions..." He broke off, then his manner softened. "Take him home, Julia," he said more gently. "He won't fit in here."

"That's giving up."

Forest Hill might take him on." He reached for a pad. "I'll write you a reference."

"Forest Hill's for delinquents."

The Director put his pen down slowly.

"Didn't you think of this before you took this boy on?" His eyes narrowed analytically. "Tell me, Julia, why *did* you take him on?"

"Let's stick to the point," she snapped.

"I've made my position clear."

She paused, taken aback at how quickly they'd reached this point of no return.

"Then I don't see how I can very well carry on here myself," she responded quietly.

"Julia, get the kid afternoon supervision through an agency. There's one right in Lexington."

"I'm talking of the principle."

"Well, you must do whatever you feel is most comfortable." He massaged his wrist as he spoke, as if the conversation were giving him pain right there. "I did warn you at the beginning that we don't like having parents as members of the staff. You can't be objective. I guess this proves my point."

A brief, taut silence fell. She took a long, slow breath to calm herself. She couldn't really trust anyone else, even the professionals, to do what was right for Adam. Who better to care for and love a boy than his mother? She didn't need the money: she was only doing the job as a means of giving something back. If she wanted to work with disadvantaged children, she had one right here who needed her desperately. It was a responsibility she welcomed, even cherished.

She stood up.

"Very well, then," she said with dignity, "I'll clear my locker right away and leave." And, turning on her heel, she left the room.

•

Over the following days, Julia set her mind to devising a program by herself for Adam's socialization and development. His only hope of a happy, integrated life was to catch up with his peers. To become, in effect, a typical American twelve-year-old boy.

This meant learning social skills. It meant understanding the concept of property and ownership. Behaving politely in company. Smiling even when he felt like scowling. Laughing *with* people rather than *at* them. Wearing acceptable clothes, eating with fork and spoon and not fingers, suppressing belches, waiting to be offered food rather than grabbing it first, and generally showing basic consideration for his fellows. It meant understanding the unfamiliar technology all around him, too: how electric light, the television, the radio, the telephone all worked. And learning to navigate safely through the minefield of everyday dangers: the traffic, glass windows, power sockets and, even in the kitchen, respecting such hazards as the food processor and the waste disposal unit.

But above all, it meant language.

He had a basic difficulty making "k" and "g" sounds, so that "car" became "khar," an Arabic-sounding guttural, and one of his favorite words, "crazy," had a bizarre charm all its own. The problem went deeper than just vocalization, of course. Partly, his own language was just so inscrutable. She began to think again of trying to decode it. Sometimes she thought it sounded like Finnish, or perhaps Hungarian—which was related anyway, and he was, after all, a gypsy. She got Walter Schreiber to agree to come over. Walter was a polyglot, and if anyone could pinpoint a language or dialect, he could.

And yet, the problem was also conceptual. There were times, for instance, when he'd learn the name of an object perfectly, only to prove unable to apply the word to another object of the same kind a moment later. It was as if his world was composed of an infinite number of particulars, each with its own individual name which, though sometimes sounding the same, were in fact unique. *This* book was called "book" in the same way that *that* book was, but to him they appeared to share no general quality of "book-ness." Man's glory lay in his ability to think in abstract and categorical terms; lose this, and he became less than human. However much progress she felt she was making, she always in the end came up against this fundamental conceptual blindness, and then she'd be cast back into despair, feeling he was as far from her reach as ever.

She'd already rearranged Sam's study into a nursery, but now, much to Sandy's detached amusement, it became a *learning center*. Books that had been stowed in packing-cases or on high shelves now came down within reach. Sam's computer, previously standing with its face to the wall on top of the filing cabinet, itself now a cupboard for project work, was reconnected and placed back on the main desk, to join the crayons and drawing-blocks, alphabet cards and basic books for teaching colors and words. She stuck up posters of stylized animals and flowers, all painted in bright primary colors, along with number charts and elementary clock-faces with movable hands for telling the time. On a side wall she fixed a blackboard on which, with his hand guided by hers, Adam had scrawled CAT and MAN, while above the mantelpiece she'd affixed a large pinboard filled with his drawings. He had a remarkable, if selective, aptitude for drawing; by far his best were done from his imagination and depicted animals—mostly bison and some kind of mountain ibex—all remarkably well executed by comparison with his childlike scribblings of houses and cars. At first she supposed he'd copied these out of books and once, out of curiosity, she checked unsuccessfully through some of Sam's wildlife manuals, but it was only later that, going through a box of books as yet unpacked, she was surprised to find they most closely resembled prehistoric cave-paintings in the south of France.

Part of her questioned what she was doing to him. She'd sit him in front of a book showing a peanut with a silly human face, for instance, holding his fingers over each letter in turn as she laboriously spelled out "p . . . e . . . a . . .," and she'd ask herself why on earth *should* he need to know the word for peanut? Why couldn't he be an artist and remain pure of society, using just the pen and brush as his means of self-expression? But she recognized the realities of life. The first instinct of any society was differentiation. You either belonged or you didn't, you were either in or out, a member or an outsider, Greek or barbarian, Jew or gentile. Children were the cruellest differentiators of all; they'd pick on the slightest oddity of another and use it to exclude them. If Adam were to belong at all, he had to belong wholly. And that, at root, meant developing in him the same needs as in the society around him—material needs, needs for approbation and recognition, for comfort, success, achievement. Didn't it even mean deliberately imposing these on him? To belong in modern Western society, he had to believe in the importance of looking presentable, behaving properly, aspiring after owning possessions of his own and, yes, even envying those who had more than himself. The conclusion was appalling. But worse still was the penalty for non-conformity.

She'd toss this dilemma back and forth until she grew numb with confusion. And then he would do some little thing, perhaps break into a spontaneous cascade of laughter or say, quite unbidden, "Mumma, lovely Mumma," with all the softness and tenderness those large dark eyes could hold, and she'd be filled with such joy and love that nothing could matter more than just that this boy should live happy and at peace from one moment to the next. He was her boy, and she was his Mumma. Wasn't that enough?

And so, gradually, the new regime got under way. The days started with a sports training session with Sandy at dawn—though, as often as not, that fell apart in frustration after a few minutes—then followed with lessons morning and afternoon, broken sometimes by a trip to the supermarket or a nature ramble round the woods, and ended with the television hour before bed. Throughout it all, Adam allowed himself to be chivvied and cajoled, bribed and berated, with apparent goodwill and heart, and yet, when those soft and tender eyes grew distant and pensive, she couldn't rid herself of a feeling that his thoughts were far, far away and that he was somehow, for some purpose, biding his time.

•

On the Friday morning of the first week of the regime, as a treat, she decided to take him to the zoo. Her first thought was the main Boston zoo in Franklin Park, but even in the short time she'd known it the area had become a wasteland of druggies and muggers, and so, instead, she drove him cross-country to the small but well-stocked zoo at Stoneham.

Despite the warm early May day, it was almost deserted. The moment Adam climbed out of the car, he scented the air in puzzlement, then dropped to a low crouch. Sighting a knot of antelope beyond a line of palisades, he slid across to the cover of a tree and stared out, chittering like a cat after a bird that lay outside its reach. Julia began wishing she'd waited until the following afternoon when Max was coming over: Max would know how to read his reactions. Every few steps into the zoo, he'd freeze and listen, his brow furrowed and his ears keened, straining to read the unfamiliar cries and squawks around him. At a sudden snarl from the tiger cage, he shied back in terror. The sight of a cage of birds of paradise in plumed splendor quickly calmed him, however, and within moments he was happily cooing and rocking his head from side to side.

At a cafeteria, she treated him to his favorite chocolate chip ice cream and, allowing him to wander free, sat down with a cup of coffee in the warmth of the first real sun of the year. Above her spread a grand maple, already bursting into leaf, while in the cages all around she sensed the pulse of life quickening. She sat back and felt a small, contented smile cross her face as she let her thoughts go back to the previous evening.

William had called to invite her to dinner at a private club on Beacon Hill. It had been a wonderful evening. He'd been so attentive and shown such interest in her small-time domestic problems that she'd really let herself go on talking far too long. Whenever she tried to change the subject to something closer to his own world, he'd kept steering the conversation back to Adam. He took a close personal interest in the boy, he'd confessed, not only out of a sense of responsibility but also out of a growing fondness for her. She'd felt touched and a little flattered, too. She couldn't remember when she'd had such an easy, pleasant evening. She'd never felt so completely relaxed since Sam had died. Even in Sam's company, looking back now, she'd never felt entirely *at ease*; he'd been too quick-witted, too fond of academic repartee, too intellectually provocative. Maybe, beneath it all, she'd held back something of herself, too: with one marriage collapsed, could she ever *trust* another? But with William it was different. He was considerate in conversation and a good listener. He made talking easy, and she felt he valued what she had to say, and this, in turn, made her rise to the moment. More than that, he always gave her the odd feeling that he already knew everything she had to say and so there was never any reason to hold back.

She was so deep in her thoughts that she almost lost track of Adam. Then she spotted his red and white baseball shirt over by the monkey house. He was standing with his face pressed against the outer wire-mesh barrier. She hurried over, but as she drew closer some impulse slowed her steps. Inside the cage, close against the bars, stood a small and scanty-haired pygmy chimpanzee. Adam and the chimp seemed to be engaged in some kind of exchange, chattering and jabbering by turns. As she watched, the animal peeled back its gums in a yellow-toothed grin and bobbed gently up and down; Adam responded with a matching grimace. It laid its head on its shoulder and gave a deep, yearning sigh; Adam responded likewise. The sigh struck at her heart. Was he merely copying, or *communicating*?

The animal reached out its paw, stretching through the bars as far as it could. Adam reached out his own hand, finding a gap where two sections of the mesh had come apart, and strained to touch the small human-like fingers. Their fingertips inched closer and closer, but never quite met. The chimp gave a small, pitiful yelp. Adam answered with a growl. Withdrawing his arm, he shook the wire violently. The chimp struggled vainly to squeeze its body through the bars. Adam was growing angry now; Julia recognized the signs and knew that at any moment he'd hit flashpoint. She called to him, but he ignored her. Before she could stop him, he grasped the wire mesh in both hands and, ripping the staples apart with all his strength, widened the gap enough to clamber through. The chimp was now dancing up and down in a frenzy of excitement. Adam threw himself on the bars of the main cage. Under his onslaught, one slowly began to bend.

Behind, from across the concourse, came a sudden angry shout. A keeper in a white overall was running across. The man was almost up to the netting before Adam turned. He faltered, then let out a howl of terror. The keeper forced his way through the broken netting and cornered Adam against the bars, but the boy slithered from his grasp and, in a flash, climbed free. Darting away in a wild zig-zag across the path, he was quickly lost in the labyrinth of small alleys that intersected the zoo.

Ignoring the keeper's enraged shouts, Julia set off after him. She found him cowering behind a small shed at the back of the cafeteria, and she slowed to let her thoughts catch up with her. She understood his terrified reaction to the keeper with the white coat. But what kept forcing itself to the front of her mind was not that. It was the scene she'd just witnessed between the boy and the chimp. And it left her with the uncomfortable feeling she had unwittingly been party to a display of empathy of a far deeper, elemental kind than ever he shared with her or others of his own kind.

11

O

EVERY MORNING THAT WEEK, JULIA WAS WOKEN BY shouts and the clattering of stones in an empty tin can as Sandy tried to rouse Adam in his attic eyrie. Berating him for being a lazy slug, the girl would drag him downstairs and force him out of doors for his training session. First came exercises on the spot, then she'd attach a clothes-line to his wrist and literally take him on a run through the woods. Next came ball practice on the front lawn, where she'd fixed up a basket on the flagpole. Watching from the kitchen as she made their breakfast, Julia would smile to hear Sandy's crisp schoolmistress voice as she tried to get him to perform various simple maneuvers with some kind of understanding of the point of it all. The idea of passing—that is, giving up the ball—quite eluded him, and this usually drove Sandy to a frenzy of frustration.

"Throw it," she'd yell across the lawn. "Toss it. Chuck it. Oh, for God's sake, give it here." She'd snatch it from him, then lob it back; he'd hang on to it tightly, and the process would start again. "Let go of it, dimwit! Open your hands, like this. Let *go* of it, dope-head!"

By the Saturday when he was due for his first lesson from Scott, he could execute a perfect pass over a good thirty feet. But something always went wrong. That same day, for instance, after barely five minutes' practice, Sandy stormed into the kitchen and slammed the door. She poured herself a glass of orange juice and sank into a chair.

"I give up," she sighed. "He always messes everything up. He threw the ball into the pool and now it's stuck in the middle."

"We'll fish it out," replied Julia mildly.

"You can't. The pole's broken and won't reach."

"Well, I think it's time the cover came off anyway and we had it filled." She placed a jug of milk on the table. "I'll go and get him."

She went to the living room window. A thick plastic covering lay across the pool, trapping the orange basketball in the center where it sagged. The dredging net had snapped and clearly wasn't long enough to reach. Adam appeared from the side of the garage, carrying a long plank. He was naked and barefoot except for his tracksuit pants. She was about to tap on the window but he seemed so preoccupied in his task that she held back. After some thought and deliberation, he laid the plank in a diagonal across one corner. Then, with the stunted pole in one hand, he crept carefully along the plank to the mid-point and, stretching out as far as he could, scooped up the ball in a single sweep.

She let out a small cry of delight. He might look backward, and goodness knew what he'd score in an IQ test, but undoubtedly remarkable talents lay locked inside that tousled head of his. All that he needed was time and the milk of common human affection. If Sandy was being hard on him, that was just because she couldn't let herself be seen doing a *volte-face* too obviously. She was cautiously warming to him, though. Scott had shown the lead, and this basketball offered the perfect means of communication. She really had Max to thank for it all. She'd invite her to supper the following evening; she'd cook something special. She wouldn't "jump the gun," but surely a modest celebration was in order.

She rapped on the window. Adam looked up. His deep-set eyes filled with pride and he did a small dance on the plank. With a laugh she beckoned him indoors for breakfast, her heart swelling with joy.

•

It was to be a short-lived joy, however. Julia drove them early to the school sports center. Scott was already there waiting, and Julia retired to the stands to watch.

Scott put Adam's passing through its paces and, though there'd been a good deal of prompting from Sandy, he declared him "team material." Then he demonstrated the basic techniques of dribbling, showing him how to pat the ball low and fast against the ground while running and dodging obstacles at the same time. With much repetition and encouragement, Adam eventually picked it up and finally dribbled the length of the court, copying the older boy's movements with surprising skill. The rest of the team was beginning to arrive on the court now, and soon Scott called for a warm-up game. He divided them into two teams, putting Adam with Sandy, and without further ado he blew his whistle.

Within a moment, Julia realized it wasn't going to work. Adam had no sense of the purpose of the game and he seemed quite unable to distinguish between one side and the other: to him, players were all alike, not team-mates or opponents. At one point, Sandy passed him the ball, but for all the yells of "Run with it!" he stood stock still, and when the opponent who'd been guarding him squared up to him, he simply handed it to him. A howl of derisive laughter spread across the court. The ball was still in play, and Sandy regained possession. She was instantly blocked by two hefty players and, as she tried a dribbling feint, one of them grabbed the ball from her and, jinking past, sped off down the court. Adam saw this. With an enraged cry, he pursued the other player across the court and knocked the ball out of his hands, then ran back to Sandy and gave it back to her. He stood, looking puzzled and wounded, as cries of "Foul!" echoed about him. Scott called to play on, with growing impatience.

From then on, the game only went downhill for Adam. Unable to understand the purpose, let alone the rules, he simply got in everyone's way. He scored the ball without dribbling and tackled players on his own side. Gradually it dawned on Julia that what he lacked at root was a basic sense of competitiveness. He just wasn't able to put on an aggressive posture in play. Sport was a formalized game of pretense, of feigned warfare. For Adam, action flowed directly from impulse, and without the specific impulse there was no need of action. Why pretend? His innocent simplicity was one of the qualities she loved most in him. And yet, as always, she'd barely had time to warm to the thought when its corollary sent a small chill through her. His lack of a competitive instinct was two-edged, for it also implied that if the impulses actually were there—if, for instance, he was provoked to real anger or aggression—then violent action would surely and swiftly follow. A boy who couldn't pretend in the way of a normal, civilized person also couldn't mediate his urges in a normal, civilized way.

As the whistle finally blew and the players grouped around their coach, leaving Adam standing alone, shunned and forlorn, she found herself filled with the familiar doubts again. Did she really want him to belong to the "civilized" world if it meant destroying his sweet innocence?

•

The afternoon was warm and the air still, and rich yolk-colored sunlight fell slantingly through the woodland, shimmering off the silver birches and fluorescing the mold-green trunk of the ancient holm oak that overhung the river. Julia had found a small patch of grass on the bank and was sitting down alone with a book. She couldn't remember the last time she'd managed to snatch a moment during the day to be by herself.

A blackbird squawked through the glade behind, while from a branch of an oak tree high above came the shrill alarm call of a magpie. Adam was somewhere up at the top of the grounds, probably playing about in his hut or rooting around the woods for mushrooms. Sandy had gone to the Blanes' next door to play tennis; Julia could hear distant peals of laughter from their garden. She read a couple of pages, but she was too tired and the warmth of the sun too soporific. She closed her eyes and in her mind she found herself relating to William the events that morning at the sports center. It hadn't worked out, but they mustn't give up. While Scott favored Adam, Sandy would follow suit and there'd be harmony at home. Perhaps by dint of practice the lad would eventually learn the rules even if he didn't really grasp the reasons. Once again, patience and love were all he needed.

•

The boy heard the laughter. He held back for a moment, his head cocked on one side, then slowly he began to creep forward. His footfalls made no sound. A few yards from the clearing, he stopped. Out in the open, the two girls were playing a game. He stood watching from the cover of a thicket of firs, his eyes moist with profound sadness.

•

Sandy caught the frisbee neatly in her left hand and spun it back across the lawn. Rackets and balls lay idly against the slack net, and the icebox remained unopened on the summerhouse steps. Scott and his friends were late, as usual. Kirsty plucked the frisbee from the air, rolled it expertly along her arm and sent it skimming back.

"What d'you think?" she called.

"Nice one," replied Sandy, catching the frisbee.

"I mean, summer school in Florence."

"It would never wash with Mom."

"What's the big deal? The insurance paid up, didn't they?"

"It's not the money."

"Oh, I get you. Why can't she look after Adam by herself?"

"Because."

"To hell with because."

Hearing voices from the house, Sandy turned to see Scott and a group of friends sauntering down the lawn, some in tennis gear, others in school casuals. Pete, a tall, clean-cut boy with curly fair hair and a footballer's physique, had brought his dog, Oscar, a large black Patterdale.

"What kept you guys?" Kirsty called out, flicking the frisbee low and hard towards Sandy.

Sandy missed the reply, for at that moment Pete unleashed his dog. It caught sight of the frisbee sailing across its path and bounded forward with an excited bark. She caught the frisbee just in time and held it above her head, out of the dog's reach. The dog reared onto its back legs, snapping at empty air.

"Hey, Oscar!" called Pete. "Easy there, boy!"

Sandy danced back, switching the frisbee from hand to hand out of its reach. Suddenly it lunged right upon her and knocked her to the ground. Still playing the game, she tried to keep the frisbee away, but the barking turned to an ugly snarl and, before she realized what was happening, the creature was on top of her, tearing and scrabbling at her clothes and snapping at her face and neck. She rolled aside in genuine alarm, but the dog kept on coming. She could hear Pete shouting vainly in the background.

Just then a shrill cry from the woods split the air. Fleetingly she caught sight of Adam's stocky figure breaking cover and racing forward, and a second later she felt the dog hauled bodily off her. She scrambled away to a safe distance from where she watched with growing horror as the fight grew increasingly vicious. Pete was running frantically around in circles. Scott was advancing with a racket, shouting furiously, but he couldn't get close enough to break them apart. Adam's shirt was ripped and his face and arms were badly gashed. Once he managed to fling the dog off, but instantly it rounded and, hurling itself back on him with a ferocious snarl, sank its teeth into his thigh. He reacted more with surprise than pain. For a moment he just stared into the white-rolling eyes, then slowly he bent forward and, working his fingers in between its teeth, began to pry its jaws apart. Relentlessly, inch by inch, he broke open the clamp until he'd released his leg. But he didn't stop then. Tightening his grip further, he gradually wrenched the writhing animal's jaw wider and wider apart, bending it back on itself like a wishbone until, with an audible *crack*, it snapped. With a final blood-curdling cry, he swung the screaming dog round in a wide arc and hurled it right over into the woods, where it crashed against a tree and fell, limp and smashed, to the ground.

Pete rushed over to the mangled corpse.

"He's dead!" he howled. "The sonofabitch killed him!"

Scott had flung aside the racket and was advancing menacingly.

"You've asked for it now, ape-dick!" he growled.

Pete closed in from the side, his fists balled. Cornered, Adam began backing away. He shot Sandy a desperate, bewildered glance. Before she could intervene, he had slipped past the other two and was darting like a hare towards the woods. A few yards into cover, he stopped and looked back uncomprehendingly, then with a long, pained howl he blundered off out of sight.

Furious and indignant, Sandy rounded on Scott and his friend.

"Why did you do that?" she cried.

"Why did *he*?" snapped Scott.

"Hold it! That brute *attacked* me. You all saw." She was shaking with rage and shock.

"She's talking shit," Pete flung over his shoulder as he bent to pick up the limp body of the dog. He heaved a great sob. "I'm gonna kill that mother."

"Damn right," agreed Scott grimly. "He'll get what's coming to him."

Kirsty broke in. "Back off, Scott. Sandy's right. The dog went crazy. If it wasn't for Adam . . ."

"Shut your face," snarled Scott, his handsome features twisted in a coarse and ugly grimace. "Sandy had better wise up. He's nothing. Shitty at sports. Talks like a gook. Look at him: he's an ape!" He began jumping up and down in an impersonation of a gorilla, then yelled towards the woods, "Hey, you there, get the hell back to the jungle!"

Sandy stood speechless. Through her tears she stared in appalled silence to witness this unwonted, unwanted side of the one whom she'd so long and secretly worshipped.

•

That night, Sandy waited until the house was quiet. By the light of the moon, now almost full, she tiptoed downstairs into the living room. Under her arm she carried the folder of secret letters. A sudden, eerie sound from outside froze her dead. A mocking laugh, or just a trick of the wind? She shivered. Her hand hovered on the light-switch, then she turned away, afraid of being visible from outside. She stepped swiftly over to the fire grate and felt around for a box of matches. One by one she set the letters alight, holding each sheet until the flame had reached the last corner and was all but burning her fingers. Then she took the poker and crushed the cinders to ash and finally, feeling older and wiser, retraced her steps slowly to bed.

In the morning, she woke early and went for her run. She left Adam undisturbed this time: there'd be no more Saturday basketball for him. Besides, he'd gone to bed in a terrible state. They'd taken him to Lexington General for a tetanus jab and to have the cuts on his hands and leg dressed properly. He'd gone berserk, and the nurse had had to send for two orderlies to restrain him, and it was only when Mom insisted they took their white coats off that they were able to calm him. The sight of the needle, too, had sent him cowering and gibbering into a corner, and they'd had real difficulty in giving him the injection. In the car on the way home, Mom explained she believed the people had done something terrible to him at the halfway house which had caused this phobia. Sandy felt sorry for him; everything was so very difficult for him. Yet, in his way, he was decent. And brave, too, Scott or the others hadn't moved a muscle to help her.

Mist hanging in low skeins above the ground swirled about her legs as she struck off across the lawn towards the woods. Soon the first trees loomed up in the pearly, translucent light, and she slowed to find the path. To her left stood Adam's strange hut... She caught her breath. All over the rough stonework of the base and the branches and scrap timber that made up the walls of the small, conical structure were daubed vicious, four-letter obscenities, while on the planks that formed the door was sprayed a large black swastika. Her mind flashed back to the sound of mocking laughter she'd heard during the night. Too sickened to continue her run, she turned her steps back towards the house, her heart heavy with the certainty of who had done this deed.

12

○
─────────────

JULIA WAS ABOUT TO START FILLING THE LAWN-MOWER
from a drum of gasoline in the garage when she heard
the sound of a car coming up the gravel drive. Ralph
Singer had only just driven off; perhaps he'd left something behind. It was Max, slim and elegant in a simple
summery silk dress. Julia returned the younger woman's
greeting warmly; she'd been looking forward to her visit.
The mowing, the first of the year, could wait for another
day.

"You're good and early," she said.

"The city's no place to be on a day like this," responded Max. "Who was that creep I met in the driveway? He nearly ran me into a tree."

"That was Ralph Singer."

"But you don't like the man. And I can see why."

"I didn't call him. He just turned up. To see how
Adam was."

"And how is the poor kid?"

"Fine. He's really remarkably hardy." She steered
Max toward the garden, wanting to have her alone for a

while. "Dr. Singer happened to be passing on his way back from golf. He's very conscientious," she added with a trace of irony.

"Yeah, very commercial. And it's Sunday. Wait till you get his bill. That'll pay for his golf club membership."

"The bills are taken care of. You know, William and his friends. William Cray."

Max caught her eye as they emerged into the early evening sunlight and gave her a complicit smile.

"Seems I hear that name a lot," she said. "Is he married?"

"Widowed."

"Ah-*ha*."

Julia felt herself blush. "It's not like that," she hastened.

"Why not? You're young, Julia . . ."

"William's a friend," she interrupted briskly. "An old friend of Sam's from college days. He's been very kind to us, and he takes a great interest in Adam. He's in Boston a lot. We have supper together from time to time. That's all." They were meeting again the next evening, but somehow she didn't want to admit it. Perhaps it was too precious.

"I'm happy for you," said Max, still with her knowing smile.

They had reached the far corner of the house; they could either turn indoors or head down towards the river.

"Let's not go in just yet," urged Julia. "It's too nice."

"I'm always happy to talk," responded Max, perceptive as ever.

As they sauntered across the lawn, with the volatile scents of spring dancing in the warm air, Julia began to relate the events of the previous day. She told her first

about the setback at the sports center and then about the
terrible incident over the dog. She felt a strange detachment, as though she was somewhere else, viewing herself
from a remote vantage point. Everything around seemed
to take on a peculiar acuity. The sun glinted off the waxy
new shoots of the rose trees in dazzling pinpricks, and
the slightest detail—a pebble on the lawn, the flaking
paint on the garage wall, the small irregularity in the balustrade—all this seemed to possess a surreal sharpness.
Yet her mind was dull, confused. She struggled to find
the words. Everything about Adam seemed so contra-
dictory.

"He simply doesn't seem to possess a competitive
instinct." She shook her head. "I always thought that was
a sad but essential human quality. The thing that drives
man on and on. I mean," she persisted, "he's just not
aggressive like most people. He only went for that dog
because it attacked Sandy."

Max gave her a long, considered look, as if wondering how far she really wanted a serious conversation
on the nature of man.

"You're assuming we are all innately aggressive,"
she remarked quietly. "That's a contentious point."

"Well, aren't we? We've lost our primitive simplicity
and innocence. That's what Sam was always saying."

Max's glance hardened.

"That's the lapsarian view, and not everyone shares
it," she responded. "Primitive man was an out-and-out
savage. It's dangerous to look upon the wild state as the
pure state."

She paused, as if unsure how far to take the point.
Julia held her eye.

"Go on."

"Well, there are people like Konrad Lorenz who believe civilization is degenerative. They say it's a form of unnatural selection. Just like domesticating animals: it keeps genes alive that would otherwise disappear in the natural world. They believe society should purge itself of the weak and eliminate their genes from the pool. Of course, we all know where that leads."

"But there are still primitive tribes today in remote corners of the world, living in their little Edens."

"And who don't know violence? That's an adman's fantasy." She looked out over the sloping ground to the river caught in the flattening rays of the sun, and a quiet intensity entered her tone. "Ever heard of a Malayan tribe called the Semai? They were always held up as the text-book case: a people innocent of any concept of aggression. There was no murder or brutality; they didn't even have a word for 'kill.' A blueprint for paradise, okay? Well, back in the '50s they were recruited by your countrymen against the Communist guerrillas. As soon as they were taken out of their nonviolent society and ordered to kill, they went berserk. They became possessed by a lust for blood. They became—quite literally, in fact—drunk on blood." She paused, her face pale and set hard. "It's a kind of insanity that comes over people, primitive and civilized alike. Have you read any of the GIs' accounts of the massacre at My Lai? These were just ordinary boys from ordinary backgrounds, simple decent kids just out of school. They shot the peasants like rabbits. They raped and impaled young girls, they bayoneted children, they scalped old men, they slashed open pregnant women. They laughed as they did it and they ate a good dinner that night."

Julia shuddered.

"Animals!" she muttered between clenched teeth.

"Not exactly," responded Max, always precise.

"Anyway, that proves my point. As a species, we are innately aggressive."

"I do believe we have a *propensity* for violence. But I also believe we can override it. That's exactly what civilization *is*."

For a while they strolled in silence. Julia's thoughts were in turmoil. They were not really talking about the generalities of human nature: no, this whole conversation was actually about Adam. Was Max saying that, depending on the circumstances, Adam was as capable of violence as anyone else? No, she protested silently to herself, he wasn't like that! He was innocent, natural. He'd been dragged out of his Eden into their vicious, deceitful world. And that was their shame. *Her* shame. He was like a true wild animal, pure and natural. In fact... here she recalled the incident at the zoo... sometimes it seemed he almost *was* one of them.

She looked up to find Max watching her with her cool, penetrating dark eyes. Momentarily caught off balance, she cast around for something to de-intensify the moment. They had come round in a circle and reached the pool. She'd taken the plastic cover off but hadn't begun filling it yet.

"D'you know," she said with a weary smile, "the water people are asking two thousand dollars to fill this thing. Two thousand! I wouldn't have emptied it if I'd had any idea."

"Pray for rain," said Max distantly. "Rain's free."

"Come on, Max, I rely on you for serious advice. Since Sam's gone, who else can I turn to?"

"Seriously, then, shop around."

The conversation dried up there, and for a while Julia found herself still staring inanely into the pool. She ought to have the cracks filled and the walls painted first. What would that cost? The money really didn't matter. She turned to find Max had dropped to one knee and was peering closely at the ground. She leaned over to see what was absorbing her attention. Pouring out of chinks in a paving slab and over the grass verge was a seething mass of tiny blackish-brown ants.

"*Tetramorium caespitum*," declared Max. "Two colonies, fighting to the death. Can you see?"

Julia looked closer. Two armies of ants were locked in mortal battle in those few square feet, and one was quite distinctly winning.

"It's a massacre," she breathed. "See: we aren't any better than animals."

"Only they're fighting for territory, not some ideology." Max stood up. "You know, it bugs me when people say that man is the only creature that kills his own species. It's just not true. Look at these ants. Even chimps kill other chimps, too. Hyenas, lions, langur monkeys—all kinds of species engage in lethal battles, infanticde, even cannibalism. Someone once said that if baboons had nuclear weapons, they'd destroy the world in a week."

"So, we're no worse than animals, and no better either?"

"Well, we haven't quite destroyed the world—yet." Max paused. "No, man is as aggressive as any other animal, but there's a difference in his *kind* of violence. His motives, if you like."

"His motives?"

"Animals fight over the necessities of life—food, shelter, territory, and so on. Man does that, too, of course.

But he has a propensity for ideological violence as well. *Gratuitous* violence."

"Exactly! We're fallen creatures."

"A propensity only, though," she cautioned. "We also have the ability to rise above our drives. We can use our minds, our faculty of reason, if we only choose to. That's the key difference."

Once again silence fell. By now they'd reached the river's edge, and the evening shadows were creeping in. In the center the last rays of sunlight danced on the ripples where the shallow spate broke over a scattering of boulders. Quite suddenly, Max grasped her arm. She was laughing, and her eyes gleamed with the triumph of inspiration.

"I've got it!" she cried. "Hire yourself a pump for fifty dollars and *pump* the water into your pool."

It took Julia a moment to come down to earth. Gradually the notion filtered through her consciousness. She caught Max's expression and grinned.

"Brilliant! That's exactly what we'll do." She turned toward the house. "Come on, let's have a drink. I think we deserve one."

•

From the darkest depth of the trees, Scott scanned the expanse of lawn that lay shimmering in the bright moonlight. Apart from the occasional car passing in the distance, all was quiet. Twenty yards ahead, nestling into the slope, stood the house, its rear façade a patchwork of lights. From time to time, two figures crossed the living room window—one was Julia, the other the visitor in the red Rabbit. From Sandy's room on the second floor flickered the bluish glow of a television. The attic at the top was in darkness, but as he watched the small window began slowly opening.

He looked across at Pete and grinned.

•

All evening Julia had felt distant, self-absorbed. She'd taken Adam up some food on a tray and left half behind in the kitchen. Over supper, Sandy had teased her for being "out of it," and it was only when the girl had gone upstairs to do her homework, leaving her alone with Max in the living room, that she realized the root of what lay on her mind. Were we all just animals, and, for all our ability to control ourselves, nevertheless driven by the instincts and impulses of animals? That was what Max had been suggesting that afternoon. Or were we, as she herself believed, different in *kind*? Because we had a moral nature. Because we were spiritual beings.

As she sat staring into the fire with a glass of wine in her hand, she tried to reconcile this thought with what she'd witnessed at the zoo. If man and animals were different in kind, then real communication could not be possible across the divide. And yet she'd seen Adam *talking* to the chimp.

Finding the moment at last, she steered the conversation around to the issue and began to recount in detail what had happened that day at Stoneham Zoo. Max listened in total silence, her face betraying no reaction.

"It was quite extraordinary," Julia concluded finally. "They could have been speaking the same language."

"Perhaps, in a way, they were," Max replied after a thoughtful pause.

"Chimpanzees in the Caucasus? Hardly!"

Max tilted her glass to examine the wine for a moment, then looked up.

"A pygmy chimp, you said? *Pan paniscus*?"

"Yes."

"Interesting. Did you know the pygmy chimp is our closest living relative? Virtually identical to our ancestors the australopithecines, the precursors of *hom. sap.* Like the famous fossil, Lucy. Sam did a lot of work on Lucy. You must know about her."

"She was almost one of the family," smiled Julia. "Only Lucy is—what?—three million years old."

"And Adam is just twelve."

"Exactly."

She stared again into the fire. A puzzling thought had long nagged at the back of her mind. She knew Max was a genetic scientist and she knew, too, that she'd been working with Sam, but she'd never properly understood on *what.* Had they been doing genetic research on prehistoric man? Surely that wasn't possible anyway. He'd often said how frustrating it was for paleontologists, only having dry old bones to work on from which you couldn't reconstitute the genetic material. What, then, really had brought them together?

Her thoughts were interrupted by Max.

"It might not really be *that* surprising," she was musing to herself. "After all, genetically speaking, we're ninety-nine percent ape and only one percent human."

"My God, is that true? Quite an important one percent, though!"

"But still only one percent. The rest of our DNA is identical to that pygmy chimp's."

She shifted uncomfortably in the chair. "But I don't see that explains his special empathy," she objected. "You or I couldn't communicate like that."

"We might possess the genes, only they aren't expressed."

"And they are in Adam?"

"Maybe."

"Anyway," she hastened on, "what really counts is what happens to him here, in actual life. That's what conditions his behavior, his feelings, his attitudes, his values."

Max's expression had sharpened.

"I can't really agree," she responded. "Behavior is basically genetic. Society provides the soil and rain, if you like, but the seed contains the code. Ever heard of the Mexican salamander? Now there's a strange creature: it develops either feet or flippers depending on whether it's born on land or in water. You'll say this proves that the environment is supreme, I know, but if you look a little closer you'll see it shows just the opposite—that the genes are, in fact, the prime determinants. If this goes for feet and flippers, why not for nonphysical things like faith and feelings too?" She paused, as if aware this was sounding like a lecture, but she went on nevertheless. "I'm quite convinced that all we are and do is genetically programmed. The program is flexible, sure, but it is *prior*. The whole glory of humanity, Julia, lies in that one per-cent."

Julia was shaking her head.

"I don't like the sound of that," she said.

"Truth is often uncomfortable."

"Truth depends on where you look at it from. Try telling a maladjusted child from a deprived background he'd be just the same if he'd been brought up in a wealthy, middle-class family."

"And Adam?"

"Well, I suppose he'd make an interesting test case," she responded, feeling the intensity of Max's scrutiny. "I mean, on the one hand being brought up here in these surroundings," she gestured around the room, "and on the other, being genetically . . ."

"Genetically?"

"Whatever he is."

Max's lips softened in a smile, but her dark eyes remained steely.

"Whatever else could he be, Julia?"

"I don't know." She shivered. "It's just that I get these strange feelings. Sandy says she finds him spooky."

Max's laugh rang out brightly.

"Come on! Relating to chimpanzees doesn't mean he's *related* to them! He's just a gypsy kid, and I guess the gypsies out there just live close to wild animals. Period."

"Yes," replied Julia uncertainly.

"Look," said Max after a moment, "if something's really worrying you, we could run a couple of simple tests."

"Tests?"

"Just to prove the point." She gestured to the grate. "How does he react to fire, for instance? All animals hate fire, chimps included. Fire's a hundred percent human thing. And then we could try him out on the 'false-belief' test. He'll pass that, unless he's autistic, but his pal the chimp won't. And there are other things we could look at," she added but left it there.

"Let's wait and see, shall we?"

She offered her more wine, but Max glanced at her watch and said she really ought to be getting home. Julia invited her to stay over, but she had an early start the next day. She prevailed upon her to have more coffee, however, and putting on a record of the Enigma Variations, made a deliberate effort to change the subject to a lighter topic.

•

For a moment Scott lost the short, chunky figure, but there it came again, fleetingly caught in profile against the outline of the roof. As he watched, the boy slid down the side of the building and dropped noiselessly onto the deck. He looked about him, and as his gaze turned in their direction he froze. Scott swore softly. Could he see them? They were a good thirty yards away, and hidden in deep shadow. Then, moving silently, the boy slipped over the balustrade onto the grass and, skirting the pool, headed toward the garage on the far side of the house. For a while he rummaged around in among the pile of lumber stacked against the garage, then with a nervous glance back across the open lawn he went inside. In the moonlight, Pete was nodding in satisfaction. They'd got him in the bag.

Running in a low crouch, they quickly covered the distance to the garage. Scott gestured to his friend to take the rear, while he himself made for the tall wooden door and slid noiselessly inside. It was pitch dark. Thin spears of light filtered through chinks in the roof. The outline of an estate wagon. Strong smell of gasoline, swimming-pool chemicals, grass mowings.

"C'mon and show yourself, Adam," he called boldly.

Total silence. Not even the sound of breathing. He fumbled for the light switch. He felt cobwebs, rough wood paneling, a cable, then at last the switch. Light flooded the high barn. He started violently. Adam was standing no more than three feet away from him, as still as stone, staring him full in the face. Scott swore an oath and balled his fists.

The blow caught Adam on the side of the head. He spun around and fled deep into the garage. Scott came forward more slowly now; nothing too rough, just to teach the kid a lesson. Suddenly Adam saw a small door and lunged for it. He fumbled desperately with the latch, then burst through. A split second later came a howl of agony. Scott arrived at the door to see Pete felled and the figure of the boy darting away across the lawn toward the wood.

"Missed him!" spat Pete, scrambling to his feet.

Together they raced across the grass. As they reached the line of trees, they separated. A few yards inside, Scott stopped and, melting into the shadow of a tree, he scoured the thick darkness and honed his ears for any sound. A distant hoot of a bird, a rustling among the leaves, Pete's footfall through the undergrowth. Otherwise silence.

Suddenly Pete's cry.

"Watch out!"

Scott caught the sweep of an arm, twenty feet away. Instinctively he ducked. A stone glanced off the trunk just inches above his head and whizzed off into the foliage. Sudden rage surged through him. He wheeled out from cover and charged forward, blundering through the snagging brambles and whiplashing branches. The boy took to his heels, he darted and jinked this way and that like a terrified rabbit, but within half the length of a pitch, Scott had brought him down in a flying tackle. Pete closed in from the wing, and together they set about beating the living hell out of the little alien jerk.

•

Max started up the car and made a tight U-turn in the gravel. With a wave to Julia standing on the porch, she headed down the drive. In her rearview mirror she could see the slender figure courteously waiting until the car was out of sight.

For the first fifty yards the drive was open and bathed in bright moonlight, then it plunged into dark woodland. She was rounding the bend, with the road ahead just coming into view, when suddenly the sweep of the lights picked out a cowering figure. In the brief instant the beam passed, she recognized Adam, his face gashed and pouring with blood.

With a cry, she rammed on the brakes and rushed out over to where the boy crouched at the base of a broad birch tree.

•

It was well past midnight when she finally left the house. She'd helped Julia and Sandy clean and patch the boy up, though despite cuts and contusions he had remarkably escaped serious damage. Julia had scoured the woods for the attacker, but found no one. She was convinced that Scott next door was behind it, and vowed to see his parents first thing in the morning. Sandy had maintained a tight silence, busying herself with tending the injured boy. Max had been for calling the police, but Julia had refused, saying it was an affair between neighbors.

Finally, Max had left. She drove slowly, deep in thought. As she turned the bend where earlier she'd caught Adam's figure in the sweep of her headlights, she felt a sudden, sick jolt. Her mind flashed back to the very first time she'd seen the boy, almost exactly in that same spot, caught in her headlights. Something about that incident had always lingered in her mind as an unresolved puzzle, and now she understood. Her very first thought then had been that this was a cat, possibly even a fox. Because its eyes had glowed green.

She drew up at the road, her pulse drumming. As anyone knew who'd taken a flashlight snap with a cheap camera, the human eye reflected *red*. Red, because of the tiny blood vessels in the retina. Equally, anyone who'd seen a cat in their headlights knew that a cat's eyes reflected green. Cats, like foxes, owls and other animals with night-adapted vision, possessed a tapetum, a mirror behind the retina which reflected back the incoming light for a second use, and this gave a greenish glow. But humans were not nocturnal creatures; we had not evolved this night-vision capability. Our eyes reflected red. And yet Adam's were definitely green.

She was trembling, and a thick swell of nausea gripped her throat. She closed her eyes. The logic was unassailable, the conclusion inescapable. Gradually, through some filter of her senses, she became aware of a strange ferrous smell. She looked down to the seat beside her at her pale jacket, heavily blood-stained, and her mind flashed back to the terrible moment when she'd found the boy and struggled to haul him into the car, thrusting her jacket at him to help staunch the bleeding while she'd reversed furiously back up to the house. Now as she stared at the boy's blood still wet on the jacket, an idea slowly took shape in her mind, an idea so definitive that it would confirm or allay her crazy suspicions once and for all.

Quickly she turned off the car heater and wound down the window: she didn't want the blood drying out too quickly. Then, ramming the car into gear, she swung out into the road and headed away in the direction of Boston. She drove fast, heedless of speed limits and traffic lights. She'd almost made it home when, on Beacon Street, a police car passing in the opposite direction wheeled around and began to follow in pursuit, but she slipped off down a side street and, cutting across the main grid, wound her way through the back streets until she reached Putnam Avenue. Instead of turning off to her condominium, however, she carried on toward the river and the gaunt concrete block, towering dark and forbidding in the moonlight, that housed the Department of Biogenetics.

Grabbing the jacket, she hurried up the front steps and let herself in with her electronic passkey. The building was empty, and the corridors were unlit but for dim safety-lights set into the skirting board. Not wanting to risk the elevator, she took the stairs to the fifth floor. There she strode down the corridor to her lab and, once inside, laying the jacket carefully on a stainless steel tray, began the laborious process of salvaging as much of the plasma as she could. Within an hour she had produced a small vial of the red-black fluid, to which she added a sterile non-clotting agent, then placed it in the refrigerator. Finally, late though it was, she reached for the phone. She needed help. There was only one person at MIT who had precisely the knowledge and expertise to do what had to be done.

13

JULIA REPLACED THE PHONE AND STOOD FOR A MO-
ment drumming her fingers on the desktop. She'd been
trying to call William all day to invite him to supper at
home, rather than meet at the appointed restaurant, but
he couldn't be reached. She glanced at the clock on the
study mantelpiece: she'd better start getting ready soon.
Through the window she could see Sandy coming up the
drive on her way back from school, scuffing the gravel
as she went. Sandy had made her promise not to speak
to Scott's parents until she'd tackled him herself at school.
But whether it was Scott or someone else, was it safe to
leave two youngsters alone in the house anyway? She
ought to stay. And yet she couldn't just stand William up.

She glanced in at the large, open-plan living room.
Adam was prowling up and down like a caged beast.
He'd ripped off the bandages and sticking-plasters, but
the wounds were healing and the worst swelling had sub-
sided. He might be prone to colds and other complaints
of civilization, but he did possess astonishing powers of
recovery. For a moment he stopped by the window and

peered out with a fearful, haunted look in his eyes. Poor boy, she thought: he's terrified they'll come and get him again. But then she realized that he was not staring at the woods but up at the sky. She followed his line of sight. High above the trees, in the center of a clear blue sky, so pale and diaphanous as to be barely visible at all, hung the ghostly image of a perfect full moon.

Curiously troubled, she backed silently away and went into the kitchen. Sandy was already in and rummaging around in the fridge.

"We're out of Slush Puppies," she said accusingly without looking up.

"I didn't get to the shops today."

"But they're my favorite! The pest has been at them."

Don't act so spoiled, she wanted to snap: *you're not the only child in the house*. But she checked herself and changed the subject.

"Well, what did he say?"

"He wasn't at school. Kirsty said he fell off his moped."

She gave a short, derisive laugh and reached for the phone.

"That settles it," she said.

Sandy stepped forward. "No, wait—"

"Leave it to me."

"No, it's better if I confront him directly. He'll own up to me."

"Sandy, I can't go out without having this thing settled."

"Don't be silly, Mom. Go and have a nice time and forget about us."

"I'll get someone to come in."

"Mom, I can handle Scott. Or whoever."

Julia hesitated, wondering who she actually could ask to come over. She thought about the neighbors on the other side, but relations had been strained since Adam used their greenhouse for target practice. One by one, she thought of all the people in the street, then those who lived further afield—various parents of Sandy's school friends, a professor and his wife who'd recently moved out to Lexington from Harvard, even a supervisor at the Unit who lived on the edge of town. Gradually it dawned on her that she had no one she could call upon in a situation like this. There was only Max, but she lived in Cambridge, and she wouldn't think of imposing on her anyway. Otherwise, not a soul. For the first time, with startling clarity, she saw that all the friends they'd known when Sam was alive had gradually slipped out of their lives—some perhaps because they were strictly Sam's friends, but others because of Adam and his behavior— leaving them increasingly alone and isolated. In this context, her friendship with William Cray was all the more necessary.

"Very well," she said reluctantly. "But keep locked in. I shan't be late back."

•

The night air was heady with the floral nectars of spring. Thin wisps of cloud stole across an infinitely black sky, veiling and unveiling a bright full moon by turns. From the road, muffled by the unfurling foliage, came the intermittent sound of cars passing. From the woods behind came a sudden sharp rustle of leaves and flapping of wings, followed by a smothered squawk, and then silence. Far off, from down by the river, rose the long,

plaintive cry of a night bird. An answering call floated
across the still air from the fir copse.

Sandy wrapped her coat tighter about her and stared
up at the moon. The night had a chill edge and a heavy
dew had settled over the ground. She felt angry and
betrayed. She'd sent Scott a message via Kirsty arranging
to meet him here. In her heart she knew the answer, but
she needed to hear it from his own lips. Part of her prayed
he'd greet the accusation with a laugh and show her some
unmistakable token of his innocence, but another part
told her this was the real world. The world of her childhood dreams had gone up in the flames that had con-
sumed her childish letters. She sighed. So, this was what
it was like growing up: everything changing, nothing remaining stable or reliable or ever quite what it seemed,
people you trusted letting you down, people you admired
and loved turning out mean and worthless. Things had
just been getting back onto an even keel after Mom's
divorce and the move over here, and now it had all been
upset again with Sam's death and this stranger coming
into their household. Why couldn't time stand still as it
was for a while and just for a moment everyone stop their
crazy mad rush after change and novelty?

At least, that was one thing about Adam: he lived
for the moment, not yearning after some ever-receding
horizon. He didn't know the meaning of discontent. Or
he hadn't, until Mom had started teaching him to want
more, turning his wants into needs so that he could be
manipulated like the rest of us. She was *compromising*
him. Sandy glanced across to the house. Though the attic
window was unlit, she knew Adam was up there. Poor
boy. His ambition was not to have but just to *be*. That
was why he was rejected by everyone. He threatened all

they stood for, and their only response was to attack and bully him.

Her thoughts were interrupted by the sound of footsteps up the gravel drive. She came around the front of the house to see Scott strolling toward her with a cool, confident smile on his broad face. A faint scent of aftershave wafted ahead of him on the low breeze, stirring treacherous feelings within her. Jabbing her nails into her palms, she stood her ground and waited for him to reach her. She could handle this.

•

From the small attic window Adam watched the two figures out on the lawn below. He could read the burly, fair-haired boy's expression as clearly as if it was day. Their raised voices floated sharp and clear on the still air. He frowned as he listened. Something was wrong. The boy's tone pleaded innocence, but that was not what his face said.

After a while he pushed them out of his mind. He had far more serious business in hand. Raising his gaze to the sky, he stared unblinkingly for several minutes into the perfect full moon. His lips began to move, but no sound came out. They fluttered more quickly, in silent chatter, then slowly, from deep in his chest, broke a long, humming note that gradually modulated into a low, rhythmic incantation.

"Atta," he chanted. "Atta."

By slow degrees the imprecation grew more urgent and his breathing came faster. Froth appeared at the corners of his mouth, his eyes began to roll and he began to sway from side to side. Keeping his face lifted up to the moon, he sank to his knees. His eyes were turned back to the whites, and the chant became broken up into hoarse, panting gasps. Finally, gradually, he grew calmer and quieter. Tears began to flow down his cheeks and a beatific smile spread slowly across his face. For a full minute he knelt before the open window, quite motionless and calm. Then he grew more troubled again. He heaved several long, deep breaths and the peace ebbed from his being. His face regained its taut and harrowed look and the old fearful, haunted stare returned once again to his eyes.

It was time.

With slow deliberation, he bent forward and reached for the two flintstones.

The pyre was not large. It lay on the floor beneath the window sill, in the center of a rectangle of bright moonlight. Small dry twigs formed the base, while thicker branches and sections of old batten completed the pyramid. Spread out on the floorboards and radiating out in all directions lay the photographs, the largest one making the head, the two smallest ones the eyes and the others the arms and hands, legs and feet. The stack itself covered the center of the body, the seat of the vital organs—heart, stomach and genitals. To the side, outside the shaft of moonlight, lay a heap of thicker logs, to be added when the fire had caught, along with a pile by the window consisting of tennis rackets and notebooks, riding boots and gowns and various other personal effects he'd culled from the attics and from drawers and cupboards over the house.

Checking finally that it was all properly aligned to the moon, he squatted on his heels and reached forward to the base of the pile, where the twigs were smallest and driest. Then he took up the flints and struck one sharply against the other.

The first spark jumped wide and died on the boards. The second, better aimed, sprang deep into the tinder. He blew carefully, but the glow quickly expired. The third, however, leapt onto a piece of crumpled paper and began smoldering at once. Gently, carefully, he coaxed the spark into a flame. It spread quickly at first, then faltered, running out of material. Tearing a leaf from a notebook, Adam thrust it into the gap and blew steadily until, quite suddenly, it burst into flames. Within a second the twigs had caught and the fire had taken hold properly. Greedily now the flames curled around the logs, tightening their grip every second, until with a fast-growing roar they enveloped the entire pile in a blazing embrace, flinging a column of fiery sparks up along the low rafters, out through the open window and into the night.

•

Sandy pulled away and backed off down the slope. Scott had confessed finally. His words struck her like arrows. *He had it coming, wasting Pete's dog like that. Listen, Sandy, that kid's bad. He's no brother of yours. He's a freak.* He followed after her and, grasping her by the wrist, spun her around to face him. Suddenly he went dumb, as if further self-justification would only serve to condemn him more. She could say nothing either: she had nothing left to say. She felt a great sadness. He was a stranger to her, speaking a foreign language and in her heart she did not know him.

A curious sound gradually filtered into her consciousness, a distant crackling, like crumpling paper. She cast about her before realizing it came from behind her, from the direction of the house. She whipped around to see a flickering red glow in the attic window. A moment later, a shower of sparks burst forth into the dark sky. Flames licked around the window frame.

"Adam!" she shrieked.

She scrambled up the slope, skidding and slipping on the dewy grass, and raced around the side of the house. She burst in through the back door and tore upstairs to the top.

The attic door was locked. She hammered with her fists and yelled his name, but all that returned was the cracking and splitting of burning wood. Acrid smoke coiled through the gap at the foot, quickly filling the narrow landing. By now, Scott had caught her up. Thrusting her aside, he hunched his shoulder into a battering ram and hurled himself bodily at the door. With a splintering crack, it burst open.

She rushed inside, only to be beaten back by the dense, suffocating smoke and the ferocious heat of the blaze. Beyond the curtain of flame she could just make out the figure of Adam over by the window, poised for flight. Scott blundered forward after him, charging his way through the flaming debris. Just as he was about to fall into his grasp, Adam scuttled through the window and, with a stricken howl, dropped out of sight.

•

From the deep shadows, tight against the garage wall, Adam watched the firemen hose down the blaze, until finally nothing remained but thin twists of steam and smoke filtering through the charred window, garishly lit in flashes by the beacons of the fire engines encircling the house. From time to time he let out a sob of frustration, and his thickset features contorted with fury and pain.

He backed deeper into the undergrowth. The night

was rent with a raucous commotion—sirens wailing, engines roaring, radios crackling, men yelling. Julia, now arrived home, was rushing in and out of the house, fraught and flustered. Sandy was standing coolly on the deck, her back turned to all the activity, and was staring into the darkness, perhaps looking for him. Not more than thirty feet away from where he crouched, Scott was pacing up and down like a circus-master. His face wore an expression of triumphant vindication.

Adam felt his eyes narrow, and he tightened his stare on the older boy's face. The whole of his being became focused in that steady, venomous glare. It was a glare of the most intense hatred, of furious frustration at a holy mission thwarted, of incandescent outrage at an obscene blasphemy committed. And it bespoke the terrible inevitability of a righteous revenge.

•

Julia looked around the devastated attic. Morning sunshine filtered in through the heavy polythene sheeting that the firemen had battened over the window, casting a diffuse light over the black and charred wreckage. Her eyes smarted from the fumes of scorched wood and smoldered plastic that still hung in the air. Builders were due any minute; God knew what it would cost to repair the place, let alone to replace the sodden, begrimed carpets throughout the house. Her eyes smarted with tears of frustration, too: any normal boy would be punished for such a thing, but how could she punish Adam?

Her eye fell upon a charred piece of card projecting from a pile of ashes. As she bent to examine it, she frowned. A citation of Sam's: what on earth was that doing there? The firemen had swept most of the loose debris into this pile, which lay beneath a fine silt of dust and ash. At night, by the light of their lamps, she hadn't noticed, but now, as she probed deeper, she began unearthing one bizarre fragment after another. A piece of Sam's academic gown. The handle of his tennis racket. Bits of burnt photographs and, deformed and discolored among the half-burnt lumber, the silver photograph frame from her bedside. A cold shiver prickled her skin. What did it mean? This was more than just a commonplace act of arson: it was a deliberate, calculated ritual of some sort that held intense significance for the boy. Some kind of cremation rite? But why of Sam? Sam was dead and buried. She shook her head. What sick, disturbed notions were going through that boy's head?

With a troubled sigh, she collected up the scraps of photograph and left the room. She went carefully down the narrow attic stairs, still greasy for all the swabbing, and along the main corridor where the carpet lay rolled up ready to be removed. As she passed the guest room where she'd made up a bed for Adam again, she paused in thought. The bed was untouched, the room unused. Adam had not been seen since; he'd taken to the woods. She knew he hadn't gone far, though, for in the early morning, too worried to sleep, she'd gone in search and found, inside his small hut of stones and branches, a bedding of straw and dry leaves that bore the fresh imprint of a body. She'd left food out on a plate by the back door, but it hadn't been touched when she checked at breakfast-time. God help us, she thought; were they reduced to treating him like a dog that lived in a kennel and took its food by the back door? The thought sent her mind flashing back to her conversation with Max the previous day. *Animals hate fire*, Max had said. *Fire's a hundred percent human thing.* Well, at least that was something, she thought grimly. She could forget *that* absurd notion.

Abruptly she turned and hurried downstairs. First things first. Get the house fixed up. Sort out the repairs and redecoration. Get back to some kind of normality.

•

Sandy returned from school at lunchtime. She'd come back to help clear up, she said, but Julia could see she wanted to talk. Finally, at the kitchen table, over an uneaten sandwich, she came out with it. Angry blotches stood high on her cheeks.

"They're all so *stupid*!" she fumed. "Even Kirsty. I thought at least *she* was different."

"Adam?" sighed Julia.

"Everyone's talking about the fire. They're making a big deal out of it. Adam's a 'sociopath,' a 'nutcase,' a 'menace to society.' Kirsty said she and Scott have been forbidden to have anything to do with us while he's here. What do they expect us to do? Send him back?"

Julia bit her lip. The last doors were closing against them.

"I'm sorry, darling," she said.

"Sorry won't help. We shouldn't have gotten into this in the first place. We should have *thought*."

Julia reached across the table for the girl's hand. It was slack, unresponsive. It was all her own fault: if she hadn't dragged Adam into their lives, none of this would have happened. Her eye caught the charred photograph stubs lying on top of the day's unread mail and newspapers. What *had* she brought into the household?

"What do we *do*?" pleaded Sandy. "We can't change people's hang-ups. What about us here, too? We can't hide the matches forever."

"He didn't use matches," said Julia quietly. "They're still there."

"And we can't lock him outside forever. It's hopeless." Unconsciously, Sandy had been forming the photographs into a pattern. Gradually she seemed to become aware of what they signified. She separated one from the rest, a full-face shot of Sam, burnt in half from forehead to chin. As she gazed at it, she gave a small shudder. "It's weird."

Julia cleared her throat. They needed a simple and safe explanation.

"Arson's a strange thing," she began. "The cause is invariably psychological. Generally it's the result of some intense frustration. The problem is, it's no good punishing the fire-starter: that'll only reinforce his resentment." She hurried on, eager to put her own mind at rest, too. "In Adam's case, it's hard to see how we *could* punish him anyway. What could we take away from him that he actually wants? He doesn't especially need clothes, food or even basic comforts. That's the whole problem."

"The problem is we don't *understand* him, Mom," said Sandy quietly.

"Arson is arson," Julia heard herself protest. "What else is it?"

Sandy fell silent for a moment and stared at the surreal face she'd composed from the fragments. At last she spoke, softly.

"It's more like voodoo."

Julia gave a short laugh. "Rubbish!"

"Think, mother. What does it mean to burn a person's picture if you're someone like Adam? He's kind of *primitive*. I remember Sam once saying how hard it is to get primitive people to let you take their picture. They think you are stealing their soul. Maybe Adam thinks that Sam somehow is *in* his photographs."

"But why ever should he *burn* them?"

"He wants to do what's right for him. Now, he knows Sam is dead—he saw him in the casket, right? But he wasn't at the funeral. He never saw him being buried."

"I still don't see."

"Use a little imagination, Mom," sighed the girl despairingly. "Maybe where he comes from they have some elaborate ritual to send the dead off to the afterlife, something very important, like the Romans putting coins in the dead person's mouth to pay the ferryman. I don't know exactly, I just think the whole thing looks like some primitive ritual. Too bad Sam's not here. He would have known."

A frisson rippled through Julia. She'd been struck by just the same notion.

"Well, I suppose if he thinks it has done the trick, we can all sleep easily now."

"What if he doesn't?"

"So, what do you suggest, Sandy?"

Sandy held her eye steadily.

"I think we should take him to Sam's grave," she said quietly. "And *show* him."

Julia frowned. This whole area was fraught with peril. Who knew what unnameable dormant impulses might be disturbed by tampering with the darker side of the boy's psyche? For people brought up in a tradition of reason and causality, Sandy's proof would dispel any doubt. But what might it provoke in a mind such as

Adam's? They simply couldn't tell. The human psyche was too sensitive and volatile an instrument to meddle around with in ignorance. And yet how could they stand by and do nothing? Besides, the whole idea behind socializing Adam was to treat him as one of us. Let him be exposed to the light of reason, and then led another step along the path of integration.

She drew a deep breath.

"I don't like it," she said, "but very well, we'll give it a try."

•

Max rose from the lab bench. She gripped the side to steady herself. Her head swam, and a dreadful dryness clutched at her throat. Beside her, perched on his stool, Murray was still muttering in astonishment over a batch of agarose gel plates. He'd have been still more amazed if he'd known what he was really looking at. She'd told him the material was from a transgenic man-chimp fetus being developed *in vitro* at a research unit attached to the Minnesota Zoo. She'd nearly blown it, for of course a chimp had forty-eight chromosomes, not forty-six as with this specimen. She'd managed to talk her way around it, though, and to persuade him to run a full hybridization analysis. She felt bad at not leveling with him, but she couldn't. If her billion-to-one hunch *was* right, then absolutely no one in the world must know until she'd had time to work out what the hell she should do with the knowledge. All she knew now was that she had to be first with it.

She fumbled her way to the window and peered out at the stream of traffic flowing steadily down Memorial Drive into the full afternoon sun. Beyond lay the river, framed to left and right by broad-spanning bridges that reached over into the bowels of Boston city itself. She had stared at this view countless times and knew every detail intimately, but now it seemed one-dimensional, lacking in depth and meaning. Nothing else in the world existed at this moment except the bombshell exploding in slow motion inside her brain.

Distantly, she calculated it was Tuesday. She hadn't slept for over two days, surviving on foul laboratory coffee and some cocktail Murray brewed from undisclosed chemicals he kept hidden in his desk drawer. Was fatigue playing tricks with her judgment? Yet she'd seen the evidence, in black and white, on the gel plates. Murray was refusing to commit himself until he'd rerun a batch of tests, but Murray was a perfectionist. The results he'd got so far were enough for her. Either they'd got something hopelessly wrong, or else the incredible was, in fact, true.

She shivered, although the room was hot and stuffy. How could it be possible? She worked back in her mind over every step of the critical subtractive hybridization test they'd run on DNA extracted from the sample of Adam's blood, but she could find no flaw. She knew deep down that they'd done it right—this was Murray's job and he was number-one in the field—and the results were quite simply unambiguous. The genetic differences thrown up were too great for a simple procedural error, anyway. Too great for this case to be merely a statistical aberration either, or some blip way off the scale of the standard distribution curve. No, they were dealing here with something—some*body*—entirely different.

Genetically, Adam was quite unlike any other living human being on this earth.

Man forms a close, homogeneous family. The genetic diversity within the human family is very small: only about 0.03% of our total DNA blueprint differs from one race to another. Our nearest relative, the pygmy chimp, as she'd told Julia just the other day, differs genetically from man himself by just about 1.0%. This is close enough for man and chimp to share a vast range of common features and to define a branching-off point as recently as four or five million years ago, and yet far enough to make *homo sapiens* an entirely different species endowed with his own unique gamut of characteristics and faculties. But, by the analysis they'd just done, Adam stood somewhere in the middle. His degree of diversity from the human norm, as estimated by the subtraction technique, was about 0.1%. One in a thousand parts. That put him ten steps removed from the nearest chimp. Yet three steps from the nearest human.

What in God's name *was* this boy?

14

○

STANDING BENEATH UNIVERSITY BRIDGE, MAX stared into the swift brown river. She found her gaze fixating on a battered, tar-smeared chunk of polystyrene caught against a mooring-ring. She blinked hard but couldn't break its grip. Gradually the piece of flotsam transformed itself into a head—Adam's head, with its dark, deep-set eyes and rugged, prominent brow. Her thoughts sped back to Sam and their last supper together in Venice, and through her ears echoed his tales of the *almas*, those mysterious wildmen of the mountains sighted from time to time in the remotest wastelands of Asia and Mongolia. And she heard again his awed reply when she'd asked if they were real: *Yes, Max, I sincerely believe they are. Absolutely real.*

She wrenched her gaze away and for the first time became aware of the din of cars thundering over the bridge overhead. A cold easterly wind was whipping up the waves against the current as it funneled in the bottleneck of the river. She felt chill to the marrow. This was all crazy. She was worn out, her judgment all to pieces.

There simply *were* no more mammal species left to be found. Cuvier had said so, as far back as the 1800s—though, actually, four species had been found since then. But hadn't every inch of the world been explored and mapped by now? Surely there just weren't any unexplored regions left. Or were there? Couldn't there still be stretches of high, inaccessible wasteland in the Caucasus, the Pamirs and the mountains of Mongolia, where not even the local nomads had set foot? But then, if these *almas* did exist, scratching out however exiguous an existence from the bare mountain crags, wouldn't they most likely turn out simply to be ordinary human recluses, outcasts, even vestiges of lost nomadic tribes that had wandered further and further away from their fellows until, perhaps over centuries, they'd developed the feral looks and habits that gave them the appearance of being a race apart? Were these creatures man, or man-*like*?

Abruptly, she turned and headed back toward the tall, drab concrete department block and the car parked behind. She knew where to look first: Sam's books. She herself had helped Julia pack them up and send them to the Department. Sam *must* have known who or what Adam was. He had *recognized* him. Maybe, with luck, he'd left some clue and all his knowledge had not gone with him to the grave.

•

Little had changed at the Peabody. The cramped, antediluvian elevator still groaned its way up to the fifth floor, where the small reception area still offered the current editions of *Cultural Survival Quarterly*, *American Scientist* and *Physical Anthropology* scattered over the low tables and still played host to gossip and banter and tales of expeditions swapped over beakers of coffee. Sam's old office even bore the faint aroma of his pipe tobacco. On the bookshelf, peeking out of the eye socket of a dusty neolithic skull, still stood his funny little toy plastic dinosaur, and on the wall, askew, hung the Persian miniature she'd bought him in the early heady Cambridge days when she'd thought there was a real chance he would leave Julia. With a stab of pain she recalled the bleak day he announced that they were moving to a new house in Lexington. It was then she'd known it would never happen: this was not the act of a man who ever intended to leave his wife. Then he'd had his illness, during which period Julia was constantly at his side and inevitably regained much lost ground, leaving Max in the wings to snatch what brief and discreet moments she could. He'd come out of it with a desperate thirst to live life to the limit, and he'd started talking again about leaving Julia and setting up with her. This time, though, she'd hung no hopes on it; she would wait and see if his actions matched his words, and in the meantime she'd enjoy his company for as long or as short as fate ordained.

Her thoughts were interrupted by a tap on the door. His old secretary came in with a cup of coffee, and then, with a kindly word, closed the door and left her to her work. Max looked around for the books. No replacement had yet been appointed to Sam's chair, and the room had largely become a general depository, packed with surplus furniture and specimen boxes and pieces of research equipment. In the corner, behind a filing cabinet, she spotted the cartons from Lexington. Shifting the cabinet, she pulled out the cartons and settled down to her task.

The first two yielded nothing relevant, but on the

third she struck gold. Sitting cross-legged on the floor, she began to skim the books and periodicals in turn. Her starting-point was Dr. Myra Shackley's book, *Wildmen*. Quickly she realized that it was important first to eliminate what an *almas* was *not*. These were clearly not cases of feral man—that is, escaped or abandoned children raised by wild animals, such as the famous wild boy of Aveyron. Nor were they to be confused with the Yeti or the Sasquatch, such as "Bigfoot," which were not hominids at all but belonged to the ape family. No, these were in the family of man.

Delving deeper, she turned up a stack of reports of *almas* sightings collected over the years, mostly by Russian scientists. She read the accounts of the anthropologist Boris Porschnev and the doctor-anatomist Dr. Marie-Jeanne Kofman; she read Zhamtsarano and Rinchen; she skimmed through the work of Pronin and Burtsev. Gradually, inescapably, she began to form the conclusion that these were no figments of the primitive imagination that had worked themselves into tribal folklore but actual man-like creatures that did indeed exist, albeit in tiny numbers, scattered across the inaccessible mountain hinterlands from Asia through to Outer Mongolia. But who were they? It was here that Porschnev went a step further and advanced a theory so utterly incredible that at first Max found herself sharing the ridicule with which it had apparently been greeted by the scientific community. But then she thought of the evidence lying on those gel plates back at her own laboratory, and her scorn rapidly died.

In one book, a passage highlighted in fluorescent marker caught her eye. It gave the account of a recent encounter between a shepherd and an *almas* in southwest Mongolia. She read carefully the description the shepherd gave of the strange creature. "Half man and half beast, with reddish-black hair," the account ran. "The face is hairless and the abdomen sparsely covered with hair. The back of the head has a conical shape as it were, the forehead is flattened and there are prominent brow ridges and a protruding jaw... He has broad shoulders and long arms... Almas are easily frightened, suspicious, though not aggressive, and they lead a nocturnal life... They are usually to be seen at dawn or dusk... They prefer to stay in places far away from man, in mountains, for instance..."

She went on to read about a female *almas* at the end of the last century named Zana, who'd been caught and brought to a village in the Caucasus, where she'd been successfully domesticated. She was described as having a large face with big cheekbones, a muzzle-like protruding jaw and large eyebrows, and she was said to be capable of running extremely fast. She produced three surviving children by her captor, all of whom had descendants. These half-breeds, it seemed, had exceptionally powerful bodies and were fully able to speak as humans.

All along, one thought kept hammering through her brain: *This is Adam they're describing. Adam is an* almas. *A modern Neanderthal.*

She turned away, trembling with excitement and dread. She felt a sudden urge to slam shut the lid of the Pandora's box, to unknow what she knew. Almost hoping for refutation, she cast around for someone on whom she could discreetly test her theory. The Peabody was crammed full of anthropologists; down the road, the Agassiz was bursting with zoologists and paleontologists. Someone could tell her where she was going wrong. She was reaching for the University internal phone-list when the answer hit her: Bernard, Sam's assistant. Bernard was a lean, dry-witted man of about her own age with a sallow Latin complexion and small, bright lizard eyes. She'd met him several times, and she knew intuitively that she could get him to talk without divulging too much herself. She glanced at her watch: it was gone six. He might have gone for the night. Hurriedly she packed away the books, careful to put the ones she'd been consulting at the bottom, and, with a final glance around to check she'd left no trail, left the room. Bernard's office was just down the corridor.

●

Max had chosen the bar because it was nearest campus and it served food; she knew she had to eat, but she took one glance at the menu and pushed it away. She smothered a mad inner giggle: had we come all this way, survived the billennia, to feed off shrimp hushpuppies and smoked duck leg with guava curry glaze and fruit plantains, served with Inner Beauty Hot Sauce? She ordered a Sam Adams beer instead. A wave of tiredness swept over her, quenching her unnatural hilarity. She must not give in now, either to fatigue or to hysteria. Remain calm, clear, controlled. She looked around. The bar was filling up. One or two faces she recognized from the department: this was the nearest bar off campus. Behind the grill bar, in a tee-shirt bearing the legend, "Grills Just Want To Have Fun," the barman was busying himself making miniature Warhols on the side-plates— purple cabbage here, slice of orange there, a wedge of melon, a daub of pink apple relish just *so*...

Beside her, Bernard was eating the nibbles in fistfuls.

"A real hard act to follow," he was saying. "Plus the funding he brought in."

She pulled herself together. He was talking about Sam. She'd asked him the question herself.

"I guess that's why they haven't filled his chair yet?"

Bernard smoothed a hand across his blue-shadowed cheeks.

"The big money was starting to come through just when he died. He had this plan for a unit in behavioral anthropology—you know, applying what we know about other races to our own. Kind of social engineering."

"You don't like the idea?" she asked, detecting disapproval in his tone.

"I liked the dough."

"Who was kicking in for that?"

"Washington, via an outfit calling itself the Foundation. Ever heard of a Dr. Cray? Cray was the link." He leaned forward confidentially. "My guess is it was PAC money."

Her responses were slow and she took a moment to register. Dr. William Cray, Sam's old friend from college days, the man who was now befriending his wife Julia. How had Sam got tied up in Political Activity Coalitions? Everyone knew about these lobbies and how they ran politicians with pay-offs and the promise of jobs and contracts after their term of office; they called it the "revolving door" relationship of government and commerce. She'd always thought of Sam as an idealist and a true-blue American, above grubby factional politics. Perhaps she'd been wrong. Wherever she delved, she kept finding suspect motives. Or was this just the paranoia of tiredness?

"But you know all that," Bernard was continuing through the final mouthful of shrimp crackers. "He was going to get you in on it."

"Me?"

"He said you were the best in the business." His lizard eyes flicked over her. "On how genes control behavior."

"But I work with animals!" she protested, stung to think that Sam could have been using her for some undeclared purpose of his own.

Bernard looked pointedly across the bar as a wild whoop rose from one particularly raucous table by the window.

"So?"

Another wave of fatigue, greater than the last, washed over her, and she knew she wasn't going to be able to hold out much longer. She racked her brains for a way to bring the conversation around to the burning issue. Picking up Bernard's point, she gestured toward the window.

"You know, I once read somewhere that if you could reincarnate Neanderthal man, clean him up and put him on the New York subway, you wouldn't be able to tell him apart."

He laughed. "Yeah, maybe we're really primitives."

She stared into her drink. "I've often wondered," she mused, "what those cavemen really were like. How they *looked*."

"Ask the guys at the Agassiz. They've done reconstructions."

"Seriously, what do *you* think, Bernard?"

"Well, I guess . . ." he began, glancing to check she was actually serious. "One thing is for sure: they're not your typical cartoon caveman—you know, the hulking, shaggy, ape-like dumbo dragging a club in one hand and a woman in the other. That was a complete wrong turn made by a Frenchman at the turn of the century. The skeleton he reconstructed turned out to be from an old man crippled with arthritis. Besides, Neanderthals were just as varied physically as us moderns. The European ones are the classic kind—heavy, beetle-browed, with a low, sloping skullcap, and so on. The ones found in the Levant and further east are much less *primitive* looking. Much more like us."

"Like what exactly?"

"Hey, you want a lecture?"

"Sure, give me a lecture."

"Well," he began after a gulp of his beer, "seen from the side, the head would look slightly elongated, kind of streamlined—kind of like a football. From the front," he indicated on his own face, "a sloping forehead, pronounced brow ridge arched over each eye-socket, heavy cheekbones, a strong, projecting nose, maybe a slightly receding chin. Overall, the guy would be stocky but extremely robust, built more like a wrestler than a runner. Think of an Eskimo or a Lapp or some other cold-adapted people. He'd be capable of extraordinary endurance, too, like withstanding extreme cold and going without food for days on end." He broke off. "Max, why am I telling you all this?"

"Because you fascinate me, Bernard. Go on."

He smiled a little uncertainly, but continued.

"Okay. Well, he certainly used fire. He cooked his meat, probably in a pit like a good old New England clambake. Then there's the evidence of broken bones that have clearly been reset, and some people deduce from this that he had a social conscience, perhaps even a religion. Certainly, they had quite elaborate burial practices and rituals: you find them buried with their tools and implements, goat horns in symbolic circles, even flowers. They must have believed in an afterlife. Not so different from many primitive tribes today."

"Could they speak?"

"Their brains were actually bigger than ours today. That doesn't mean they were more intelligent, of course, but brain casts do show slight bulges in the left hemisphere." He tapped above his left ear, where the main speech area was located. "They've tried reconstructing vocal tracts from skeletons. The first stuff suggested that Neanderthals had only about half the phonetic range of modern man. But they've just discovered a hyoid bone in a skeleton in Israel and that's changed the whole picture. So I guess they could speak pretty good. And they probably had the complex social structures that go with language, too."

"They'd pass muster on the 'T,' then?"

"Cognitively, I'd say a Neanderthal was every bit as competent as us. Culturally, though, he'd appear very backward."

In the pause that followed, she struggled to find the least chink in the identikit picture. But she couldn't: this *was* Adam. Finally, she drew a deep breath. There was one thing she had to know.

"Can he . . . could they . . . breed with us?"

"Probably—it depends on how you categorize them. Are they a genus of our species, *homo sapiens*? Or just plain *homo neanderthalensis*, a distinctly separate species that branched off maybe three hundred thousand years ago from *erectus*, the common ancestor? The current thinking is that they're an earlier branching. We are, as it were, different twigs on the human bush—but nevertheless a little twig of phenomenal success. Still, that's not to say Neanderthal man couldn't interbreed with anatomically modern man and produce fertile offspring. Lions and tigers can, can't they? But the really interesting question is: *did* they?"

"Well, did they?"

"Fossils don't help here. There's confusion about whether hybrids exist. The telling evidence is genetic: no mitochondrial DNA from Neanderthal man exists in us moderns. So I'd say, on balance, they didn't." He sat forward more eagerly. "But then you've got to ask, *why not?* Why, in fact, did they die out so abruptly about thirty thousand years ago? That's a fascinating question. They apparently lived alongside pre-modern man in the Middle East for tens of thousands of years before. Maybe they didn't come into direct contact—after all, the human populations were tiny compared with today's. The idea of a titanic clash between the two races, a struggle to the death between the old nomadic hunter-gatherers and the new, settled pastoral peoples is really just a myth and good fodder for novels. You don't even need theories of competitive exclusion, either, since I doubt there was really all that much competition over resources. No, I suspect it is something simpler. Perhaps climatic change killed them off. Perhaps disease. Either way, a tiny increase in mortality rate would have quickly led to their extinction—just two percent would have been enough. Whatever the threat was, they just couldn't adapt. And within no time they were wiped off the face of the earth."

"Completely?"

"Sure. Completely."

"Too bad."

He laughed shortly.

"Science is a religion, Max, you know that. It needs

its mysteries. For God's sake, let's hope no one ever finds some frozen tissue and manages to clone a Neanderthal."

"And if someone did?"

"There'd be a lot of egg on a lot of faces."

"But seriously, Bernard. What if?"

He paused, as if to give scale to the implications.

"It would be the biggest thing ever to hit the scientific world," he said quietly.

Max felt dazed. For a while she let the conversation drift off the point. He began asking her about her own work, trying to shift the balance of attention onto her, but she was too tired, too mind-numb, to respond properly. As soon as she felt she decently could, she put a bill on the counter and rose. Thanking him and explaining she hadn't slept for two days, she excused herself and left. She'd call him up next day and thank him again, but in the meantime she knew she had to get home to bed before her legs collapsed or her brain exploded or both happened simultaneously.

•

Her sleep was beleaguered by dreams. She saw grunting creatures, half primate and half caveman, shuffling around frozen primordial forests hunting wild boars and strange, shaggy mouflon. One, crouched over a kill with blood up to his elbows, bore the face of Adam. His eyes glinted emerald green. He rose, and slowly the others began to advance too. Suddenly she was in full flight, stumbling and tripping through the forest, while the thick panting behind her grew closer...

She woke, drenched in sweat. She fumbled for the bedside light. The clock read three. From the small photoframe beside it, Sam's face smiled out at her. Confident, even arrogant. Somehow this photo had escaped the clear-out and worked its way back here. Briefly she gazed into the two-dimensional eyes and wondered who this man had really been. She'd known nothing about Cray and Sam's project, nothing about his political involvement and nothing about his plans to bring her in on it. Had he been planning to exploit her love and loyalty all along?

She sank back into the pillows. Everything was such a tangle, without shape or sense. Had he already known in Venice what he would find in the Caucasus? Was that the real purpose of his trip, the *coup de theatre* that would launch the project? "Social engineering—the genetic angle." She swallowed a shudder. How little she had understood the man she'd loved.

And she thought of Adam. To Julia and everyone else, Adam was just a plucky, bewildered kid who'd been dragged out of his primitive habitat and thrust into an alien world. On a different level, he had an entirely different significance. He was potentially the "biggest thing to hit the scientific world" because he, and he alone, held the key to the single great question that had obsessed mankind from the dawn of consciousness: *who are we, and where do we come from?* Were we risen out of grunting, gibbering bestiality by the glory of our minds and reason? Or were we a corrupted, decadent species in its last throes of existence, fallen from a lost age when we were noble savages? Were we innately peaceful or innately aggressive? Good, or evil? Throughout time, the answer had always been ideological, conditioned by our view of ourselves. But here was Adam, a living specimen of what we once were, the man we all had been a brief three hundred thousand years ago before our paths branched. No studies of animal behavior, for all the millions of dollars poured into them, could tell us a fraction of what this one boy could. His species had evolved in the meantime, of course, biologically as well as culturally, just as our own had, but so very much more slowly. And he still carried the genes of his distant fathers. Through him, if we listened very carefully, we could hear the echo of our own forefathers, too.

What should she do—what *could* she do? Suddenly her own work at the lab seemed very petty in comparison. Where did her future lie? Back there, scratching around for crumbs from other peoples' bigger budgets, or here, where there could never be a more pertinent, critical issue for humanity to address nor, for a scientist seeking to establish her name, a greater opportunity to earn a permanent place in the history books?

Abruptly she got up and threw on her clothes. She fumbled her way out of her apartment and into her car. The night was clear, and above the glare from the city lights, the stars burned brightly in their infinite orbits. A sense of awe gripped her. At the Department block, she stood for a minute staring into the heavens with a strange feeling of intimacy, a sort of empathy with the cosmos, as though she had been groping blindly in the dark all her life and had suddenly lifted a corner upon the workings of the universe.

Mastering her emotions, she turned and headed for the labs. The first thing was to make sure that every shred of evidence, every plate and assay slide, was safely under lock and key and every accessible file and data register in the computer was wiped clean. Only then could she settle down to work out what to do with the time bomb ticking away in her hands.

15

○

TAKING ADAM BY THE HAND, SANDY LED THE WAY UP
the trim-mown pathway to Sam's grave. Julia followed a
step behind. The warm afternoon air hung slumbrous
over the cemetery. Julia had come here every week since
Sam had died and she noted the smallest changes with
the eye of familiarity—fresh flowers here, a new urn there,
and halfway up the broad path, the unadorned grave of
an old woman whose children, according to the gardener,
were in a bitter lawsuit over her will. Some distance away,
beneath the white clapboard chapel with its chiseled stee-
ple pointing confidently up to God, a burial was in progress. Fleetingly Julia wondered if showing Adam an
interment would bring the point home better, but she
decided to leave it to Sandy. The girl seemed to know
what she was doing.

As they approached the grave, Julia fell back. She
felt uneasy. She watched from a short distance as Sandy
led Adam to the grave-side and, producing the photograph of Sam she kept in her own room, tried indicating
by signs that Sam lay dead and buried there beneath the
ground.

Adam looked peaky and nervous. He'd disappeared for three days. She'd been beside herself with anxiety, fearing something serious might have happened to him, or that he'd got into trouble, perhaps started on a spate of fire-raising. She'd watched the television news closely and kept the radio tuned to a local station. She'd told herself that if he didn't turn up by that morning, she'd go to the police. In the early hours of the previous night, he'd stolen back home. Before breakfast, going to check his hut, she'd found him curled up beneath the deck, nestled into a roll of underfelt the decorators had thrown out. She couldn't guess how far afield he'd been, except that his jeans were ripped as though he'd been climbing rocks and his sneakers were full of gravel; besides the river, the nearest gravel she could think of was at a quarry five miles away. Traces of blood and what looked like pigeon's underfeathers clung to his tee-shirt, but otherwise he'd kept himself very clean. He'd eaten his breakfast ravenously, without attention to his manners. For once, Sandy had overcome her distaste; she'd even brought him various of his bits and pieces that she'd salvaged from the fire and laid them on the kitchen floor in front of him in the way of a homecoming offering. She was very keen to try out her idea.

"Adam! Stop that!"

Sandy's sharp reproach jerked her to attention. Adam had fallen to his hands and knees and was scratching away at the earth, tearing away fistfuls like a dog burrowing after a rabbit. Sandy was trying to drag him off. Aghast, Julia hurried forward and, gripping him by the shoulder, spun him around to face her. A wild, desperate fervor glistened in his eyes.

"No, Adam, you mustn't!" she cried. "Sam is asleep.

Don't disturb him. Let him be.''

He tilted his head on one side for a moment, then wrenched himself from her grasp and attacked the earth again with renewed frenzy. Appalled, Julia slapped him hard on the cheek. He recoiled instantly, with a gasp of dismay. She'd never hit him before.

"That's wrong!" she hissed. "Bad! You mustn't disturb the dead. He's gone. His soul is in heaven.''

She stabbed a finger urgently upward, to the sky. His eyes followed where she was pointing. Slowly his mood changed. His resistance slackened and, screwing up his eyes against the glare, he gradually rose to his feet and stood staring unblinkingly into the infinite blue sky. He glanced down at the grave, then up at the sky again, as if finally making the connection, and his rugged features began to relax. A look of wonder, almost of devotion, spread slowly across his face, and from his lips came a soft, low mutter that formed itself into a word, that word.

"Atta.''

Atta? It didn't sound like "Adam" after all. What did it mean? She caught Sandy's eye. Sandy was smiling. Spontaneously she reached out and grasped each of her children by the hand. For a full minute, thus linked, the three stood together over Sam's grave, in silence and harmony.

•

Max drove fast, erratically. She was so self-absorbed that she missed the Lexington exit and had to do a long loop back, and that only served to fuel her anxiety. She'd slept like the dead, through the alarm clock and several phone calls. One was from Julia, on the machine. Adam had *set fire to the house!* She'd called back immediately, but there'd been no reply. Instantly she'd imagined the worst: arson . . . a disturbed kid, the neighborhood pariah . . . the police involved . . . the boy removed . . . questions asked, investigations set in motion . . . Within minutes, she'd taken a shower, swallowed a mouthful of juice straight from the carton, grabbed a slice of half-shriveled pecan pie and set off in her car. Once clear of the city, she hit the gas. The sun dazzled her full in the face, and at one point she narrowly missed a bad crash while passing a truck. She had to get to him before they did. They? Who were *they*? On the return loop, she eased up. There was no "they." She alone possessed the knowledge. *No one else knew!*

As she reached White River Drive, she slowed down further. She hadn't thought what she'd say to Julia. Should she tell her? But what would she actually *say*? "Julia, there's something I feel you ought to know: the boy you adopted, the boy you took into your home as your son and Sandy's brother is actually not one of us at all. Julia, you're harboring a modern-day caveboy." She let out a peal of crazed laughter. It sounded insane! All right, she could go through the evidence point by point, but was that necessarily right? Julia might not *want* the knowledge. It would put her in an impossible dilemma. Even if she kept the boy, her feelings would never be the same. She wanted a son, not a freak. More than likely, she'd try the noble route but end up getting rid of him, sending him back to the agency or having him placed in some penitentiary for juvenile sociopaths and fire-starters and other social misfits. She would certainly tell other people: she couldn't keep the secret to herself, for how else would she justify getting rid of him? She'd tell the adoption people, she'd tell this man Cray, she'd say to the world, "I thought he was just a disturbed and backward kid, and I brought him into my home and gave him a mother's love, but then he turns out to be this creature, a freak, a throwback, not really a person, not really a proper human being."

Max caught her breath. What was she saying: they might get rid of him? Was that to be a possibility? No. It was unthinkable. Julia must not be told.

Max reached the house to find the estate wagon gone. She learned from the decorators that they'd all gone to the cemetery. The *cemetery?* she thought with a flush of alarm. Relax, she told herself; they've probably just gone to change the flowers on the grave. She paced up and down the drive, waiting. Five long minutes later, she heard a car turn into the drive. She stepped forward to greet them, trying not to betray in her manner her racing pulse.

Sandy was first out of the car and came running forward, chattering eagerly. Julia called out a cheery "Hi" and delved into the back for some shopping. Then the rear door flew open. Out leapt Adam. With a whoop, he flew after Sandy. Max felt her mouth go dry. He was so *like us*. Give him a wash and brush-up and put him on the subway... In disbelief she watched the figure disappearing around the side of the house. There he was, a stocky, muscular young lad with thick reddish-black hair and striking, even handsome features, and dressed like a typical kid from the neighborhood, tumbling out of an estate wagon in Lexington, Massachusetts, yelling and whooping like any high-spirited twelve-year-old. She blinked hard. Was she seeing things, or imagining them?

Julia had come up and was talking animatedly about the cemetery. Something wonderful had happened, it seemed. In a daze, Max followed her indoors. In the kitchen, Julia put a pan of water on to boil and asked her what she'd like to drink.

"Vodka," she croaked.

"I'll join you," said Julia, taking the pan off. "I feel just in the mood."

•

Max took her glass outside onto the deck. An oversize sun the color of molten glass was inching down behind the tree-tops, casting long horizontal shafts of caramel light across the ground. Over by the flagpole, Sandy and Adam were playing a game of ball. She watched as Sandy's shot flew wide and the ball rolled down the slope into the pool. Adam began after it, but stopped some way clear of the edge. The pool was about half full of water; in one corner fed a broad black pipe, connected to a small electric pump.

Julia followed her gaze, and chuckled.

"Another twenty-four hours should do it. It was a perfectly brilliant idea of yours, Max." She paused. "Something wrong?"

"I was just watching Adam," Max mumbled.

Adam was inching gingerly toward the edge of the pool. He peered in, then quickly shrank back.

"It's the water," explained Julia. "It scares him stiff. He still won't take a bath, and I have the devil's own job even using the hand-shower on him. Poor Adam and his phobias. That's the next thing we have to tackle, now that we've sorted out this business about Sam."

Max avoided her eye. How could any understanding of our own kind possibly relate to Adam? He was remote to us: unreachable and incomprehensible. He was simply not the normal American adolescent Julia wanted to see him as, and to interpret or predict his behavior as though he were was to make a dangerous false assumption. God knew where it could lead.

"Julia," she began, "I think you shouldn't assume too much about Adam."

"Exactly!" agreed Julia, to her surprise. "That's just what I've been thinking. We need to know what we're dealing with. We've proved we can get through to him, but we've got to make sure we get it right. No one has really tried to analyze what makes him tick." She beamed the full intensity of her gaze on her. "We need help. Your help, Max. Now, those tests you mentioned—"

"Excuse me?" queried Max.

"Cognitive tests. We could start with the false-belief test."

"I'm not sure he's ready for that."

Julia laid a hand on her arm.

"Then whatever you think. I'm frankly out of my depth."

Max took a breath, then checked herself. Why not? She could learn things about him herself that no amount of gene assays could ever tell. Every single thing about the boy was of astonishing importance. Catching the bright, expectant expression on Julia's face, she began to see that here was a heaven-sent opportunity to study Adam for herself within the best possible framework.

"Take him to a real shrink," she urged disingenuously. "I'm not a professional in that field."

"Never! They're a bunch of charlatans. He's had three look at him and they've all come up with something different. No, you're the person, Max. He trusts you. And you care."

"Well, let me think about it," she replied.

"Thanks," said Julia with sincerity.

•

William Cray replaced the phone with the taut self-control of a man who watched his blood pressure and, drawing tighter his silk dressing-gown, went to the ormolu escritoire that concealed the drinks cabinet and poured himself another nightcap. Through the French windows he listened to the sounds of the hot, thundery Washington night. From close by came the peaceful lapping and dripping of his own water garden, disturbed by nothing more than the occasional flick-flash of a carp breaking the surface; beyond the high security wall lay the other, more violent face of the city with its sirens and car-horns and those more ambiguous sounds—the car backfiring that could be a gunshot, the squeal of a tire on a still-warm road that might be a human scream. Tonight this all-American juxtaposition of order and anarchy, of the haven at home and the jungle in the streets, left him unmoved. His thoughts were preoccupied with Eliot Lovejoy's ultimatum. Time was running out fast. It had started so promisingly, but the fact was that the material collected to date was embarrassingly scanty. All kinds of dramas had been going on in the Wendell household, but somehow they weren't getting the right *answers*.

He turned back to his desk and his eye fell upon the photos of his two children. Why was he doing all this? For *their* sake? Not for Howard's, resplendent there in his West Point passing-out uniform, before Vietnam shot his nerves through and he became a Wall Street drifter, forever needing to be pulled off minor drug and fraud raps. Not for Mary-Ann's either, shown here giving her college valedictory speech, before she fell in with a left-wing set and married a black rights activist in Berkeley. Not for what they had become but for what they could have been. For the country that had given them the promise which they would have fulfilled had it not been for the bad elements within it, the cancers destroying all that was wholesome and harmonious, the worms within the apple pie. The country had to be led back to its old civilized values. All that was bestial, savage, primitive and regressive in man's nature must be identified, isolated and extirpated. There could be no task more important. That was why he was putting every ounce of his own energy and the Foundation's resources behind this project.

With refreshed purpose, he reached for the files and reread the latest transcripts. There was Julia, speaking to him off the page as clearly as if she was in the room. He frowned briefly. He didn't like this part of it. Perhaps he should never have begun these evenings but kept her at a professional distance—at arm's length, literally. He was deliberately using her. Normally that wouldn't have caused him a moment's worry. But things were happening between them that he hadn't planned for. She was growing dangerously fond of him and, he had to admit, he was beginning to feel the same about her, too. God *damn* it! The weakest element was always the human factor.

He turned back to the transcripts. At the reference to "tests," his frown deepened. What tests? Swiveling his chair around, he stared thoughtfully into the aquarium behind him. A piece was missing. They needed someone on the inside. Someone who could work with them, someone with a motive, political or personal, which could be manipulated. The ideal candidate was staring him in the face. Close to the family, with a background in genetics, she could prove just the very person.

He turned back and reached for the slim file entitled, *Dr. Maxine Fitzgerald.*

16

○
_____

MAX ALLOWED HERSELF TO BE PERSUADED BY JULIA
and, during the days that followed, she threw herself into
the task of assessing and recording everything she could
about Adam. She worked fast, though the work was too
great and, she sensed, the time available was all too short
for a properly scientific study. She shot rolls of photos,
she took reels of tape recordings, she wrote pages of notes
and observations. Each night, back at the labs, when
everyone had gone home, she'd file it all away on disk,
locking these carefully away at the back of the chemicals
cabinet. Such physical records she'd collected she took
back to her apartment and hid in her wardrobe: his drawings of strange bison-like animals, a flint he'd chipped to
a razor edge, samples of the acorns and mushrooms she'd
found on the floor of his stone hunt, an old sneaker he'd
worn through at the toe.

Under the guise of playing a game or getting his size
for clothes or any other excuse she could think of at the
time, she managed to take systematic measurements of
his bone structure and his musculature, and these she

filed away under *Anatomy*. She borrowed a video camera from the Department and taped his movements, his facial gestures, even his strange method of locomotion, and by playing it back frame by frame proved her theory about his toe-first gait. She made notes on his metabolism, too, and managed to obtain a good set of readings of pulse and blood pressure at various stages of exertion, which she filed under *Physiology*. In all this, she enlisted Sandy's cautious support, persuading her that it was all for a project connected with the work of one of her colleagues into the physical adaptation of kids from non-American racial stock. She took pains to understand Sandy's motivation and state of mind. Sandy, it seemed, saw herself as having saved Adam and, in some fundamental way, she felt he belonged to her. She had virtually appointed herself his guardian, taking responsibility for what happened to him. It was thus vital to Max to ensure her involvement, but she couldn't help sensing her resistance, almost suspicion, and so she was careful to tread warily.

By the end of the first week, Max found she had accumulated an astonishing amount of material. Her files bulged on *Genetics*, *Behavior*, *Cognition* and *Language*, mostly packed with raw information as yet unanalyzed. One file, however, remained stubbornly empty: *Brain*.

For some days she puzzled over how to fill this gap. No single description of an organism was alone true. Take Adam's phobia for water, for example. She had a good behavioral description on film: she had him physically shunning a hose-pipe directed at him. She could conceive a plausible psychological description in terms of race-conscious memories of glacial floods, or more simply some childhood bathing trauma in which he'd nearly drowned. She could describe his reaction at the physiological level, too: pulse, blood status, skin resistance, pupillary reflex, sweat glands, capillary erection, and so on. She could guess at what went on at the biochemical level, and possibly even the nuclear cell level. None of these by themselves gave the total picture, however; all were components, offering one face of a multifaceted truth. But they all had one thing in common: they were outward manifestations of events in the brain, in those two fist-sized lumps of porridge-colored matter. The mind, in her view, *was* the brain. To understand what was different about the boy's mind, therefore, she had to know what was different about his brain.

But how, and where? The obvious place was the Boston Children's Hospital, which boasted the very latest body scanners. But no radiologist would see a patient without a referral from his own doctor.

"We'll get Dr. Steiner to refer him," suggested Julia promptly when she told her the problem.

"I don't think that's wise."

"Wise? Max, he'll get paid for it. All right, I'll speak to William."

"No, no. Let's not involve him either. You know how people are: they'll only want to put their two cents in. Before you know it, there'll be shrinks crawling all over the place."

"Just say what we need and William will fix it."

"Leave it to me, Julia. Trust me."

Then she had a break. Late the following evening, as she was about to leave the labs, she was going through the pile of papers in her in-tray and caught the headline in the Institute newsletter: *MIT in NMR breakthrough.* Of course! Here at MIT, on her very doorstep, some of the leading work on nuclear magnetic resonance scanners was going on. Next day, she met the radiologist over coffee. The timing couldn't have been more fortunate. His team was actually looking for volunteers to test the equipment and, subject to a disclaimer, he agreed to run the boy through it. She fixed an appointment for two days' time—in the late morning, when Sandy would be at school.

Doubts over the ethics of what she was doing began to assail her. The web of deceptions was growing ever wider: Adam, Julia, Sandy, Murray and now the radiologist. She reminded herself it was all for a higher moral purpose, but even this rousing notion failed to still her nagging doubts. She recalled reproving Sandy for her cynicism, but the girl had been right: altruism really was egotism in disguise. What the hell? she thought finally. Men climbed mountains because they were there. She was studying Adam because *he* was there. Period. Get hung up in moralizing and you got nowhere. All that mattered was the result. In the big picture, the ends justified the means. And screw the rest.

•

A pale slip of moon cowered behind restless clouds and cast a timid greenish pall across the grass tennis court and up the shallow slope above, illuminating the rear of the tall house in a flat gray wash, only to dissipate itself in the balconies and casements. At the other end of the court stood the small octagonal summerhouse, lost in its own shadow, within which sun-chairs and tennis equipment lay stacked against the wall and, hanging high on a nail just inside the door, the spare key to the back door of the house. Behind, the trees thickened into blackness. The wind rose a degree.

Adam crouched at the foot of a silver birch, staring up into the sky. His face bore a look of angry betrayal. From time to time he peeled back his lips to bare his teeth and stuttered in a silent chatter. The clouds prowled past in unending procession, alternately masking and revealing the inky sky. Occasionally he'd catch a glimpse of a star, brighter than the rest, shining through the shifting screens, but they never parted enough to reveal a constellation, let alone yield sight of the small speck of proof that he so yearned for. Five nights in succession now, he'd climbed out and crept into the woods, each time searching from a different vantage point for the sign that would tell him that what was necessary had been fulfilled. But in clear visibility or poor, at dusk, midnight or dawn, he never saw anything. Anything at all.

For a while his gaze combed the rear face of the silent, unlit house. Somewhere *he* was in there. The boy who had thwarted him in the completion of his duty. The one who had committed the blasphemy. The one who must be punished.

Turning away, he padded noiselessly back through the woods and, following the path the badgers took, wound his way down to the river. There he fell once again to a crouch and began working his way through the smooth gray-white pebbles, searching for ones that were just the perfect size and weight for his purpose.

●

Julia glanced across at Adam in the passenger seat beside her and contrived a relaxed smile. She always felt nervous about taking him out, even just to Cambridge. She wasn't sure how he'd react to the scan, either, and his mood was not promising. In the last couple of days,

he'd been sullen and withdrawn; he'd refused to coop-
erate with Max and once he threw a bad tantrum when
she tried to make him repeat one of her tests.

She sighed; nothing was ever straightforward. Maybe
they were pushing him too far too fast. She hadn't imagined Max would take the bull by the horns quite so obsessively: she really was pressing forward at a breakneck
pace. Maybe she'd lost her sense of proportion in her
enthusiasm to be *complete*. That was often the problem
with scientists; Sam had been just the same. They could
never get the general drift of things; they always had to
pick and analyze and probe down to the very last detail.
Fine, if it was a pile of dusty bones or some genes in a
test tube, but here they were dealing with a whole living
person. Perhaps after this scan she would call a halt.
Sandy would be relieved. She had always been skeptical
about the value of putting the lad under the microscope,
and she was becoming openly hostile to the program.
That morning, in fact, her exasperation had broken its
bounds.

"Why can't you leave him alone?" she'd cried. "This
is his home, not a laboratory! He's not one of Max's
horrible zoo experiments! I don't trust her. She's only
doing it for what she can get out of it. You wait: we'll
find it all written up in some scientific journal. 'A Social
and Physical Anatomy of a Caucasian Gypsy Orphan.' I
can't see what good it can ever do *him*. Look at him!
He's perfectly miserable."

Julia had told her not to be so ungrateful. Max was
giving up an immense amount of her time to help them.

"What help?" Sandy had demanded. "She's not a
doctor or a psychiatrist. She's a geneticist."

"She's a scientist," Julia had replied. "She spends

her day applying her mind to solving problems in an orderly, scientific way. You're not a psychiatrist yourself either, darling, but you found the answer to that fire business through applying your intelligence. Right or wrong?"

At that, the girl had mumbled something under her breath and stalked off to collect her things for school.

Julia slowed as they approached the river and checked the address: the Department of Experimental Bioelectronics, on Amherst Alley. Briefly she wondered why they weren't meeting at Max's lab or even at her apartment—neither of which, she realized with a touch of surprise, she'd actually visited. But her mind was occupied with navigating and eventually, after taking a wrong turn, she found the building. Max was waiting for her in the parking lot and came forward with a bright, confident smile. She told her everything was ready and they were waiting for Adam inside. Her manner radiated quiet professional competence and, feeling reassured, Julia returned her smile with relief.

•

Max double-locked her apartment door and stood in the small hallway, waiting for her nerves to settle. Finally she let out a long, slow breath and, without putting down the folder of radiographic photos, went to the kitchen to fix herself a coffee. Changing her mind, she went into the living room and poured a vodka.

It was gone four, and she'd only just left the radiologist. She sank into a chair, exhausted. It had taken every ounce of her diplomatic skills to keep Julia and the man from discussing the results there and then, and Julia wasn't so dumb as not to realize they were quite extraordinary. It had been just as tricky, too, once she'd seen

Julia and Adam off the premises, to get the radiologist to explain their exact significance while at the same time playing it down so as not to arouse his interest overmuch. Jesus, she breathed, a close call. Not again.

She drew the blinds and took the phone off the hook, then settled down to go through the folder. One by one she studied the computer-generated photos of segments of Adam's brain. They showed the brain from various angles—some in section, some in profile, others in the round, viewed from within as well as from outside, with the gray and white matter, the vesicles and the bone distinguished in brightly varied colors. She lingered over one that revealed the whole organ, awed by the sheer beauty and power of that small walnut-shaped cluster of matter. Here were expressed the genes that controlled the body and all its processes of motion and emotion, of action and reaction, and of those two quintessential human capabilities, conceptual thought and verbal speech.

She looked closer. The complex folding gyra of the cortex bespoke a typical human brain. But even from a gross visual inspection, the differences were apparent. Adam's brain was clearly large for his age, although not disproportionate to his body weight. From side view, it was noticeably elongated—unusually well developed in the occipital region at the back where the visual centers lay, and correspondingly less pronounced in the prefrontal lobes where the higher cognitive functions took place. This suggested Adam possessed relatively superior eyesight—a fact she already knew—but also certain conceptual deficiencies, such as a poor sense of the future and of the ability to plan for it. True, he didn't seem interested in the morrow or in allowing for it; his actions, just as his feelings, were always immediate and lacked any sense of premeditation. Along with his auto-centric view of the world, that made him into the innocent Julia saw. She herself, however, saw a different boy emerging from these plates. The radiologist had unwittingly summed it up: "This kid's not just backward," he said, "he's goddamn *primitive*."

She turned to a photo of a section of the deep, midbrain structure. This showed the amygdala, the part of the limbic system which, along with parts of the hypothalamus, controlled the emotions of rage and fear. What had he seen that was so significant? She pulled a copy of Gray's *Anatomy* from the shelf and compared an illustration. Had she mistaken the scale, or were the amygdala in Adam's brain significantly *larger*? Her thoughts turned to the controversial book by Mark and Ervin back in the '70s, entitled *Violence and the Brain*, which advocated curing violence in U.S. cities by mass surgical amygdalectomy. She frowned. Adam might be disturbed enough to start a fire, but he'd never actively attacked anyone. It wasn't *in* him, as Julia would say. Was it?

She went to the window and stared out. At the back of the dismal concrete school block that lay across a stretch of trash-blown wasteland cordoned off by a rusty chain-link fence, two truant figures were bent in a doorway in some patently illicit act, doubtless swapping dollars for dope. She turned away, disturbed by the thought that within each of those lost heads lay an instrument more powerful than all the world's computers put together. She returned to the photo plates. The very same power lay there, beneath Adam's skull. In fact, the most striking thing about these scans was not the differences but the similarities. Adam represented a precursor of ourselves, an echo from our primitive past, who'd evolved separately along a parallel track. He might lag behind us on speech and conceptual thought and exhibit slightly accentuated primitive drives, but cognitively, he was just as aware as we were. And he had the same capacity to use his intelligence for good or bad as any one of us, from those school kids to the Pope or the President.

She swallowed back her vodka. She'd get over to her own labs and write up the results. What was the next step? Adam was showing signs of stress. Maybe she'd been applying the pressure too hard. Tomorrow was Saturday anyway, and Sandy would be around. Maybe she'd give it a break for a day or so. Take a badly needed break herself, too. Resolved, she reached for her car keys and within a minute she was on her way to the labs.

•

A car pulled up in the road. Voices shouted farewells. A door slammed. The car roared away. And down the drive swayed the tall, athletic figure he had been waiting for.

The night was close. Moonlight filtered through the pacing clouds. Dry, pent-up growls of thunder threatened an imminent storm. Adam crouched lower into the undergrowth, as still as rock. Only his eyes moved, following the figure as it wound an erratic path down the drive toward the house. His grip closed over the small, round pebbles in his pocket, muffled in a wadding of moss. Silently, he rose and slipped through the woods, tracking the older boy in parallel as he moved inexorably into the ambush.

The front door, set within its grand porch, was locked, and the boy fumbled his way in the dark around the side. His foot struck a watering can, sending it skidding away with a loud clatter; he swore roundly, then rebuked himself with a hissed *Ssh!* The back door, too, was locked. He groped under a small ornamental stone vase for the key. It was gone. He grumbled a curse. He glanced at his watch, then at the unlit house, and finally set off down the slope and across the grass to the summerhouse for the spare key.

Like an invisible arrow, Adam darted beneath the skirts of the trees alongside. The other boy was five paces from the summerhouse when he tripped over the cord and fell forward onto his face. Suddenly, for a brief moment, the moon came out bright and full, illuminating the scene like day. As the boy eased himself groggily to his knees, Adam broke cover. He slipped a stone into the sling, took aim and with a single rapid twist let it fly. The small missile shot through the air low, fast, hard, smack into its target, and with a muffled grunt, half of surprise and half pain, the boy toppled over.

Some while later, when his work was done, Adam removed the small pegs stretching the cord taut and replaced the key beneath the stone vase. Then, just as the first heavy clots of rain were beginning to fall, he turned and quickly retraced his way home through the woods.

•

Sandy woke early. There'd been a storm in the night and she'd slept badly. Wearily she dragged herself out of bed and slipped on her tracksuit and trainers. It was Saturday: she'd put in an hour's easy run before basketball. As she passed the spare room she saw the door was ajar. Inside, Adam lay curled up on the floor beneath the window, fast asleep. She closed the door quietly and made her way downstairs.

Outside, the dawn sky was gray and lusterless. For a moment she hesitated on the doorstep; the earth was sodden, and a low, chill wind bit in through her clothing. Briefly she wondered why she was putting herself through all this. Did she want a place in the school basketball team as a means of gaining acceptance by Scott and the others? Maybe in the past. Now she was doing it for herself.

She headed off across the squelchy grass and down the path, now a muddy trickle, that led aslant through the woods and, skirting the Blanes' property, wove its way down to the river. She counted her breathing aloud, marking time with her step. The trees had swollen with the recent heavy rain and closed over the paths, brushing her cheeks with their soft wet leaves as she passed. Gradually her muscles loosened and her step grew lighter, and soon she'd reached that exhilarating moment she loved above all when she seemed to shed her body entirely and become a dancing kite wafted along by the wind, a being without weight or substance, made only of air. She was afloat, flying among the treetops, weaving through the canopies, rising higher and higher to touch the clouds...

A hand...

Purple-red, swollen, a hand reaching out of the trees at her. She saw it out of the corner of her eye a split second before she felt its touch on her face. She choked on a scream. Swerving to the side, she crashed into a tree-trunk and collapsed, momentarily winded.

She turned, sick with horror. Out of the tree hung an arm, upside down, swaying limply. Beside it, twisted in a branch, hung the other arm. The body itself was half buried in foliage. On the ground she noticed a shirt, stained where the rain had not quite washed away the blood. She craned forward, feeling nauseous and faint. The body had its back to her, but she recognized instantly the short-cropped fair hair. With a cry she staggered to her feet and stared up into the depths of the tree.

Strung up by his feet from a high branch, roped there by the wire of the tennis net, hung the body of Scott. He was naked to the waist. Deep in the flesh of his back, a series of jagged gashes oozed wetly from swollen welts. As she reached forward, hardly daring to touch, a gust of wind swung the body around to present the face. She recoiled with a throttled gasp. The eyes were open and staring, the whites veined with blood. His forehead and scalp hung red and loose like the dewlap of a turkey, while his mouth, agape, was jammed with leaves. Motionless, inert, sightless, he swung slowly back and forth following the whim of the wind.

17

○

JULIA WAITED FOR SANDY IN THE CORRIDOR OUTSIDE
the room where Scott lay comatose. A pervasive scent
of air freshener masked the sickly underlying hospital
smell of medication and disinfectant. From time to time
a doctor or a nurse would pass and cast her a professional
smile of sympathy. She glanced at a clock on the wall: it
was close on noon, and Max would soon be arriving at
the house. An impatient clatter of heels interrupted her
thoughts, and she turned to find Loretta Blane, ashen
and grim, bearing down the corridor with Kirsty, her
daughter, in tow. Loretta was carrying a suitcase, no
doubt with clothes for her boy.

Julia stepped forward.

"I'm so very sorry," she said. "If there's anything
we can do..."

"You've done quite enough already," responded the
other woman, steering Kirsty ahead of her toward the
door of Scott's room.

"I don't understand who could possibly have done
such a thing," persisted Julia.

Loretta paused. The overhead light glinted off her sunglasses, giving her the appearance of a magnified fly.

"Don't you?"

"Surely you don't think Adam—"

"That's for the police and the lawyers to decide. Now, if you'll excuse me."

At that moment the door opened and Sandy came out, pale and upset. She moved aside to let the others enter. Kirsty brushed past without a word, casting her a cold stare. Through the door, Julia caught a glimpse of Scott lying propped on his side, his back and legs swathed in bandages. Sandy stared after them as the door closed, looking angry and hurt. Julia drew her quietly away. They walked in silence down the corridor, through the large reception lobby and out into the leaden, overcast day. As she climbed into the estate wagon, Sandy turned to her.

"They think it's *him*, don't they?" she said. "They've made up their minds that he did it. But he *couldn't* have."

"Of course not, darling," she replied gently. "Let's get home."

She paused for a moment with the key in the ignition as the memory of that morning flashed through her mind. She'd been woken by the sound of screaming and leapt out of bed to meet Sandy racing up the stairs, white with shock, imploring her to come quickly. She'd rushed in her dressing gown across the lawn and into the woods. She'd sent Sandy to fetch the Blanes, and together they'd cut the boy down. But she'd never forget those bulging eyes, that stuffed-open mouth and that wattled scalp. Or those cuts. And the particular, distinct pattern they made—a triangle within a circle. Instantly she'd recognized the strange mark. It was the very same she'd once seen daubed in pigeon's blood on the floor of Adam's attic. There could be no doubt. This work bore Adam's signature.

"Well, *I* know," Sandy was saying. "He was in his bedroom, fast asleep. I saw him."

Julia checked herself. Let Sandy keep her illusions, at least until the truth came out openly. The police would soon bring the facts to light. The fire was one thing, but this was a case of actual bodily assault, maybe even attempted homicide. Not just mildly crazy but positively *criminal*. They'd take Adam away. They'd lock him up in a home for delinquents. The psychiatrists would have a field day; they'd subject him to all kinds of tests and torments, they'd pump him full of antipsychotic drugs, the agency would annul the adoption and the Blanes would crow vindication. *They'd take him away.* Her boy.

And yet, this bizarre mark could always be a coincidence. By itself, it was only suggestive, not conclusive. In fact, as evidence it could be quite misleading. She wouldn't be thanked for misleading the police. No, best to keep her suspicions to herself. Leave it to Scott to make a firm identification, and face the problems then. Even so, in the meantime, something had to be done. What if Adam were to try it again?

She drove for a while in silence. As they reached the four-way stop by the shopping plaza, she took a right. Sandy looked across in puzzlement.

"Where are we going?" she asked.

"To buy window locks."

"What on earth for?" cried the girl.

"You know as well as I do he can climb out when he wants to."

"But it poured last night! If he'd done it, there'd be

mud all over the place. And there wasn't: I looked. Anyway, Adam wouldn't hurt a fly. Except in self-defense.''

She pulled up outside the Grand Union and cast her daughter a long, serious look. She knew what had to be done and she sought for the right way to present it. She took the girl's hand.

"Sandy, listen," she began. "You and I know it wasn't Adam. But until Scott clears him, no one will believe us. Everyone will think he did it. In revenge. Tit for tat. Scott's friends might well try and settle the score. Adam needs to be kept in at night for his own sake. Out of harm's way. In the daytime there's always one or the other of us to look after him. But not all night long. If he's allowed to go out on his own as I'm afraid he does, he'll be asking for trouble. Believe me, darling. It's for his own good."

Slowly Sandy's manner eased and she gave a small, grudging nod.

"I still don't think it's right," she said. "He trusts us. We should trust him."

Julia squeezed her hand reassuringly.

"Come along, angel. The sooner we're through, the sooner we're home."

•

Max hurried over after receiving Julia's call. She arrived to find a patrol car in the drive and a burly, corn-haired cop prowling around outside the house. Julia and Sandy had already left for the hospital, and he wanted to take the opportunity to ask Adam a few questions. Adam, he told her frankly, was the prime suspect. Herbert Blane was a big shot in the county with powerful connections, and he'd got it into his head that the boy was the culprit. He certainly had the motive and the opportunity, but there was no hard evidence. Any footprints had been washed away by the rain, and neither the weapon that had dealt the stunning blow to the victim's temple nor whatever implement had been used to lacerate his back had been recovered. Whoever it was possessed considerable strength to string a young man weighing a good one hundred and fifty pounds up by his heels like that, a strength he himself thought was way beyond the capabilities of a twelve-year-old boy. Still, the forensic tests would tell. Plus, of course, Scott's testimony when they could get it.

Max showed the officer into the playroom and left him with Adam. From the corridor she could hear the man trying to get sense out of him, repeating his questions over and over again with increasing frustration. "Did you go out at all last night? Were you in your room all the time? What time did you go to bed? Hell, kid, don't you have a tongue?"

She smothered a grim smile and slowly, deep in thought, wound her way upstairs. Maybe she would find some answers in his room. Her knowledge of his physique told her that it could easily have been his doing, and in her guts she knew it was, but she tried to remain scientific and not jump to conclusions. She hoped to God that evidence would remain circumstantial and the whole affair would blow over. Anything at all that focused the spotlight on Adam was dangerously unwelcome.

She went down the corridor to the spare room which was serving as Adam's bedroom while the repairs to the attic were being finished. She stepped inside and went over to examine the window. The catch was closed, but he could easily have shut it on his return. She threw up the sash and peered out. Her eye fell upon a tendril of creeper crushed against the clapboard in a way exactly consistent with someone climbing out. She dismissed the evidence: Adam, she knew, was in the habit of climbing out at night, and nothing here proved he hadn't damaged the creeper on some previous excursion.

As she took a step backward, however, she trod on something hard and lumpy. In the pocket of his jeans, lying on the floor. She bent down. The knees of the pants bore green marks, clearly from the bark of a tree—but Adam wasn't in the habit of climbing trees. Then, dreading what she'd find, she slid her hand into the pocket. Buried among a wadding of moss were three perfectly round white stones. From the other pocket she recovered a stretch of cloth that she recognized as the sling she'd seen that day at the hunting shack. So here was the missing weapon.

Instantly she slid the damning evidence into her pocket and, casting a final glance around the room, hurried back downstairs. As she passed the playroom she recalled the officer's words: *the forensic tests will tell. Plus, of course, Scott's own testimony.* Those were risks she couldn't cover; this was one she could. She slipped swiftly out of the back door and, controlling her pace, strolled past the pool and down the slope to the edge of the river where she reached into her pocket and one by one sent the small pebbles skimming across the glistening water.

•

Sandy tapped on Adam's door and let herself in. He was sitting on the floor with his face pressed close to the television screen. A sitcom was showing, but as always he seemed to be looking at it rather than actually watching

it. Above the sound of canned laughter she could hear
the tinny *tish, tish* of a disco beat coming from the stereo
earphones slung around his neck. He had his back to the
window. The night was warm and the window was open
a couple of inches—now its fullest extent since the decorators had fitted the stops.

"I brought you a drink," she said.

He took the beaker of juice with a short grunt and
turned back to the television. She sat down on the carpet
beside him and, wrapping her arms around her knees,
pretended to watch the program. Out of the corner of
her eye she observed him. She'd never seen such a look
of profound sorrow before. Instinctively, she put her arms
around him and drew him toward her. Slowly his rigid
body unlocked and softened into the embrace. Keeping
his gaze fixed on the screen, he gently laid his head on
her shoulder and let out a tremulous sigh.

"I know it wasn't you," she whispered. "I'll stick up
for you."

•

An underlying tension spread throughout the household. News came from the hospital that Scott was off the
danger list. He'd come around briefly and told the police
that he hadn't had a chance to get a glimpse of his as-
sailant. But the Blanes weren't leaving it there. Julia wrestled with the rights and wrongs of keeping her evidence
to herself. She couldn't contemplate delivering Adam up
for punishment, but she'd only feel justified if she made
a renewed effort to get to the bottom of it all, to understand *why* he had done it. If they could be sure nothing
like it would happen again, then she felt it was legitimate
to keep quiet. Cure was far better than correction. It

meant taking up the analysis again, however. There was no other choice.

On the Monday, with her approval, Max started her tests again. She persisted for several days, but it soon became clear that she wasn't getting any results. Adam seemed distracted, lost in a world of his own. He couldn't be made to concentrate for any workable length of time, and however patient Max tried to remain, this inevitably led to tantrums. Julia couldn't shake off a worrying sense, too, that something further was already brewing. It manifested itself in a host of small ways. At the start of every session, for instance, he'd be set a free-association drawing exercise; hitherto these had been random pictures of houses and cars, even once or twice that bison-like animal like something from one of Sam's cave-painting books, but now he only drew one thing, and always the same— a moon surrounded by stars—and she couldn't help noticing that while the constellation of the stars stayed fixedly the same, each day the moon grew one degree fuller.

That act of violence shook her very conception of Adam himself. Was this really the doing of an innocent child of nature? Was he merely reacting in that immediate, instinctual way of his, retaliating for an injury with a primitive, Biblical eye-for-an-eye response? Or was the degree of the violence really quite excessive, even gratuitous? Couldn't one see an ideological motive behind the bizarre symbolism of the cutting? Was he, in fact, already corrupted? These questions burned constantly in her mind. Twice she'd been on the point of opening up to Max, desperate for an answer, but each time she'd held back. Max was a friend, a close friend even, but she couldn't be sure how she'd react if her loyalties were put to the test. In the final analysis, where *did* Max's loyalties lie?

Adam wasn't her son, her responsibility, her problem.

Towards the end of the week, she decided she had no choice but to confront the issue. It was late afternoon, and she was seeing Max off to her car. Max had the trunk open and was rearranging some electronic equipment to make room for her briefcase.

"That looks serious stuff," Julia remarked, seeking an approach.

"My *real* work, the kind that pays the bills." Max smiled to suggest no barb was intended. "It's a new radio-tagging device. I've got to check it before we can use it in the field."

Julia stirred the gravel with her toe.

"I know these past days haven't been very productive," she began, "but I would like to feel we're getting warm."

"Sure, the picture's building up."

"I mean, I wish we could say something, anything, with certainty. The poor boy's looking so despondent. I even wonder if it's right to keep him cooped up at night. I caught him the other night trying to break the locks. He was frantic. If he starts to feel trapped . . ." She trailed off. "On the other hand, it's too dangerous to let him loose."

"Dangerous?"

"I mean dangerous for him." She drew a deep breath and corrected herself. "No, I don't. I mean he could do something bad, something terrible, to someone else."

"Someone *else*?"

"Let's be frank, Max. With all you know about Adam, you must admit that everything points to him as responsible for what happened to Scott."

"It had occurred to me, Julia."

"Well," she went on briskly. "I think we should work on the basis that it *was* him and just hope we're proved wrong."

Max considered her carefully.

"What about the forensic tests? How tricky is this man Blane?"

"He and Sam used to get on fine. Played golf, sat on charity fund-raising committees together, that kind of thing. Since Sam went, he's changed his tune. I think he'd do a lot to see the back of us. I wouldn't put it past him to get Scott to change his evidence." She paused. "I'm telling you this in confidence, as a friend. A friend of Adam's, too, with his best interests at heart."

"I know, and I appreciate it. I share your suspicions, Julia. And I wouldn't want to see him taken away any more than you. I've gotten kind of close to the case."

"Close to Adam, you mean," Julia corrected her mildly, then gave a self-deprecating smile. "That's the trouble. One can't be objective about one's own child. The question now is, what shall we do?"

"Nothing."

"Nothing?"

Max slammed the lid of the trunk to emphasize her conviction.

"We just go on as we are. No changing course." She climbed into the car. "I'm off in the morning on this field trip. I'll call you Monday when I get back. We'll pick it up then, okay? And we'll see if we can pull it all together." She reached out and pressed Julia's arm. "Don't worry. Just take it easy. We'll get there. Believe me."

Julia watched as the car headed off down the drive. She felt a great weight lifted off her shoulders. She'd confessed her worst fears and found Max already there and on line. Of course Max had her own angle, and that was fine so long as it worked to Adam's benefit. As she turned toward the house, she caught a glimpse of the boy's face at the window, staring out at the sky, his deep-set dark eyes so lost and vulnerable. They'd sort this thing out between them, at home.

•

Adam kept watch all that night. Crouched unstirring beneath the window, he peered out into the sky. His gaze followed the large yolk of the moon as it rose over the treetops and gradually veered around to the west until it slipped from sight behind the eaves. He watched the twilight grading into ever-deepening darkness, and he waited with diminishing hope through that indefinable moment in the early hours when the cycle of the night passes its turning point and the darkness begins to ebb once again before the oncoming dawn. The first bird had started up its song and the dawn star was brightening when he finally stirred.

He uncoiled and stretched, then he went to open the window. It wouldn't move. He stretched his arm through the gap up to the shoulder, but the stops prevented the sash opening more than a few inches. With a frustrated stutter, he pulled back and cast around him.

He had to get out.

He padded over to the door and slipped out into the corridor. There he hesitated, listening. The house was quite silent. He tiptoed up the narrow wooden stairs to the attic and let himself into his old room. The smell of charred wood and scorched plastic lingered behind the odor of fresh paint. Through the putty-smeared window filtered the tentative pallor of dawn. Even as he reached to open it he saw there, too, the small bright metal stops set fast in the frame. He thrust it open its full few inches. Heady summer night scents flooded in through the narrow aperture. With a thwarted cry he turned and retraced his steps down the stairs.

The plate-glass windows in the living room were sealed. The windows in the kitchen and in the study were locked. A bolt secured the sash in the playroom. He tried the back door, then the front. He was growing frantic. He prowled from room to room, pulling at windows and wrenching at doors. As he blundered through the hall, he swept Julia's purse off the table. It fell onto the tiled floor with a muffled *clink*. Instantly he spun around. Within a second he'd opened the bag and had the keys in his hand. A low gurgle passed his lips. He knew about keys.

He slipped unseen out across the grass, through the woods and onto the road. A paperboy caught a glimpse of a stocky figure cutting across the front yard of one of the older mansions in the row, before losing it behind the garages. Later, a patrol car would report sighting a kid out jogging who answered to the boy's description, crossing a disused car lot behind the shopping mall and heading toward the edge of town, beyond which there was little other than a couple of antique shops and the cemetery before the saw-mill and the forest itself; but at the time the patrolman on duty thought nothing special of it and continued on his way without a second glance.

Dawn was breaking fast now, and Adam found it hard to keep to a straight line without the risk of being seen. He had to skirt open spaces and hug close to buildings and fences, and before long he'd begun to lose his sense of direction. But he managed to reach his destination and scale the wall unseen. The roads were filling with the first commuters and it was already light enough to see trucks on the distant highway. A plane soared high overhead, scoring a trail in the brightening sky, and in the distance came the faint whine of a high-speed saw. He melted into the trees at the edge and, burrowing out a nest for himself in the undergrowth, settled down to wait for dusk.

•

Julia slept badly, troubled by nightmares. Shortly after six, she slipped on her dressing gown and went downstairs to the kitchen to make a cup of tea and take an aspirin. Dimly she registered the room felt strangely cold and drafty. When she'd gone into the hall to fetch the tablets from her purse she found the front door swinging ajar in the early morning breeze and the contents of her bag lying strewn across the tiled floor, the keys gone.

Instantly she understood. She flung the door open and started down the front steps. She called Adam's name, but the trees returned her cry. She hobbled painfully over the sharp gravel and broke into a run across the dewy grass toward his small stone hutch. No sign of him there. She looked about her. He could be anywhere. In her heart she feared that this time he would never come back.

Slowly she retraced her steps to the house. She'd been foolish to think of incarcerating him. She should have brought the old blanket he liked to sleep on into her own room instead and kept an eye on him herself. If she was going to lock the house up, too, she should at least have hidden the keys properly. What would the police make of it? A boy under suspicion of attempted homicide goes missing? A clear confession of guilt.

Once indoors, she checked all the rooms, just in case

she'd been over-hasty, but he had indeed fled. She raised
Sandy and got her to look in the woods and by the river,
and later in the morning she herself drove to the disused
quarry a few miles away and searched the empty sheds
and the abandoned workings, but without success. Back
home, almost as a matter of routine, she left a message
on Max's answering machine reporting the news, then
she went about her daily business as normally as she
could. This had happened before, and she tried to tell
herself there was no cause for special anxiety. During the
afternoon, Sandy found the front-door keys in the grass
at the base of the flagpole, and from that they deduced
roughly the direction the boy had taken. But that only
served to revive her worries for, far from taking to the
woods and the wilds as before, Adam had evidently been
heading for town.

•

Max had worked late each night that week in an attempt to catch up on the work she'd been neglecting. Project Adam was reaching a critical phase, and she'd taken a
tactical decision to appease Gerald, her head of Department, for the time being and so avoid trouble in the labs
until she was ready to move on her own front. As a gesture
of cooperation, she'd agreed to join one of her colleagues
on Project Noah, a zoologist working at Bronx Zoo, on a
weekend exercise to test a new lightweight radio ankle-
band which had been developed in the Department of Radiotronics at MIT. The plan was to test the device in the
wild, using deer as being the closest local alternative to gazelles, and a team of two was needed to track, stun-dart
and fit the bands. She'd arranged to meet the zoologist
that Saturday evening at a hunting lodge deep in the Cats-

kill mountains, about four hours' drive west of Boston; they would set out the following dawn and find two specimens, one of each sex, and fit them each with the new ankle-band tags. She would then return home, leaving her colleague on the ground to track the deer's movements using a normal radio receiver. These tagging devices were the latest in a new fashion for armchair zoology: they could even be monitored by satellite and relayed to the researcher in the comfort of his laboratory. Max, however, belonged to the old school; she was a field worker and believed in on-the-ground tracking.

She spent the full Saturday morning at the labs filing a carefully couched report for Gerald on his electronic mail system, and early in the afternoon she drove around to the Department of Zoology to collect the stun-dart rifle she'd arranged to borrow. Finally, in the early afternoon, she went back to her apartment to pack a holdall and prepare for the short expedition. She was already concerned about being away from Adam for just the weekend, but when she received Julia's message something told her that this crisis was unlike the others. This time Adam's disappearance was really serious. By a lucky chance, she caught the zoologist just as he was leaving and, pleading sudden illness, managed to postpone the exercise to another weekend. Then she hurried to her car and headed out of the city on the familiar route to Lexington.

•

Max left Julia busying herself with the roses and strolled down toward the river. She found Sandy sitting on the bank, dangling her feet over the cutaway edge and lost in her own thoughts. She sat down beside her and let the silence lengthen. The air was syrupy with early summer pollens, and she felt a numbing glaze of timelessness hanging over everything. The river was low and its chatter softer than usual, and idly she picked out a path of dry stepping-stones across to the other side. She glanced at Sandy; the girl's face wore a thoughtful frown. She followed her gaze to a clump of stunted wild irises sprouting precariously from a tangle of sedge caught in the rocks a few feet away. The next spate would wash them away.

Sandy finally let out a despairing sigh.

"What's the *point* of it all?" she said. "All that blind, desperate push to do better, reproduce more, survive longer. It's so wasteful."

"You're right about that," agreed Max gently. "Mother Nature can be really profligate. See that iris there? It's got more chromosomes in each cell there than a blue whale. We ourselves probably still possess the blueprint for making a tail, maybe gills too. Thank goodness they don't get expressed."

Sandy smiled briefly, but soon her frown returned.

"Why does it have to be such a struggle, though? Why can't everything reach some kind of balance and then stay in its place?"

"Nothing remains constant, Sandy. It's all in flux. That's the rule of the universe. But the system is built to cope with change. It *expects* change." She plucked a stem of vetch from the grass beside her. "This particular flower here won't seed now, but the species won't die out because of that. Surplus is built in. The same applies to us, too."

"*Nobody* is surplus!" cried Sandy. "Everybody deserves to be treated as equally special, even if they seem like a misfit."

"I was talking on a species level. On an individual

level, I agree, everyone is equally important." She paused, before adding casually, "And that goes for you and me. And Adam."

Sandy turned to her with eyes blazing.

"Well, I wish more people thought so! No wonder he's run away. He's been frightened off. He even gets punished for things he didn't do. I *told* Mom it was stupid to lock the place up. She tried to explain that it was for his own good, but *he* didn't see it that way. And now look what's happened. It's obvious what everyone will think. Poor Adam. It looks as if he's headed into town. He might survive in the woods, but not there. He'll get hungry and steal something, then he'll get caught and that'll be it. For good." Her blue eyes were now filled with despair. "I've been trying to work it out. Last time he ran away, after the fire, I thought it out. I tried to figure out his motivation. I think I got it right."

Max hesitated. An idea was taking root.

"Remind me about the fire, Sandy. Who actually discovered him?"

"This doesn't have anything to do with the fire."

"Just tell me."

"Well, Scott was the first one into the room."

"So, Scott disturbed him? Scott *thwarted* him?"

"What are you driving at? Adam didn't do that terrible thing to Scott." She was growing upset. "I wish everyone would stop trying to find reasons to pin the blame on him. I could give you a dozen reasons why it wasn't him."

"I'm not saying it was, Sandy." She swallowed. The truth was dawning on her now: Scott had interrupted Adam in the performance of his ritual and he'd paid the price. "But let's just suppose for a moment," she continued. "We know Adam thinks very literally. He tries to burn Sam's effigy. You show him a grave. You demonstrate to him that Sam is dead and buried. May he should be dead and *cremated*."

"You're playing with words."

"With ideas. Ideas of this kind are very potent in the primitive mind. After all, he didn't try to *bury* the photographs and clothes, did he?"

"I don't know where that gets us," responded the girl shortly. "It doesn't explain why he's run off or where he's gone. I think it's something to do with feeling rejected. He's not trusted at home and he's ostracized outside. All because he's different and doesn't fit in."

She had touched a critical nerve. Was Adam rejected because, at some silent, unconscious level, people recognized he was of a different kind? Very probably. Max would have liked to explore the girl's idea further, but there was a more immediate issue to deal with. Adam had to be found. And now she had the vital clue.

She let the conversation trail on for a reasonable while, then she rose and, with a few words of comfort, left. She retraced her steps up the slope to the house. Believing she had a four-hour drive into the mountains ahead, Julia didn't try and press her to stay. Max refrained from mentioning that she'd canceled the field trip; she wanted to be free to investigate her hunch as she pleased. The sun was already dipping below the crowns of the trees when she said goodbye and set off. At the end of the drive, she pulled up and glanced in the mirror to check she couldn't be seen from the house. Then, instead of taking the road to the highway, she took a right and headed in the direction of town.

18

○

THE TOWN WAS ALREADY SETTLING INTO ITS GENTLE
evening mode. On the main street, realtors and antique
dealers were shutting up shop and heading to their country clubs for the cocktail hour, and from the railroad station flowed a steady stream of sedans bearing commuters
with flushed faces and loosened ties to the white mansions
in the leafy residential avenues. Here and there, outside
a soda bar or a movie theater, teenage kids loafed in
small groups, the boys sporting beach shorts and the girls
in leopard-print denims, but otherwise the town was gradually draining of life. As she drove through the emptying
streets, Max felt a disturbing sense of incongruity. All
about her a typical evening in a quiet New England town
was unfolding, with all its citizens going about their affairs
secure in the known order of things, while at the same
time, somewhere in hiding in this very town, lurked a
strange, alien child whose existence posed unanswerable
questions to challenge that familiar order, a boy who came
from a different world, a different epoch, a different *genus*,
and yet was in truth as much an heir to all this as any of

the rest of this comfortable, self-satisfied town.

She'd been this way only once before, and that had been in the depths of winter, with the trees bare and the snow ploughed in steep banks at the roadside. Twice she mistook her way, but finally she came to a small roadsign, half concealed by a fulsome maple, that pointed her toward the cemetery.

The main cemetery gates were locked and chained. In the fading light she could see the flicker of a television in the adjacent keeper's lodge. She followed the low brick wall round the side to what appeared to be a service entrance. There she pulled up and got out. The last rays of the sun were already gilding the tips of the cypresses, abandoning the path along the perimeter wall to the cool afterlight. Overhead flew a squabbling drove of starlings in search of roosts, and somewhere in the distance a chain saw coughed and died, and all was silent.

She followed the path up the slope until the wall gave way to a thick yew hedge interlaced by a stout wire-mesh fence. Just at the place where wall joined hedge, however, the fencepost had been bent back to make a narrow gap, evidently where the local kids climbed in and out. With a nervous glance around, she squeezed through, snagging her loose red dress, then headed quickly for the cover of a wooden fence. Behind this stood some heavy-duty gardening equipment and a large pile of grass mowings and dead flowers that gave off the sour, steamy smell of compost. Ahead of her spread the cemetery, a broad, rolling slope of grassland intersected by broad pathways and toothed with gravestones glowing purple-blue in the twilight. Her pulse was beating hard. What if they had security patrols at night? How would she explain herself? What the hell *was* she doing here, anyway? The flaw in her logic was that it made assumptions about *his* logic. What evidence did she have for believing he'd headed here? None at all. Only her hunch. Pretty smart for a scientist.

She decided it was safer to act boldly. Reaching among the discarded flowers for a bunch that looked least wilted, she broke cover and strode purposefully out into the open. Not a soul was about. Far ahead, the white clapboard chapel stood silent and serene; the keeper's lodge lay out of sight behind the walls of the memorial garden. Suddenly she realized she couldn't remember where the grave was, and she was forced to make the chapel her starting-point and work her way from there. A cool evening wind was pressing in from the east, urging the darkness along with it. A shiver of fear prickled her skin as she saw her line of retreat being gradually absorbed into the encroaching shadows. All the pathways looked the same. She felt over-conspicuous, too, in her red dress. Quite suddenly she lost her nerve. She was turning to go back when she caught sight of a movement some distance away in the parallel avenue. She froze. Peering out into the gloaming, she began to make out a bent figure with its back to her, busily digging and scraping. She crept forward and crouched behind a tall gravestone.

It was Adam. He was kneeling beside a grave, bent forward facing the headstone. In both hands he clutched a slate with which he was furiously scraping aside the earth and piling it into a mound on the side.

She was about to start forward when she stopped dead. Through her mind whirled her own words of that very afternoon: *Scott disturbed him . . . Scott thwarted him.* And what had happened to Scott? Her pulse gave a sick lurch. Jesus Christ, she breathed, what are we dealing with here? She couldn't intervene to stop him, but equally she couldn't stand by and watch him robbing Sam's grave.

And then the answer came to her.

•

She had never used the dart rifle before, and despite the numerous times she'd watched Steve and others darting animals in the wild, her hands were trembling badly as she unpacked the lethal-looking weapon from its case in the trunk of her car and selected two tranquilizer darts from their pods in the ammunition tray. The darts had been carefully prepared in advance, for the dose was critical. Too little of the drug, and the animal could escape with the dart embedded in its flesh; too much, and it might not recover. It all depended on the weight and size of the target. How did Adam compare with a stag from the Catskills? She'd have to chance it.

She watched from a point outside herself as she crept back through the gap in the mesh fence, the rifle slung over her shoulder. From afar she observed the figure that was herself stalking like an Indian from grave to grave with grim and steely purpose. It was not the self she knew who crawled on elbows and knees until within range and, lying concealed behind a headstone, took aim, centered the crossed hairs of the sights on a fleshy part of the boy's upper thigh and, with breath held, gently squeezed the trigger.

The report echoed round the open cemetery, scattering roosting birds and whipping her back to earth. The instant the shot rang out there came a sharp cry from Adam. He gave a violent jolt and, half rising to his feet, staggered a few steps forward. He spun round defiantly, then his legs abruptly buckled beneath him and he collapsed with a grunt onto the mound of earth.

Not daring to look around her, she grasped the rifle and hurried over to the unconscious figure. Falling to her knees, she quickly checked his eyes and pulse: she'd never seen any creature go down so fast. He looked all right but very heavily drugged. How long did she have? An hour or two, perhaps more. She eased the dart out of his flesh, causing a small swell of blood to bubble up through his jeans. Slipping the dart into her pocket, she bent to haul him up, but at once fell forwards on top of him: she hadn't reckoned on the dead weight of all that muscle and bone. She tried hoisting him to her shoulders in a fireman's lift, but he was just too heavy. She dragged him by the shoulders a few yards, but realized she wouldn't be able to make it all the way back to the car. Then she remembered seeing a wheelbarrow behind the wooden fence, and in this way she finally managed to trundle him in a wobbling, erratic path back down the avenue and along the grassy slope to the perimeter hedge, where she hauled him through the gap and down the path to the waiting car. There she hoisted him onto the back seat and stowed away the rifle in the trunk, then sank into the front seat, shaking violently in a welter of shock and exhaustion. It was only when she was starting up the car that the full import of what she was doing hit her. And, to compound the felony already committed, she knew she had no intention of turning him in to the police or even taking him back home. Her plan was tantamount to kidnapping.

•

The journey to the hunting shack deep into Worcester County seemed interminable. She drove carefully, keeping rigorously within speed limits. From time to time she glanced anxiously over her shoulder at the inert body slumped over the back seat, afraid he might come round before they'd arrived. As the night grew darker and the roads narrower and as she left the light and other signs of human habitation further behind, she felt a tightening dread in her stomach. Here she was, in the middle of nowhere, with a disturbed boy of inordinate physical strength and dangerously unpredictable temper. She had witnessed what he was capable of doing when provoked. No one had any idea where they were. There wasn't even a phone at the shack. By the time she finally drove up the pebble-strewn track and reached the overgrown wooden lodge, she was shaking so badly that she could barely get the key off the hook in its hiding-place under the eaves or get it to fit in the lock.

She returned to the car to find Adam stirring drowsily. She eased him carefully to a sitting position and coaxed him to his feet. Slowly and painfully, she hobbled him indoors and laid him on a mattress on the wooden floor. The dose must have been very powerful, for no sooner had she got him to lie down, after a brief, bewildered, drug-drunk protest, than he fell into a deep and torpid sleep.

She retired to the bedroom and went to sleep on top of the bed with all her clothes on, leaving a chair propped against the door to give her a few seconds' warning, in case.

o

She slept fitfully, and she fell into an exhausted slumber only when the sky was already growing pale and the first lone birdcall filtered through her open window. She woke gently to a strange, persistent whistling sound and opened her eyes to find Adam kneeling beside her, blowing into her ear. She recoiled instinctively, then realized to her surprise that he was smiling. He handed her a tin cup full of water. It was cold and sweet, and she knew it had come from the mountain stream in the gorge a short distance away. She glanced around the room; the chair was still against the door but the window was wide open. Sunlight poured in, and from her watch she saw it was gone nine. Adam had been up all this time and he'd made no attempt to hurt her or even to escape. Carefully, she handed him back the cup half drunk and gestured for him to finish it. He took it in both hands and drank it back. A broad smile wreathed his strong, prominent features, then it broadened, and he let out a long cascade of laughter. She was puzzled: didn't he associate her with what had happened the previous night? Could he be *so* volatile? Or was his memory so short that he'd actually forgotten what he'd been doing?

Cautiously, not yet trusting his mood, she let him take her by the hand and lead her into the kitchen. There, on a plate of plaited leaves on the floor, lay a pile of raw mushrooms and berries of various kinds, mostly unripe, and beside this a small, squirming tangle of grubworms. Breakfast. He was chattering excitedly now and tugging her to sit down. She swallowed hard: she was going to have to go through with this. Squatting, he picked up a fat white grubworm and offered it to her. It dangled and wriggled in his fingers. Nausea rushed to her throat. With a gesture to suggest such a delicacy should really be his, she selected the safest-looking mushroom she could and, trying to convince herself it was a plain boletus from the fields and not some amanita culled from beneath the trees, took a nibble from that instead. He let out a silvery peal of laughter and pointedly dropped the grub down his throat. She gave a convulsive shudder and squeezed her eyes shut. His laughter rose. It was a *game*.

Never could she have foreseen his reaction to this new environment. It was as if he rightly belonged here, in the forests and mountains. Any notion of blaming her for dragging him away from the cemetery—if, indeed, he made the connection—seemed forgotten in his new-found happiness. He had found a place that felt like home.

Astonished that such a transition could be so rapid and intrigued to see how far it went, she tried him out on various things he'd grown familiar with in those past months. She played some Whitney Houston on her car stereo, she offered him an old college basketball sweat-shirt of her own, and later she dug out a tin of corned beef and some semi-stale crackers from the larder, but he showed no interest in these. By midday he had dis-carded his tee-shirt and track shoes, and from then on went about just in boxer shorts. Were his responses *so* immediate that the only reality for him was the absolute present? She wondered if he thought about Julia and Sandy, but when at one point she mentioned Julia's name, such a threatened, disorientated look came over his features that she dropped that line. And yet, what did she have to offer him instead? When was she going to return him—indeed, *was* she going to? She didn't know: for the moment she, too, was living moment by moment.

He went off exploring on his own, for shorter or longer periods, but he never came back without some new find, whether just a bird's tail-feather or, as toward the end of the afternoon, a live hedgehog. He carried this prickly living ball in a pouch made from an old sack and ceremoniously presented it to her. After appropriate noises of appreciation, she handed it back and watched with mounting unease as he hung the pouch safely from a branch and set about preparing a thick paste of brown clay; he was evidently going to bake it whole, prickles and all, in the way of the gypsies. She couldn't stand by while he killed and cooked the creature, but at the same time she dared not intervene to stop him. Instead, being without any provisions to her own taste, she took a risk and drove to the small store that lay a few miles away down the mountain to stock up with the basics of civilized life—bread, milk, coffee, beer, vodka, juice, tacos, burgers, fruit. When she returned she found he'd made a fire in a small pit in the ground, laid the hedgehog in its clay cladding in this and then covered the whole with earth and leaves. The meal, a New England clambake, à la Neanderthal, was ready at sundown. When the moment came, Adam dug away the earth and broke open the clay casing. It came away with spines and skin and all, leaving the naked cooked flesh like a rolled turkey breast. She drank a large vodka to steel herself. The meat was soft and tender, however, with the color of hare and the flavor of a gamebird. Washed down with beer and buried in bread, she had to admit it was really quite palatable.

They sat round a campfire until it became dark and chilly and she could see he was growing restive. Night, she knew, was the time he came alive. Here he would be free to roam as he pleased. All the while, however, she remained watchful and took care not to overstep the bounds. Over the course of one short day, he seemed already to be reverting to his natural state. That would present its own set of unfamiliar dangers. Besides, she didn't quite trust such a rapid transformation, recognizing that it could change back again just as fast. Even so, she sensed that he really felt he belonged here. *He's in his natural element here*, she recalled saying to Sandy that time she'd brought them both up to the shack. And then, ever present in the back of her mind, was the thought of what this could mean for her work. She had a mass of physiological data on him and stacks of behavioral material on how he related and reacted to the alien cultural environment of middle-class North America. But the most fascinating question still remained unanswered: how did he really live among his *own* people, back home in the remote Caucasus? Now, here was a place as close to the wilds as anyone could reasonably get in modern America. Could there ever be a better opportunity to study him in his natural state?

•

William Cray stared out of the airplane window. The day was so clear that he could almost count the tiny toy yachts that lay harbored in the reefs of Martha's Vineyard, and as the plane crossed the narrow strand into Cape Cod bay and wove its way along the coastline by Plymouth and Kingston, he fancied he could see the faint, mauve photochemical haze in the distance that marked the city of Boston.

He returned to his thoughts with a frown. This was a crisis. Adam had been missing for four days now. Julia had called him with the news even before he'd picked it up from the transcripts. She was extremely worried and convinced the boy had run off for good. She'd been on the very point of finally alerting the police, but he'd managed to persuade her to hold off for a while yet. He'd had enough trouble with the county police already, and he'd had to bring Eliot Lovejoy in on it. Through contacts of Eliot's in the Massachusetts State forensic department he'd learned that the tests definitively linked Adam with the attack on the Blane kid, and he'd had to spend the last two days calling in cards at a very high level to get the damning evidence spiked. The boy's disappearance now would only be seen as an admission of guilt. Should Blane senior find a way of bringing the case to court, there'd be the devil's own job to get Adam off that. He'd end up in a state center for juvenile offenders under tight official control, and all hope of continuing the experiment would be irretrievably lost.

The crisis gave him less and less justification for forestalling Eliot, too. Only the previous day, the man had stormed into his office, insisting that the experiment could no longer be conducted in the risky and unreliable conditions of a private household and demanding that the boy be located at once and brought along to the Center. An acrimonious dispute had ensued, which served only to bring out bitterly their fundamental differences. The Center, of which Eliot Lovejoy was Director, had been set up and funded by the Foundation to study the biological basis of human behavior. Genes controlled behavior: control the genes, and you controlled behavior. They both agreed on this principle, but fell out over its applications. Lovejoy was a biologist, not a social reformer. He was only interested in the scientific work itself, not its end-uses. Cray himself, however, along with a small number of like-minded men—Sam Wendell among them—was interested in practical applications in social engineering. Control behavior, and you could build a better society. What they could learn from observing Adam in a real social situation was far more valuable than anything gleaned from the artificial environment of the laboratory. Lovejoy had left the meeting angry and dissatisfied, and Cray knew he wouldn't be able to stand up to the pressure much longer.

It was vital to find the boy. He'd been gone for four days. Now, Cray happened to know that Maxine Fitzgerald had been absent for just the same time, too. He also happened to know—for he'd started taking a close interest in the young woman's movements—that she had cancelled the field trip at the last minute. No one knew where she was, though he'd get an update from her head of Department, Gerald Reihart, when he met him in an hour's time. He'd set up the meeting before this business had blown up. His plan was to offer the Department money from Foundation funds to set up a small and highly confidential unit, specifying Max to head it up. Its remit would be couched in such a way as to conceal its true scope, but the subject in question was Adam. He'd considered offering Max a job at the Center direct, but he knew she'd never stomach the kind of work that went on there. No, the only way to harness her talents and exploit her special rapport with Adam was to use her within her existing set-up. The project would be strictly classified, and he'd structure the reporting system so that not even Reihart knew what she was up to.

But now it looked as if she was involved in Adam's disappearance. How much had she worked out? Had she made her move before he'd got to her? He should have nailed her a whole lot earlier. He closed his eyes as the plane began its descent into Boston and turned his mind to more pleasant thoughts. He'd fixed a date with Julia that evening. He thought of her smile, her eyes, her scent, and imagined the shape and feel of her naked body. He felt weary, hounded, and—damn the consequences—he yearned for the comfort of her embrace.

•

Over the days that followed their arrival at the shack, Max found herself growing increasingly fond of Adam. Almost despite herself, she began to see him as a child in need of love, respect and care, rather than the scientific opportunity he had come to represent. By degrees, he was slowly winning her heart.

The forest and mountains were his natural habitat, and he flowered here in a way he never had in the mannered, urban confines of Lexington. She was amazed to see how quickly he shed the effects of Julia's development program, which, as Sandy had rightly perceived, had been aimed at turning his simple wants into fundamental needs. The moment he stopped being able to fend for himself independently, he was trapped. But she needn't have feared. Here, in the semi-wild, he reverted perfectly readily to his natural state. He roamed around semi-naked; he slept in a small hut he'd made at the back by re-arranging the wood-stack; he refused Coke and burgers and instead he drank water and ate berries, wild mushrooms, green walnuts and unripe chestnuts, using his hands rather than a knife and fork, and he hunted for his meat, mostly birds and rabbits, which he liked to eat charred black on the outside and raw in the center. Apart from a lingering fondness for candy, the only food he liked from the store down the mountain was potatoes, which he threw into the ashes of the fire until the skins were burnt to carbon. He reverted, too, to his old habit of hoarding food. One evening, she was startled to see him on his knees in the woods, scratching a hole in the ground, and for a terrible moment her mind flashed back to the cemetery and she saw the specter of that unsatiated primordial drive surfacing again, but when later she went to investigate, she found he'd merely been burying a cache of elderberries and acorn buds, all carefully wrapped in protective layers of maple leaves.

He was a creature perfectly adapted to his environment and, perhaps in that above all, he won her admiration. He moved through the woods as silently as a shadow, alert to the smallest sound. From time to time, he'd freeze rock-still to scent the breeze or read the call of a bird. He seemed to possess an extraordinary empathy with his fellow creatures, too. He even killed with a kind of respect, and only ever to satisfy his needs, never gratuitously or excessively. She had the feeling that he was all of one piece with the natural world about him, and she found herself filled with respect for this supremely adaptive human creature.

She felt filled with pity and sorrow, too. However superior this was to his urban life, it was still not his own proper home. However much she befriended him, and even loved him, he was fundamentally alone. He assuredly had a family back where he came from, a father and mother, maybe sisters and brothers, too. But here he was on his own, bereft of others of his kind. He was like one of her gazelles, captured in the wild and incarcerated in a zoo—yet with one major difference: she could re-engineer her gazelles and return them to their habitats. Whether in human society or here at large in the wild, Adam was condemned to remain in an alien and essentially friendless world. The tragedy of his state only really struck her when, late one night, she went round to the wood-stack at the back of the shack to check he was all right and found him staring into the starry sky, uttering soft, plaintive cries with a look of such desperate yearning on his young face that she sank to the ground beside him and hugged the poor, homesick boy with all the sorrow and compassion in her heart.

In the daytime, however, he was invariably bright and lively, full of innocent high jinks and boyish tricks. His silvery laugh from the yard filled her with joy, and there were times when some prank of his would reduce her to tears of laughter. He loved being tickled, for instance, and would lie on the ground and make her drive him to frenzies of giggles, dragging her hand back each time she tried to stop, until she could withstand his infectious laugh no longer and collapsed beside him herself in equal paroxysms of mirth.

Towards the end of the week, she decided this could not go on for ever. Adam might live in his immediate paradise, but she lived in the real outer world. This was her *work*: she had to turn the experience to useful account. She decided to make a trip back to Boston. She'd check in at the labs and fetch back various necessary pieces of equipment—a tape recorder, a video camera and her desktop computer—and she'd settle down to keep a proper record of each day.

She chose the Saturday, reckoning the labs would be quietest then, and in the middle of the morning she bade farewell to Adam, telling him she'd be back by dusk. Her feelings were in turmoil. Over that short space of time together, she had grown very close to him. Yet she knew she couldn't hide him away forever. Sooner or later, and certainly when eventually she published her work, she'd have to declare him. What would his life become then? Would he ever have a moment's peace and solitude? She felt sorry for the hurt she was causing the others who loved him, too; she'd called Julia twice and was left feeling wrung out by the bravely concealed pain in the woman's voice. And yet, she always came back to the same point: what was all that compared with the importance of the work itself? But there again, was it right to use Adam like this? He was not a laboratory animal. He was not a feral child, a freak oddity way off the end of the human scale. He wasn't like Victor, the wild boy of Aveyron, or Genie, that Californian girl discovered at fourteen confined in a small room and tied to a potty chair since the age of twenty months. He was a fully formed, normal member of the human race, the genus *homo*, only he belonged to a different branch. Within his own species he was completely normal. He had the full rights of a full human.

He must have sensed the inner conflict in her mood, for when she left he clung to her in a strange, intense embrace, and as she drove off down the rocky path, she looked back to see his solitary, forlorn figure staring after her from the porch of the empty house.

•

She was at the computer terminal when she heard a footstep in the corridor and, a moment later, the lab door opened. Her heart sank. Gerald was the very man she wanted to avoid. A sly smile spread across his square, freckled face and he took a step into the room. He was dressed for golf, with a spotted cravat and a diamond-check jersey, and his ginger hair lay carefully sleeked back in ripples. He perched on the edge of her desk and his eye flicked over her work. She snapped her notebook shut and cleared the computer screen. His smile didn't falter.

"Working weekends? Catching up, huh?" He picked up a folder and glanced at the coded title. She took it back with a glare. He raised an eyebrow in mock reproof and tut-tutted. "Writing up your field test?" He held up his hand. "Don't say anything. I know you cancelled."

"Something came up. You'll get your report."

"Like tomorrow?"

"Like one day. Give me a break, Gerald."

"You want a break? Have I got a break for you!" He drew closer until she could smell his breath freshener. His smile hardened and a gleam entered his eye. "I'm serious, sweetheart. You want to hear?"

With a sigh she pushed back her chair and listened. He spoke with suppressed excitement. He'd received an offer from a "certain source" to fund a high-level, classified research program in behavioral cybernetics, aimed at identifying the genetic regulatory systems that ultimately determined key aspects of human behavior. A separate, autonomous unit would be set up within the Department, and she had been specifically named to head it up. The work was highly sensitive, but highly rewarded too.

"C'mon, Gerald," she replied when he'd finished. "You know that's not my field. I deal strictly with animals. Endangered species."

"Man is an animal, honey," he replied. "And an endangered species."

"You're talking about genetic manipulation for social control."

"The purposes don't concern me."

"They concern *me*. Check out the motives before you take the money."

"Look, Max, we're just here to do the research. That's our function. Leave the application to the politicians."

"I don't believe this! You want to know why I don't work in human genetics? Just that: because I can't be sure what some other Joe will do with the results. That's why I stick to animals. Okay?"

"Very high and moral," he responded, his smile hardening. "Listen, what do you think your own work with these goddamn gazelles is ultimately about? Adding to the sum of knowledge for the hell of it? No: everything we do is about *control*: controlling Nature, controlling our environment, controlling our own selves and our societies." He rose to his feet and faced her. "You think the people funding your work on gene modification really give a damn about whether a bunch of gazelles survive or not, when whole species are disappearing every day? Be real, Max. Sure, it gives everyone a nice taste in the mouth, and it's great for raising funds, but in the end everything has to do with *us*: how can *we* survive in an environment which is changing too fast for our own natural evolution to keep up?"

"I don't see it that way. Nor, I'm sure, does the World Wide Fund for Nature, the National Institutes of Health . . ."

"You don't think? Wise up, Max." He stood up and stabbed a finger at her. "We now control our own evolution. We have stepped outside the whole dumb process of natural selection. We're on the brink of being able to choose what we want to become. We can write our own destiny. And the language is genetics. You'd better believe that's what it's all about. If you can't hack it, you'd better quit the field."

She had stood up, too, in instinctive posture echo.

She fought down her rising anger.

"I'm clearly not the person for your new job," she said finally. "Whoever gave them my name doesn't know me very well."

"Oh, I wouldn't say that," responded Gerald, his cover-all smile returning. "A lot of people are taking a lot of interest in your work, Max."

"My work?" she asked sharply.

"I think you know what I'm referring to."

"My project is on schedule..."

His eyes narrowed. "I'm not entirely blind, you know. I know when my staff is doing non-Department work during Department time. Like certain assay work on hybrids?"

She felt an involuntary flush betray her. Had he got something out of Murray? Murray believed that she was working on a man-chimp chimera. She glanced nervously up at the chemicals cabinet; it appeared untouched. She looked back down quickly, conscious of Gerald's scrutiny.

"Spare time work," she said tightly. "Nothing to do with you."

"Everything in the Department is to do with me," he replied sweetly. He reached out a conciliatory hand towards her. "Forget all that. Look, we're talking money. Serious money. Plus one, maybe two, full-time assistants. Your own lab. Hell, Max, it's a big break."

She looked away, fearful of betraying herself. She had to play for time.

"I'll think about it."

"You do that." He went towards the door, then turned. "Get off your high horse, Max. Come down to earth. I'd hate to see you pass up this chance."

"I'll think it over, Gerald."

•

She stared after him at the closed door, then went over and turned the key in the lock. She hurried back to her desk and riffled through the drawer. Was she imagining it, or were the files in a different order? Surely she'd left the assay plates folded *inside* the computer print-out? She unlocked the chemicals cabinet and reached carefully inside. She could swear things had been disturbed. Or had they?

Who was this "certain source?" The whole project stank. It sounded the kind of business Bernard had said Sam was involved in. "A lot of people are taking a lot of interest in your work, Max." Like who? Gerald himself? How much *did* he know? God, she thought, maybe he's got into my computer files! She remembered when Murray suspected he'd been hacking into his own. She'd re-coded all her accessible files, but what if . . . ?

She hurried back to the terminal and called up the code for Project Adam. The menu was still complete, the files intact. But how could she be sure they hadn't been penetrated, perhaps even copied?

Slowly, methodically, she set about removing the records. She copied the computer files onto her own mini-disks and then erased all record from the mainframe database. She emptied her desk, the filing drawers, the chemicals cabinet, and packed the files into a cardboard carton. She went through Murray's own filing system, too, and eliminated all trace of the differentiation analysis he had run for her. Finally, she went to the annex room that contained the cryostat and unscrewed the clamps that held down the lid of the large stainless-steel drum. Wisps of liquid nitrogen vapor coiled out like smoke. Slipping an asbestos glove on her hand, she raised the rods one by one with a pair of tongs until she'd located the small transparent plastic vial containing the unused serum she'd extracted from the sample of Adam's blood. With a pair of tweezers she removed the orange marker tape and replaced it with another bearing the code *GDD/018/33M*, a regular reference that indicated this belonged to dorcas gazelle number 33, male, modified with chamois genes from batch 18. She slipped it back on the hook at the bottom of the rod next to number 32 and quickly replaced the lid.

Within a few minutes she was hurrying down the back stairs and out through the emergency exit at the rear of the block that led directly to the car park. It took her three journeys to carry down her desktop computer and mini-printer and the large carton of files and data. As she opened the trunk of her car, she saw she'd still got the dart rifle and the radio-tagging equipment. She glanced at her watch: she'd pass by on her way and just hope someone was there to check the stuff in. After that, she'd stop by the apartment to make a few calls and to pick up her camera, tape recorder and a few clothes. And then she'd get back to Adam.

Adam. What the hell *was* she going to do about him?

She had to think ahead. The moment she published her findings, the moment she even submitted her first paper to the *Scientific American* or to *Nature*, the boy would quite simply become, overnight, the hottest scientific property in existence. Everyone would be after a piece of him. It might all break even before then if Gerald had in fact hacked into her files. Even if he hadn't, somehow the whole story was bound to leak. Something like this just couldn't be kept under wraps forever. Maybe

Julia had already reported Adam missing, and before long the police would come looking for him. The fuse was already smoldering on the time-bomb. Wasn't there some way she could save him from the inevitable, while at the same time fulfilling her own ambitions? Did the claims of her career necessarily have to be in conflict with her concern for Adam? There *had* to be a way to reconcile both. A way that would preserve Adam.

She was starting up the car when the perfect idea occurred to her. At the first intersection, instead of turning left to the Department of Zoology to return the equipment, she took a right directly to her apartment, and within fifteen minutes she was on the road heading west back towards the mountains.

•

The night was dark and moonless, the forest black and impenetrable. Occasionally her headlights picked out the form of a bird or a badger, which lingered fleetingly, then vanished. The track was unfamiliar. It grew steadily steeper and rougher, and more than once she swung the car aside to avoid a boulder or a pot-hole, only to scrape the side on a sharp projecting branch. At one point, an overhanging bough struck the windshield with such force that Adam, beside her, let out a sharp cry. She glanced across at the boy; in the light of the headlamps reflected from the pale rocks and the clawing sinews of the tree-roots, his face bore an expression of fear and foreboding. She turned back to the winding track with clenched teeth. She mustn't flinch now.

She had no idea where she was or where she was going, only that she had to get as deep into the mountains and as far away from human habitation as possible. In the back she had packed a small box with some of the provisions he still liked—candy, ginger cookies, popcorn. She'd added a penknife, some fishing-line and wire for making traps and several boxes of matches, as well as his red sweatshirt, jeans and track shoes which he'd discarded earlier, together with various other pieces of survival equipment she knew he wouldn't be needing but which she'd packed because, when all was said and done, he was just a young kid and she couldn't bear to see him go out into the harsh wilds quite unprepared and unprotected.

A lump rose in her throat. She glanced at his wrist on which she'd crimped the radio ankle-band. At least this would keep her in touch with him. He might be far away, but he'd never be lost.

Eventually, as the ground grew steeper and more craggy and the trees gave way to wiry, spiky scrub, she found a small rocky shelf and pulled up. To one side, a cliff rose sheer before her, profiled against a sky only one degree less black; to the other, the land fell away into the pitch dark from which she'd come. The air was sharp and cold, and a restless wind combed the spars and hollows. She took out the box of provisions, then drew him out of the car. She led him some way up a narrow path deeper into the undergrowth, then pressed the box into his hands. His face lengthened, and such a look of sorrow filled his large, dark eyes that briefly she faltered. *Do it quickly*, she told herself. *That way it won't hurt so much*. She drew him to her and closed her arms round him in a quick, strong embrace. Then she turned him round and pointed him towards the wilderness.

"Go now," she whispered.

He turned and let out a small stuttering whimper,

but she pressed him forward.

"Go!" she urged.

He fumbled a few steps forward, then hesitated, wounded and perplexed. She couldn't bear this. Fighting against the tears, she stumbled back to the car and climbed quickly in. Within a moment she was lurching and bouncing this way and that down the rocks and rubble, and once, only once, did she cast a glance back over her shoulder at the small, stocky, bewildered figure of the boy she had deliberately sent back into the wild.

19

○

JULIA DRESSED SWIFTLY, SILENTLY, NOT WANTING TO wake the sleeping figure lying sprawled among the tousled sheets of the large double-bed, and yet reluctantly, too, not wanting to steal away into the night without one last kiss, one final living touch. As she rolled a stocking up her leg, she paused to contemplate his face. Through the half-open door filtered a dim shaft of light from the sitting-room of the hotel suite, casting a warm parchment glow across the bed. With his eyes closed and his features relaxed, he looked so youthful, so vulnerable. As though sensing her gaze, he stirred and, stretching luxuriously, turned face-down into the pillows.

She finished dressing quickly. Whispering a soft word in his ear and brushing his silver hair with a kiss, she turned away and quietly let herself out of the room. As she made her way down the thickly carpeted corridor, in the silence and emptiness of a hotel in the small hours, she felt a twinge of excitement, a small reckless thrill of danger and abandon. The warmth and soreness spreading through her body recalled the love they'd made, reminding her how fine it had been and how badly she'd needed it. And as she crossed the large marble and gilt foyer, conscious of the discreetly knowing eye of the hall porter upon her, she could scarcely suppress a smile of pleasure and satisfaction. She felt renewed, rejuvenated, reconstituted in herself. She could cope with anything.

•

She waited until the school bus had disappeared from sight, then turned her steps back towards the house. Under her arm she carried a clutch of travel agents' brochures from the mail box. They'd remain unopened; the thought of holidays was out of the question until Adam had been found.

He'd been gone for over a week now and the atmosphere at home was like a second bereavement. At first, Sandy had blamed her, but after a day of carping she'd decided to think positively and had set about restoring their spirits. She'd dragged her along to a showing of *Blame it on Rio* in the school theater, insisting that a comedy would take her mind off things; she made them play cards together in the evenings, rather than watch television or read alone, and generally she strove to keep up a brave front of normality. Julia responded in kind, though no amount of contrived gaiety could cover up the long, laden silences that fell in between. The holiday brochures had been Sandy's idea, too: her summer semester was shortly coming to an end, and everyone at school was making plans for the vacation. But would theirs be a trip to Disneyland for three or a tour of northern Italy for two?

Her hopes and fears varied with her mood. One minute she would feel optimistic and tell herself he'd be all right: he was a survivor, used to living rough and fending for himself. The next, her spirits would fall and she'd imagine he'd had an accident, hit by a truck or beaten up or even shot for trespassing, and he was lying bleeding in some culvert or comatose in some hospital, and no one knew who he was or where he belonged. Something would happen to give her a flash of hope, only to dash it a moment later. One morning, for instance, she found the food she religiously left out by the back door each night had been nibbled away, but later just a few yards away she found the unmistakable signs of a badger.

Time and again, she was on the point of calling the police, but she held back. This was a card to play only as a last resort. She called Max's number constantly, but she never got a reply. No one at the Department had seen her recently, either. A sneaking suspicion crept into her mind: wasn't it rather a coincidence that both were missing at the same time? Then, eventually, Max called from somewhere deep in the Catskills—the line was terrible—and Julia berated herself for imagining anything more sinister than the simple truth that Max had been held up on her field trip.

But thank God for William. He was always there to give support and help. She'd left it a few days before calling him, not wanting to upset him unnecessarily in case Adam had just wandered off on one of his short jaunts. But in the end she'd had to turn to him. With his usual concern, he'd jumped on a plane and come up. They'd had a wonderful evening—a wonderful *night*— and he'd done all he could to calm her anxieties. He'd gone a bit overboard at dinner, with some perfectly far-fetched notion that Adam might have formed some strange attachment to Max and gone off looking for her. Was there anywhere that the boy might have headed for? The only place she could think of was the old hunting lodge Max had once taken the two children to, but that was far away, in the depths of Worcester County, miles from anywhere. William had seized upon this and made her promise to ask Sandy if she could remember anything to locate it. She smiled to herself. It was very sweet of him, but way off-beam. He was clutching at straws out of a desire to make her feel better.

She made herself a cup of coffee, tasted it and pushed it away undrunk. She sat down at the study desk to pay some bills, but couldn't wrap her mind around the task. She rearranged the periodicals on the side-table, fanning them out just as Sam used to keep them; although she'd cancelled the subscription, they still kept arriving, and somehow she was pleased they did. Yet today she felt different. Sam had become remoter, more of a stranger, and this small act of devotion seemed like a hollow ritual.

She glanced at the phone. Should she call William at the hotel? Better to play cool, she decided. Then she thought this was being adolescent and called the hotel, only to be told he had already checked out. She replaced the receiver with a pang of hurt. He could at least have called her before leaving. Maybe he had tried to when she was out, seeing Sandy off to school. He'd now be on his way back to Washington. She bit her lip. She mustn't allow herself to become too dependent. If her life felt empty, it was up to her to do something positive about it. In the depths of her heart, she felt sure that Adam was not going to come back. What would she do? She couldn't go back to the Unit: she'd burned her boats there. She had set out to make a home for the boy and, in the process, she'd sacrificed her career and alienated her friends and neighbors. William represented a new life, a new chance, and perhaps just for that he was growing dangerously precious to her. She must guard against falling for him too deeply—or was it already too late? To restore the balance, she needed Adam back. Why, oh why, *had* he flown the coop? Had she really made the home *so* unhappy for him? He always expressed his feelings directly, and if he'd left home it must be because he simply wasn't happy there.

She turned away, finding the thought too bitter to bear. There was nothing she could do except stand by for the phone to ring and bring her the news, good or bad. Then at least the waiting would be over.

When the phone did ring, she started violently. She snatched up the receiver. It was William. Her pulse quickened. He was at the airport, he said; his plane was about to leave and he could only speak briefly. He wanted to know what Sandy had said about the whereabouts of this hunting lodge. Assuming a businesslike voice and trying not to read hidden meaning in his tone, she gave him the scanty information Sandy had provided her. His flight was closing and he hung up in a hurry, without any mention of their night together or any proposal about fixing another date. She put the phone down deep in thought. She knew it had been good for him, too, but he wasn't the kind of man to talk about it. She wasn't going to push it. From now on, she was going to be dependent on herself alone. She wasn't even going to dispute his notion of helping. If he wanted to chase hares, that was his affair. Why would Adam run away from home in order to be with Max? It was an absurd idea.

Abruptly, she headed for the kitchen. She'd sit down with a fresh cup of coffee and go through the holiday brochures. She would live on the assumption that all would work out.

•

With a screech of tearing metal, the limousine grazed its belly on another boulder. William Cray hauled the wheel over to avoid a deep pit, only to score the fender on a projecting rock. The track was growing steeper and narrower. He muttered a vicious oath. If he stopped, he'd lose momentum and be unable to start again; if he didn't, he'd as likely get stuck further up anyway. He accelerated. The car slewed to the side, its rear tires spitting pebbles. What the hell was he thinking of? He should have come in by chopper. Or at least taken a jeep. And a guide, too: despite the large-scale map spread out on the seat beside him, he'd lost his way twice already and even now he couldn't be sure this was the right track.

Lurching and grounding by turns, the limousine forged slowly higher up the course of the dry riverbed. On either side the trees crowded closer in—black spruce and balsam fir and mountain oaks choked by the quicker-growing evergreens and tangled in dense undergrowth. Suddenly the track swung to the left and there, in a small clearing in the woodland, no more than a hundred yards away and yet almost out of sight above the rim of the windshield, stood a one-story wooden shack. Here the track ended in a small shoulder dug into the hillside. He pulled up and clambered stiffly out. Outside the car, he felt very vulnerable and wished he'd come armed. The strange flintstone that had arrived with Sam's personal effects and which he now carried in a cloth in his pocket was all the armament he'd brought.

As he reached the edge of the clearing, he stopped. He was already out of breath and sweating heavily, and he felt the sharp warning pains of an angina attack. An eerie, pent-up silence gripped the forest, as though a hand were clamped over its mouth and at any moment it would tear free and burst into a scream. He glanced uneasily about him. He saw poison ivy here, poison sumac there. Was that a biting spider? A hornet hovered close by his cheek. The sun beat down, hard and pitiless. He swallowed, his mouth dry. He was a city man; nature in the raw unnerved him.

Screwing up his eyes against the glare, he peered out across the tall, rough grass. The shack looked unoccupied. The windows were shuttered, the door was closed and the screen door drawn to, and the porch was empty of chairs or other signs of the living. A glint of sunlight off the chimney cowl made him look up sharply. A loose shutter rattling in the sluggish breeze briefly startled him. Was he alone? Max, he knew, was back in Cambridge, but not with the boy. Bracing himself, he took a step forward.

The shack itself was locked up, but with the blade of a kebab skewer he found at the back he managed to slip the catch on a small window at the back and, with some difficulty, he climbed inside. He waited for his eyes to grow accustomed to the dark, and then in the pinshafts of light filtering in through chinks in the shutters he began his examination.

The woman clearly intended to be back. A portable computer lay on the desk in the main room, with a couple of yellow legal pads beside it. The diskette slots were empty. He uncrumpled a piece of paper from the waste-paper basket, but it was merely a shopping list: penknife, fishing line, wire, matches, sweatshirt . . . On the mantel-piece he found an Instamatic camera with fifteen shots used. There was only one bedroom; women's clothes spilled out of a holdall on the bed, and the wardrobe was empty. In the kitchen, he found just one glass, one set of cutlery and one plate and bowl in the drying-up rack. In the fridge, a carton of milk, still within its sell-by date, several Hershey bars, some English muffins, butter, an unopened carton of Florida orange juice, and in the freezer compartment a bottle of Stolichnaya and a pack of beefburgers. Nothing to suggest there'd ever been more than one person here.

This was crazy! It *had* to be the place. Irritably, he climbed out again and searched the outside. By the gar-bage bin, which had been cleared, he found a pile of green walnut shells and a handful of unripe chestnuts. So what did that prove? Further afield, in a hollow scraped into the earth, he found evidence of a fire, and not far away, in a clump of wiry grass, a heap of pigeon feathers and a rabbit pelt. Who was he to say the woman didn't live off the land up here? It was a goddamn hunting lodge, after all. He was standing a short way off, angry and perplexed, when his eye came to rest upon the wood-stack at the back under the eaves. No: not directly un-derneath the overhang. In some distant recess of his mind that struck an odd note. Surely you'd stack wood in the dry?

The logs had been arranged to form a small hovel shaped like a corn stook. Inside, the floor was laid with leaves and fine twigs. Mud crudely plugged the gaps in the lumber, and grass was wedged into the cracks at the top where the logs met in a point. In one corner lay a

strange collection of objects. These he took out into the
light to examine: several ring-pulls, a couple of quarters,
a crumpled ball of tin foil, a piece of broken mirror, the
brass casing of a spent .303 shell. A hoard of baubles.
Gleanings. Glittery bric-à-brac that caught the primitive
eye.

And then he found the final proof. Hairs. Short,
reddish-black, wiry, thick, curly head-hairs. Max's hair
was long and gently wavy, dark but not reddish-black,
and, he dared guess, fine. There was no doubt: this was
Adam's hair.

And it confirmed the conviction forming in his mind
over the past few days. Max knew about Adam. And she
knew now what he was. She'd smuggled him up here to
carry on her own "tests" on him. She was a geneticist;
without doubt she'd run the same analysis as Eliot had
and come to the same conclusions. She was fully in the
know. Would this make the way smoother, or tougher?
He badly needed to meet her face to face.

Twilight was beginning to fall. From the woods came
chilling cries and grunts. A moth blundered past his cheek.
The boy was out there somewhere, lying in hiding, watching, perhaps waiting. His nerves grew shakier. He'd somehow imagined he'd find him there and, by displaying the
flintstone, lure him away with him and back to Julia's.
But out here, in the raw wilds, that seemed increasingly
absurd. Risky, too. What if he'd misjudged the boy completely and, instead of evoking loyalty and respect, the
sight of the flintstone provoked rage and aggression? How
could a man of his age and fitness hope to defend himself
from this wild brute of a boy? He was quite alone, miles
from anywhere; his only link with the world outside was
the phone in the car, and he was probably out of cellnet

range anyway. He'd established the boy's general where-abouts, but that was as far as he could go. He'd have to call in the Center. They'd have ways of tracking him down. The social experiment was over. Eliot would get his material.

Quickly, nervously, he went around covering his tracks and removing all signs of his presence, then with mounting unease he cast a final glance around him and stumbled back across the open ground to his car. As he climbed in and started up, he was seized by a sudden attack of wild, irrational panic. Crashing the great tin whale back and forward, he turned around and set off down the rubble-strewn channel, careering like a pinball between the trees and the rocks, smashing his head on the roof one moment then half winding himself against the wheel the next, yet despite the screech of ripping metalwork, despite, too, a stabbing pain in his heart, never for one moment letting up until he was well out of the forest and onto the safety of familiar roads. Finally he pulled up by a truckers' diner and, slipping a nitroglycerin tablet under his tongue, lay back in the seat until he had grown calmer. Then he reached for the car-phone. He'd get the men in right away.

•

The boy crouched beneath the jutting slab of rock of his den. He honed his ear to catch the sound being carried in broken snatches on the wind. A shiver rippled through his body.

Dogs!

All through the day a terrifying giant metal dragon-fly had buzzed about the sky, disappearing one moment only to swoop around the blind side of the mountain the

next. In its belly it carried men. Through an open panel
he could see dogs on leashes. It would hover over the
rocky crags, flattening the grassy scrub beneath and raising a wide circle of dust, then lift its tail and wheel off out
of sight with a shuddering roar. He'd hear the plangent
beat of its wings now returning, now receding, until finally, as the sun was dipping behind the peaks and the
reddish-white rocks began to give back the warmth they'd
absorbed during the day, silence descended over the wilderness. Only then had he cautiously emerged from hiding and settled down to prepare for the night's hunting.
He'd been looping a snare across a small dry runnel
between two stunted thornbushes when suddenly, from
afar off, borne on a waft of the wind, he'd caught the
faint, throaty yelp of a hunting dog.

   The cries were coming closer now. He flattened his
back against the rock. Already he could hear the crash
of boots through undergrowth. Three dogs? Four? And
men, too: two, or possibly three. The minutes lengthened.
A sudden rise in the breeze swept away the sound, and
for a while it seemed they'd gone to ground or headed
off elsewhere. But then, abruptly, the yelping returned,
much closer, a frantic, choking, greedy sound that chilled
his blood. He inched forward and peered out from his
vantage point. Beneath him, the mountainside fell away
in a rugged sweep. There, way down below, in among
the thinning trees, he caught a flash of movement. Suddenly they broke cover: three men advancing at a stumbling run, each with a dog straining on a leash, heading
in a direct line toward him.

   He slid his chipped stones into the box Max had
given him and hid it at the back of the rocky shelf under
a covering of earth and leaves, then he slipped out into

the open and made for higher ground. Twilight was falling fast, and soon he would have the advantage of darkness. Scrambling over rocks and down gullies, he'd managed to put a good distance between them when he heard a far-off shout. They'd found his den. In the fading light, he could just make out two of the men; one was trailing his red sweatshirt and jeans before the excited dogs, while the other, carrying a pack on his back with a tall projecting wire, seemed to be speaking into some kind of telephone.

He thought fast. Some way toward the setting sun lay a small flat plateau with steep sides that narrowed to form a natural funnel, ending in a sudden sheer drop of a hundred feet or more. He knew: he'd already marked this as the perfect spot for herding bears or deer or other animals that might inhabit these mountains and were too large to trap or stone and driving them over the edge to their death on the rocks below. Doubling his pace, he headed into the sun.

Behind him, the cries of the dogs grew louder as they gained the fresher scent. He ran like the wind, skimming and sliding over the winding, rock-strewn paths until he reached the flat channel. The last spokes of sunlight streamed out from the high peaks directly ahead of the mouth of the funnel, momentarily dazzling him. He slowed as he reached the lip. Way below, now lost in darkness, stretched the bed of sharp, rough boulders. Taking a deep breath, he lowered himself carefully down the sheer rockface. A few feet down, his foothold crumbled away, and for a moment he was left hanging by his fingers. Frantically he scrambled onto a firmer ledge and gradually managed to work his way down until he came to a narrow shelf that ran horizontally along the length of the deep gully. Inching along this shelf, he soon reached a broader, gentler path that would back up to a point overlooking the plateau. As he doubled back, he stopped to collect an armful of stones.

By the time he'd reached the top again and found himself cresting one of the steep sides that hemmed in the narrow channel, the trackers had already arrived and were hurrying forward, three abreast, dragged along by their dogs into the dazzling splinters of the dying sun. He fell to a crouch.

As the funnel tightened, the men were forced to break formation and proceed in line. The dogs were yelping ravenously now. The sunlight glinted off the tips of the men's rifles. The first one broke into a run. The channel narrowed further. At that moment the sun exploded in a sudden, final burst. Blinded, the man threw his arm up to shield his eyes. His dog was straining forward, its claws tearing at the rock. Suddenly, the ground fell from beneath it and, with a howl of terror, it vanished over the edge. A second later, dragged forward by the leash, the man followed. His falling scream died with a distant, muffled crunch. The second dog was too close on his heels and it, too, disappeared, writhing and twisting over the edge. Its handler let go of the leash and, swayed, dazzled, on the brink. Adam rose to his feet. Taking aim, he wound back his arm and with all his might catapulted a stone at him. It skimmed through the air and smote the man below the ear, knocking him off balance. He clawed vainly at the empty air, and for a split second it seemed he might recover, but slowly he toppled backward and, with a bloodcurdling shriek, disappeared from sight.

The third man had dropped to his knees and was sighting his rifle in Adam's direction. There was a crack, and a bullet shimmied off a boulder, sending a splinter of rock fizzing past Adam's face. He fell back to a crouch. The dog, released, instantly bolted forward but it was hemmed back by the steep wall. With its frantic barking ringing in his ears, Adam slid quickly away into the deepening shadows and retraced his steps to the rockface, knowing that no dog could follow him there. He would climb down to the bottom of the gully and make his escape that way.

He had found his way to the narrow shelf and was halfway along, spread flat against the rockface, when in the far distance he heard the ominous threshing of mechanical wings. It grew gradually closer and louder. Suddenly the giant metal dragonfly rose up from the very bed of the gully. From its underbelly two lights, each as bright as the sun, swept the rocks. Suddenly one found him, then the other swiveled onto him. With a cry, he shrank closer against the rockface, unable to escape the blinding floodlight that pinned him there, while slowly, like a beast preparing to pounce, the terrible monster hovered ever closer.

•

Since returning to Cambridge, Max spent every available hour in the Peabody Museum library, reading up all she could on Neanderthal man. She was interested to see how far her own work, when published, would fit in with the current paleontological interpretation of the fossil and stone record and how far established reputations might suffer. In science, results were denominated in dollars, and a lifetime's career might hang on the refutation or confirmation of a chance discovery.

She found surprising congruity between her own factual data on Adam and the speculative reconstructions of the experts. Nothing in the fossil record, for instance, suggested that Neanderthals were cognitively inferior to ourselves in the complexity of their problem-solving, planning or even symbolic thought. True, we possessed larger frontal and prefrontal brain areas, but this didn't necessarily imply superior cognitive awareness. The key characteristic of man, as indeed of all primates, was adaptability, and in this respect Adam had shown himself supremely well endowed.

But here the congruity began to falter. One of the perennial questions that cropped up was: were Neanderthals "savage"? The answer given largely depended on the fashion of the time. Originally the split human bones found at a Yugoslavian site had been taken to suggest cannibalism, but a recent interpretation had suggested that this was merely the result of the crushing weight of the overlying rock. Paleontologists looking to portray Neanderthals as good neighborly cousins of ours pointed to the residue of flowers and pine boughs on the graves in the Shanidar caves in Iran, indicating a people of refined cultural sensibility and religious belief. On this basis, they promoted Neanderthals to a level of innocence far above that of modern man. They might have been aggressive, but only in the way animals were—that is, in defending territory or struggling for scarce resources. Not gratuitously or ideologically, as with modern man. Here Max paused. Did sensibility preclude aggressivity? Surely not: hadn't the music of Wagner accompanied the march to the gas chambers? The argument went back and forth. It was a debate between men with blunt instruments groping in the dark. Adam would change all that. He would flood light on these eternal questions. For he *was* a savage. He had shown himself capable of extreme, ritualized violence. Was it unreasonable to infer that his own fore-bears had practiced the same kind of savageries upon each other, too?

The two species might be physiologically as akin as lions and tigers, in Bernard's phrase, but Adam was proof that there were fundamental unbridgeable differences. She remembered once staring out of his playroom at the flagpole and feeling it would forever be beyond him to comprehend the concept of a national flag. Deepest would always be these differences of culture—differences of morality and behavior, of belief and ideology. But, above all, whether cultural or cognitive, the one faculty Adam so patently lacked was the very one that stood as the crowning glory of modern man: the ability to reason. Reasoning was the chasm that irreconcilably separated Adam from his anatomically modern kin. It cast him on the far side of an unbridgeable divide. It made him forever a savage, lost in the dark ages of ignorance and super-stition and set apart from us, his civilized cousins. This was the key lesson he had to teach, not simply to resolve an age-old academic squabble. What he had to teach us was about the nature of ourselves. He held up the mirror to us.

That day, around the middle of the afternoon, she rose from the desk and left the library. She had read all she could and had formed the framework for her analysis. She looked in briefly at the lab and left a note for Gerald in his electronic mailbox, saying she had considered the offer and wasn't interested. She stopped by her own apartment to fill an overnight case with a change of clothes, then climbed back in her car and headed first for Lexington. She owed Julia a visit.

On the way she stopped at a gas station and called

her up instead. She'd rather not have to face her and see her suffer, knowing that a single word of the truth would release her. She couldn't tell her: she *mustn't*. Life was short, and an opportunity like this wouldn't happen again in a million lifetimes. It would be stupid, even irresponsible, to pass it up out of sentimental regard for one person and their minor sorrow. Anyway, Adam had run away by himself to start with, and it was just as likely he would still be at large anyway if she hadn't found him. Sooner or later, she recognized she would have to tell Julia everything. But in the meantime, she simply didn't have the emotional energy to face the confrontation and risk the consequences. If Julia had the slightest suspicion she'd had a hand in Adam's disappearance, she'd be onto the police, or at least William Cray, straight away and they'd be on the track within minutes. Where would her work be then? Where would *Adam* be?

She drove fast, anxiously. The first thing she'd do when she arrived was get a radio fix on the boy, to set her mind at rest.

The last rays of the sun were just dying behind the fir trees and a smoke-blue twilight was mopping up the undergrowth beneath when she finally arrived at the shack. Without stopping to unload, she unlocked the trunk and took out the radio receiver. This was a lightweight black aluminum box with two dials on the surface, one to register direction and the other intensity, and, projecting from the front, the signal finder, a small probe sheathed in black foam and resembling a microphone. Hurrying to catch the last of the light, she hastened past the shack and scrambled up a steep track between the trees that led to a small rocky outcrop a hundred feet or so above. This commanded a fine view of the distant crags, with nothing between to create interference. Briefly checking the setting, she flicked the switch up and pointed the box towards the mountains. For a moment, no signal appeared to come through, and she readjusted the settings. Then suddenly, very faintly, the machine gave out a slow, staccato *blip, blip*.

She laid the instrument on a rock slab and swung it through ten or fifteen degrees either way until she'd found the strongest signal, then marked it on the dial with the cursor. She breathed a sigh of relief. Fine: the boy was safely out there, up in the mountains, just about where she'd left him. She was about to turn back and retrace her steps when gradually the signal began to fade. She frowned; the selenium batteries in the wristband should be good for three months at least. Or was it the receiver itself? As she reached to examine the instrument, she nudged it slightly out of line. At once the signal returned, as clear as ever. She checked the cursor; it registered a direction two degrees to the left. Impossible! That meant a distance on the ground of perhaps a quarter of a mile, covered in just a matter of seconds.

With a drumming pulse, she took another reading. Sure enough, the source of the signal was continuing to swing to the left. Only a bird could travel at that pace! And then, dimly in the distance, she heard a faint, familiar throb in the sky and, a moment later, standing out stark against the sun's afterlight, the speck of a helicopter crossed her field of vision. It must have been two or three miles away, heading southeast. With growing horror and disbelief, she pointed the receiver set directly at the helicopter and kept it locked on as the throbbing receded into the distance and, with it, the *blip, blip* grew gradually fainter.

•

As he hit the Saw Mill River parkway, heading up-state into Westchester County, William Cray put his foot down on the accelerator. They'd found the boy, and he wanted to be there when they brought him in. Preferably ahead of Eliot, too, who was flying in from Ann Arbor, where he'd been attending a bio-cybernetics conference at the University of Michigan. Headlights at full beam, the limousine bored fast and deep into the night. Road signs glared back at him briefly, then flashed past. On either side, the rolling woodland stretched into darkness, punctuated here and there by the lights from small clusters of habitation.

He heaved a sigh. Poor Julia. She would be devastated. What would they tell her—what would *he* tell her? Fabricate some story about the boy being run down by a truck, or drowned, the body disfigured beyond recognition . . . ? He'd comfort her, pick up the pieces, see her through her grief and remorse. Damn it, he swore softly; why had he gone and muddied things? She was a fine woman and deserved better. But life was tough. Tough on himself, too: his own feelings as well were at stake.

But toughest of all on Adam. Very soon the boy would come face to face with Eliot Lovejoy. He gave an involuntary shudder as he thought of the experiments performed on the primates under Eliot's direction. The man believed in a mixture of aversive conditioning and cortical ablation. William swore again to himself. He should have gone direct to Maxine Fitzgerald in the first place and done a deal with her. Still, all that was academic now. His side of the experiment was dead. Adam was now Eliot's material.

As he swung the limousine off the parkway toward Pleasantville, he reached for the car-phone and called up the Center. The chopper was due to arrive in ten minutes, he was told. On the outskirts of the town, he turned down a broad, freshly surfaced road toward a sprawling complex of low laboratory buildings. Around the perimeter ran a high chain-mesh fence, affixed every few yards with large KEEP OUT notices between concrete posts topped with barbed wire. These posts were angled outward at the top, in the manner designed to keep people out— first, when the complex had belonged to the Defense Department, to ward off pacifists and antinuclear protesters, but more recently, since it had been taken over by a major pharmaceutical corporation as a research center for testing new drugs, their function was mainly to keep animal liberation activists at bay. He smiled grimly: the posts ought to be re-angled inward, for their purpose now was to keep this most valuable human property *in*. As the car was waved perfunctorily through the checkpoint at the main gate, he made a mental note to speak to Eliot about security generally. But then maybe it should be left as it was: wiser not to advertise to the rest of the employees on site what was going on in D-wing. The discreet, low-profile approach was the way they'd always worked it.

He pulled up outside the wing. This was a two-story modular concrete building, with a windowless brick structure added on top where the experimental animals were housed. It stood apart from the rest of the complex, having its own car park and small canteen for the handful of staff, and a separate access off the main perimeter driveway. Lights burned in the lower rooms. A brief glance at the cars parked there told him Eliot had not yet arrived. Good.

He was heading towards the front door when he heard the mechanical purring in the distance, coming rapidly closer. Within a few moments, a sleek black helicopter was gently dropping out of the inky sky, its lights beaming down on the large yellow "H" marked out on the tarmac behind the building. He positioned himself at the edge of the circle and, as he stood buffeted by the downdraft as the chopper touched down, he was joined by Lovejoy's deputy. Two lab assistants came forward at a crouching run, carrying a stretcher. The door in the side of the helicopter slid open and the limp, inert body of the boy was lowered out. For a brief moment, Cray felt a stab of pity at the image of this deposition, then he stepped briskly forward. What was one human's suffering, one single life, in the greater purpose? This was a sacrificial lamb, come to save mankind.

As he walked alongside the stretcher into the light, he gazed down at the unconscious boy. He was wrapped in an army blanket up to the chin. His eyes were closed and his face, with its strong, almost sensual features, lay in peaceful repose. One arm slipped free and trailed to the ground. Cray reached to lift it back. As he did so, he noticed a small, flat band of transparent plastic around his wrist. Imbedded into the plastic he could see a tight coil of copper wire, some tiny electronic components and a dime-sized battery of the kind that powered cameras and watches. With a flash of insight, he recalled the purpose of Max's aborted field trip and he made the connection. He knew exactly what this was. And, barely a second later, he perceived how he might turn it to his own purposes.

As the assistants laid the body on an inspection couch, he signaled to one to snip through the fixing stud and free the wristband. Smoothly, as if it were merely an identification tag he'd had put there himself, he slipped it into his pocket. Much later, long after Eliot had arrived and they'd cracked a bottle of bourbon to toast the triumph, William Cray excused himself to go to the men's room. Instead, he took the rear stairs up to the top. There he opened the fire-escape door that led onto a narrow parapet and, reaching up as far as he could, lodged the wristband out of sight on the top of the roof. Then he slipped back downstairs and rejoined Eliot in his office.

20

IT WAS AFTER MIDNIGHT WHEN MAX ARRIVED, UNANnounced, at Julia's house. Barely moments after she'd rung the doorbell, footsteps came hurrying forward. A security spotlight sprang on above the porch and a brief second later the door swept open. With her fair hair drawn back from her forehead and her complexion smoothed with night-cream, Julia's face registered the sequence of her feelings—first hope, then disappointment and finally anxiety.

"What's the news? Have they found him?" she rasped.

"I came to ask you that," replied Max, instantly regretting she hadn't just phoned again instead. "I hope I haven't woken you."

"I was still up. Come in. You look shattered."

Wrapping her silk Chinese housecoat tightly around her, Julia ushered her into the living room. The smell of wallpaper glue and fresh paint hung faintly in the air. The room lights were low and the television was on with the sound muted. On an occasional table stood a bottle of brandy and a half-empty glass, and on the floor beside the armchair lay a telephone. She turned on a table lamp and, with a brief interrogative glance, fetched a glass from the cabinet and poured Max a brandy. She raised her own.

"*Slainte*," she said. Her voice was slightly thick. "So, no news?"

"The police haven't been in touch?"

Julia's expression sharpened.

"No. Should they have?"

"You've heard nothing at all from them?"

"Max, is there something I should know? Tell me quickly! Get it over with."

"No, no, I don't mean that." Max braved a reassuring smile, but her mind was racing. "If he'd had an accident or anything," she heard herself saying, "you'd be the first to know."

"Assuming they could identify him." Julia reached down for the phone. "Max, this is madness. I've made up my mind. I'm going to report him missing. I don't care if he gets into worse trouble. I want him back."

Numbly, Max sat back and waited as Julia made her calls. She had the numbers of the various police departments already written down on a small card. First she called the local precinct officers, then the county headquarters and finally the state police. No, there were no reports of a missing boy answering to the description. Then she called Information for the number of Worcester County police. Max sat forward with a start. Why should she try them? Did she *suspect*?

"Just a crazy idea." Julia shrugged self-deprecatingly. "I had a notion he might have tried to follow you to that hunting shack of yours."

"But I didn't go there," replied Max, holding her eye firmly.

"I know. Silly, isn't it?"

Max sat biting her lip as Julia put the same question to the Worcester police. But again they'd had no report of any such missing boy. Julia replaced the phone and cast her a slantwise smile.

"Well, so much for my crazy idea."

Max said nothing. Her thoughts were whirling in dizzy spirals. If not the police, who *had* it been in that helicopter? And what had given Julia that idea in the first place? This whole thing was getting beyond reason.

Julia sank back in her chair, defeated.

"They say when you don't know, you can still hope," she said bleakly. "But I can't even hope any more now."

"Don't give up. He'll turn up. Believe me."

Believe me. How hollow that sounded. For a moment silence fell. Julia reached down to check she'd left the phone properly on its cradle. She poured them both another drink. She drew a breath to speak, but checked herself. She stared into her brandy for a while, then looked up and caught Max's eye.

"Let's talk about something more cheerful. How did your field trip go? Did you catch your deer? You know, I've always wondered how you people do it. My father used to go deer stalking in the Highlands. He always took along the very best gillies, and still he'd often come back with an empty bag. I suppose it's different now. Technology, and all that."

Max allowed her to talk on, occasionally responding in monosyllables. She knew she ought to get back home to Cambridge, but she felt too tired, too brain-numbed, to stir herself just yet. Her own apartment, too, was so far removed from the action; she'd never know what was going on from there. Maybe she would stay over this time and hope to be there when the fateful call came. She was relaxing, feeling the warmth of the brandy seeping through her body, when with the delay of exhaustion she heard a word of Julia's echo through her mind: *technology*.

She jerked upright in her seat. My God, she thought. Of course!

•

The Department of Radiotronics operated from a warren of small rooms in the basement of the Physics block, and it was here that Max put her question to the young technician who had designed the ankle-band radio tag. She'd tagged a deer in the Catskills, she told him; all had gone fine, but when she'd gone back a few days later to check, the radio receiver wouldn't pick up a signal. Either the tag had sprung a fault—which the technician wouldn't hear of—or the beast had been shot and taken home, perhaps by one of the weekend hunters who came up from as far afield as New York City, but certainly well outside the range of the receiver. It was vital to her study to recover the tag. By appealing to the young man's technical pride, she coaxed him toward offering the solution she already had in mind.

"You'd have to link into a satellite," he said with a helpless shrug. "And we don't run those babies."

"Okay, who does?"

He scratched his ear.

"Well, first off, you need an orbiting sat, not a geostationary one. Call up one of the big telecom companies. Give the transmission frequency and they should give you a fix. And just hope the sat's overhead when the little brute bleeps." His face suddenly lit up. "Hang on! Over in Geophysics they've got time allocation on Landsat. Maybe they could spare you a few nanoseconds. You could flutter your lashes at the guys there. Try Joe. He's crazy about brunettes."

She pecked him a kiss on the cheek.

"Thanks, pal. You're the best."

Less than twenty-four hours later, she was standing in the map-room of the Department of Geophysics, poring over a large-scale map of northern New York State with a puzzled frown. The tiny *bleeps* from the tag on Adam's wrist had been picked up by the satellite as it passed overhead in orbit at approximately 0233 hours that morning, then transmitted back to earth where they'd been logged and converted by the computer into a grid reference. She checked the computer printout on the desk beside her that gave the map coordinates: 41° 08′ 30″ N; 73° 40′ 51″ W.

As she traced the coordinates on the map and obtained a fix, her frown deepened. What the hell went on at Pleasantville, New York State?

•

A hundred yards down the turnoff to Pleasantville, Max drew up on the shoulder and got out. She reached for the small black radio receiver on the passenger seat and swept it carefully from side to side until she'd obtained the loudest *bleeps*, then she climbed back into the car and headed off in that direction. Slowly, step by step, she homed in on the target. The beacon took her in a route that skirted the town and ended down a broad newly surfaced road enclosing a complex of laboratory buildings behind a high mesh fence. A signboard identified this as the research division of a leading pharmaceutical corporation. She felt sick. What in Christ's name was Adam doing here?

She curb-crawled along the perimeter fence, discreetly projecting the receiver through the open window. *Bleep, bleep*: louder and louder the signal grew until finally she'd pinpointed a building standing separate from the rest. She pulled up close to the fence and studied the structure as well as she could in the semidarkness. It looked more recently built than the others and more expensively equipped, too. For a moment the windowless story at the top puzzled her—it was too big to house generators or utilities—until suddenly she understood. This was a unit for animal experiments. And, judging by the scale of it, not for rats and rabbits, either, but primates. Primates, like man.

The building itself looked deserted. Apart from one downstairs room, the windows either were in darkness or glowed dimly with blue lab safety lights. Here and there a light came on and a figure, perhaps a cleaner, appeared fleetingly at the window, then moved on. Somewhere inside, Adam was being held. And between stood the impenetrable fence. To avoid suspicion she drove on until she could do a U-turn, then coasted slowly back. All the time she felt a rising desperation. It was hopeless. She had no identification, no pass, no cover. She'd never get past the first security point. Suppose she got herself caught deliberately? She had only one weapon, and it was a strong one: she knew all about Adam. She'd confront whoever these men were who'd kidnapped the boy, she'd threaten to go to the press and the media if they didn't release him, she'd kick up so much shit . . . But she knew this was false bravado. In truth, she was quaking. If they could raise him, they could just as easily bury her. And with all he clearly meant to them, they would.

By now she'd reached the main gate. She'd just have to front it out. She fumbled in her purse for her MIT ID card and, taking a deep breath, swung the wheel around and headed for the white boom. The guard barely looked up; a telltale bluish reflection off his glasses told her he was probably watching a mini-TV under the counter. He nodded at her proffered pass, and a moment later the boom rose.

She parked tight in around the back of the building and tried to consider rationally what to do next. Break in? Impossible. There was a small louvered service door to one side, but she could see from there that it was bolted. Nearby stood a fire-door, but that would only be openable from the inside. All the windows appeared fastened. She got out. It would have to be the frontal approach again. Adrenaline burned in her veins. Briskly, she walked around to the front entrance. Inside sat a uniformed security man at a desk. Behind him, an IN/OUT board was fixed to the wall. The name at the top read, *Dr. E. Lovejoy.* He was out. She assumed a bright smile; it felt like a mask that would drop off at any moment.

"Hi, I'm Maxine," she said, "Dr. Lovejoy's niece." She affected to understand his puzzlement. "I guess he didn't say to expect me. My uncle's always in the clouds. Is he in?"

"No, ma'am. Everyone's gone."

"He didn't leave a package for me?" Her face fell. "Some assays he wants me to check, and I need them now. He must have left them in his office. Mind if I take a look? Or will you?"

The man hesitated. His eyes bored through her mask. He wanted to oblige yet also to protect himself, and either way he couldn't leave his desk unattended. The moment stretched interminably. She intensified her pose of innocent helplessness.

"You have ID, ma'am?" he asked eventually.

She showed him her MIT card. He pushed a register forward.

"Sign in here. Name and address. You go through the door there and it's on your left. Hit twenty-seventy-seven to unlock it."

She thanked him and walked as calmly as she could over to the door and punched in the number. The door opened at a touch. Beyond, the corridor stretched the length of the building, lit and carpeted more like a clinic than any lab she'd ever worked in. She put her head around Dr. Lovejoy's door. The lights were on, and from the comfortable teak and leather furnishings she deduced this was the Director's office. She was drawing away when a flickering light from a CRT monitor on a small conference table caught her attention. She went over to look. It was a video-tape held on freeze-frame, half obliterated by a horizontal white band, but slowly she began to make out the image. She caught her breath. With a trembling hand, she pressed the "Play" button. The image jerked to life.

It's Adam. He's in some kind of a tank filled with water. Swimming. No, Christ alive! Not swimming. *Drowning.* Threshing and splashing around desperately for his life. There's a large disk-like platform in the middle of the tank which he's frantically trying to get a handhold on, but it's fixed to a central column by a gimbal so that every time he tries to grasp it, it dips and he slips off. He can't quite drown, because there's a narrow shelf around the edge at the bottom, and by standing on tiptoes on this ledge he is just able to keep his nose above water— or he might be, if he weren't in such a state of frantic panic. A harness is fixed around his waist and chest and attached to an overhead boom, and whenever he is in real danger of drowning, he gets hauled out, choking and spluttering, only to be lowered gently back in a moment later. On his head he wears a skullcap such as severe epileptics have fitted to locate the focus of their seizures, and from this feeds a lattice of fine wires which bind together at the crown like a topknot and, from there, lead in turn to a cable that loops away along the boom. Large white disks fixing electrodes in place are attached to his chest, thorax, wrists and legs. There is no soundtrack. The whole scene takes place in an eerie, dehumanized silence.

As she watched, his panic gradually turned to rage, to blind vicious fury. He began to claw at the skullcap, he tore at the wires, he ripped at the disk-like platform with his teeth, he wriggled and writhed to free himself of the harness. And then, as though indicating the focal point of the experiment, the camera slowly zoomed in on his face and his rolling eyes and his livid blotched cheeks and on his wide open mouth, contorted in a silent howl of pain and rage.

She recoiled in horror and disgust. Gradually, a matching rage took hold of her, too. She burst out of the room and stormed down the corridor. Room by room she searched, slamming doors and overturning equipment, heedless of any concern except finding and saving the boy. At the end of the corridor, she came to the fire-escape stairs. Of course she knew where he'd be! She flew up them two at a time to the top floor. Pushing through a heavy fire-door, she found herself in a long, low, dimly lit corridor. Here the floor and walls were of plain concrete, and the air hung hot and heavy with the familiar odor of animal fur and feces. To her left stood a service elevator and, at intervals beyond, a series of metal-studded doors, each with a small barred window set high up. Beyond these again stood a bank of cages in which, as her eyes grew accustomed to the penumbra, she could make out large, hairy ape-like forms. A low chittering filled the air, punctuated occasionally by a shriek and a sudden flurry in the shadows.

She peered in at the window of the first cell. It appeared to be empty. She turned to the one opposite.

There, in a far corner, lit only by a small amber sodium lamp above the door, half naked and curled in a fetal crouch, cowered the form of Adam.

She wrenched at the door handle. It was locked. She could see three keyholes. She cast about her for an implement to break it down. A fire extinguisher, a bucket of sand, a mop and a pail for swabbing down, but otherwise nothing. She was growing frantic when suddenly a whirring noise made her freeze. She spun around. The elevator light! The whirring grew louder. Instinctively she sought a hiding place. The elevator had reached the top just as she backed away through the fire-door and pressed herself flat against the wall beyond. The elevator doors shuddered open and heavy boots stomped across the concrete floor. Craning forward, she peered through the wire-glass window. A heavily built man wearing green denim fatigues and an intercom on his belt was making for Adam's cell, carrying a bucket. Behind him, he'd left the elevator open. At the door, he stopped and, with a brief glance through the peephole, pulled out a large ring of keys leashed to his belt.

He had undone the first lock and was bending to unlock the second when she struck. Every ounce of her determination went into the action. All in one seamless movement, she slipped through the fire-door, snatched up the fire extinguisher, wielded it around in a high arc and, well before the man had had time to straighten, before even an oath had fled his lips, she'd brought it crashing down. The blow caught him high on the shoulder, flinging him violently back against the door. His head smote the metal-studded door and he sprawled unconscious across the concrete floor.

She scrabbled for the keys. She fumbled, dropped the ring, almost snapped one off in the lock, but finally she managed to find the one that fitted and, with a twist of the handle, the door opened. She rushed over to the boy.

"Adam!" she cried, grabbing him. "Come! Quick!"

But he merely shrank further back into the corner, chattering in terror, his hand held up to fend her off.

"It's me, Max!" she hissed. "I'm getting you out of here! Hurry, for God's sake, *hurry!*"

She hauled him to his feet. He felt like a dead man in a sack. She dragged him toward the door, but with a terrified whimper he struggled free and flung himself back into his corner, hiding his head in his arms. She cajoled, she shook him, she tried the touch that had calmed him in the woods at Julia's house the very first time she'd met him, but nothing worked. Vital seconds ticked by. She was growing frantic. Finally, she thought of addressing him in his own language. There was only one word of his own she could recall.

"Atta," she said urgently, pointing to the open door. "Atta."

Gradually he uncoiled his head and a glimmer of hope entered his pitiful eyes. She grasped him by the hand and tugged him to the door, repeating the strange word over and over again. At the sight of the keeper lying unconscious on the ground, he recoiled, but with a firm shove she thrust him past the body and, hoisting his arm over her shoulder, she half pushed, half dragged him across the corridor to the open elevator. As she was about to bundle him inside, she glanced back to see the man was beginning to stir. His hand fumbled groggily around for the intercom. Instantly, she steered Adam away and through the fire-door. Sliding and tripping, she managed to get him all the way down the stairs when, just as they reached the bottom, the shrill ring of an alarm bell shattered the silence. Through the fire-door window there she could see the security guard hurrying down the corridor, followed by two men dressed in green fatigues.

They were trapped! Suddenly she remembered the fire-door she'd seen from outside. It lay down a further short flight of steps that twisted back underneath the staircase. A glass box, to be broken in emergency, housed a key. With her elbow she smashed the glass. Just as a siren was going off in the distance, she broke through the door and tumbled onto the grass outside.

At that instant, a bank of floodlights burst into life, bathing the whole building in searing brilliance. Grabbing Adam by the collar, she hauled him off to where she'd parked her car and flung him bodily into the back. Climbing into the driver's seat, she fired the engine and roared off with tires screeching back along the route she'd come. As she approached the main security gate, she slowed.

The boom was lowered. But her luck was holding. A Federal Express van had drawn up ahead of her at the post. Just as the guard was waving it to pass, she pulled forward and tucked in close behind. As the boom rose and the van drove away, she drove through tight on its tail. A moment later she was speeding away down the perimeter road and heading toward the parkway, with every second taking them further clear of the nightmare. It was five or six miles down the road that the physical reaction caught up with her. She pulled off onto the shoulder and hurried outside to the verge where, doubling up, she retched emptily into the bushes. Finally, cold and trembling, she returned to the car and, taking the boy in her arms, wept with pure relief.

•

The drive was long and tiring. More than once, overcome by a wave of fatigue, she nearly swerved off the road. Adam lay curled up on the backseat, staring out up at the stars, saying nothing. Eventually she stopped at a service station for gas and a snack, then pulled over to the side and climbed into the back with him. Her sleep was short and broken by the constant arrival and departure of heavy trucks. Adam lay in her arms, sleeping deeply. She woke after an hour, cold and stiff. She stared out across the floodlit parking lot and noticed a gray sedan she could swear she'd seen before. A trucker swaggered past and leered in through the window. Then a police car drew up and two officers hurried purposefully into the diner. She felt uneasy, exposed. It might just be paranoia, or tiredness, but could she be sure? Freeing her numb arm from under the boy, she climbed back between the seats to the front, and a moment later she was on her way again. She fancied she saw the gray sedan pull away after her, and for several miles she drove with her eyes fixed on the rearview mirror, but evidently it had turned off for it never reappeared.

The sky on Adam's side was perceptibly lightening as she reached Boston, and in the city the first signs of daily life were already stirring. She felt dislocated and dazed, as though she was waking from some horrific night terror. The first birds were in full song when finally she drew up on the gravel outside the low, white-slatted home of the Wendells. Adam was still asleep, curled on his side with his knuckles pressed against his eyes.

She got out. The cool, damp early dawn air smelled fresh and sweet, and suddenly she was gripped with a wild, untameable exhilaration. She wanted to laugh and cry at the same time. As she leaned on the doorbell, she realized she hadn't the least idea what she'd say to Julia. Somehow it didn't matter. All that counted was that Adam was safe. And this was where he had to be. There was nowhere else.

Julia must have seen the car through the hall window, for she flung the door open. Wild hope, hope beyond words, rose in her face.

Max stood quietly and calmly on the doorstep.

"I've brought him back," she said.

21

○

JULIA WAS AGHAST AT THE SIGHT OF THE BOY. HIS face bore a cadaverous, ash-grey pallor and his eyes, narrow and haunted, darted about nervously like a lizard's. He seemed to have developed a convulsive facial tic, too, and whenever anyone came too close or moved too suddenly, he'd instinctively flinch away. It reminded her of the state he'd arrived in from the halfway house, and yet this was worse, as though he'd been deliberately beaten and brutalized. He refused the sweatshirt she tried putting on him and cast off the blanket she wrapped around him, yet he was shivering uncontrollably, so she turned on the central heating and gave him the run of the fridge and larder. He ate ravenously, grabbing the food in his hands and hoarding it close to him as he squatted in the corner, just as he had done before she'd begun teaching him manners. But she watched her returned prodigal son through eyes brimming with joy. Let him be as he was: she wasn't going to try and correct or coerce or condition him anymore. From now on, he could go his own way; she wouldn't force him to fit into theirs.

She laid a mattress on the floor of the attic where he'd always been happiest and covered it in a pile of blankets, and together with Sandy and Max she helped him upstairs and put him to bed. Back in the kitchen, she made mugs of cocoa for all three of them and, sitting her down at the table, forced Max to tell her story. Haltingly, forgetfully, often losing track of where she was, Max explained what had happened. She said she'd thought about Julia's hunch that Adam might be trying to make for the hunting shack and she'd followed it up. They'd both remarked on his extraordinary sense of direction, she said and then began explaining that we possessed tiny particles of magnetite located in our nasal bridges, which were vestigial in developed peoples like ourselves, but still probably active in many nomadic races, and this provided a homing capability, somewhat like a pigeon's. On this assumption, she'd taken a map and drawn a dead straight line from Lexington to the shack in Worcester County. She'd computed roughly how much ground he would be likely to cover in the time elapsed, and then gone in search. She'd found a long, narrow lake in the foothills of Mount Wachusett which lay directly across his path, and there she'd lain in wait for him, knowing that at whatever point he reached it, he would be forced to skirt it, and, with impassable rocks hemming in the east side, he'd be likely to seek a way around the west. Eventually, in the early hours of night, just as she was giving it up as harebrained lunacy, she'd spotted a small, stocky, forlorn figure staggering across the moonlit plain. And that was it.

"Astonishing," breathed Julia when the story was done. "Unbelievable."

"Well, there it is." Max spread her hands. "So it

wasn't such a crazy notion of yours after all, huh?"

"Brilliant," said Sandy fervently. "I wish I'd been there."

Julia rose to her feet. "Come along now. It's almost time to be getting up. Max, let me fix up the spare room."

She led the two upstairs to catch a couple of hours' sleep before the day began. Having settled Max into the spare room, she hesitated on the landing, uncertain whether to go back down or try and rest herself. She felt too stirred to sleep. As she stood there, she glanced out of the landing window. The sun had broached the tree-line and was spilling straws of gold aslant the lawn. How beautiful the world suddenly appeared. A fresh day, full of fresh hope. Just at that moment a tiny glint caught her eye. It flashed again, way across the woods by the road. Sunlight reflecting off glass? *What* glass? As she peered out through the soft muslin light of the dawn she fancied she caught a movement in the undergrowth. She peered harder, but nothing appeared to stir. She turned away: it must have been some trick of the light. Or of her own imagination. Lately she'd been seeing a lot of things that weren't there. Even just now with Max, downstairs. All that business about magnetic particles in our noses had sounded a trifle specious. Coincidental, too. But then, anxiety played hell on the nerves. She shouldn't trust her instincts right now. Anyway, what did it really matter how Adam had been rescued? He was found, and that was all that mattered.

On impulse, she tiptoed up to the attic and quietly opened the door. The mattress was empty! The boy was nowhere in the room. She shot a glance at the window. It still bore its locks. Oh God, she thought, I should have had them off! She flew down the stairs toward her bedroom. She would put on a coat and scour the grounds: he couldn't have got far. As she burst into her room, she stopped dead. There, on the bed, curled up with his knuckles pressed tight against his eyes, lay Adam, fast asleep.

•

She began to worry about Max's nerves, too. The slam of the front door as Sandy left for school brought Max hurrying downstairs. Every time the phone rang, she started. She would fall abruptly silent in the middle of a conversation, and Julia would turn to find her staring anxiously out of the window, fiddling with her bracelets in a state of curious agitation. When she asked her what was wrong, Max replied it was just exhaustion from two nights without sleep, and yet when Julia pressed her to go back up and get some rest, she said she felt she had to stay up and around. At one point, she went outside for some fresh air, and even that decision appeared to involve a considerable internal struggle. Watching from the window as she disappeared haltingly up the drive, Julia was shocked by the nervous hesitancy in her step and she nearly went out after her to make sure she was all right. Max returned after just a few minutes, however, and then it was to say that she had better be getting back to the labs.

Julia saw her out to her car. Max wound down the window and cast her a long, urgent look. She started to say something, then broke off. Julia felt she couldn't let her go like that.

"Something's the matter," she said.

"Julia, listen. I want you to take precautions. Keep all doors and windows locked."

"Come along, it's okay now! Anyway, I'm not going to keep him cooped up indoors again. That was exactly the trouble before."

"I'm serious." Her hazel eyes were pinched with anxiety. "Just for a day or two until he's settled. Don't answer the door. Check out anyone who comes. You never know."

"Relax," smiled Julia. "You're overwrought. Go home and get some proper rest." She paused. This wasn't the note she wanted her to leave on. "You've been so wonderful, Max, I don't know what to say."

"Just say you'll do what I ask."

"Of course I'll take care. And you do, too, bless you."

Max was about to say more, then seemed to realize it was fruitless. With a pained frown, she started up and pulled away. Julia watched the small red car drive away until it was out of sight, then turned back indoors, deep in thought. She went upstairs to her bedroom and, taking care not to disturb the sleeping boy, tiptoed through to the bathroom. She slipped off her housecoat and quickly wrapped her bath-towel round her. She caught sight of herself in the mirror and considered her reflection for a moment. Not bad for a woman only just the right side of forty, but these past weeks had taken their toll. Her eyes hollow and sunken, and running a hand through her hair revealed the straw turning to silver. As soon as school ended, they'd take off on holiday. Three tickets to Disneyland.

She slid the cabinet door open and turned the shower on full pressure. For a while she stood beneath the pounding jet, feeling its force gradually easing away all the weariness and anxiety. She reveled in the thick, steamy heat and the lash of the water upon her naked skin, and as she soaped and sponged her body she slowly began to feel the stirrings of feelings long forgotten until so recently . . .

She choked back a scream.

A dark shape loomed up through the cabinet screen. The door shook violently. Adam's face zoomed close up through the blur, wild and frantic, shouting above the din of the shower. He wrenched at the door desperately. A welter of panic seized her. He'd been watching her undress. She'd provoked him. She shrank back against the tiles.

"Adam!" she screamed. "Stop it!"

But her cries only made him redouble his attack. Suddenly the entire door frame jumped its tracks and came away in his hands. He thrust it aside and, with a howl, grabbed her through the steaming cascade of water and hauled her out. He half dragged, half pushed her across the bathroom and flung her onto the carpet on the bedroom floor, then fell to the ground beside her and, seizing her head, twisted it to face him. From the ferocity in his gaze she knew that to plead or protest would only provoke him further. Let him do what he wanted; she was utterly naked and powerless. Trembling, she closed her eyes and, just covering her breasts with her hands, lay still and submissive, waiting for the inevitable to begin. Hot tears welled up beneath her eyelids. So this was how it had to end. After everything.

She waited for the first brutal touch, but none came. Through half-open eyes she saw him drag the counterpane off the bed. He's going to strangle me, she thought. But a moment later, she felt the counterpane settling softly over her body, covering her nakedness. She opened her eyes fully. A look of tender anxiety now filled his face and he reached forward to stroke her cheek, whimpering softly. From time to time he'd flash a petrified glance towards the bathroom, then he'd turn back to her and press his face close to hers, cradling her head back and forth.

Suddenly, she understood. The water! With his phobia, he'd thought she was trapped inside the shower, drowning. He hadn't come to rape her but to *rescue* her!

Relief and joy flooded through her. She wanted to burst out laughing.

"You're so sweet and kind," she murmured. "Sandy's right: you'd never hurt a fly."

For a fleeting moment the picture of the triangle within a circle flashed into her mind, and she stiffened. It wasn't quite as simple as all that. But then that was different: he'd been provoked. Reaching up, she drew him down alongside her and nestled him up against her breast. Together they lay there on the soft carpet in a sweet embrace, while in the background the shower still beat pitilessly down upon the tiled bathroom floor.

•

The meeting had been inevitable. The moment that she'd paused at the landing window and caught a glimpse of the white automobile watching the house from by the trees, Max had known it was imminent. Under pretext of going for a walk, she left the house and marched up the drive to face whoever it was. She had to draw their fire. The man in the back of the car looked vaguely familiar. A silver-haired, distinguished figure, he introduced himself as Dr. Eliot Lovejoy. He offered her a simple choice: did she want to talk right there or someplace else? Max had returned to get her own car. She would have any dealings well off premises.

As she turned out of the drive into the avenue, the white Plymouth pulled out behind her. It followed so close on her tail that she could see her own car reflected in the chauffeur's mirrored sunglasses. She drove through Lexington and, some way beyond, drew off the road onto a patch of rough ground. Ahead stretched the white palisade of a stud farm, behind lay a golf course, while opposite, hidden deep among the trees, rose a thin reed of smoke from a quarry. Cars and trucks passed sporadically, but otherwise the place was deserted. No help nearby either, she realized as the car wheeled around in the clearing and came to a halt, blocking her exit.

She got out and waited in the dazzling sun for the tall, well-dressed man to come toward her. He took up a stance a short distance away.

"Okay," he began tightly, "so what's the deal?"

"I'm not looking for a deal."

"We have a common interest, Miss Fitzgerald." He modulated his tone. "Now, we could work together. Or we could have a problem."

"Who the hell are you?"

"You wouldn't know about the Foundation. We're just a small group of right-minded people. Working for a better America."

She gave a derisive laugh. It was only much later that she recalled the name of the organization and made the connection. At present, all she could think of was Adam and the cruelty he'd been subjected to in that infernal laboratory.

"Torturing defenseless kids for your country?"

"Let's avoid the emotive language, shall we?" He

took a step closer. His eyes shone with a fervent brilliance. "Let's not beat around the bush, young lady. You and I know what this boy really is. He's unique. He is the greatest scientific find of our lifetime. He can tell us things we can't possibly learn from any other place. This boy is a walking echo from the past. His genes carry the pattern of our ancestry. He holds the key to who we are and what we have become. And why we behave as we do. That's why we need him. And why we're going to have him."

"Not if I can help it, Dr. Lovejoy."

"Listen to me!" He paused and gestured about him. "Look around this fine world of ours, Miss Fitzgerald. Everywhere you see crime, violence, aggression. As a scientist you must ask yourself, Why? Is our society sick because man is fundamentally sick? Is violence part of our psycho-chemical make-up? Is aggression *wired in*? Is it genetic? If so, can we identify the genes responsible? Is it an organic function? If so, can we lesion it?"

"Not that old fascist crap," retorted Max, stepping back.

He came a step forward to close the gap.

"Wait a minute! Look at the evidence. Look how inner-city crime correlates with organic brain dysfunction."

She felt her heat rising. This was a perversion of sociobiology she felt very passionate about.

"Come on, human behavior can't be explained in simple terms of brain structures!" she exclaimed scornfully. "That begs the question. Pointing to activity in the hypothalamus to 'explain' a person's anger doesn't answer the question of why it's active in the first place. Create a threatening environment and of course you'll get aggressive behavior in response. Build a less threatening society and you'll get less aggressive behavior. That's just obvious. It doesn't take psychosurgery to prove it. Or cold-blooded cruelty."

"Seventeen-X-three is an experiment," Lovejoy retorted. "Conducted under the conventions regulating animal experiments in laboratories."

"You mean Adam?" Her temper was skidding dangerously out of control. "He's not an animal, for God's sake! He's a human being."

"Is he?"

"Of course he is!"

"That's a matter of definition." He spread his hands in a gesture of mock helplessness. "I'm not aware of any special regulations governing experiments on Neanderthals."

"Bastard," she muttered between clenched teeth. She glared at the tall, eminent-looking figure, wondering how a man could hold such beliefs and live with his conscience. "Do you have a child, Dr. Lovejoy?" she asked.

"Two sons. Both at high school. And let me tell you, I care deeply about the kind of world they're growing up in."

"God spare them from ever getting into your hands!"

"You're letting your feelings override your judgment, young lady. I accept that you are fond of that boy. But the feelings of one junior genetics researcher are, frankly, of very little consequence. Our work does matter, though. We need him. We were getting some useful results on aggressive responses to phobic deterrents when you made your little entry. Sure, it means a little discomfort. All progress does."

"I've got nothing to say to you."

He mollified his tone, and a cajoling smile spread across his face.

"Let's not get into a philosophical debate. Now, listen sensibly. I have a proposition. Let's work together. Let's collaborate. You can share our research findings. You can run your own experiments. When we're through with the kid, you can publish. We're not trying to make a name for ourselves. And don't think about the money. You'll have all the resources you can need. Whatever you're making at MIT, we'll double it. That's our part of the deal." His eyes hardened. "You know the boy. You know the family. It'll be up to you to get him back to the Center. That's your part."

She shook her head.

"No deal."

"Think hard. The boy could easily disappear again."

"I said no. Never."

"Then I should warn you . . ."

A sudden surge of fury seized her. She rounded on him.

"Let *me* warn *you*, Dr. Lovejoy. Yes, I do know the boy. I know who he is and who you are and what you've been doing to him. Adam stays right where he is. If he 'disappears,' it'll be on every TV screen in America within twelve hours. Now, excuse me, please."

"Miss Fitzgerald . . ." he warned, grabbing her arm.

She broke away. "Don't touch me! I have nothing but contempt for you and what you do in the name of science."

Quaking with rage, she stormed off to her car. Spitting up the dirt, she spun it around and headed towards the road, only to find her path blocked by the white

automobile. The chauffeur was shaping up for a confrontation, but at a sign from Lovejoy he drove the car
clear, and a moment later she was on the open road and
away.

•

As one day eased itself into the next, Julia gradually
began to feel more at peace. A drowsy midsummer calm
settled over the household, and she felt a fullness and
contentment she hadn't known since the early times with
Sam at Cambridge. She spoke to William by phone every
day, and on his next visit to Boston she felt secure enough
to spend the whole night until dawn with him. He seemed
reluctant ever to visit her at her own home; she understood, and she respected him for it. In a way, too, she
preferred to meet "off premises" as it were: this affair
was her own independent business.

As for Adam, she kept the doors and windows unlocked even at night, but so far from attempting to escape
again, he wouldn't let her out of his sight. He tailed her
from room to room like a puppy, and at night he slept
on her floor—not even by the window, as he usually
preferred, but between the bed and the door so that he'd
be alerted if she left the room. At times his clinging was
almost excessive—he went into small fits of jealousy if
she kissed and hugged Sandy, for instance—but she was
careful not to deny him the least part of the comfort and
reassurance he sought.

She abandoned the training plan, too; the playroom
remained unused and the educational toys in it untouched. As for food, she allowed him whatever he asked
for, whether it was raw hamburgers or chocolate-chip ice-
cream topped with ketchup. Sandy welcomed him back

gladly, too. She began taking him with her on her morning runs again, although he generally gave up after no distance at all, and in the afternoons after school she'd often play jakari or softball with him on the front lawn.

There were still the old problems, however. Sandy had to keep him occupied downstairs, for instance, while she herself snatched a shower. They both had to give up swimming, too, for the first time he saw Sandy dive into the pool he threw a hysterical screaming fit and couldn't be calmed for hours. Nothing she tried would relieve this phobia, and washing him at night became a complicated ritual involving damp face-cloths and sponges kept well out of sight of the washbasin. She was still worried that, at the deepest level, he wasn't happy, too. Sometimes she'd wake at night and find him lying with his eyes open, staring across the room through the window into the starry night with a strange, sad look on his face, a look both haunted and wistful. At other times, such as when the doorbell or the telephone rang, he'd shrink back into the corner, uttering monkey-like chirrups of alarm, and she'd have to hold him tight to her for a good minute to calm him down. But on the surface, by and large, he seemed to be settling back in well, and every day that passed he became more his old, cheerful, mischievous self.

They planned a long touring holiday in August. They bought a small colonial silver vase for Max as a token of their thanks, though they couldn't reach her for several days to give it to her. One evening, they all went to the movies to see a Walter Matthau comedy, and Adam laughed as loudly as the best of them. The next evening, she saw William again; it was by way of a farewell night, for he was off to Europe the following day for a fortnight's vacation. He invited her to join him, but of course she couldn't. Once again, she returned home with her confidence and optimism refreshed. Over breakfast, she asked Sandy what she thought about throwing a small party, though the idea fizzled out when they tried to list the people they'd actually ask. Sandy had already tried to heal the rift with the Blanes. She'd given Kirsty a card for Scott, who was now back home and convalescing, though when no reply came she guessed it had been intercepted by their parents. She had her school friends, of course, though she didn't invite them home. It really didn't seem necessary: they were sufficient unto themselves. They were a family, they had their home and the days were long and warm and for most of the time quite carefree. Even, to Julia's relief, the police seemed to have given up looking for evidence to connect Adam with the Scott case, and though she was conscious of their watchful presence in the background, at least that nightmare hadn't become a reality. In all, the traumas of the past weeks seemed to melt away, and it seemed right to enjoy the gentle respite and take a welcome ease.

•

The boy could easily disappear again. The words drummed constantly through Max's mind. She had to find a solution, but she didn't know where to begin to look. She roamed the streets of Cambridge, staring blankly into shop windows or stopping abruptly on the sidewalk as she wrestled with some new argument, and from the weird glances she received she realized she had taken to talking aloud to herself. She looked in on the bars where her friends hung out, but she couldn't follow a conversation through and, too distracted to try, she would slip away again, leaving her drink barely touched, and continue pacing the sidewalk. Movement itself at least gave her some sense of making progress, but by the end of the second week she finally gave up in exhaustion. The answer she sought was not to be found out there, but within herself.

That evening, she drove to the ocean. There, standing on the empty beach, with her shadow lengthening out into the great grey expanse of the Atlantic and the twilight shouldering its way over the sill of the horizon ahead, she came to a momentous decision.

Adam's life was in danger. He had to be saved.

Not by stealing him away again, however, for there was nowhere he could run to and remain safe. If they could find him in the remote crags and gullies up in the mountains, they could find him anywhere. Not by making the Wendells' home a fortress either, for no amount of locks and fences would keep a professional out even if it succeeded in keeping the boy in. Nor yet by confessing the whole truth to Julia and urging her to sell up and take him back to England where he might, just possibly, be beyond the reach of Eliot Lovejoy.

There were only two possible solutions.

One was to take him back to where he'd come from. Literally.

She spent a while investigating this option seriously. A batch of twelve gene-modified gazelles from various zoos around America, now grouped at the Bronx Zoo, were scheduled to be airlifted out to Pakistan in three days' time. Each animal would travel in a special, double-skinned wooden crate. Now, it might just be conceivable to find a way of smuggling Adam aboard. At the other end, appropriate use of *baksheesh* might slip him through immigration. But then what? How would she get him to

Soviet Caucasus? And, most of all, how on earth would she find his people in all that vast wilderness? They were, by definition, a lost people. The secret had died with Sam. It was impossible.

The other was the solution of last resort. It tugged at the roots of her mind, demanding attention, but time and again she shrank from confronting it. The implications were mind-numbing. It might be her desire, even her duty, to save the boy's life, but at *this* cost? Did she have the right to play God with his very make-up? And yet, as the options failed, she found herself being driven inescapably into this final corner. Perhaps by fronting it out with Lovejoy she had bought Adam a little time; perhaps she hadn't. Either way, she knew, the man would get his way sooner or later. Adam was condemned to live all his life under that threat. Sometime, next week if not this week, later if not sooner, a van would turn up at the house, or a car would draw up alongside in the street, or maybe even a sniper with a dart-gun would draw a bead on him just as she herself had done, and before he knew it he would be right back in that laboratory nightmare again, and this time for good. And why? *Because he was what he was.* He was the victim of his own uniqueness. His only certain escape, therefore, his only real hope of living a halfway normal life within our society, was to become different. To lose his uniqueness. To become, literally, one of us.

She had already worked out hypothetically how she might do it. Conceptually, it was simple. From his blood plasma she already had a full analysis of his genetic make-up. Murray was working on precisely the same analyses, but for modern human kind. Subtract the first from the second, and what did you get? Those genes that we possessed and Adam didn't. He was a primitive, a backward savage dredged up from the mists of time, simple soul lost in the dark realms of superstition and unreason. We, on the other hand, were creatures of enlightenment, complex social beings who had achieved mastery of the planet by the application of our vastly superior intelligence and, above all, the supreme faculty of reason. Intelligence, reason, law, social order, technology: it all amounted to one thing that set us above our caveman cousins—*civilization*.

She would take Adam out of the dark and into the light. She'd make him leap the millennial gulf that separated us. She'd bypass the slow and random grind of evolution, and in a single step she'd raise him to our own level. She'd make him one of us.

She'd give him the gift of civilization.

His birthright.

22

○

CONCEPTUALLY IT MIGHT BE SIMPLE, BUT PRACTICALLY it was like searching for an ant on Mount Everest. With as many base pairs in a single human cell as there were people on the globe, the prospect of finding a single specific gene cluster—and the key cluster at that—filled her with despair. She turned back to her earlier subtractive hybridization work. If Adam differed genetically from ourselves by a mere 0.1%, and if, by extrapolating from McKusick's *Mendelian Inheritance in Man*, she was right to conclude that the basic number of separate human genetic functions was of the order of 5,000–10,000, then this equated to an effective difference of probably no more than ten gene clusters. With all the new techniques for probing and sequencing, would it really be so difficult to identify these? If she knew what she was looking for, of course, she could readily develop a restriction enzyme to isolate the particular segment and then, by means of a regular plasmid vector, clone it to produce useful quantities. This was routine procedure in any genetics lab. But that was the nub of the problem: she didn't know *which* ten.

Finally, after several days of fruitless work, she realized that her underlying thinking was at fault. It took Murray to point out her obvious mistake. One morning in the labs, seeing her driven to the limit of frustration and exhaustion, he came over and put a tentative arm around her shoulder. Wedging his glasses higher up his nose, he peered at the autoradiography plates she'd been staring at in the hope of making some sense of the disordered wiggles and blobs.

"Still on your man-chimp, huh?" He stepped over to the door and flicked on the red light in the corridor. "You saw Gerald's memo on extra-curricular activities?"

"Gerald can go screw himself." She sighed wearily. "I turn the job down. So he stops my pay-check. Says the budget's been held up."

"Bullshit! Take it higher, Maxie."

"He's got all the aces. Anyway, this," she went on, pointing to the plates, "is my meal-ticket. So long as he doesn't cancel my pass-key before I'm through, I don't care what the hell he does. I can work anywhere. I don't need any aggravation from him."

"You're not thinking of quitting?" he asked with sudden feeling. He turned quickly back to the plates. "Looks like you've got problems. You want to talk about it?"

She began elaborating her story, explaining that the embryo in the host chimp's womb was growing to term, and that, using samples of fetal blood, her job was to identify the key genetic differences between this creature and man himself, with a view to matching these with observed behavioral characteristics after birth. The story grew flimsier the more she went on. But Murray was scarcely listening; as always, he was more interested in the problem than its context. As he examined the plates and the reams of print-out, his frown deepened. Finally he perched on her desk and scratched his head.

"Have they done ultrasounds?"

"I guess so. I don't have the results."

"I mean, have they *see* this thing? Christ, Maxie, it's going to look goddamn human. Meet it in a dark alley and you won't be able to tell the difference."

"That's what's puzzling me," she hastened. "I figure only a handful of functional gene clusters are different from yours and mine."

"Jesus," he breathed.

"The questions is," she went on, pressing home, "*which* ones?"

He pondered for a moment, then shook his head.

"That's not how I'd go about it."

"Okay, wise guy. What would *you* do?"

"I'd look at modifications of shared genes, not at entirely different ones. I'll show you what I mean. Take fetal hemoglobin, for example." He reached for the print-out and spent a moment riffling through, then tapped a finger on a mass of close print. "Here. Alpha genes on chromosome 16. What do we have, then?" He began scribbling down a notation in the margin; he could read the four-letter AGCT code as though it were his mother tongue. "Look. $5'-\zeta-\psi\zeta-\psi\alpha-\alpha2-\alpha1-3'$. Right?" He tapped the *psi-alpha* symbol. "A pseudogene, okay? It has sequence homology with the alpha genes but normally it has a mutation that prevents its expression. An evolutionary remnant of a once-active globin gene."

"So?"

"Maxie, you aren't using your *eyes*. Take a real look. I said, *normally*. In human beings. But this gene here doesn't have that mutation suppressing it, see? It's active. I guess it's still active in your average chimp." He paused, evidently seeing the point was slow to sink in. "You've got to look for *clusters we share but where there's been a modification.* In the hemoglobin case, we've all dropped this piece of our vestigial past. This little monster hasn't, and that gives us a clue how close it'll be to its chimp mother. But if you want to see how close it'll be to Joe Doe, you want to look at mutations which have *added* something to the pot. Right?"

Gradually the message percolated through her weary, blurred mind. He was right, and more so than he knew. At the pace evolution progressed, there simply couldn't have been time for modern man to evolve significant new genes from his Neanderthal cousins. To look for quite different gene clusters, therefore, was likely to be fruitless. Better to look instead for differences *within* existing clusters. Almost certainly, the basic "genes of civilization," whatever the hell that meant, were already present in Adam, only in a dormant or low-active state. What gave us our superiority was probably no more than minor mutations which cancelled out inhibitors or promoted the genes to work more actively. The place to look, therefore, was in the regulator mechanisms of the genes.

"Civilization" was not a single set of faculties or aptitudes, of course, but a complex pattern of behavior. Behavior itself was the product of a subtle interaction between the external environment and the internal chemistry of the brain. Genes didn't code directly for behavior as such, merely for amino acids in the peptide chain of a particular protein. Linking behavior to the activity of a protein was extremely difficult. Sometimes it was possible:

serotonin had been linked with aggressive behavior, for instance, and a single gene cluster had been identified that coded for that. But more complex behavior was polygenetic, involving numerous genes operating at once. Was she looking for a whole bunch of separate genes, each with its minor mutation? Or was she looking for one master gene which regulated those others? How the heck could she even begin to know, let alone find the answer?

She felt a timid hand on her shoulder again.

"You look beat, Maxie," said Murray. "C'mon, let's get out of here. I'll buy you a cup of coffee."

•

Day followed night in a seamless blur. They worked behind locked doors and drawn blinds. Midday became indistinguishable from midnight. The trash bins spilled over with empty take-out cartons and drink cans, the floor was awash with computer print-out and every available surface was piled high with agar plates and X-ray sheets and bits of other genetic assay equipment. They took it in turns to fetch take-outs and to grab spells of sleep on a couch she'd set up in the corner. Once in a while she called Julia to ask how things were there and to check on Adam. She didn't know how long the line would hold; she could only be sure that time was running out ever faster.

She'd been forced to make a deal with Murray, for the task was too great. In return for his help, she offered him an equal share in any results. She'd face up to the implications of that later, and in the meantime she kept consistently to her story about the transgenic embryo. His input was unavoidable anyway, for as a key member of the national human genome program he had access to the entire gene library so far developed.

Once again, the concept was simple. They would work by elimination. First, they'd identify the gross differences between the test material and the human template. They'd eliminate all but the regulator sequences. These they'd fine down still further by ignoring any which were too small, too repetitive or which controlled genes whose functions were known to be irrelevant. And then they'd see what they ended up with.

In practice, however, it proved a nightmare. Hours of assay work ended in the bin. Promising leads fizzled out to nothing. Grand expectations turned out to be false hopes. She was growing desperate. Murray was becoming disillusioned. He started asking difficult questions as the startling genetic closeness became increasingly apparent. The stock of Adam's blood plasma, too, which she withdrew in smaller and smaller quantities from the cryostat and only when Murray was out of the room, was threatening to run out. She herself was beginning to make contingency plans should it all come to nothing. In a last-ditch attempt to save the boy, she'd publish and be damned. She'd write up her data for *Nature* and *Scientific American* and send copies simultaneously to *Time* magazine, the *National Geographic*, *People*, the *Washington Post*, the *New York Times*. She'd let the world know who he was. There'd be mass TV interest. Nationwide network exposure. Interviews. Movie offers. He'd become a household talking-point, she a household name. Julia would never forgive her, of course, and Adam himself would be corrupted. But at least, under such a glare of publicity, no one would dare attempt to abduct him. He'd be spared Dr. Lovejoy's experiment chamber.

And then the breakthrough came.

It came quite unexpectedly. She herself found it. She was plowing routinely through a print-out listing gene sequences on the short arm of chromosome 16, around band p15. She had moved on to check through another long list of bases before a query registered itself in the back of her mind. She went back to the string. There, in the central portion of a precursor regulator segment of just some six hundred base pairs, she found a section which, when checked against the listing from the library, had clearly not undergone the same mutation as our own. She went over it three, four, five times. No, she wasn't mistaken. This regulator was, quite simply, switching off this gene in Adam's case and, in its modified form, switching it on in ours. And, by the look of its structure and position, this gene could itself very well regulate several others. Could this conceivably be the master gene they sought?

She took the print-out over to Murray's bench. For a while he stared at the sequence she'd ringed, making small grunts and tilting his head this way and that as if to get a different angle on it. He reached for a pen and made some calculations of his own. He tapped some data into the computer and carefully studied a listing that came up on the screen. He pushed the print-out away, frowned, shrugged, nodded. Then with a deep breath he slowly took off his glasses and stood up.

"That's it," he said in a snipped voice. "That's it. We got it." He flapped his arms by his side and sought around for some displacement for the feelings about to burst. Suddenly he let out a long, wild whoop and flung both fists triumphantly into the air.

•

Instantly, she had to face two questions.

One: should she? And two: *could* she?

Introducing modified genes *in vivo* merely into animals, as she knew all too well from her work with gazelles, required endless submissions for official approval. But doing the same to a human being? In 1983, Martin Cline from UCLA had inserted engineered genes into patients suffering from beta thalassemia; his experiment hadn't been approved in the States and it was not successful either, and he was subsequently reprimanded and demoted. At a conference more recently she'd met the head of the hematology unit at the National Heart, Lung and Blood Institute who told her he'd been applying for permission to insert an artificial gene, using a mouse retrovirus, into human cancer patients. Even though the gene had no therapeutic value and was merely a "tracer," this had entailed months of detailed submissions to the NIH and the other guardian bodies of safe practice in genetic engineering. In both cases, extensive tests had been carried out on mice. Here, she wasn't even thinking of running any tests: there simply wasn't time. In the other cases, moreover, the patients had given their informed consent. Adam couldn't. Julia might be empowered to do so on his behalf, but Julia was not to know anything about it anyway. There was no way around it: what she was contemplating was grossly, shamelessly and unequivocally unethical.

And then, could she actually do it? Getting a gene into the appropriate target cell and keeping it there involved a whole separate series of problems. However, this was precisely her specialty. With her gazelles, she had designed a specific retrovirus to carry the foreign chamois genes right into the cells' chromosomes. Could she maybe modify this, or would she have to start from scratch to construct a new vector? And, if the catalogue of obstacles wasn't already long enough, how would she get it physically delivered? It was reasonable to assume that, being a behavior regulator, the gene would be expressed mainly in the brain. So, she needed a vector that was carried by the blood and passed easily through the blood-brain barrier. You could inject a gazelle in the butt and get it into its bloodstream that way. But Adam, with his terror of needles? And not just one injection, either, but a whole course? Maybe a shot every day for weeks, even months?

Leaving Murray working on a probe to isolate the exact section, she let herself out of the building and strolled, blinking, into the dazzling afternoon sun. As often, her steps took her toward the river. In the shadows beneath a bridge she noticed the figure of a young black kid rolling up his sleeve and tightening a tie round his arm with his teeth. She looked away; in any American city it was an unremarkable sight. Fleetingly she wondered if drug addiction had a genetic component and, if so, you could incorporate a vector in every shot to switch off the gene responsible for the craving. She chuckled at the idiocy of the idea, a harsh, brittle laugh that didn't ring familiar. She was overtired. The sun coruscated from the water's surface, mesmerizing her. She should go home, take a pill, get some sleep. But her thoughts were locked on their rails. Adam was no junkie; that wasn't the way. But narcotics weren't the only substances people shot up regularly. People with quite minor complaints often had to take daily injections. Some even had to inject themselves. There was a diabetic in Experimental Biology who gave himself a tiny injection before every meal. She'd seen him in the canteen. He had a neat little needle, just like a fountain pen, with a screw cap and all. You never really even noticed him do it. A quick flick of the pen-top, slip open the shirtfront and in it went, just a few millimeters, into the stomach. He said it hurt no more than the faintest sting. Amazing.

Her mind suddenly jerked to attention. She stared at the junkie, now walking away, on air. A smile broke over her lips. She snapped her fingers. Jesus, she thought; that's it.

•

"*Prazosin*," she read. "Trade-name 'Hypovase.' Prazosin hydrochloride. Used to treat raised blood pressure. *Adverse effects*: dizziness, weakness, frequency of passing urine, fainting... Cases reported of unconsciousness after the first dose. *Dose:* By mouth. 0.5 mg three times a day for seven days, increasing to a maximum daily dose of 20 mg."

She closed the large *Pharmacopoeia* with a definitive snap and rose to her feet, scraping her chair on the linoleum floor. Heads looked up from desks; someone hissed Sssh! She replaced the book on the library shelf and tiptoed down the aisle to the exit. She knew exactly where to go for it. Half the guys in Biochemistry ran a sideline in under-the-counter prescription drugs. A single dose of 20 mg should do the trick nicely.

•

Julia spread a blanket on the grass and unloaded the tray. Adam grabbed his beaker of orange juice and emptied it in one gulp, then held it out for more. She cast Max a smile as she refilled it. His needs were always a priority.

"Come and sit down, Max," she said. "Adam will

be here, beside me. No, you've had enough to drink for now. Yes, you can have more later, when everyone else has got theirs. Sandy, pass the sandwiches, there's a love. Cucumber," she informed Max wryly. "And Earl Grey tea. So, how have you been? We've missed you. You look to me as if you've been working too hard again."

Max pulled a face. "We had a bunch of problems on the project."

"And it's all sorted out now?"

"Sure, it's all fine."

A brief silence fell.

"You know," began Julia quietly, "I almost miss work. The people, the gossip, the structure. Even the problems. I envy you, Max."

"You can't be all things all the time. You gave up your career to have another child. A fair swap. One bunch of problems for another." She glanced at Adam; he was sitting absorbed in unpicking an old raffia shopping-bag. "I almost forgot," she went on, reaching into her bag. "I bought you all a box of candy."

"How very kind," said Julia. "Let's have them afterwards. Keep it away from Adam. You know he's a devil for sweets. Come on, do tuck in. And tell us all that's been going on."

After tea was over, Max offered around her candies. Wisely she handed Adam his own in case he grabbed the whole box. Then Sandy sprang to her feet and dragged the boy off to play softball. Julia stretched out on the blanket. The sky was a cloudless, infinite blue. A plane was scoring a trail high overhead with a sound like softly tearing tissue-paper. The afternoon air was drowsy with the scent of roses and honeysuckle. She looked across at Max, sitting with her chin on her knees and her dark hair shimmering in the sunlight, staring out into the heat haze that hung in the middle distance, and she felt a sudden swell of feeling for this young woman. She genuinely *cared*. From the first, she'd taken a real interest in Adam and treated him in a way none of their friends in the neighborhood ever had. How ridiculous to doubt her motives. That had merely been the product of her own anxiety. Projection, wasn't that what they called it? But all that was now behind them, thankfully.

Max must have sensed her scrutiny, for she turned. Julia couldn't find words to express what she felt. She let out a long sigh.

"Hot, isn't it?"

"Great."

"It's going to get hotter, they say."

Max merely smiled distantly, as if preoccupied with her own thoughts. A moment's silence fell.

Suddenly, the peace was broken by a cry. A second later, Sandy came tearing around the side. Her face was ashen and her eyes wide with alarm.

"It's Adam!" she cried breathlessly. "He's fainted. Come quick!"

•

Julia put down the telephone and stood for a moment, staring at the table-lamp and bookshelves reflected in the study windowpanes. The night beyond was pitch black, and a cool breeze filtered in through the open sash. She bit her lip. So, that was what it had been. All along. Diabetes. "Early-onset diabetes mellitus," Max had called it. Fortunately, however, in a mild form. Insulin-dependent diabetes most often struck children and adolescents, she'd said. The victims just suddenly stopped producing insulin. And Adam was one.

Max had taken urine and blood samples away with her at once and had them analyzed later that afternoon by a pathologist friend who did this every day of his life. It tied in with Adam's general thirst and now the fainting-fit. His system was producing too little insulin, resulting in an excessive blood-sugar level. Maybe this accounted for everything.

This time she'd felt she ought to call Ralph Singer. Diabetes was a well-defined physical condition, well away from the grey area of psychology. Max had seemed very reluctant to see the doctor involved over this, just as she had been over the referral for the brain scan. Maybe here, as then, it wasn't really necessary. Couldn't it be contained simply by a change of diet, by cutting down on sugars and carbohydrates? Max wasn't sure this would do, however, given such a sudden onset. Julia had asked about pills. There were oral hypoglycemic drugs, Max had told her, but these weren't really any more effective than diet. The common alternative was injections of insulin.

"But Adam would never let a needle anywhere near him!" she'd cried.

"Give me twenty-four hours," Max had replied coolly. "I'll come up with the answer. If I don't, then by all means let's bring Dr. Singer in. Now go to bed, Julia, and don't worry."

She went to the living room and poured herself a brandy, then returned to the study and spent an hour with *The Family Practitioner* and *Household Medicine*, reading up all she could on the condition. Everything that Max said was right. Well then, she'd go along with Max's suggestion. Max knew all the right people in the medical and scientific world, and all her advice in the past had been absolutely sound. A time came when there had to be more trust and less suspicion. And anyway, if she didn't feel entirely comfortable, she could always call in Ralph Singer for a second opinion.

•

Towards the end of the following afternoon, while Sandy was still at school, Max arrived carrying a small black attaché case. She led Julia into the study and shut the door, then she opened the case. It contained the kit for a diabetic.

"Here," she said triumphantly. "I said I'd come up with the answer. I have a friend in Biology who's been a diabetic all his life. His doctor is a specialist. I discussed Adam's case with them both. Remember, I've got a full physical analysis of the kid, better than any medical record. It'd take your man Singer a month to get that data. Anyway, I went through it all very carefully. And this is exactly what he needs. Should I show you?"

She first demonstrated the syringe. It resembled a draftsman's pen with a short, fine needle. This was sheathed in a spring-loaded cowl which, when locked, protected the needle and prevented accidental discharge, and when unlocked, slid back to let the needle penetrate the skin a small amount. The insulin was a clear liquid that came in little polythene cartridges. With a quick pumping action of the case, a pressure could be created around the cartridge, so that once the needle was inserted just a fraction beneath the skin, a light touch on the release button at the back was all that was necessary to deliver the right dose. In addition to several spare needles, there was also an expanded polystyrene box which contained fifteen cartridges, each giving the equivalent of a week's supply. These were to be kept in the fridge.

With this, Max told her, Adam could keep to his usual diet, including sweet foods: indeed, if ever he missed a meal and went faint, it could mean he was low on blood sugar, and so a packet of candy should be kept on hand. The insulin preparation included zinc to make it slow-acting, so that one shot a day should be sufficient, and Julia could give him it whenever it seemed most convenient. Although the dosage level was low—his condition was relatively mild—she'd best keep a close eye on him for the first few days until he'd stabilized. Beyond that, it should all be plain sailing.

Max stayed only to deliver the kit and demonstrate how to use it, then said she had to be getting back. She left before she'd even had a chance to see Adam, but she promised to call later to see how the first time had gone.

After seeing her off, Julia returned to the study. For a while she stood toying with the syringe in her hands, wondering if it could really be that simple. If a specialist doctor had prescribed the treatment, knowing all about the patient that Max could tell him, then there probably wasn't any call for a second opinion. At least, she should give it a try. If she kept a close eye on the boy, as Max had advised, she could catch anything before it went wrong. She spent a while practicing loading and cocking the syringe until she had mastered it. Then she went to find Adam. She would start right away.

He was sitting on the kitchen floor, fiddling with an Action Man paratrooper, pulling it about in the random way he played with toys. She got a box of his favorite chocolate chip cookies and, sitting down opposite him, began the old copy-cat routine. First she bared an inch of her own tummy and, laughing and chatting, made a pretense of pressing the needle into the flesh. Then she reached over and did the same to him. Back and forth the play-act went until at one moment, in a single swift movement, she unlocked the cowl catch, let the needle prick into his flesh, pressed the release button, then withdrew it and locked the cowl again. There was a second before he let out a small grunt, more puzzled than pained, then he took the syringe from her and pressed it harmlessly back into her stomach. She mimicked his grunt, then laughed and gave him a cookie.

"Tickles, doesn't it?" She chuckled. "Here, have another biscuit for being so good."

She let him play with the syringe until he grew bored, then quietly took it off him and, judging her moment, got up and slipped it into a high cupboard. She turned again to find him blinking hard and rubbing his eyes. He twitched his head a few times as if to shake something off, then he blinked once again and, with a strange shrug, returned to the Action Man. This time he stood the model upright and, step by step, marched it across the floor. For a moment he stood it to attention before him, then suddenly he knocked it down so sharply that its head fell off. Shaking with small shudders of laughter, he screwed the head back on again and repeated the game.

She went to leave a message on Max's answering-machine to say all had gone remarkably well, and returned to find him playing happily by himself. Could it really be working so fast? Maybe: it was only a question of getting a hormone balance right. He certainly did already seem somehow more *himself*. As she watched him, she felt a warm glow spreading through her. It was worth anything to see him happy like this. To see him being his real self.

•

The boy stared out into the clear dark night. Carried faintly on the breeze came the distant sounds of cars, doors slamming, laughter. A bird called from the far woods. An owl? Behind the garage a snuffling betrayed a badger digging for roots. A badger? He suddenly wasn't sure. These sounds were familiar, yet not as he knew them.

He raised his eyes to the stars. He sought to disentangle their patterns. Here was the Crow . . . No, there it was. He scoured the heavens for the Pole star. He always knew his way from that. He blinked. Something seemed to be crawling inside his head. He rubbed his eyes. That was a bit better. Everything was clearer.

He searched the sky again. What was he looking for? Would he know it when he found it?

He reached out a hand to steady himself against the window-frame. His voice came from a different person.

"Father?" he croaked. *"Father?"*

THREE

SUMMER

23

○

AT FIRST, THE CHANGE CAME OVER ADAM GRADUALLY, but the effect was cumulative. As each day went by, his development seemed to accelerate at an increasing pace, so that by the end of the first fortnight Julia looked at him and found, to her astonishment and delight, an entirely new Adam was emerging. It was as though a light had been switched on in a darkened room.

One by one, and with no prompting from her, he began to adopt the manners and habits she'd tried so hard to inculcate into him in the early days. One night during the first week, she'd woken in the early hours to find he'd disappeared from her room, but only to discover he'd taken himself up to his attic and was asleep on the mattress beneath a clean white sheet. The following morning, he got himself up and came down for breakfast early, before Sandy left for school. Another morning at the start of the second week, he decided he was going to eat the same as her—muesli with fresh fruit, rather than his usual cold porridge. When she offered him a spoon, he took it and began using it with considerable dexterity. She noticed he used it in his right hand, too, something she'd never seen him do before. Two days later, for the first time, he eschewed the floor and sat up at the table with the two of them. And the morning after that, he appeared dressed in jeans and an inside-out tee-shirt, and he'd even made some attempt to comb his hair.

Julia could only marvel at the sheer speed of the progress he was making. In a single day he would make strides that she'd failed to achieve with him in months of struggle. It was amazing to witness what a difference the right treatment could make—and dreadful, too, to imagine how long he might have gone on if they hadn't diagnosed the root of the trouble. All along, he'd been physically, not mentally, ill. The blame lay partially with Ralph Singer. Why hadn't the doctor spotted the problem during the check-ups? Medical practitioners were all alike: they only ever saw what they expected to find. Everything was becoming crystal clear now. The nomad diet evidently contained something that Western food lacked, something that triggered off the body's own production of insulin. She wondered with alarm whether he'd suffered lasting damage through lack of sugar to the brain Max frankly couldn't say; she thought not, but only time would tell.

This extraordinary turnabout affected not only his outward behavior but his very personality as well. As the days passed, it was quite clear he was growing brighter, more alert, more eager to learn, *cleverer* overall. He appeared to be developing a stronger sense of his own self, too, and a new willfulness entered his manner. At the same time, on an emotional level, he seemed somehow more restrained. His moods were distinctly less volatile and his reactions less immediate; he would consider his responses to new situations quite carefully, rather than react with his previous spontaneity. But that was all part of the same new and welcome process of healthy socialization. The boy was growing up. As Sandy put it, he was at last becoming like the rest of us. She could hardly wait to tell William when he got back. She wasn't going to risk causing him misplaced worry by telling him on the phone when he called. She'd keep it as a wonderful surprise.

•

Nothing, however, was more surprising than his sudden new grasp of language. One morning—it was the day of Sandy's end-of-year dance—he took Julia by the hand and led her into the playroom. There he sat her down on the floor and, reaching for an alphabet teacher, made her read through the book with him. "A is for apple," she recited, "B is for ball, C is for cat," and so on to the end. As she turned the final page, he pointed and said, in a clear voice, enunciating each syllable distinctly, "Zebra." Then he took the book from her and went through it again by himself. "Apple," he began. "Ball. Cat. Dog. Elephant." Julia watched, enthralled. He wasn't actually reading the words, of course, but he was naming the objects. He was *speaking*.

But could he put words together into phrases? That was the next step. Could he then form sentences? She fetched a bowl of fruit from the kitchen and placed it on the floor between them. She put two apples out before him and pointed to them.

"How many apples are there, Adam?" she asked.

With barely a hesitation, he reached forward and touched each quickly with a finger.

"One, two," he said.

"Two *whats*?"

"Two apples."

"And what are those?" she asked, pointing to a bunch of grapes.

"Grapes."

"The grapes are in the bowl." She paused. "Where are the grapes?"

"In the bowl." He was rocking back and forth on his heels. "More?"

"And these?"

"Oranges. One, two, three oranges." Each word was so clearly spoken. "Three oranges in the bowl."

"That's right! You're brilliant, Adam."

He grinned.

"Adam's brilliant."

She held his eye as the significance of his reply gradually dawned upon her. Adam...is...brilliant. If he could grasp the simple syntax of language, could he apprise the structures that lay beneath it? Was he, for instance, capable of simple logical reasoning? Carried along on a crest of this breaking wave, she decided to try an easy syllogism. The deduction was intuitively obvious to anyone raised in a tradition of logical thought but, on all the evidence she'd had to date, quite beyond a wild gypsy child like Adam.

She pulled the fruit bowl between them.

"Listen carefully, Adam," she began. "All these things in this bowl are called fruit. These grapes are in this bowl. These grapes are therefore...?"

"Fruit," he replied instantly. "More?"

"All fruit is good. Oranges are fruit. Therefore oranges are...?"

"Good." He took an orange, bit off a section of the peel and sucked the juice. "Very good," he said.

She took him around the house, pointing out one object after another. He was insatiable, like a thirsty plant in a drought. It was as if all these familiar things he'd been living among, which, she believed, existed for him just as a myriad of innumerable separate entities, without connection or common link, were now forming into patterns and families. He would repeat the name of each after her, then link them together—"red chair, wooden chair, soft chair"—suggesting for the first time that he'd begun to perceive categories. She was increasingly struck by his native intelligence, too, and every new revelation brought with it for her a pang of regret that she had ever thought of him as backward. His brain simply hadn't been getting the right nourishment; that was what had been retarding him.

Before lunch, she played once again the familiar routine of the injection pen. This time he seemed to register a slightly sharper prick than usual, but when she took the bull by the horns and explained carefully that it was necessary to make him better—and he was feeling better already, wasn't he?—he appeared to accept this as a sufficient explanation and, handing her back the hypodermic after a short but careful examination, asked abruptly for his lunch. He chose a bacon-burger and potato chips, and later cleaned out Sandy's Jell-o from the fridge. Afterwards, he took himself off to the living room where he switched on the television and sat gripped to a soap opera. But this time, instead of watching it with detachment as a series of moving images that occasionally provoked an outburst of inappropriate laughter, he seemed to follow the drama as though it carried a proper meaning for him. Far from trailing her around the house, too, he seemed quite content to stay in the room on his own, leaving her free to catch up on her calls and correspondence in the study.

After half an hour there, she heard his footsteps approaching down the corridor. When he came in he was carrying her car keys.

"Out," he said, pressing the keys into her hand. "Out in car. Shops."

"What do you say, Adam?"

"Please, Mumma."

She smiled and rubbed a hand through his thick dark hair. In the hallway, she noticed him looking at himself in the mirror and patting down his hair where she'd tousled it. She smothered a grin. She'd never thought she'd see the day when he took a pride in his appearance. Again, at the shopping plaza, she caught him looking at his reflection in the shop windows. It was when they were inside the Grand Union she saw him staring at a pretty girl at the check-out that she realized that he was developing in other ways, too.

That evening, after she'd got Sandy dressed up for her dance and finally, after much agonizing over her appearance, driven her to the school, she took Adam upstairs to get him ready for bed. Instead of allowing her to wash him, he edged her from the bathroom and locked the door behind her. When he finally emerged, in place of the boxer shorts that sometimes covered his nakedness and frequently did not, he was wearing proper pajamas. She felt the bitter-sweet twinge of sadness a parent feels to witness their child's innocence giving way to shame.

That night, she tucked him up and kissed him lightly on the head. And as she went downstairs to wait for

Sandy's call to collect her, she looked back over the astonishing progress he'd so rapidly made. Growing up inevitably meant growing apart, but so long as he was growing into himself, into the real Adam that had been stifled for so long, she could do nothing but rejoice.

•

Sandy sat apart on the wooden balustrade, watching the others laughing and flirting in their couples. Inside the marquee, the band had broken into a rendering of "Twist and Shout." Across the lawns trailed lines of garden flares and Chinese lanterns like the tendrils of a jellyfish, converging on the warm, rich light that glowed from within the tent. Forming the backdrop rose the rear façade of the mansion, its pinnacles and gables profiled against the pale midsummer night sky. She smoothed a crease from her cream taffeta ball-gown and sighed quietly. She'd had her hair done specially, she'd spent ages thinking what to wear and taken great pains over her make-up, all for her mother's sake. Her mother, she knew, had hunted high and low for the right dress and thrown herself into the preparations as though it were a wedding and not just a school dance, all for *her* sake. She mustered a small, wry smile. It was rather absurd really, pretending she was one of them. Sure, various friends had come up to chat or ask her to dance. She'd danced a couple of numbers; she'd even attempted a Dixie stomp with the year's valedictorian, but then the music switched to a smooch and they'd separated, leaving the floor to real couples and their closer clinches. She'd gone outside into the warm night, where the air was sweet with the nocturnal scents of flowers and where, wafted across from the shrubbery, betrayed only by stifled giggles and the occasional sudden glow of a cigarette, she caught the resinous incense of an illicit joint. She felt at ease here outside, listening to sounds of the party from apart. She was familiar with being alone. The disappointment no longer hurt as it used to.

Gradually she became aware of a commotion inside the marquee. Voices rose in a cheer. The band stopped playing, then with a long roll of the drums burst into a rendering of "Yankee Doodle," the school basketball team's song. Through the open flaps of the tent she could see a tall, slightly stooping figure surrounded by an excited clamor of friends. As the crowd parted, she caught a brief glimpse. She gave a start. It was Scott, supporting himself on a walking-stick. She barely recognized him: his fair hair had grown long but his face was lean and hollow, and his white tuxedo hung loose about his wasted frame. A moment later, the press surged around him again and swept him from her view, and the band started into a brisk Chuck Berry number.

She glanced at her watch, trying to ignore the thumping of her pulse. It was nearing eleven. She'd give it a little longer, then call Mum. She whiled away a few minutes chatting to a fellow tenth-grader about white-water rafting in Colorado, then went for a stroll to the foot of the lawns where a barbecue, tricked up in Mexican style, was dispensing tacos and tortillas. As she was returning to the balustrade, she heard a voice from the darkness.

"Hi."

The figure of Scott detached itself from the shadows and hobbled stiffly towards her. He must have seen the look on her face, for he tapped his leg with his stick and chuckled.

"So I won't play for the Lakers, what the heck?"

He came closer. In the light from the lanterns and

flares his broad, strong face looked gaunt, almost ascetic, and his eyes glowed from sunken hollows. They both began to speak at the same time, then broke off, laughing. She launched in first again. She wanted to say everything she felt all at once. How sorry she was for not visiting him more often in the hospital. That things were different now at home, that Adam had been ill all along but now they'd found what the trouble had been and he was genuinely becoming a new person, that the past should be buried and she'd like him as her friend again but she'd understand if he felt he couldn't be.

"I'm truly sorry," was all that came out.

"I've had a lot of time and done a lot of thinking, Sandy." He hesitated, trying to articulate what he wanted to say. "I wrote you a few times, but I didn't mail them. You know how it is. Mom, Dad, even Kirsty. They only see it their way. For me, it's over and done. Forgotten."

"And forgiven?"

"I guess I've forgotten what there is to forgive." He chuckled. "Hey, c'mon! Let's dance."

"With that leg?"

"Fred Astaire, eat your heart out."

He reached for her arm, but stumbled and smothered an oath. Laying aside his walking-stick, he leant on her arm and limped onto the dance floor. Heads turned; faces registered surprise, amazement, envy. The crush parted before them to form a clearing, and there, in the center of the sprung wooden floor beneath the tented roof, they shuffled and hobbled their way through the dances like runners in a three-legged race, seeing one through to the next until the lights dimmed and the band struck up the final slow farewell number.

•

Adam sat up in bed. He blinked hard. He shook his head. He hammered his skull with his fists, but he couldn't dislodge it. It lay inside, stirring sluggishly like a slumbering beast waking. Every now and then the creature would writhe violently and speak with a voice. He pressed his thumbs into his ears and uttered a cry. Yes, that was it! That was the voice of the demon within. Pretending to be his own thoughts. Apeing his own voice.

He scrambled out of bed and, ripping off his pajamas, fell to a crouch beneath the open window. Naked, he felt better, more like his real self. Then he became aware he was shivering. He'd never felt cold here before, not even in the winter snow and ice. He stared out at the night sky. It was almost too pale to see stars. He began to search the heavens as he'd so often done, but even as he scanned the constellations he heard the small voice whispering doubt in his mind. *You dumb fool*, it said. *Your father is buried. He lies beneath the ground. You saw the grave. He is deep in the earth, while you look for him in the sky. Idiot!*

He fell back. No! It's not true! That's the voice of lies! Please, father, show yourself. Please, Atta. *Please.*

The voice was laughing now, life the soft, self-satisfied chuckle of an older, crueller child. He beat his head on the wall, once, then again and again, harder and harder, but he couldn't drive out the terrible mocking laugh. Words flew into his mind like fiery arrows. Words he knew and yet he didn't. They sprang up from some deep and terrible well of blackness. He thrust his hands over his groin, shamed by his own nakedness. He struggled to his feet. If he slipped away, maybe he could cheat it. If he ran fast enough he might shake it off. He groped for the door, suddenly conscious he couldn't see in the dark properly any more. What was happening to him?

He stumbled down the steep attic stairs. At the bottom, he hesitated and cast about him. Driven by some inner impulse, he slid into Sandy's room. The scent of her clothes, her make-up, her body, all stirred in him a dreadful mixture of terror and excitement. On the bed lay her slip, her panties, her small personal things, all laden with her scent. Sick with fear yet in the grip of a terrible necessity, he gathered up the clothes and pressed them to his face. A heavy ache swelled in the pit of his stomach, a sweet agony he'd never know before, a fire shooting and curling through his limbs. Panting, trembling, fainting, he thrust the ball of clothes over the furnace raging between his thighs and, pressing hard, yielded himself up to the overwhelming urge as one violent convulsion after another discharged through his body.

Distantly he heard the note of a car engine. Lights swept the bedroom ceiling. A car drew up on the gravel outside. He peered out of the window. Sandy! Suddenly he saw his own father's face, stern and angry. He heard voices—not the insidious whisper of the snake within but voices of his own people, the priests and old men, his uncles and brothers, chanting the song that heralded the ritual initiation to manhood. He backed away, choking. What had he done? It was profane, impure! He cast around him. What was he doing in this room? He was vile, he'd broken taboos, he'd sinned. *Sin*, whispered the voice. *Sin and shame*. In disgust he threw the clothes aside. Yet even as he was turning towards the door, the voice checked him. *Be clever*, it said, *cover your traces, no one need know*.

He grasped the small bundle of clothes and shuffled quickly out of the room. As he passed the window on the landing, he glanced out. Beneath, in the center of the gravel drive, against the pale midnight sky, stood Sandy and a tall figure with long fair hair whom he recognized at once, kissing.

•

A whoop came across the lawn from the flagpole where Sandy had set up the basket. Julia looked up from the barbecue. Adam had scored a goal. Sandy retrieved the ball and lobbed it to Scott, who hobbled a few paces and tossed it in a high spiralling arc. It dropped perfectly into the basket. Sandy cheered, Scott laughed. But Adam glowered. Retrieving the ball, he took up a position a good ten yards further back and wound up for a shot.

Julia glanced across at Max.

"Who'd ever have imagined it?" she sighed.

"Yes," mused Max in reply, watching the boy closely. "He seems to be developing quite a competitive spirit."

"I meant, Adam and Scott playing together. You know, he's putting whole sentences together now. And you can *reason* with him, too. It's truly wonderful. And at last we can go back to living in some kind of civilized order. I spent the morning putting all the stuff back in the living room. It feels like normal again." She paused, sensing that Max wasn't listening. She watched her run a hand through her long dark hair; she could see the hand was shaking. Beneath her light make-up, dark lines ringed Max's eyes and her complexion, usually peach-like, was the color of cold milky coffee. "Max," she began, "are you all right? You don't look yourself."

"I've just been under a bit of stress lately."

"I thought you said it was all sorted out."

"There's always something."

"Still, you've got nothing to worry about on this front anymore," she responded, meaning to cheer her. "It's really incredible. You've only got to ask him to do something and explain why, and he'll do it. I thought I'd have terrible trouble with the injections, but now I think he actually *wants* them. Yesterday, he took the syringe out of my hand and gave himself the shot. With none of the usual lead-up, either."

She scooped the sausages and burgers onto a plate and called the others over. There was food enough for a legion. This had been meant as a party for Sandy to celebrate the end of the school year, but it had turned out just a family affair. She'd been astonished when Sandy had suggested inviting Scott. He'd arrived with a bunch of flowers; his company itself was peace offering enough. Maybe now the rift with the Blanes would be healed and harmony would return to their relations. But then again, Kirsty had pointedly stayed away.

Sandy came over and filled plates for herself and Scott, then took them away to the poolside. Julia was helping Adam to his own when she heard a loud splash. She hadn't warned Scott about that! She spun round. Adam was frozen. His eyes darted towards the pool and a look of terror flashed over his face. He stood rigid, his whole body shuddering. Max reached for his wrist to feel his pulse, but within a few seconds a strange calm came over him. He blinked, shook his head, looked around him as if uncertain of his surroundings, then turned his eyes to Julia and fixed her with such a gaze as she'd never seen before. It was a look both of complicity and compliance, of knowing and unknowing, a look that was at contradiction with itself. His eyes said, *I know, I under-*

stand, *I have been here before*; his half-smile said, *you respond first, I'm waiting for you, I'll match my response to yours.* It left her feeling that he had seen right into her and knew every thought that passed through her mind.

"Adam, are you okay?" she fumbled.

"Great," he replied with a careful smile.

She turned to Max to break the lock of his gaze.

"Well, it looks as if he's got over *that*." She turned back to the boy and tried to deintensify the moment. "Come and sit down with us, darling. On the blanket here. And after lunch we'll go for a walk around the golf course, shall we? We can go around the edge, through the bamboos and thistles, there's a drink station too. Sam used to be a member. You'll love it, Max."

"Sure," said Max, her eye fixed hard on the boy.

•

Max had gone indoors to make a call. Mumma had gone to see if Sandy wanted to go on the walk. A *walk?* How boring.

He reached for Max's empty wine-glass and closed his fist around the slender bowl. He tightened his grip until it cracked. He felt the jab and stab of splinters in his palm, but he gripped it tighter, then tighter still. Finally he let the blood-sticky shards drop to the ground. It hurt like it never would have hurt before. But he was still smiling. From now on, no one would ever tell what he was really feeling.

•

William Cray eyed Julia closely as he sipped the bourbon she'd handed him, and wondered what tack to take. He'd flown in the previous evening from Zurich,

Switzerland, and called at once to fix a date. He'd suggested, to her surprise, that he come to pick her up at her home: he wanted to take a look at the boy himself and estimate the measure of the damage. This whole project had been nothing but a series of crises. The idea of exploiting the radio tag had worked beyond his wildest imaginings—he'd foreseen a confrontation between the Fitzgerald woman and Eliot, but he'd never thought she'd have the balls and the brawn actually to snatch the kid back. She'd had her confrontation and temporarily blocked Eliot, but now the whole thing had blown apart again. What the hell *was* this crap about Adam being diabetic? The transcripts had been faxed to him in Europe, but there'd been nothing he could do at that distance. Had he really been on vacation and not on a high-level scientific mission for the White House, with Eliot Lovejoy in tow, then he'd have cut it short at once and flown back. The worst was that Eliot had somehow got sight of the transcripts on the final day, and on the flight back the inevitable fight had ensued. Once again he pulled rank and forced the man into line. But how much longer would the line hold? If those idiot women were meddling about with home-spun medication behind Singer's back, God knew how it might be affecting the kid. Max was patently up to something.

"Julia," he began again, "I do think Ralph should check Adam over. With all respect, your friend Max isn't a doctor."

"William—" she warned.

"There's something I never told you, Julia," he began quietly, steeling himself to tell the lie. "The fact is, my son Howard is a diabetic. So you see, I know quite a bit about the condition. The dosage is absolutely critical.

Howard was hospitalized for two weeks while they got the level right.''

"It's working. That's all that matters." She gestured above her in the direction of the attic where Adam was lying asleep. "You should just *see* the difference. He's a new person. I'm over the moon."

"Even so." He cast her a look of grave solicitude. "I'd like to have that insulin checked out, Julia. Some brands have side-effects."

"Come on, William. Don't let's talk about that. It seems ages since I've seen you. I want to hear all about Europe. Did you get to the Italian lakes? They're so lovely at this time of year."

"I'm going to insist, Julia." He dropped his gaze in assumed sincerity. "I've always felt like a father to the kid, you know that. I guess I do more than ever now, when I think of Howard."

She reached to refill his glass.

"What is it about you, William?" she smiled. "You always get your own way. Of course, if you really think it's necessary. Shall I fetch you one of the little sachets?" Seeing his slow, determined nod, she headed for the door. "Wait and I'll bring it in. And then let's go. I've booked at the country club. They've got a new chef."

While she was out, he glanced around the room: nice furniture, expensive rugs, some interesting Mayan stuff. Sam had taste. He was examining an antique porcelain vase when she returned carrying a small white polystyrene box. She opened it in front of him. Inside lay a row of slim, cartridge-shaped sachets. She handed him one. He slipped it into his cigar-case and gave her a conspiratorial wink.

"Not a word to Max, huh? She'd only misunderstand." As he patted the cigar-case, he glanced discreetly at his watch. He had a lab standing by to analyze the stuff as soon as he could get it to them, but he wasn't going to be able to get out of dinner. The sooner it was over, the sooner he'd have the answers he was dreading. He stepped over to the door and held it open for her. "Shall we get going?"

•

The night was close and charged, and distant thunder rolled dryly across a taut sky. Julia waited for the black limousine to disappear from earshot, then closed the door. She went around turning off the downstairs lights. Briefly as she puffed up the sofa cushions in the living room she paused and frowned in hurt. All evening William had been sneaking glances at his watch. He'd dropped her back home and hurried off, refusing even a nightcap. Had something happened on vacation? Had he *met* someone? Don't be silly, she reproved herself sharply. He just didn't feel comfortable sleeping in his old friend's bed—it was quite understandable. Yet to leave *so* abruptly?

She wasn't going to let it get to her. She had more than enough cause for comfort and satisfaction right here. As she stood with her hand on the light-switch, she surveyed the new room. Gone were the white drapes, the empty shelves and Martha Walker's ten-dollar plastic sheets, and back were the things that belonged here, the things that made it a normal home.

24

○

AS THE FOURTH WEEK OF THE TREATMENT BEGAN, MAX began to suffer from an accumulation of nervous tension. She had attacks of paranoia in which she saw Lovejoy's agents watching from doorways, following in cars, dogging her steps. She heard clicks on the line and was convinced her phone was being tapped. She couldn't return to her apartment without half expecting to find Lovejoy himself lying in wait to blackmail her with evidence of what she was doing, nor switch on her answering-machine without dreading a call from Julia saying that Adam had "disappeared" again. It wouldn't be long now, only just a short while, before the genes would be on site and active and the old, native Adam would be finally beyond their reach.

None of her fears had actually yet materialized, but in the meantime she was going slowly deranged. Her conscience, normally well tamed, began to torment her. It pained her to witness the alacrity with which Julia had seized upon the phony diagnosis. She almost wished she'd been more discerning, more critical: that would make the betrayal easier to live with. But then it was too late to go back and undo the trickery. It was, after all, just the latest in a train of deceits leading back to before she'd even met her. From the very first moment she'd decided to say nothing about her affair with Sam, she had established a pattern from which it was now impossible to deviate. Relationships took their character from the first and last acts that circumscribed them. Even if it were possible to unweave the web, it would now be wrong to do so. Maintaining the lie had become the lesser evil and telling truth the greater.

To add to her frustration, she was witnessing these astonishing, unparalleled changes in Adam without any proper means of recording or analyzing what actually was happening. Science was measurement. She should be measuring changes in protein synthesis at cell level, in the chemical composition of his blood, in the level of neurotransmitters in his cerebro-spinal fluid. She should have spliced a tracer into the genes and be tracking them to their exact site in the brain. Even in regard to his external behavior, she should be running all kinds of cognitive tests and systematically monitoring his responses to both the physiological and emotional levels. All she had to show for these first weeks of one of the world's most extraordinary and daring experiments was a couple of notebooks of her own subjective observations which she'd written up at the end of each day.

As she lay in bed one morning, she thought through her position carefully and came to a decision. Adam was clearly progressing by leaps and bounds, but behind it all she knew it was a race against time. Could she *finish* him before they came to get him? Without any scope to make decent scientific study, crude expediency had to be the order of the day. This thing had to be brought home fast. She would accelerate the program and step up the dosage. She'd recall the vials and double the concentration.

She hauled herself out of bed and took a shower. The morning was already hot, but she felt cold and shivery. She took a handful of pills to settle her stomach, slipped on her clothes, put some color on her cheeks and fumbled her way downstairs into the blinding sunlight. She felt tired and and slow and one degree removed from the world. Twenty-odd miles away Adam would be already up, alert, thirsty to learn, poised to leapfrog another millennium in this one day. She climbed wearily into her car. She had to keep going, but she was already slipping badly behind. The program was running away with her, careering off under its own control, and in her heart she knew she could never hope to catch up with it now.

•

"Try this," said Julia, coming out onto the deck, handing Max a steaming mug. "Wild thyme. One of the oldest remedies in the world. Forget your modern-day pills and tablets." She paused. "You really don't need to keep coming over every day, Max. I don't mean we don't love to see you—of course we do, always—but you've got your own work to think of. He's *better* now. Just look."

Max followed her gaze over the balustrade to the front lawn beyond. Adam was sitting on a blanket, leafing through a book of nursery rhymes. She began to get up. She should be recording this.

"There's time in plenty for that," said Julia, urging her back into her seat. "Drink up."

Max sipped the infusion. Her stomach lurched at the

bitter oiliness beneath the thin mask of sweetening. No doubt the ancients relied on the placebo effect, too: the more vile a medicine tasted, the more effective it must be. She swallowed hard against the rising bile. Then she remembered her purpose in coming. This was the perfect moment.

"It could use some more sugar," she said, rising.

"Stay there, I'll go," responded Julia at once.

"No, no. Leave it to me."

Max crossed the living room and followed the corridor to the kitchen. There she emptied out half the mug and filled it with hot water. Then, listening to check no one was coming, she opened the fridge and reached inside for the small polystyrene box. She would take it to the lab, concentrate the fluid in a centrifuge, then slip it back the following day, before Julia had a chance to notice. It would be far easier not to have to find an explanation.

Automatically she glanced inside. Ten sachets left. She was closing the lid when she paused. There had been fifteen to start with. She checked the wall calendar. Yes, they were only in the fourth week of the treatment. There ought to be *eleven* left: three used, and one in the pen. Her mouth went dry. Had Julia been giving him more than one shot a day? God knew, the experiment was uncontrolled enough without the one constant becoming a variable.

She took the box back outside with her and held it open.

"I only count ten, Julia," she said levelly. "Is there something I should know?"

Julia met her eye. "There must be some mistake."

"There's no mistake. One is missing."

"I really have no idea."

"That's not true, Julia. You know it."

Julia lowered her gaze. "I'm sorry. I didn't tell you in case you misunderstood. Perhaps I shouldn't have done it, but he was so persistent."

"Adam wanted more?"

"Oh no, not Adam. William."

"William *Cray?*"

"His son is a diabetic, you see, and he knows a lot about it all. He took one of the capsules. Just to check. For us."

Her world was reeling. "Jesus, Julia," she exclaimed, "are you telling me you gave that man one of these vials? Oh my God."

"What's wrong?" asked Julia, now white-faced. "He was only going to check the dosage. He said it could be critical. His own son spent weeks in hospital before they got it right."

"Don't you trust me, Julia?"

"Of course I do! I just thought it wouldn't do any harm to check. You'd want to know, too." She reached out a hand. "I'm so sorry, Max. I didn't mean it like *that*. Believe me."

Max drew away. "What's between you and this man?"

"Does it matter? The fact is, he wanted to help."

"Oh God, Julia, you're so *naive!*"

Max's hand tightened around the box. This was catastrophic. Who really *was* this man Cray who'd wormed his way into Julia's affections so as to spy on Adam and what they were doing with him? She recalled her conversation with Bernard and, more recently, with Gerald. Slowly an ominous pattern began to form in her mind. She rose to her feet.

"I need to make a call."

"Of course, of course, help yourself."

Slowly, like one walking to the gallows, she made her way through the house to the study where she wouldn't be overheard. On the desk lay Julia's address book. She flicked it open to "C." The entry for William Cray gave a 202 prefix, the area code for Washington, D.C. It showed two numbers, one most likely a central switchboard and the other a private line. She dialed the switchboard.

"The Foundation," responded a pleasant female voice from the other end. "How may I help you?"

Max's throat went dry. It was all fitting together. She already knew the answer even as she formulated the question.

"Do you have a Dr. Eliot Lovejoy there?"

"Dr. Lovejoy's not in the office at present," came the reply. "Can I give you his laboratory number?"

"Thank you," she mumbled. "I'll call later."

She replaced the receiver and stared out of the window at the thick foliage already tinged with a foretaste of autumn red. The pattern now at last made sense. And the common link was Sam.

Sam. Once again, her thoughts returned to their final night in Venice. He'd known exactly what he was after on that expedition and where, in all that remote wilderness, he would find it. He was going for a specimen of Adam's species, to bring it back to Lovejoy and his laboratory. She herself was to be a part of the plan; that she'd gleaned from Bernard. Sam's feelings for her had been entirely cynical. He hadn't loved her at all. He'd used her to satisfy his lust and to advance his ambition. Was this the man she'd believed in, respected, given the finest of her love to? She felt sickened. Nothing was pure. All was defiled by deceit. Everywhere you turned ran the currents of deception. The *bastard*.

She clenched her fists and steeled herself to face the immediate crisis on her hands. As she considered the new evidence, the pain gradually hardened into determination. So: Cray was in possession of the capsule. He would have it analyzed, and then what? Would he remain silent and cowed, as Lovejoy had been for these past weeks under threat of exposure? One thing alone she felt certain of: a man who'd been so careful to remain invisible so far in all this would want the affair to remain invisible. His first instinct would be to do a deal.

She glanced at her watch. She'd get back to her apartment. If there had to be a meeting, she'd hold it on home ground.

•

William Cray sat very upright in the back of the cab as it jostled among the flow of homebound traffic leaving Boston for Cambridge and the suburbs beyond. He was seething, but he had no one to blame but himself. The project was *fucked*. He should have let Lovejoy have his way from the outset. Now what the hell did they have here in this boy? Genetically, trash. A polluted heap of shit.

As the cab swung off Storrow Drive, he felt in his pocket for the card with the woman's address. As he did so, he felt the touch of the flintstone, cold as gun metal, on his fingertips. He had his plan of action. He would drag out of her exactly what she'd been pumping into the kid. Then he'd go to Lexington and, by whatever means it took, he'd get the boy out of there himself and ship him once and for all to the Center. Tough, Julia, he thought grimly; it's gonna hurt, but it's either you or me. After that, he'd have to face Eliot. He hadn't told him about this latest disaster—he'd had a biochemistry lab in Washington analyze the "insulin," and it was human genetic material—but now he'd have to come clean and hand the sample over to him. And then it would be for the Center to try and salvage what they could of their spoiled specimen. God *damn* the bitch!

As they arrived, he told the driver to wait. When he'd done his business, he'd get the cab to take him to a car rental agency. He'd drive himself to Lexington; he didn't want witnesses. He climbed out. Max's red Rabbit stood in the parking bay. Briskly he walked around to the side of the clapboard house and rang the bell marked "Fitzgerald." There was no reply. The outer screen door was swinging gently in the light breeze. The inner door was unlocked. He knocked and stepped inside, then made his way up the narrow wooden stairs. As he reached the landing, he heard a voice from within.

"Come in, Dr. Cray. I've been expecting you."

•

Cray listened with mounting horror as Max described with cold precision, even pride, exactly what she'd done. Much of the technical detail passed over his head, but he grasped sufficient of the gist. He paced around the room, refusing a chair. She remained standing, too, quite composed and unflustered, with one eyebrow slightly arched. A coffee-table strewn with periodicals separated them. Finally she came to an end. For a while he was too numb to speak. He felt ice-locked with disbelief.

"You are a very foolish young woman," he whispered. "Do you understand what you've done? You have destroyed that boy."

"On the contrary," she replied calmly. "I've saved him."

"Don't play word games!" he snapped.

"I've saved him from spending his life as a human experiment in that little Auschwitz you and your friend Dr. Lovejoy call a laboratory."

"By subjecting him to your own idea of genetic improvement? Exactly who is playing Nazi doctors here?" He stepped up to the table's edge. "You are the vivisectionist, meddling with a living person's genes."

"I don't need to justify myself to you."

"Indeed you can't."

A flush had appeared high on her pale cheeks. She gripped the side of a chair and her knuckles whitened.

"You were abusing him like an animal!" she hissed. "Worse, even. At least there are controls on animal experiments. Don't forget I saw some of your 'tests.' They were deliberately stressful, cruel and degrading. I call that immoral."

"And engineering him into some kind of genetic hybrid is *not*?"

"No more than modifying any creature to help it survive. That's what we're doing to save endangered species."

"The case is hardly parallel. Adam is a human being."

"Dr. Lovejoy didn't seem to think so. He didn't even want to accord him animal rights, let alone human ones." Her large hazel eyes were blazing. "Think of it from Adam's point of view. He's being given a helping hand to adapt to our society. Soon he'll be like us. One of us.

That's got to be better for him than being cooped up in a cage, probed and tormented all the rest of his life."

Cray cleared his throat. You could never win on the high ground of morality.

"This is not getting us anywhere, Miss Fitzgerald."

"Fine, then let's stop." She paused, her temper cooling. She considered him carefully, then managed a small, arch smile. "I think you might end up agreeing with me if only you'd let yourself," she mused. "But then, you have a vested interest. I'm sorry we can't be on the same side. We might even have worked together. You, with me." She assumed an unconcerned tone. "I'd have thought my work would have interested you. A master gene that codes for certain patterns of behavior we call civilized. The genes of civilization. Right up your alley. No?"

For a moment, he hesitated. Of course, this thought had occurred to him. This was exactly the kind of work the Foundation was set up for. Imagine! A master gene that coded for all the values of a civilized society, that encapsulated all the benefits mankind had achieved since the dark ages! The key to the disorder in society, to crime and corruption, to drug abuse, to violence, to all the anarchic and vicious drives so evident in every block in every street in every city of the entire country. One would screen offenders for deficiencies in the gene. Even latent offenders. Isolate society's trouble-makers in an ultimately clear, scientific way. Then what? Co-opt them, segregate them, lock them away, recondition them, maybe *re-engineer* them. Christ, if she could do it to goddamn gazelles, why not to the bums and hobos in every downtown American city?

But first, the boy. The key question here hadn't yet been asked.

"Tell me one thing," he said quietly. "Can the gene implant be reversed?"

Her manner grew cool and professional again.

"Provided the gene bonds to its site correctly, then each successive injection will take Adam further along the path. Once in its site, the gene is effectively ineradicable. Cumulatively, it's a step function. A threshold will be reached when, to all intents and purposes, Adam will *be* a member of our species: he will think, feel, act, *even reason* like one of us. I believe we are very close to that moment." She held his eye. "The short answer is, No. The process can't be reversed."

He allowed the silence to lengthen. There was no deal to be done and nothing more to be said. He'd got the bad news he'd come for. At the door, he hesitated.

"We should have had this conversation earlier," he said. "We have more in common than you think."

She held out her hand. Her half-smile was hard, watchful.

"I'm glad we understand one another," she said.

"I think we do," he replied steadily. "Goodbye, Miss Fitzgerald."

•

Max watched the dapper, silver-haired figure disappear briskly down the sidewalk into a cab waiting two doors away. She poured herself a vodka and downed it with a shudder. She'd handled the meeting well, she thought. She'd got the miserable little shit in a corner. She'd held out just the right hint of a deal, but with just a few more shots Adam would be safe anyway and there'd be no need to play for time any more. A master gene that coded for civilization, what rubbish! At best, genes could only be responsible for dispositions towards certain behavior, tendencies to act in this way or that. And there was always the power of the mind, of reason, to override these. Still, he'd swallowed it, like the good home-grown fascist he was. He'd go running back to Lovejoy and they'd get in a huddle, and next thing she'd know there'd be some deal on the table again. Well, they could stuff it.

She glanced at her watch: the labs would be empty by now. She'd better get moving. It would take the better part of twenty-four hours to concentrate the plasma. As she hurried through her bedroom to the bathroom beyond, her eye fell upon the photograph of Sam on the bedside table. She hesitated for a moment, then abruptly turned on her heel. In the bathroom she filled the sink with cold water and stood splashing her face until gradually all the hurt and rage began to ebb away.

•

At first Julia burst out laughing.

"Don't be so silly, William!" she cried. "I've never heard anything so absurd!"

But William was not laughing.

"Oh come along," she chuckled, "you can't be *serious*."

The look in his penetrating blue eyes was deadly serious.

She looked at the flintstone in the palm of his hand. So what if it had been dated to x-thousand years BC? So had half the specimens in Sam's cabinets, and sacrificial knives like this among them, too. That was no *proof*. She glanced at the thin file on the table between them, lying open to reveal a sheaf of photographic plates with what looked like rows of blurred supermarket bar-codes. Here she was less sure. William said these were genetic fingerprints and they proved the case definitively. How could she know? On the other hand, why should he invent such a ludicrous, far-fetched story? She felt dizzy. The floor beneath her was swaying like the deck of a ship.

"William?" she whispered hoarsely. "Tell me you're joking."

"I'm sorry, Julia," came the short reply.

"Please say it's not true."

"Think, Julia. Think."

Adam, her Adam? Impossible! This was the modern day! Those people were extinct! They belonged in the Peabody, along with the mammoths and dinosaurs. The subject of long-winded scholarly papers. Sam's kind of work.

Think, Julia, think. Gradually, grudgingly, by permitting the unimaginable hypothetical a moment's elbow-room, she began to see that the pieces might indeed fit all too neatly into an entirely new picture.

First, there was Sam. She thought of his lifelong obsession with the prehistoric origins of mankind, his fixation on the roots of man's nature, his absurd notion that prehistoric man might still survive in remote wildernesses of the earth. She thought of all those behind-closed-doors meetings with Cray and the others, and of the new project he'd been involved in with Washington that brought money into the family in unwontedly large sums. She thought of his final field trip, planned to penetrate the wildest regions of the furthest Caucasus.

Then she thought of Adam himself. She thought of the boy she'd first glimpsed in the hospital cell in Turkey, the strange, feral creature who'd stowed aboard a plane just so as to stay close to Sam's coffin. She heard Martha Walker's phrase, "an undomesticated animal with the strength of an ox and the manners of an ape." She pictured Adam as the boy at the zoo who'd shown an eerie rapport with the chimpanzees. Adam, the fire-starter. The kid who lived rough, slept on leaves, ate berries and raw meat, who'd brutally attacked Scott and scarred him with that ritualistic mark which she knew matched one of Sam's prehistoric artifacts. And then, set against all this, she saw today's boy, the sweet, obliging, bright, well-behaved young lad who dressed himself properly and ate normal food and was beginning to speak the language. A boy who was undeniably *one of us*.

No, no! Was she going crazy?

"William?" she pleaded.

He gripped her hand. His piercing blue eyes bored hypnotically into hers.

"Julia, listen to me. If we don't act now, they'll come and take him away."

Suddenly she was seized with panic.

"No! Who? Why? They can't take him away! He's my son! I adopted him. What are you talking about?"

"If they find out."

"Let them! I don't care *what* he is. I love him just as much! It doesn't matter where he's from. I don't care a fig about all your genetic rubbish. *He's my boy!*" She struggled to keep her voice down; Sandy was out with Scott, but Adam himself was in his attic room upstairs. She clutched her head. The world was swimming about her. "Look at what the treatment's doing! He's perfectly *normal*! Ask Max if you don't take my word. Go on, ask her!"

Cray cleared his throat. He laid a hand on hers.

"You've become very precious to me, Julia. I wanted to spare you this, but I guess I've got to tell you." He drew his breath. "That stuff you're giving him. It's not insulin. Or anything like it."

"What do you mean?" she choked. "Of course it is!"

"I had it analyzed, as I said. I didn't tell you the results because I didn't want to upset you. I care too much for you. I didn't want you to have to go through even more of this."

"Come out with it! What's Max been doing to my boy?" She was approaching hysteria.

"Keep calm, Julia. Everything is okay. I've got it under control." He pressed her into a chair and sat down opposite. "There's something about your new Adam you should face up to, Julia. Listen carefully. The real Adam is not the kid you see now. The real Adam's the one who savaged Scott Blane."

"How did you know he did that?" she demanded hoarsely.

"I have my contacts. The forensic tests proved beyond a doubt that Adam did it. I had the report hushed up. For your sake and his, Julia. I had hoped it would blow over and he'd change. But I'm afraid leopards don't change their spots."

"For God's sake look at him!" she persisted. "I don't know what you're saying. There's nothing wrong about him."

"That drug you're giving him. It's designed to alter behavior. To suppress his instincts. To *tame* him. This isn't the real Adam."

"I don't care!"

"You may not, Julia. But others will. The police will.

So will the authorities generally. And all kinds of not-too-pleasant people will start taking a very close interest. All he has to do is lose it one more time, and he's done for. I can't buy him off a second time."

"There won't *be* a second time, William. That's what I'm trying to tell you."

"Julia," he warned, "you know from the Unit how little it takes to get a kid committed. Now, Herbert Blane is looking for ammunition. He's not satisfied with the forensic results. Any chance to pin anything on Adam, he'll take it. Suppose something does happen. Suppose questions start getting asked about who he is, or *what* he is . . ."

She felt lost, cut adrift. She sensed she was being presented with false alternatives, but she couldn't unscramble her mind to see another way out. She wanted to shout aloud, "Can't you see it doesn't matter a damn what race, color or creed or even species he is? He's *Adam*! He's the boy he is. Why should you want to take him away?" But she couldn't speak. She felt paralyzed and drowning.

"What are you suggesting we do?" she asked finally, trying to rise above her rage and bewilderment.

He leaned forward. "Just a precaution."

"What kind of precaution?"

"We need a doctor's certificate giving the kid a clean bill of health. Saying that if he stays on these drugs, he's perfectly safe. Sane. Balanced. No danger to society. Do you get me?"

"I'm not sure."

"Listen. I've got Ralph Singer standing by." He held up a hand. "You must put any personal antipathies aside. Singer is the man for the job. He has everything ready.

He'll give the kid a thorough, basic medical, and that'll be it."

"What if *he* asks... questions?"

William smiled reassuringly.

"Ralph is an old friend. Why do you think we picked him?"

"Well, I suppose it can't do any harm. I'll make an appointment."

"Julia, this must be done *now*. I said he's standing by."

"Now? At this time of night?" She was appalled.

"Exactly! Don't you understand? It's *urgent*. And we've got to be *discreet*."

He reached forward and shook her arm. All the time his penetrating blue eyes were fixed on hers. She felt under a spell. Her feelings were in turmoil. None of this was really happening. Any minute she'd wake up. And yet she felt herself talking and acting as though she were there and in full possession of her faculties. She listened through this film of unreality as he continued pressing her to act at once. A doctor's certificate would put Adam in the clear, he said, and she'd never have anything to fear it the truth ever did come out.

"Do I have any alternative?" she asked, defeated.

"None, Julia. Believe me. Trust me."

She rose to her feet and moved to the door like a sleepwalker.

"What shall I pack?" she heard herself asking. "I'd better put some things together."

"Don't worry: they've got everything at the clinic. All right, just a teddy-bear or whatever he has."

"I'll leave a note for Sandy."

He had risen to his feet, too. He touched her arm.

"No, Julia. You stay. Your place is here."

"I must be with him!"

"You need time to get over the shock of this thing. Then you need to be here for Sandy. You'll have to think how to break it to her."

"But Adam?"

"Don't worry. He'll only be in for the night. You can come and pick him up in the morning. Just call up first to make sure he's all through. I'll take him myself."

"But—"

He pressed her arm more firmly. His eyes bored into hers.

"No more, Julia. Just show me where he is."

•

It all happened so quickly she didn't have time to reflect. Numbly, as if still under the spell, she led William upstairs to the attic. In a voice she didn't recognize as her own, she told Adam that he was going to go with William on a midnight adventure. Adam, perplexed, grasped her hand and demanded if she was coming too. With a trembling voice she mumbled something about coming along later. She couldn't bring herself to lie directly.

She made him dress, suggesting his most comfortable clothes, then took him downstairs and straight out into the drive where William was waiting in a car. The night was hot and humid, as it had been for days, boding a storm that refused to break. As the boy clambered sleepily and obediently into the back of the car, she hurried back indoors and ransacked the kitchen for something in case he got hungry in the night. She threw some chocolate cookies, a bar of candy, potato chips and a couple of bagels into a bag and handed it through the car window to William. She made him promise to call the moment they arrived. Yes, yes, he agreed quickly and started up.

She took a step back. Adam pressed forward against his own window. He realized something was wrong. The car began to move. The boy's eyes widened with alarm. His mouth formed a silent cry. The car was pulling away now. Adam clambered onto the back seat, ramming his face against the rear window. His eyes were filled with the pain of betrayal.

She watched the car disappear down the drive until it was beyond earshot. Suddenly the trance snapped. Her hands flew up to her face and she let out a cry. In the shock of the moment and the weakness of her feelings, what had she let William talk her into doing?

On impulse, she hurried back indoors and scribbled Sandy a note saying Adam had cut himself—it was nothing serious—but she was running him up to the hospital. She checked Ralph Singer's address in the phone book, then hurried into the estate wagon. It wouldn't start: it was out of gasoline. She spent precious minutes filling it up from the gasoline cans Sam had always kept stocked in the garage. Finally she got it going and shot off down the drive. William would have a head start, but so long as she could be there to settle him in, Adam wouldn't feel so let down. That look she'd seen on his face had cut her to the core. She felt as though she'd given him away.

Clenching her teeth, she put her foot down and headed at full speed for Boston.

•

The car was speeding along the freeway, passing trucks, cars, buses. Headlights zipped past on the opposite lanes. Adam crouched in the well at the back, chattering to himself. Where was the man taking him? He didn't want to go anywhere.

He reached for the door handle. The door was locked. He rattled and shook it. The man was calling to him, cajoling him to be quiet, telling him it was all right. He caught his eyes in the mirror, pale, piercing blue eyes that fixed his own in a snake's grip. He felt his skin prickle. The voice said one thing, but those eyes said something quite different. Something was badly wrong. Suddenly, with absolute certainty, he knew what was happening.

He was being taken back to the men in the white coats.

He shot to his feet, banging his head on the roof. The man shouted at him to sit down. Adam lunged at the door. He hammered the glass with his fist. The car swung into the inside lane and began to slow. The man called out his name. Adam looked up, then let out an awestruck gasp. There, dangling from the man's hand by the very leather thong that he himself had painstakingly cut and worked, hung his father's precious flintstone.

Father?

Atta?

A sudden, terrible force rent him deep within, like the splitting of a mountain oak in a gale. Impulses flooded up from unnameable depths. Was this his *atta*, come back in another form because he'd failed to fulfill his duty? But even as he staggered, buffeted by the gale of his guilt, from the very eye of the storm came the small voice of doubt. *Your father is dead*, it whispered once more, *dead and buried. He can't be both here and there, both alive and dead. Think.*

Adam thought. The tempest in his head grew ever

more violent. Reason battled with instinct for possession of his mind. He felt riven asunder. He cried out, he beat his head, he clamped his hands over his ears to silence the voice, but on and on continued the insidious whisper. Gradually the confusion rose to a babel. A roaring deafened his ears. Sheets of red flashed across his vision. His very head was split in two, the right side a seething ferment of urges, the left a mad chatterbox of voices. One part of him stood outside himself, shouting vainly from the sidelines, while the other part, lashed into a frenzy, powered his limbs and fueled his purpose.

He reached out his hands. Gradually he closed his grip round the man's throat. Choking, the man tried to claw free. The car veered across the lanes. Lights flashed, tires howled, horns pealed. Just as they were about to hit the central crash barrier, an involuntary jerk of the man's knee swung the wheel back. Adam tightened his grip. He could feel the gaps between the neck bones. Another notch and he'd snap the cord. He felt a terrible laughter seize him. The car had slewed broadsides across the road. With a violent *crump*, a truck struck it on the front fender, sending it spinning in a crazy loop towards the side. The man was vainly biting and tearing at him with both hands, his eyeballs red to bursting. For a brief second he twisted enough to draw a choking breath before Adam applied the winch tighter still. The car was spiralling out of control now. It skimmed the side of a silver limousine, ricocheted off an emergency phonebooth on the shoulder, then shot back into the inside lane. Another truck rammed it hard from behind, sending it shooting off the metal surface and plunging along a corrugated track where, bucking and lurching, it finally came to rest on its side at the foot of a small grassy incline.

Adam was propelled forward into the front seat by the impact. He scrambled out of the passenger door and waited a few yards away as the man painfully fought his way out and, staggering drunkenly forward, collapsed onto the grass, his head flung back and his arms bent beneath his arched body. Only the feeble twitching of a trapped hand showed he was still alive.

Adam picked up a large jagged rock.

A terrible, unassuageable blood-lust bubbled up within him. Kill, kill, it shouted. Kill!

Raising the rock in both hands, he brought it crashing down on the man's head, shattering the skull. Again and again he smashed the rock down, pounding it into a formless fleshy pulp. Finally he flung the rock aside and stumbled back to the car to retrieve the flintstone. By now the ridge was rimmed with figures silhouetted in car head-lights. Voices called out through the dark. The first men were already advancing down the slope. Dropping low, he slipped along the foot of the slope and, skirting an open stretch of rough grassland, swiftly disappeared into the cover of the woods beyond.

25

○
_____

JULIA SAT UP INTO THE EARLY HOURS, BUT NO CALL
came from William.

She had found Ralph Singer's clinic in darkness. No
one answered the bell. The place was patently closed for
the night.

Even on her way there she'd felt puzzled: she'd remembered it as a normal doctor's surgery, not a place
where patients stayed in overnight. She thought she might
have misunderstood and William was taking the boy to
the doctor's private residence—more than likely at a time
of night like this. From a street pay phone she called his
service, to be told he was out of town. She left a message
to call her urgently, then headed back to Lexington where
at least she would be near the phone. By now she was
growing seriously alarmed. On arriving home, she called
William's number in Washington. His own service was
still less forthcoming.

She settled down to wait. When, shortly after midnight, Sandy returned, she seemed so elated that Julia
hadn't the heart to broach any part of the news. Maybe

she need never know until it was over. They'd get Adam back in the morning, with his clean bill of health, and the new life could start again on a safe, sound footing.

One cup of coffee followed another, interspersed with glasses of brandy, as with numbed brain she struggled to come to terms with all that she'd learned that evening and to see how it could make sense of what was happening. She'd lost Adam before—the times he'd gone missing. But this time, she'd *given* him away. *They'll come and take him away*: William's words echoed ominously in her ears. In her mind she went over and over the sequence of events, the revelations, shocks, disappointments, hopes, alarms and finally that fateful decision, and she could not imagine what had possessed her to allow it to happen. Why, at the very least, hadn't she insisted on going along in the car? She'd been another person. The shock had momentarily unhinged her. Then she began to wonder about William himself. She heard again his response when asked about Ralph Singer. *Why do you think we picked him?* Who was "we?" They'd "picked him" at the start. Had William known the truth about Adam from the very beginning? And deceived her, *used* her? She felt giddy, sick. Out of her own weakness and loneliness, she'd let herself believe she was falling in love. And now, out of blind trust, she'd let him take Adam. No, no, she cried silently: be strong, hold on. There's a perfectly good explanation. William will call. He's a good man. *Trust me*, he'd said. So she must.

And then her thoughts turned to Max. Max, her loyal friend and trusted ally throughout everything. Max had been conspiring behind her back. She had known about Adam all along. She'd contrived this whole charade about the diabetes and the special treatment. She'd exploited, cheated, *perverted* Adam. "To suppress his instincts . . . to tame him." God alive, what had been done to the poor boy? How could she have been so blind? So—what had Max once said?—*naive*?

Shortly after dawn had broken, still without news from William, she decided she could wait passively no longer. She left Sandy another note, a garbled, erratic message that ended telling her that if he called to be sure to get his number. Filled with a terrible creeping dread, she took her bag and car keys, and headed out. She was going to get to the bottom of this. And she knew exactly where she'd start.

•

From a distance, through the darkness of the wood, Adam watched the police cars and ambulances arrive. He enjoyed the wails of the sirens, the flashing lights and the sight of men scurrying to and fro. This was all his doing.

His smile hardened. These were not his people. He knew how they thought, and he could think like them if he tried. But he was not *of* them. They were the others. The ones who had carried off his father's body to their own land and dug him into the ground beneath the earth, never to rise to the stars. He fingered the flintstone around his neck. There must be sacrifices. Offerings. Burnings. Blood-lettings. His hands twitched. Turning his back on the wrecked car, he slipped away into the dark shroud of night.

He traveled through woodland, across streams and wide stretches of rough grass, skirting a quarry, crossing a railroad, until finally he came to a small cluster of farm buildings. From afar he caught the scent of a bull. The night was dark and cloudy, with a flickering backdrop of lightning, yet he could see again as if it were day. The house was in darkness. Cattle stirred in a long, low shed across a mud-caked yard. Beyond stood a bull's pen. He slid through the shadows. The bull, a black mountain of muscle, prowled restlessly, its nose-ring clanking as it butted the bars of its cage. It glowered from beneath a broad forehead. Carefully he unlooped the flintstone.

He vaulted the bars and dropped onto the dung-sodden straw. Calming the beast with a low mutter, he began gently scratching its stubbly forehead. Gradually it raised its massive head and he stroked its underneck, moving his hand ever lower down its throat until finally he felt the thick vein. The creature stretched into the caress. Then in a single swift movement, he wrenched the nose-ring up and brought the sharp edge of the flintstone down in a long jabbing stroke. It knifed through the skin, springing a geyser of black blood. With a screaming roar, the brute swung around, but Adam was already back over the barrier. The cattle were bellowing, birds scattered from the eaves, dogs began to bark. A light came on in the house. Adam stopped only to smear his bloodstained fingers on the side of the pen, making the special mark, and then he was gone. From the woods he listened to the shouts and the last crazed roars of the dying bull.

He looked up at the stars and took a bearing. His course took him through fields, across rivers and around the edge of a small town. Dawn was beginning to break and he felt desperately hungry.

For several miles he ran parallel with a road, keeping out of sight of the cars and trucks that passed from time to time. Finally, he stumbled into a broad clearing. Set back from the road across an expanse of dirt, lay a small deserted gas station and a huddle of wooden shacks. A solitary light burned in the forecourt cabin. As he crept closer, he saw a beefy figure in a check lumberjacket asleep in front of a television. Behind stood a fridge cabinet filled with drinks and snacks. The man lay slumped in his chair, his head lolling back and his neck perfectly exposed.

Adam felt for the flintstone.

•

Julia turned down a no-through street off Putnam Avenue and checked off the numbers until she came to the peeling clapboard condominium where Max lived. In the early morning light, everything seemed surreally bright and false. Parked off the street in a patch of unkempt grass stood Max's red car. A newspaper boy on a bicycle brushed past her on the sidewalk and lobbed two bundles over the fence. In the distance she was aware of the rumble of traffic as the city began to stir. She headed up the path to the front door. The name on the bell was wrong. She stared stupidly at it for a moment, then went around to check the side entrance.

No reply. It was barely seven o'clock. She rang again, this time keeping her finger on the bell. A window eventually opened and Max appeared, angrily sweeping aside her long dark hair to see who was there.

"Julia!" she exclaimed. "Hang on. I'll be right down."

A moment later, she opened the door, barefoot, in just a crimson silk robe.

"What's wrong?" she snapped.

"Where's Adam?"

"What's happened?"

"Where has he been taken? Is he here? Answer me, Max."

Max's mouth opened and closed.

"You'd better come inside."

She led the way up a set of steep stairs and across a hallway into a broad, comfortable living room. She cleared a pile of books and magazines off the sofa and gestured for her to sit down. Julia glanced around for evidence of Adam. Was she going crazy?

"Now, let's take this calmly," Max was saying. "What's this all about? I don't know anything about where Adam is. The last I knew he was with you. Has he . . . disappeared?"

"Just answer me: *where is my boy?*"

"I don't know. That's the truth."

"Don't lie to me, Max. I know what you've been up to. I know everything. William's been around."

"Ah," Max paused, then drew a deep breath. "I guess I owe you an explanation, Julia," she said finally.

"I think you do."

"I'd better make coffee. It's a long story."

•

Julia sat very still. The world was spiralling out of control. In the space of twelve hours she'd been told that her boy was of a different human species entirely, and now that, by some devious piece of genetic gerrymandering, the differences were being bridged and within no time he would become "one of us." What madness was this? She pressed her hands to her temples.

"Just tell me where he is," she said. "Where has William taken him?"

"William *took* him? You didn't say that."

"You know very well he has. You must do."

"Julia, believe me, I don't. I only met the man for the first time yesterday! He came here. He wanted me to turn Adam in. Of course I refused."

"How do you mean, turn him in? I don't understand."

"But it's okay. They will find he's not what they want. Not any more. They'd be better off picking someone up off the streets. Or the subway." She laughed shortly, with a mad note bordering on hysteria.

"How can you sit there joking, after what you've done?" cried Julia. "It's the most evil, wicked thing I've ever heard. You had absolutely no right."

Max grew deadly serious in the instant. She leaned forward.

"I *took* the right," she replied in a half-whisper. "Adam couldn't possibly survive in our world as the little savage he was."

"For God's sake! He's a perfectly normal, decent boy. Why can't you get that into your head? You've seen it with your own eyes."

"Yes, and since when? Since the treatment. Before, he was a violent little brute with the mind and instincts of a caveman."

"He was natural. Pure."

"He was *primitive*, Julia. Violent. Barbaric. Bloodthirsty. Unconstrained by morality. What we've left behind, what we *were*." She held up a hand before Julia could protest. "Don't romanticize our origins, Julia. Eden never existed. We were never those noble hunter-gatherers: we were scavengers. Hyenas on two feet. That's where the roots of our nature lie. But we've civilized ourselves. That's the difference."

"And Adam? You think you're civilizing him? You're *destroying* him!"

Max's eyes flashed with the fervor of conviction.

"No, no!" she cried. "Saving him!"

"It's us who need saving!" Julia felt her rage rise like a whirlwind. "God damn you scientists! Why must you always meddle? You take what is natural and innocent and degrade it. Adam was a child of nature, living in the light. You, with all your arrogance, you've dragged him down into the dark. With us. With all us fallen creatures."

Max had sprung to her feet. It seemed to Julia for a second that she'd strike her.

"I've dragged him *out of* the dark and *into* the light!" she hissed. "I've given him the power to reason, to think, to understand. Like us. That's my gift."

"Your curse."

Max grabbed her by the shoulders and shook her hard.

"Don't you understand anything, woman? Your friend William Cray only told you half the story. Did you know what they were doing with the boy, him and that man Lovejoy? And, let me tell you, your late departed husband Sam was part of it too. Listen to me!" she spat. "Remember the last time Adam disappeared? Do you know where I really found him? Not in the shack. Or anywhere near any lake in the mountains. In fact, you know the place. You know it as the 'halfway house.' They call it the Center. It's a laboratory. A lab for animal experiments."

"I don't believe you," choked Julia.

"Want to know what they were doing to your precious boy when I found him?" Max pressed on regardless. "Tests. Some pretty nasty tests. Water-tank tests. Involving a little bit of controlled drowning. Just to see his responses. His aggression levels. Why? Because the kid is what he is! Because he's the first goddamn real-life Neanderthal ever found. And because," her voice fell to a deadly whisper, "everyone wants to know the answer to that question of yours, *are we risen or fallen, innocent or corrupted, good or evil?*" She thrust her back. "How would you go about answering that if you had an Adam to play with? You'd make him angry, you'd give him pain, a lot of pain... But it only works while Adam is what he is. Make him no longer unique, make him one of us, and there's no experiment. I did it to save him from *that*. Do you understand now?"

Julia had shrunk back into the sofa. For a while she sat rigid and controlled. She'd become too emotional, betrayed her feelings too openly. She composed herself to move. She'd leave: she had nothing to say to this woman any more. As she rose to her feet, she felt a sudden rush of nausea. She was going to be sick. She struggled to hold her stomach down as she stumbled to the door and fumbled her way through a bedroom and into a small bathroom beyond. There, crouching over the bowl, with tears pouring down her face, she coughed and retched out all her rage and despair.

Later, when she could trust herself to stand up, she washed herself and, still giddy and shaking made her way back through the bedroom. She'd get back home. There was only pain and disillusionment for her here. As she passed the bed, she chanced to glance at the bedside table. She'd taken two steps towards the door when she stopped dead.

In a small heart-shaped silver frame, sitting between the alarm clock and a small bowl of roses, was a photograph of Sam.

•

Sandy prowled about the house from room to room. She wanted to go for a run before going downtown, but Mom's note had asked her to mind the phone. Nine o'clock became ten, and still she hadn't returned. Had something gone wrong at the hospital? Keeping within earshot of the phone, she went into the garden to pick a bunch of large white daisies, Adam's favorite flower, and took them up to his room in the attic. He'd obviously gone off in a hurry, for he'd left his pajamas. And yet his bed was slept in. He'd fainted, the note said. In bed? How could you tell if someone had fainted in bed?

Puzzled, she went downstairs to her bedroom and changed into her tee-shirt and satin running shorts, then slipped into her mother's room and took the phone off the hook. Anyone who wanted would keep calling until they got through. She hurried down and, jotting a P.S. to Mom's note in case she got back first, headed out through the back door.

The day was already close and sticky. A leaden sun struggled through a veil of cloud that lay low and suffocating over the land. She skirted the pool and plunged down the slope towards the river, lengthening her stride as she picked up speed. The earth was hard and cracked, the grass yellow and slippery. Skidding at the bottom, she veered off down the narrow, winding dirt track that ran along the river's edge. The river itself had dwindled to a meandering trickle in a bed of sun-bleached stones. At her usual place, she jumped down the bank and sprang across the stepping-stones to the other side, where she made off along the edge of the poplar plantation.

For a stretch the going grew rougher. Brambles

snagged her ankles and in places the shrubbery had closed in over the path, slowing her to a jogging pace. She had fought her way through a thick elder bush smothering the track and was turning the corner into a small grassy clearing when suddenly she jolted to a halt.

She stifled a cry.

Quite still, in the shadow of a clump of thorn bushes, staring at her with a hard, level gaze, stood Adam.

"God, you scared me!" she exclaimed. Then she saw the blood all over his hands and face and clothes. "What happened? I thought you were at the hospital. Did you just get back? Are you okay?"

She started forward and reached out a hand, but faltered.

"Adam? Did you run away? Mom'll be looking for you. Adam?"

Then he moved. He took just one step towards her. His eyes seemed to devour her, to look *into* her. Greedy, rapacious, cruel. She froze. She felt suddenly naked and exposed. She braved a short laugh, but it came out fractured.

"Hey! Stop giving me that look! It gives me the creeps. Adam!"

His face registered a blank. His eyes, wide-staring, were fixated as in a trance. He took another step towards her. Was he playing zombies? She clapped her hands. He was looking at her body now. His breathing was coming faster, heavier.

"Hey! Cut it out! Adam!"

He had come up close. His hands touched her bare shoulders. She pulled away. He came forward again. She swung her hand to slap him, but he caught the wrist in mid-flight. He bent it back like a twig and slowly forced her down onto the ground. She kicked him hard on the shin, then aimed for the swelling between his thighs, but he caught her foot and gradually, by the wrist and ankle, raised her bodily off the ground, then abruptly let her drop. She screamed. He grabbed her tee-shirt and ripped it open in a single stroke. She tried to squirm away. But he was on top of her now, bearing down upon her, his breath coming harsh, his body fetid with blood, his strength overpowering all resistance, his knees splaying her legs, and finally came the first sudden jerking brutish thrust that sent her world spinning from white to black to red and her screams spiraling up into the final mist of unconsciousness.

•

Max stared at the neat new row of capsules laid out in their polystyrene box on her lab bench. It was all coming unstuck. A brilliant program, a grand hope for mankind, the saving of a poor unfortunate kid, and all screwed up, as usual, by the human factor. She took the lid in her hand and slowly crushed it into a hundred featherweight fragments. Specks of the polystyrene leapt and clung electrostatically to the face of her wristwatch and to the plastic casing of the telephone.

She looked around the lab. It was Sunday, and the building was deserted. Even Murray's desk was clear and tidy. She'd misjudged it badly. She'd sent Cray off thinking she'd got him nicely cornered, and he'd gone straight around and snatched the boy. How could they want the kid after what she'd done to him? Wasn't that the whole *point*?

She stared at her in-tray and its increasingly angry memos from Gerald. She'd probably be fired before the week was out. What the hell? She could never go back to gazelles after this. She glanced at the row of capsules. Whatever happened, she still had the data of a discovery that could, in Sam's favorite phrase, "take her to Stockholm."

But what of poor Adam? Was he back in that grotesque torture chamber? She'd never pull that stunt a second time. Five weeks of injections: he must be darn close to closing the gap by now. Would the genes stay bound to their sites? And, if so, would they bring with them a prisoner's only ace, the ability to second-guess his captors? Given the will and the moment, might Adam seize the chance himself to make his bid for freedom? It was all down to Adam now. She could do no more to save him.

•

Julia drove home in a sick daze. More than once she nearly ran into the car in front as it slowed for an exit or traffic-lights. Knowing it was futile, nevertheless she passed by Ralph Singer's clinic. No Adam Wendell had been checked in, and Dr. Singer himself was in Florida until midweek. As the signs for Lexington came up, she accelerated. It was obvious where William had taken Adam. Why hadn't she got the address of that vile laboratory out of Max before she'd left? If there weren't any message when she got home, she'd call the woman. From now on, she'd conduct any dealings between them on the phone, not face to face. All trust, respect and friendship was shattered. And the same for William.

Reaching the house, she clambered out of the car and flew indoors.

"Sandy?" she called. "Sandy?"

Then she saw Sandy's note. She picked up the phone to dial Max. An extension was off the hook somewhere. She traced it to her own bedroom. She had the phone in her hand when, through the window, a movement caught her eye. She took a half-step forward.

Struggling up the grassy slope, tottering and falling by turns, staggered the bloodstained and battered figure of Sandy.

Julia dropped the phone and fled downstairs and out into the garden, where Sandy collapsed, sobbing hysterically, into her arms.

"Adam!" she choked, gesturing in terror towards the woods. "He's gone mad! He . . ."

"Adam's *here*?" Then she saw the gashes and bite-marks and the blood. "Oh my God, *no*!" she gasped.

Even as she began to help the girl indoors, half hauling and half carrying her, she heard the distant siren of a police car. She listened without surprise as the howling came closer and closer, turned down the drive and came to a halt in front of the house.

•

Julia stared out across the lawn to the far woods. Daylight was ebbing fast, like receding floodwater, leaving the bluish gray dusk in possession of the land. She'd spent all day at Lexington General Hospital. Sandy was staying in for the night, under sedation. The physical damage would quickly heal, but what of the psychological trauma? And what if the most unthinkable thing had happened? She'd asked both doctors separately and the nurse. They couldn't tell at this stage; it depended principally on Sandy's monthly cycle, and Sandy was in no state to answer questions of that sort. Couldn't they give her the morning after pill? No, they said, not with the medication she was taking.

Julia poured herself a brandy and shuddered as it burned through her. Just suppose...Would it mean abortion? The alternative was still more unimaginable. Pray God it didn't come to that.

And Adam. Who was this creature, her "new Adam?" How had he *turned* like that, from innocent to savage, from pure to vile?

That morning, the police had arrived. They hadn't come about Sandy but about William. The terrible news choked her. A "cold, sadistic murder," the police had called it. She thought of William and a wave of grief flooded through her. Foolishly, blindly, for something in him she'd found compulsive and essential, she had loved him. Yet whatever his sin, however cynically he'd used her and however cruelly he'd betrayed Adam, no one could wish such a punishment on any man. Adam must have guessed where he was being taken. William had provoked his own retribution. But what had he unleashed? After battering him to death, Adam had apparently gone on to wreak a trail of havoc and bloodshed. The police had launched a manhunt. All patrol cars in the vicinity were on alert. A search party had spent the afternoon combing the area where he'd attacked Sandy, with orders to shoot if he evaded capture. Households in the neighborhood had been warned to stay indoors. Even at this moment, glancing through the window onto the front, she could see the police car parked just off the drive, half hidden among the trees, while somewhere hidden in the woods towards the Blanes' house two patrolmen had staked out their positions. They reckoned the boy would try and make it home. And then what?

They'd told her to lock all windows and doors. He was a savage, the lieutenant had said. A rabid wild dog.

This was Max's doing. She had *made* him a savage. She'd given him the lust for gratuitous violence without the ability to control it. Adam was an infant with an infant's instinctual impulses. In our society, a child spent years having these impulses tamed within codes of behavior and standards. But in expecting Adam to leapfrog the gap from the primitive to the modern adolescent in a single bound, she had bypassed the critical conditioning period. She had placed a gun into the hands of a mortal two-year-old and expected him not to shoot. *She* was to blame for what he had done!

She turned away with a bitter, angry sigh. She'd better attend to the windows and doors. Yet what did she have to fear? She knew the *real* Adam and she trusted her own faith in him. Or did she? She saw once again the final look flashing over his face in the back of the car, a look of despair, hatred, betrayal. If he could rape his sister who was entirely innocent, what might he not be capable of against those, like William, whom he found guilty?

•

Adam carefully peered out through the leaves. He could see the man in the police car beneath the trees as clear as daylight. He had pinpointed the other two men, one lurking in the shadows of the Blanes' summerhouse, the other patrolling the river bank. Did they really think they could fool him?

The house stood ahead of him, across a stretch of unmown grass. The front porch and the far side were lit by bright floodlamps set high up the wall. For a moment he studied the wires leading to the house. The main power cable looped along a series of poles and met the house at the roof, where it followed the guttering a few feet before feeding down a pipe to an outside meter-box. The telephone lines came in from a separate pylon, and these fed along under the eaves to the back. He was surprised at what he seemed to know.

His hands began to twitch. His throat was dry, unslaked. The rushing in his ears grew louder. He could just make out the small voice above it. *Be clever*, it whispered; *be tricky*. He felt a shiver of excitement ripple through his hands and, suppressing a smile, he melted back into the woods and slipped round the edge in the direction of the Blanes' house next door. He'd draw them off with a little diversion.

26

○

MAX HAD SPENT THE DAY AT THE LABORATORY GOING repeatedly over the analysis she and Murray had made to identify the critical master gene and trying to calculate what percentage of the neuronal sites it might have penetrated over the five-week period. She plotted the results on a logarithmic scale and concluded that Adam must be almost ninety-four percent *there*. Time and again she cursed her stupidity in not second-guessing Cray and getting to Adam first. Even a single shot of the concentrate might have nudged him those final few percent over the threshold. She was wearily tidying up her desk when a call came through on the internal phone from the security guard downstairs. There was a cop in reception, he said, asking to see her.

She arrived to meet a tall, fresh-faced young patrolman waiting for her. He told her that a Dr. William Cray had been killed in an automobile accident late the previous night and the case was being treated as homicide. A card had been found in his pocket bearing her name and address. Could she help them trace his movements on that day? There had been a boy in the car at the time, the man added. He'd gone missing, and a warrant was out for his arrest.

She returned to her lab, deeply shaken. Adam had killed Cray and was on the run. Jesus *Christ.* Gradually the implications began to sink in. There would be a full-scale manhunt. He'd be captured and charged, or else he'd get shot resisting arrest. Either way, he was finished. Either way, *she* was finished, too. If he was killed, there'd be an autopsy; if caught, a medical investigation. Julia would see to that. What chance did the poor boy have? Perhaps if he could be persuaded to turn himself in quietly, the Foundation might step in and hush it all up. He'd escape with his life, though what kind of life would he be going to? This was nonsense: to surrender was quite against the natural instinct. It was an act that took thought and calculated reasoning, qualities he did not possess— yet. He was within an ace of gaining the reasoning ability. If she could somehow give him that final shot to nudge him into goal, maybe she could explain his chances to him and hope an appeal to his reason would override his instinct. It was a gamble, but she had to make the attempt. And that meant she had to get to him first.

Without stopping to throw off her lab coat, she swept up the vials in their box and grabbed a spare syringe from the desk drawer, then headed for the door. She had a hunch where she might find him. She'd struck lucky there once before.

•

Crash! A windowpane on the upper floor shattered, sending a shower of glass tinkling to the ground. The second stone flew in a perfect arc and smashed a down-

stairs pane. The falling glass was echoed by a rumble of
dry thunder, growing closer. A low, restless wind was
rising, stirring the moonless shadows.

Adam took aim again. A third window fell. Glass
littered the stone front steps. A light came on in a downstairs room and the figure of Scott's father in a smoking
jacket hurried across to the deck and snatched up the
phone.

Adam carefully selected a perfect oval pebble and
sped it low and hard at the center of the pane just beside
the desk. The crash of shattering glass echoed around the
trees. The man dropped the phone and ducked behind
the desk. Adam could hear the police car starting up and
leaving its hideaway next door. From the woods between
came the sound of boots crashing through undergrowth.
He laughed to himself.

Then, as silently as the shadows themselves, he
melted back among the trees and slipped back along the
invisible pathways towards home.

•

From the landing window Julia saw two powerful
headlights spring to life from the trees alongside the drive.
A moment later the patrol car broke out onto the grass
and, swinging around in a tight circle, roared away back
up the drive. Barely a hundred yards away she heard it
brake. Had they run the boy to ground at the Blanes'?

She went downstairs and turned off all the lights.
She wanted to be able to see but not be seen herself.
She memorized the emergency number the police had
given her and checked the position of the buttons on the
phone so that she could dial it in the dark. With the
windows shut, the house was suffocatingly hot. She took

a glass of iced water to the living room and stood in the shadow of the curtain, looking out over the deck and the stretch of grass beyond toward the Blanes' house. Had they got him yet? She wanted him caught and—yes— punished, and yet at the same time she wished for him to remain free. Could she ever forgive him for what he'd done to Sandy? And yet who had done that terrible thing? *Which* Adam?

•

Max crouched in the shadow of a large family vault and scanned the broad close-mown avenue with its two rows of tombstones. A short distance away stood Sam's grave. Among the marble chippings she could make out an urn filled with fading flowers. The gift of a loyal loving wife to a deceitful cheating husband.

A sharp rustling caught her attention. A fox or a rabbit, or maybe a badger, or... him? Dimly in the far distance rumbled a constant flow of traffic; closer by, a truck's horn sounded, disturbing the peace of the dead. She shivered. Her eye picked up small movements: a darting shadow, a stirring among the grass, a leaf scudding over a gravestone. She gritted her teeth, fighting to keep her imagination in check.

She glanced at her watch. She'd wait just a few more minutes, then call it off. This time she'd misread him. So, what now? He was probably working his way back home. God knew what was in his mind. It meant having to face Julia. But Julia could be in real danger. She must be warned.

•

The thunder edged closer and the first thick clots of rain began to fall, spattering down on the hood and roof and smudging the windshield to an opaque smear. Max drove with her face craned forward and the wipers on double speed. At last she reached White River Drive and slowly turned off down the drive. She'd gone twenty yards when her headlights picked out a fir tree fallen directly across her path. As she jammed on the brakes, the car skidded to a halt, striking the tree with a soft metallic *crump*.

She got out to inspect the damage. The rain was falling in long fat pencils from a graphite-black sky. The front of the car had ridden up over the trunk of the fallen tree, shoving in the bumper and buckling the fender. She smothered an oath. Then she frowned. This tree had no roots nor crown. It hadn't fallen: it had been dragged there deliberately. An ominous gong began to sound in the back of her mind. The house lay a hundred yards ahead. Through the sheeting rain she could see it was in pitch darkness. Wasn't there anyone at home? She'd have to abandon the car and go on foot. She reached inside for her small box and syringe and, hauling her white lab coat up over her head as a makeshift rain hat, she headed for the house.

•

A white coat! He knew what white coats meant. He'd seen the car arrive and recognized it. Now he knew the truth. She was one of *them*.

He tracked her from the puddles in the driving rain. He spotted a broken fencepost and bent to pick it up. Stealthily he followed her, waiting his moment. Suddenly he broke cover. With a yell of rage, he smote her across the shoulders with the post and sent her sprawling onto the ground. A small box she was carrying shot out of her hands and scattered across the gravel. She flung up her hands.

"Adam!" she cried. "Stop! Wait! Listen!"

Her voice seemed to find an echo in his mind. He hesitated, the spar of wood still upraised. She was scrambling to her knees.

"Adam, listen to me! What you're feeling, what you're doing, it isn't *you*! Look!" She scrambled among the gravel and held up a familiar pen-like object. "I can help you! This stuff can make you better. It'll make you a regular person. One of us."

His head was splitting in twain. The rushing grew louder, surging with every pump of his blood. Her words were clawing at his brain, locking under his skull like bats. And, penetrating the raging tempest, he heard the small voice echo, *A regular person . . . One of us.*

He howled aloud, tossing his head to shake off the insidious whisper. *One of us*, it repeated, luring him on. One of *them*? roared the storm. He backed away. I'm not one of you! I don't want to be one of you! Go away! Leave me!

"Adam," she called, starting after him. "Wait! I'm here to save you!"

But he was already stumbling away, clutching his head, staggering in a crazed path into the woods. She followed, her bedraggled hair streaming in the driving rain, her hand outstretched, and gaining on him. He backed up against a tree-trunk. She had the pen in her hand. She was coming forward, slowly, deliberately, holding his eye like a snake with a mouse, just like the men in white coats, the men with needles, the men with the water tank.

The roar exploded in a starburst. He gripped the

fencepost in both hands and swung it back, then brought it down sharp and hard. It glanced off her forearm thrown up to shield herself and struck her on the side of the head. She let out a short, choked cry. Her eyes widened briefly, then swam upwards to the whites, and slowly her body folded beneath her and she crumpled to the ground.

Hurling the club aside, he lumbered off toward the house.

•

Julia's hand hovered over the phone. Had she imagined a sound upstairs? The rain cloaked the house in a pounding torrent, muffling and distorting the noises of the house. Suddenly she froze: she was sure she'd heard a sharp crack, just as if someone were prising the clapboarding off an outer wall. She tiptoed upstairs to the landing. Dimly, through the curtain of rain, she could see a pair of stationary headlights halfway up the drive. Had the patrol car come back empty-handed?

There it came again! That splintering sound. From the top floor.

She slipped over to the foot of the attic stairs. A sudden gust of wind howled through the house. The attic door slammed, making her start violently. Then she heard footsteps across the boards above her. She knew those steps. She stood rooted to the spot, hardly breathing. For a long moment, all was silent.

Then the shadows at the top of the stairs came alive and a short, stocky figure separated from the background.

She recoiled with a stifled cry. In the dim light she could see his eyes burning out at her from behind their heavy brows. His hands hung by his side. One fist was tightly closed, with some kind of cord looped round the wrist. He stepped down onto the first stair. She could see him more clearly. Her hand flew to her mouth.

"My God!"

His dark hair was wild and bedraggled, and two long gashes ran down his cheek and neck. His deep-set eyes were staring and his mouth was slack as if in a trance, and his clothes were drenched and spattered with blood. Slowly, with a sleepwalker's step, he went down another stair. She backed away.

"Adam? Speak to me!"

He gave a low growling grunt, the kind of sound he used to make before... before he knew proper words. She was shaking. Which Adam was this, the one before or the one after? Or one locked in between? She edged backward onto the landing. A wave of panic suddenly choked her. She spun around and flew down the main stairs into the kitchen. Snatching up the phone, she began frantically punching in the numbers. But even as she finished dialing, she realized there was no tone at all from the phone. The line was dead.

She looked up to see the boy framed in the doorway. She reached for the light-switch on the wall by the phone. Maybe she could coax him towards the window where the police outside might see him. She turned on the switch. The flood of light momentarily blinded her. But an instant later, the light snapped off: he had switched it off at the door. She turned it on again; immediately he switched it off. On, off, on off: could she get a signal going? What were the wretched men doing out there? Then abruptly Adam seized a jar and lobbed it at the ceiling, shattering the light. In the dark she could just make him out. He was slowly shaking his head.

She bluffed a short, nervous laugh. Be matter-of-fact, she thought. Pretend nothing's wrong. Play "tea-time-as-usual." She opened the fridge door.

"You must be starving, love," she began. The words barely came out of her throat. "Would you like some baked beans? A ham and cucumber sandwich? Tell you what: a nice burger and fries. What do you say?" Keep talking, she was thinking. Already an idea was forming in her mind. At the back of the fridge lay the pen needle in its small polythene sheath. She slid it quickly inside an open pack of muffins. "English muffins? Grape jelly or peanut butter? Come on, darling, make up your mind."

She took the muffins out onto the side and reached for a large, sharp knife. Adam was watching from by the table, his eyes narrow with suspicion, ready to spring at any moment. She made it clear she was splitting the muffins in two before putting them in the toaster. She caught his eye, then slowly put the knife down, where it lay uselessly on the sideboard between them, its blade gleaming dully in the light of the fridge. No way could she get away with that.

"You watch the toaster," she continued cheerily, "while I go upstairs to the bathroom." She smiled. "Call of nature."

The hypodermic pen slipped easily into the palm of her hand. She headed stiffly for the door and went as slowly as she could up the stairs and along to her bedroom, then flew into the bathroom and tore open the medicine cupboard. With shaking hands she rummaged around for the vials of Largacil that the nurse from the adoption agency had left when they'd originally come to deliver Adam. *One shot will usually zap him out*: wasn't that what the woman had said? Let's hope to God she's right, she prayed as she fumbled frantically with the barrel of the pen. The first glass vial slipped out of her hand and fell into the sink, where it shattered to fragments. She froze, listening. Then she took another. Drawing the plunger carefully back, she managed to fill the small inner bladder with the tranquilizer, then she gave it a couple of short pumps to build up the pressure and screwed the barrel back on. Slipping the pen back in its holder, she turned to the door with a sigh of relief.

Adam was standing in the doorway, as still as a rock. He had seen it all.

•

They stood facing one another for what seemed an eternity. Then slowly he unfurled his fist to reveal the small, sharp flintstone. The sacrificial knife. In a flash she thought: that's why he killed William, to get this thing back. And an accident in a car. Just like with Sam. A cry gagged in her throat. She grasped the pen-needle tighter. She would go for him, she'd stab, strike, punish, kill. But her legs wouldn't move. She was paralyzed, and he was slowly approaching.

He held the flintstone gripped flat in his left hand, with the leather thong strung round his wrist and the full length of the blade's edge bare. Gradually he raised his arm. She backed away. She felt the rim of the bathtub against her legs. There was no retreat, no escape. She met his eye. A ferment boiled within her. She hated him, yet she loved him. She cursed him, yet she pitied him. Every fiber of her being cried out for vengeance, and yet she forgave him. She would kill him, and yet she would spare him.

She heard the hypodermic drop from her hand onto the floor. She was defenseless.

"Go on," she whispered. "Do it. Do it quickly."

His arm rose higher. She closed her eyes. She'd been fatally mistaken. He was not the child of nature, that pure and innocent echo of our past paradise; he was a brutish savage of bestial impulses and dark and untamed instincts. He was the true face of ourselves. Max had understood, and in her own way she had offered him salvation. But too late.

She waited for the blow, the searing pain, the flash of agony, wondering how it would come, seeing Sandy in her mind's eye. Sandy as a little girl with blonde locks, thinking of the sorrow and the waste of it all. But no pain came. Gradually she opened her eyes. His arm was descending to his side, and his eyes were moist with tears. Tears of pity and remorse. She had never seen him weep before.

A loudspeaker shattered the silence.

"Mrs. Wendell, can you hear this?" rasped a harsh metallic voice. Adam jerked to life. *"We have the house surrounded. We believe the boy is inside. Come to the window."*

Adam grasped the flintstone. His large, dark eyes narrowed and flickered with terror. He was trapped. Behind him, through the door, she could see the beam of searchlights sweeping across the bedroom wall.

"Mrs. Wendell?" came the voice again. *"Do you read me?"*

He hesitated, torn in a conflict of impulses. A red, feral look entered his eyes. The moment hung agonizingly in the balance. She hardly breathed. Then she moved. In a sudden explosive motion, she stepped forward and, with all the command she could muster, yelled at the top of her voice.

"Get out! Go! Get out of here!"

Taken by surprise, he recoiled. But it was enough to tip the balance. He backed away to the door. As she bore down upon him, he fled into the bedroom. At the far doorway, he hesitated, his face lit in the whirling searchlights, then casting her a final glance, half in sorrow, half in pain, he turned with a stricken howl and vanished. A moment later, from upstairs in the attic, she heard the window bang.

The loudspeaker was barking again, warning they were moving in. Shaking and sick, she made her way out onto the landing and looked down onto the driveway. A sea of men and cars surrounded the house, lights flashing and sirens blaring. Slowly, taking her time, she made her way down the stairs. Already she could hear the crash of axes as the police set about smashing down the door. But she didn't hurry. Her thoughts were with the boy, fleeing into the night.

•

Adam dropped noiselessly to the ground and crouched in the shadows at the back of the house. He glanced up at the sky again. Though the rain was easing, the stars were still hidden. He scanned the ground about him. Ahead stood the garage, unguarded. The men were all around the front, hammering their way in. He moved swiftly. He knew what had to be done.

He scurried low and fast across the short stretch of grass to the garage and let himself in at the back. Inside, it was hot and dry, and the air was heavy with the smell of gasoline and pine lumber. He slipped the catch on the back door and dropped the bar over the front.

He gathered together a pile of timber and fencing,

broken chairs and pieces of firewood, leaving a small space in the center clear. He pulled apart a bale of straw and scattered it around the edge for kindling. Beneath the toolbench stood the gas-cans. One by one he slipped the catches and began to pour. The liquid sank greedily into the dry woodwork. Soon the timber was drenched and the garage floor swimming. The last can he kept aside. On the bench he found an iron wedge. Finally he was ready.

Outside he could hear shouts growing closer. The garage door was being shaken violently. The rushing in his head was already softening into a song, a chant of the sweetest sound. He could hear his brothers and sisters singing, and the priests and the old men, too, and all his uncles and cousins. His mother was there, no longer weeping. The sound seemed to come from the very sky itself, calling him, beckoning him. He crawled into the center of the wood-pile, then emptied the final can over himself. Half fainting with the fumes, he fumbled for the iron wedge, then unlooped the flintstone from his wrist. As the garage door caved in, shattered to pieces, he raised the stone and, grasping the iron in the other hand, struck. A fat spark sprang free.

"Atta!" he yelled with his last breath as, in that instant, the fireball exploded, sweeping him in its fiery rush up to the stars.

27

○

RAGE AND HATRED WAS THE FUEL THAT KEPT JULIA
going in the days that followed. Everywhere her mind
turned she found deception and degradation. A thousand
times she re-lived that final moment with Adam, striving
to see in his act of forgiveness some glimmer of a reason
why she should forgive him. She wanted to believe that,
in the final critical moment, she had met the real Adam,
his true self, the child of nature that knew pity and remorse
and encompassed the full feeling of the human heart. She
tried to see him as redeemed by his final act of self-
sacrifice and to find in it a redemption for herself, too.
Yet she couldn't. Pure or evil, innocent or corrupted,
noble or base, what did it matter? He was what he had
done. How could anyone forgive one who raped their
daughter?

Why forgive at all? That was Sandy's question. For
her, there was no cause even to consider the notion.
She'd been right all along: her first instincts about Adam
had proved fully justified, and now she was cruelly ex-
onerated. With the forthrightness of her age, she saw only

black and white. Adam was quite simply an evil brute, a disgusting wild beast, and she wanted to block all thought of him out of her mind. It was Julia who kept trying within her own conscience to find mitigating circumstances for him, who focused on sophistries of distinction between the Adam-before and the Adam-after, who thought in terms of legitimate provocation and diminished responsibility. And by degrees she came to realize why. By exonerating him she was exonerating *herself*.

Her mistake, her sin, was one of blindness. She recalled Sandy accusing her at the very start of going into the adoption blind: she'd even called it a "blind date." The girl was right. She should have checked more carefully before bringing a strange boy into the bosom of the family. She ought to have insisted on seeing more of him during the "quarantine" period and checked out the "halfway house" with the other agencies whose books they were on. She should have approached Max with her eyes open, too. Listened to her own nagging doubts about her work relationship with Sam. Been more suspicious of her overtures of friendship. Looked for the motive behind the manner, read the subtext behind the speech.

What kind of a fool had she been? The kind, she feared, that lived with a man and never for a moment imagined he might be cheating on her. And why *had* she been so gullible, so blind? Because she *didn't want to hear*. She only saw what she wanted to find. She called and she took the echo to be real. Take William: she'd been deaf to his real motives. Take her household, too: she wanted a harmonious home with a famous husband and a happily integrated daughter, and so that was all she saw. Sandy had rightly charged her once that her work at the Unit served as much for her own charitable self-image as for the true needs of the children. And finally, above all, take Adam. She had made up their minds for them from the outset—from the moment she'd had the idea in William's car on the way back from the trip to Turkey. She'd been "angling for it all along," as Sandy had put it at Sam's funeral. She'd forced the fit, dismissed the problems, ignored the signals. "Someone's got to look after the poor lad," she heard herself saying, to which Sandy would riposte, "Why does it always have to be us?" Why? Because, in truth, it wasn't Adam's need she was fulfilling: it was her own.

Of all her rage and remorse, the harshest she kept for herself. She and no one else was ultimately responsible for Adam and everything he had done. She could advance a thousand arguments in mitigation: at the time it seemed right, she hadn't known, she'd been enmeshed in a web of calculated deception woven by those closest to her: Max, William, Sam . . . And yet, nothing removed the facts. Adam was what he *was*. He had raped and killed. Blindness and gullibility might explain but could not excuse. People were responsible for their actions, and that included the results of their actions, whether foreseeable at the time or not. If not, then who was? Deeds couldn't just go unreckoned. Someone had to be held to the account.

If time is the greatest healer, truth comes a close second. She felt that only by unburdening her heart to Sandy and telling her the full and untrimmed truth could she free herself from this ferment of anger and recrimination. And yet, to her bitter realization, even the release of confession was not open to her.

Sandy had returned home in deep shock. She spent hours in her room on her own, neither reading nor watching television, simply staring sightlessly out of the window. She moved about the house silently and nervously, like a wraith, shunning contact with anything to do with Adam, skipping quickly past the playroom door and taking the back stairs so as to skirt the attic staircase. The only modest relief she found was when Scott came to visit. Then Julia preferred to leave them alone together, talking upstairs or strolling in the garden; she'd rather not have to face Scott, knowing all that they both knew and yet hadn't admitted, and besides, it was virtually the only chance she had to get out herself as Sandy was keeping close to home. Throughout those days, an unspoken fear hung heavy in the atmosphere as the due time for her period grew closer. In the light of that, how could Julia sit the girl down and tell her the whole truth? To tell her any more than she needed to know would be a cruelty, not a kindness. To tell her who Adam really had been, the creature whose child she might be carrying, would be positively wicked. And so, for all that she yearned to open up and re-establish their relationship on the old sister-to-sister footing, Julia found this avenue blocked to her. She had to suffer the burden of Sandy's own silent blame upon her, without the chance of pleading her defense. That was her bitter harvest in those days that followed.

•

Max spent the days following her discharge from the hospital at the hunting shack, hiking during the daytime and working on her publication program in the evenings. Skull X-rays had revealed several hairline cracks, not serious in themselves, and the brain scans had shown nothing at all untoward, and within a few days of healthy exercise she was feeling fitter than she had for months.

Behind it all, however, she felt a burning drive to bring all her research data together and publish her results. Now that Adam was gone, she had no qualms about putting it in print. She'd allowed herself to grow too fond of the boy; human feelings all too often muddied the waters. The specimen himself was dead, his body burned to cinders, and now the way was clear for her to move ahead.

She marshaled her information together and sketched out the plan for a series of articles, which she would submit simultaneously to all the leading academic and semi-popular journals. She had the story complete on file, in dossiers, on computer disks, in notebooks, photographs, radiographic plates and print-outs, and all it took was the work to draw it together in a cogent and scientifically presentable form. But more important than the files by far, she possessed the key-stone to the entire edifice: a frozen sample of the boy's actual blood. She had the field to herself. Julia knew, it was true. But Julia would say nothing. The betting was she wouldn't even tell Sandy. Cray was dead. Gerald had not the least real inkling. Murray might pursue the master-gene work, but that was strictly based on *homo sapiens* material, and nothing she'd left him would even begin to suggest what they'd really been working on. Only Eliot Lovejoy knew. Now, Lovejoy was sure to have kept samples of Adam's DNA, and no doubt he would clone these in quantities sufficient for his research. But the last thing the Foundation wanted was publicity. In his overture to her, he'd explicitly offered her publication rights. Lovejoy wasn't going to steal her thunder.

The more she worked on the reports, the more her excitement grew, and she began to feel something of the driving obsessions she'd witnessed in Sam. Two elements, however, she decided to omit from any publication. First, she would avoid any mention of the "birthright" program: being so patently unethical, it would undermine her standing and, besides, without the subject available for study its success would be virtually impossible to demonstrate.

Second, and more importantly, she would offer no hint whatever as to *where* Adam had been discovered. The least clue would trigger off a world-scale hunt for other remnants of this lost branch of humanity. Massive resources would be thrown into the field; political interests would become galvanized; international scientific committees would be set up to examine "The Neanderthal Question;" magazines and television networks would probe every inch of the area from the sky, while on the ground every adventurer would be on the trail for this hidden human gold. Sooner or later, someone would strike it rich. Helicopters would ferry in the journalists and scientists, and the world's television screens would be filled with the bewildered, hunted faces of a pitiful band of human creatures whose way of life was now destroyed forever. She could visualize it now. But if all remained a mystery, she herself would stand at the core of it. Hers alone would be the source of genetic material. The blood plasma hidden in storage in the labs at the Department was more precious than moondust. A milligram would be worth millions of dollars. As soon as she'd written up the basic framework, she would return to Cambridge and move the material to a safer storage place. Then, simultaneously with publication, she would invite three world-renowned laboratories to analyze tiny samples of this material so as to validate her claim. And then the bidding could start.

She would build her name and fortune from the ashes. Sure as hell, she deserved to.

•

The computer screen flashed up the message, FILE NOT FOUND. Eliot Lovejoy frowned. He keyed in another instruction. The same response came back. He turned to Gerald.

"You sure she only used these IDs?"

"Sir, I know every ID in my department," replied Gerald smugly.

"And this was her desk?"

Lovejoy opened a couple of drawers. They were empty: of course they would be. He tried not to betray his frustration. Maxine Fitzgerald's work was of particular relevance to the Foundation's project, he explained. Too bad she'd just quit. Gerald hovered in the background, trying to suggest that the work of his other research assistants was equally good. Lovejoy ignored him. He rose and wandered about the room, picking up a gel sheet here and an assay plate there, his mind haunted by the unbelievable catastrophe in-house that had made this visit necessary. He seethed with rage as he recalled it. A junior technician in his own labs had mis-referenced a series of capsules in the gene bank and got Adam's material mixed in with a batch from a bunch of colobus monkeys. Of course, he'd fired the man on the spot; he only wished he'd throttled the idiot. If Cray knew where Sam Wendell had found the kid, he'd taken the knowledge to his grave. The stuff was, literally, irreplaceable.

He put his head around a door to a small annex room and gestured to a large stainless-steel cryostat. She might have taken her files home, but this facility she couldn't duplicate.

"Any of her work in there?" he asked bluntly.

"Sure. The gazelle plasma. Like I said, it's a co-operative project . . ."

"Mind if I look?"

Ignoring the mild protest, Lovejoy unscrewed the clamps and released the lid. Slipping on an asbestos glove hanging at the side, he reached into the frosty vapor and pulled out a flat rod on which two rows of small polythene bags were clipped. At a glance he could tell the bags contained vials of blood plasma. Each was marked with a reference number. GDD was the common prefix: evidently, *gazella dorcas dorcas*. Nothing remarkable there.

He was replacing the rod when he hesitated. Laid out as they were in pairs, it was easy to see that there were an odd number of bags. Wouldn't she have kept a control sample from each animal, and wouldn't that mean there'd be an even number? Quickly he glanced down the rows again.

"How many of these animals was she working on?"

"Thirty-two. I signed the budgets."

Lovejoy plucked a bag from the bottom hook. It bore the reference *GDD/018/33M*. A *thirty-third* specimen? He felt a physical kick of elation. With total certainty, he knew he had found it. Carefully, he held it up to the light. There was enough genetic material here to provide some very interesting experiments indeed.

•

Julia had lain awake into the early hours, unable to calm her thoughts, and dawn was already breaking when she finally sank into an exhausted, dream-troubled sleep. She woke with an abrupt start to find it was gone nine. The aroma of percolating coffee met her as she hurried down and into the kitchen. Sandy was already up and dressed in the large, shapeless Princeton tee-shirt Scott had given her. He was going to college there this coming year, and she had set her mind on getting the grades to follow him in two years' time.

Sandy handed her a cup and held her eye levelly.

"You can relax now, Mom," she said. "It's okay."

"You mean..."

She nodded. "I always told you, but you didn't listen."

"Well, I know how I felt when I was expecting you..." began Julia, automatically rising to the point, then she stopped. This was the last thing the poor girl wanted to hear. Her eye fell upon the holiday brochures. Well, it wasn't going to be Disneyland. "You know, I've been thinking, darling. We do need a proper break. Now's the perfect time. Leave the builders to sort out the mess. I was thinking of Florence. Or Venice."

"Mom, Scott's asked me to go to basketball camp with him. I told him yes."

"Ah." She paused. "What dates are you thinking of? We could go before. Or after."

"Mother, I think it's best if we don't plan anything. You know."

"Well, actually, I *don't* know, Sandy." She could feel the pain rising and was powerless to keep it down. "We have a lot to talk about. And a lot to put behind us. It's been a difficult time. A terrible time."

"There's nothing to talk about, Mom." She laid a hand on hers. "I'm sorry," she said tenderly. "It's just that I feel different about everything."

"I do understand, darling," hastened Julia.

"I know you try to," she smiled weakly. "Sometimes."

Julia looked down at her hands. This was terrible, like the parting of lovers. If she was to lose her girl anyway, then let her go in knowledge, not in ignorance. With the danger of a pregnancy past, could she not tell her the truth about Adam now? And about Max? And even about Sam? And let her, in the wisdom of her new maturity, make up her own mind?

"Sandy," she began. "There's something I want to tell you. Come and let's sit down at the table."

●

Sandy stared into the flames, almost invisible in the bright outdoors light, curling around the pile of clothes and drawings and the other hateful reminders. She reached into the carton and threw another handful onto the fire—the tracksuit, his sweatshirt, those frayed and torn jeans, his underpants, and the boxer shorts he slept in . . . She stifled a shudder. She'd always known. Hadn't she said from the very first he wasn't *one of us*?

She looked around the ruins of the devastated garage where, among the ashes and debris, she'd built the fire. The roof had gone up with the fire-bomb, and the firemen had demolished the tottering remnants of the walls. All about her lay a tangle of blackened spars and jagged, buckled beams. The trees above were heavily scorched, and behind her the drive was scarred with deep tire ruts made by the fire engines. It was all ugly, vile, unclean.

In her mind echoed the unbelievably terrible story Mom had told her. She wished she hadn't heard any of it. Wouldn't it have been better just not to know? Mom had told her because she was feeling bad herself and she wanted to be let off the blame. That was Mom all over.

She'd said the words Mom needed to hear: she'd told her she forgave her. But how could you really forgive something that couldn't ever be undone? You could only cover it up and pretend it wasn't there, like concreting over a crater. Whatever you built on top, you couldn't change the foundations.

She threw the carton itself on now and watched it roar into flame. As she stepped back from the blaze, she felt something jab her sharply in the ankle of her wellington boots. She glanced down to see a curious, sharp-edged stone sticking out of the ashes. It looked more than just a piece of rock that had split in the heat. She bent to pick it up and wiped off the soot. It was shaped in an oval, with a hole at the thick end, and it came to a sharp point and had its edges chipped to form a blade. She recognized it as one of Adam's interminable wretched stones he had littering the floor of his attic. With a swift movement, she took aim and threw it as high as she could over toward the river. It spun through the sky, flicking and flashing like a spear, and finally disappeared from view behind the tall fir trees. She didn't hear it land.

"Sandy?"

It was Mom, her voice straining. Sandy turned to see her struggling around to the side of the house with another large carton. She helped her bring it over and lower it onto the ground.

"Sam's things," said Julia shortly. "For the fire."

"Couldn't some of it go to charity?"

"No, the fire."

Together they heaved the box forward and upended it into the blaze. Tennis kit, golf shoes, field jackets, documents, certificates, maps, notebooks, a couple of pipes, correspondence, periodicals, brochures, all spilled out onto the pile, and slowly the flames began to curl around the edges. Suddenly Julia bent and reached into the smoke to retrieve a postcard, already half-scorched. She appeared to recognize it. For a moment, she stood reading the message, tight-lipped, then without an expression handed it to Sandy.

The picture, poorly printed, showed a sulky camel against a desert background. The card bore a Pakistani stamp. It was addressed to Sam at the Department and was signed "M." She read the message, and instantly she understood. Mom had said nothing about *this*. How long had she known about it?

She thought of Scott and how she would feel if this were herself, discovering that she'd been systematically deceived and cheated in love. She could well imagine the hurt and the impotent anger her mother must be feeling at this new pain, coming as it did on top of everything else. As she handed the card back, she felt a wave of pity and fellow-feeling. There were no words she knew to comfort her. Reaching forward, she pressed herself gently, silently, into her mother's embrace.

•

Max's world spiralled sickeningly out of control. She counted and re-counted, she checked and re-checked, she dredged the base of the cryostat in case the vital sachet had dropped off into the liquid nitrogen, she quizzed Murray and she scoured her files over and again. But there was no mistake: the sachet had gone. A frantic phone call to Gerald confirmed her worst fears. Eliot Lovejoy!

She was beaten. This was the only unequivocal material evidence that remained. Without it, she had no proper scientific case. The ground had fallen from under her. Nauseous with despair, she roamed her apartment, around the streets, in and out of bars, on and off the campus, looking for some solution. Could she treat with Lovejoy? Impossible: why should he need to do a deal now? Find another specimen? Impossible again. Who the heck even knew where the first one had come from? Only Sam, and maybe Cray, and they were both dead.

She began clutching at straws. She revisited Sam's former office at the Peabody and went through the carton of his books again, ransacking every page for some clue she might have missed. But no: plenty of colorful oral accounts, but no hard geographical pointers. She went to the Department of Geography and scoured the large-scale maps of the Caucasus, on the offchance Sam might have studied these and left some marginal note. Again, she came away empty-handed. On some contrived pretext, she questioned Sam's old secretary as to his exact itinerary on that last, fateful field trip, but he'd been living with nomads, by definition rootless people, and traveling wherever they took him.

The issue began to obsess her every moment. She refused to allow that, in this age of information, some record would not exist somewhere. She knew where he'd been hospitalized in Turkey, and she was seriously considering going out there to try and retrace his steps until she realized the sheer futility of it. He wouldn't have risked crossing at any border-point, so she wouldn't be able even to get an initial fix on his direction. It was hopeless.

Gradually, her thoughts began to focus on his home in Lexington. There *had* to be something she could dig up there. They'd had no contact since Julia called the hospital to see how she was. She couldn't face the confrontation. And yet, what other choice did she have?

Late one afternoon, having invited herself over to her girlfriend's in Concord for the evening, she found her tracks taking her along the familiar route to Lexington. She drove slowly, telling herself at each exit that she'd turn off at the next. But, with the same numb inevitability that had driven her there the very first time, she soon found herself in Lexington town, passing the four-way stop by the shopping mall, carrying on down White River Drive, and eventually rolling slowly down the gravel drive. Her pulse was drumming hard. She had no idea what she'd say to Julia.

Ahead lay the burnt-out shell of the garage. The drive was empty of cars. Her nerves began to ease. She crept forward, craining for faces at the window and listening through the open window for sounds from the garden behind. But the place seemed quite deserted. She drew up beside the garage and, turning the car around to face the way out, stepped out, leaving the engine running. She'd slip in the back way with the spare key they kept in the pool pump-house. First, she'd try the study and check for diaries or atlases. Drawing a deep breath, she headed for the side of the house.

As she passed by, she noticed the remains of a bonfire on the floor of the burnt-out garage. Something registered in the corner of her eye. A handle of a hockey-stick projected from a pile of charred papers. She stopped. They'd been burning Sam's things. She looked closer, and suddenly her pulse somersaulted. A passport. A padded mountaineer's glove. Some papers in Russian. A flight timetable. The stub of a receipt from the Danieli hotel, Venice . . .

And there, tucked between two journals, a charred

fragment of a map, no bigger than a postcard. It bore small, precise handwritten markings. Pencilled lines. A circle. And beside the circle, a series of numbers: 40° 19' 35" N; 44° 53' 25" E.

A map reference.

•

Slowly Max lowered the binoculars. Cold sweat prickled her skin and her pulse drummed in her temples.

A fire at *that* altitude?

She muttered aloud in disbelief, her breath freezing on the moonlit air. She stamped her feet and clapped her mittened hands to restore the circulation. Wiping the frozen condensation off the eyepieces, she focused the binoculars once again on the flickering pinprick of light just visible in the clear bright night, high up on a distant, inaccessible crag.

It *was* a fire! Jesus Christ.

With a shaking hand, she folded the map back into her anorak pouch and scanned the black void that lay between herself and the tiny, elusive flicker high up in the far distance. Quickly she slipped her binoculars away, and, swinging her backpack onto her shoulders, with the light of the moon to guide her steps, struck out across the rocky shale.

The mountain seemed to recede as fast as she advanced towards it, and the hours lengthened immediately. The going got steeper, and for much of the time she scrambled and climbed in shadow, where the rock was beginning to glaze with frost and shapes and distances played tricks with her vision. Her feet were so numb that much of the time she could only guess the toeholds.

Having gained some height at last, she paused and

looked down. Beneath her, the mountain fell away in a long sweep of loose shale, ending in a sheer drop. Some way ahead, she saw a small ledge and decided to bivouac there and grab a couple of hours' rest. She headed on.

By now, desperately weary in every limb, she began to make mistakes. She had almost made it across the broad sweep of scree when quite suddenly the ground slid from under her foot and she fell backwards. She fought frantically to regain her footing, but the surface was a mass of loose pebbles. The more she struggled, the more she slipped. Slowly, the whole mountainside began to slide downward like a sheet, gathering speed as it went and carrying her helplessly along in a torrent of stones. She struck a boulder and flew head over heels into the air. She wrestled and clawed in an effort to buck the landslip, but it was no use: she was part of it, one rolling boulder among the rest, flung headlong in the same downrush. The roaring grew louder in her ears. Stones spun wildly past her head. Violent shafts of pain stabbed her in every quarter. The sky tumbled crazily about her eyes. Covering her head with her arms and curling into a ball, she gave herself up to the stone-storm and waited for the one final jolt, greater than the rest, that would bring the blackness and the silence.

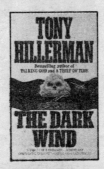
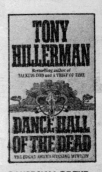
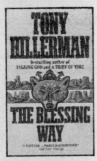